Books by Carmen Schober

After She Falls
Pretty Little Pieces

CARMEN SCHOBER

BETHANYHOUSE

a division of Baker Publishing Group
Minneapolis, Minnesota

Published by Bethany House Publishers
11400 Hampshire Avenue South
Minneapolis, Minnesota 55438
www.bethanyhouse.com

Bethany House Publishers is a division of
Baker Publishing Group, Grand Rapids, Michigan

Printed in the United States of America

Library of Congress Cataloging-in-Publication Data
Names: Schober, Carmen, author.
Title: Pretty little pieces / Carmen Schober.
Description: Minneapolis, Minnesota : Bethany House, a division of Baker
    Publishing Group, [2022]
Identifiers: LCCN 2022029124 | ISBN 9780764239304 (paperback) |
    ISBN 9780764240157 (casebound) | ISBN 9781493437320 (ebook)
Classification: LCC PS3619.C449256 P74 2022 | DDC 813/.6—dc23
LC record available at https://lccn.loc.gov/2022029124

Unless otherwise noted, Scripture quotations are from The Holy Bible, English Standard Version® (ESV®), copyright © 2001 by Crossway, a publishing ministry of Good News Publishers. Used by permission. All rights reserved. ESV Text Edition: 2016

Scripture quotations in chapter nineteen are from THE HOLY BIBLE, NEW INTERNATIONAL VERSION®, NIV® Copyright © 1973, 1978, 1984, 2011 by Biblica, Inc.® Used by permission. All rights reserved worldwide.

All emojis designed by OpenMoji – the open-source emoji and icon project. License: CC BY-SA 4.0

Cover design by Kathleen Lynch/Black Kat Design
Cover photography by Natalia Ganelin/Arcangel

Author is represented by Golden Wheat Literary Agency.

Baker Publishing Group publications use paper produced from sustainable forestry practices and post-consumer waste whenever possible.

22 23 24 25 26 27 28   7 6 5 4 3 2 1

For Jeff, Vivian, Sofia, and Leo.

Our story is my favorite.

1

"There. Done."

Georgina smiles in the mirror as Margot finishes styling the last strand. Her curly mane is tamed and glossy, and it frames her contoured face—also Margot's handiwork.

Georgina gently swings her hair from side to side. "I love it."

"You look perfect," Margot says through a mouthful of pins. "Are you nervous?"

Georgina nods. The entire day has been a blur of preparation for tonight, and now her eyes are darting between the phone in her lap and her reflection in the mirror. Messages—mostly from her ecstatic mother and excited friends—are rolling in so fast she can't keep track. "It doesn't feel real yet, honestly," she adds, wishing it did. She's worked *so* hard for this moment.

Margot smiles and slides a pearl pin through Georgina's hair. "It is real, babe. You're doing it—"

Georgina stiffens in the chair as another message arrives.

"All good?"

Georgina pries her eyes away from her father's text, but the damage is done. "Yes," she lies. "Sorry."

"You're fine. I can't even imagine your phone right now. I think you should go with the claret," Margot suggests, shifting the focus to lipstick, which Georgina appreciates. "But I also love this new peach."

She finishes up a few minutes later and showers Georgina with air kisses, so Georgina turns on some music to fill the too-quiet apartment, but her thoughts wander back to her father's text.

> Congratulations. I'm proud of you.

Five simple words, but she sifts them in her mind, searching for hidden clues. His almost-constant silence makes every word seem irritatingly important. Her fingers hover over her phone for a moment, but then she sets it on the vanity.

"You can write back later," she reminds herself, recalling the boundaries Alvin suggested she set with both of her parents. Georgina's always felt like she has to respond immediately, especially when it comes to them.

"That's the beauty of a boundary, Georgina," Alvin had explained at her last session. *"It's you choosing your own response instead of going into autopilot."* His gray eyes were encouraging under his fluffy eyebrows. *"And boundaries are especially important when your parents don't have any,"* he added with a sad smile.

Georgina takes Margot's advice and reaches for the safer, muted claret. She twists the tube and glides the color over her lips but stops when her stomach tightens. She's had light cramps on and off all afternoon, but she had plowed through them, too busy to pay much attention until now.

Worry fills her when they don't fade. Each one hurts a little more than the one before it, so she shifts in her seat, hoping a new position might help, but the next one surges harder. She gasps and suddenly stands up, lurching toward the toilet as the lipstick slips from her fingers and clatters against the tile.

She lifts her sequined dress just in time as the pain deepens and blood rushes from her body. Panic fills her as she realizes what's happening.

She's losing the baby.

"Please let it be okay," she prays instinctively, even though it's obviously not okay. She covers her face with her hands and inhales through the pain. "Please, please, please let it be okay. . . ."

When she uncovers her face moments later, she finally looks down and quickly flushes the toilet. Her muscles eventually relax again, and the shock fades, but she can't make herself move. Her feelings are rising like a cold, dark tidal wave, and it gets worse when she catches a glimpse of herself in the mirror.

Thankfully, Lance isn't home yet. As awful as she feels right now, she doesn't want him to see her like this. *She* doesn't want to see herself like this, but the bathroom is filled with mirrors, so she can't hide. She fixes her eyes on a vase of dying lilies instead and whispers another desperate prayer.

"Help me."

"Hey, Joanna Gaines! Over here!"

Georgina turns in the direction of a familiar voice and finds Corrine Jacobs grinning back at her. She eyes Georgina's gown and cashmere sweater combination. "Aren't you looking rather iconic tonight?"

Georgina smiles. "Thanks." The sweater is a little warm for late April, but she's committed to the look. Corrine stands out, too, in her drapey dress and towering heels, even among so many beautiful people crammed inside the art gallery. She's been Lance's assistant for years, and Georgina's never seen her in flat shoes.

"Lance should be here any minute," Corrine says, glancing

at her phone and typing something at breakneck speed. "They reshot a bunch at the Gulch house," she adds with a grimace. "He's not a happy camper."

Georgina nods but hides her disappointment from Corrine. She doesn't want to talk about the miscarriage yet, but she wouldn't mind his strong arms around her.

"How's the cookbook going, by the way?" Corrine asks, her smoky eyes lighting up. "Did you decide on a theme?"

"Not yet." Between the unexpected pregnancy and preparing for her new show with Lance, her potential cookbook contract is still sitting on the back burner. She's always wanted to write one, but the timing couldn't be worse.

"I think you should just do a spin on the whole country farm-house thing and roll with your Joanna vibes. Apple pie, but make it fashion, you know? That sort of thing."

Georgina smiles weakly. Corrine's referring to the *Young Southern Style* cover that earned Georgina and Lance a spot at tonight's event in the first place. Georgina's mother ran out and bought fifteen copies.

> Designers Lance Broussard and Georgina Havoc look more like the next Chip and Joanna Gaines every day as the power couple prepares to host a new design series flipping unique spaces across Nashville. Twenty-nine-year-old Havoc is rapidly following in Joanna's footsteps with a beloved lifestyle blog and cookbook talks—

The magazine gushed on for another five paragraphs, but Georgina's eyes kept coming back to those two sentences. The comparison is thrilling but daunting, and her people haven't stopped talking about it since.

"Georgie!"

Poppy McCrae loops her arm with Georgina's and pulls her toward the food. Georgina throws Corrine an apologetic look, but relief fills her. Corrine is nice enough, but she's intimidating. It could be her cool confidence, or it could be because Lance's life would instantly combust without her.

"Okay, just tell it to me straight. Do I look like garbage?" Poppy glances down at her loose linen dress, which barely hides her baby bump, then back at Georgina with an uneasy expression as a woman in Marchesa glides by. Unlike Corrine, Poppy doesn't own a single pair of heels, so she's shorter than pretty much everyone in the room.

"You look adorable, like always."

Poppy looks skeptical, but Georgina means it. Poppy's red-gold hair is tied back in a quick mermaid braid and reveals her glowing freckled face.

Typically, Georgina would've touched her bump and updated her prediction—she's sure it's a boy now—but she doesn't tonight. Her emotions are too close to the surface.

"Is this, like, your poker face, Georgie? Because it's good. Almost too good." Poppy frowns. "Are you secretly geeking out on the inside?"

Georgina forces a bright smile under her probing eyes. "I'm happy, Pop." It's not a lie—she *is* happy—but she can't shake off the heaviness of the miscarriage. "I'm just overwhelmed, I think. . . ."

"Well, you're allowed to freak out since this is literally *the* moment," Poppy continues, her eyes glowing with pride. "Like, you did it, Georgina Havoc. You really freaking did it."

Nostalgia and sadness hit Georgina at the same time as Poppy hands her a glass of champagne. "No, *we* did it."

Poppy smiles. Neither of them could've ever guessed how much *Nail Breakers* would take off when they pitched the concept to UpScale three years ago. They were just artsy Instagrammers back then with a knack for flipping furniture and staging fabulous spaces, and somehow their side hustle turned into two seasons of a wildly popular show.

Sadness tugs at Georgina as she sips the champagne. Almost six months have passed since Poppy left *Nail Breakers* to raise her daughter, Olivia, but Georgina misses her every single day. She's also a little envious. Georgina could never give up her career like that, but she thought she'd at least be married by now.

"Here comes Lance," Poppy mutters.

Georgina's mood lifts as she turns and catches his eye.

"Sorry I'm late, babe," he says, pulling her in for a quick kiss on the cheek. "Gulch," he adds glumly, finishing what's left of Georgina's champagne. "I should just burn it down at this point. Oh, hey, Pop," he adds, suddenly noticing her. "How's it going?"

Poppy returns the greeting with a tight smile. Technically, Georgina is the only one who is allowed to call her that, but Poppy lets it slide. "Hello, Lancey."

He frowns at the nickname, but his eyes drift back to the crowd. It's a mix of familiar faces and strangers in a shimmering sea of stylists, designers, and photographers, and his presence causes a fresh murmur of excitement. He looks back at Georgina with a smirk. "Are you ready for this, G?"

No. Just hold me for a second, please. That's what she wants to say, but "I think so" is all that comes out.

"Do we both go up there, or just you?" he asks, eyeing the press area.

"Um, I think just me first, maybe . . ." Georgina tries to remember the long list of instructions from the *Young Southern Style* intern, but her mind keeps slipping back to the bathroom—the silence, the blood, the lilies—and she just wants to be alone with him for a few minutes as her feelings rise and fall all over again. Tonight was the night she was going to tell him about the baby. "Hey, can we go—"

"They'll want pictures of both of us," he says, running a hand through his swishy Clark Kent hair—a trait that earned him the nickname "Superman" from his fawning fans. Georgina can't blame them. Her formerly awkward teenage self would've probably passed out at the sight of him.

"Sorry," he adds, finally perfecting the swoop. "What were you saying?"

"Um . . ." She tries again, but the words still won't come out. Poppy throws her a curious look. "Nothing important."

"One second. I'll be right back."

Her disappointment returns as he slips off again with his phone pressed against his ear, but she doesn't have time to think about it, thanks to Poppy, who drags her over to the press area without him. It's a velvety blue carpet with a million logos where they're supposed to do standard hand-on-hip poses for a gaggle of flashing cameras, but Poppy ruins every shot by talking or laughing.

"Okay, okay, one serious one," she says, finally standing still with her arm around Georgina. Georgina smiles happily as the lights burst all over again. It's the best moment of the night so far, but it's bittersweet, too. She's excited for the next chapter with Lance, but *Nail Breakers* was a wild, fabulous ride.

"My turn," Lance says, surprising her as he steps up to take Poppy's place.

Poppy smiles stiffly and steps back, and Georgina's stomach flutters as every pair of eyes moves in their direction.

"Y'all are just too precious," Corrine purrs from a few feet away, snapping pictures on her phone as Lance pulls Georgina closer.

Georgina does her best to match his confidence as the press pelts them with comments and questions, but he's better at this sort of thing than she is.

"Lance! Georgina! You both look incredible tonight!" A

stunning woman with a microphone waves them down. "Some UpScale fans have commented that you two have such different styles. Do you think that's going to be a challenge for *Trending in Tennessee?*"

There's a collective swoon as Lance smiles charmingly at the crowd. "I don't think so." He glances back at Georgina with hopeful eyes. "We're better together, right, G?"

It sounds like a champagne bottle popping or lipstick clattering—Georgina's not sure which—but whatever it is jolts her awake. It takes her a full minute to realize she was dreaming before she rolls over and presses a hand against her gurgling stomach. She drank more than she should've last night and fell asleep as soon as Lance helped her unzip her dress.

The sadness seeps in again. She'd had a cute scavenger hunt planned to announce the pregnancy, starting with clues in the entryway and ending with a new super-sleek rocking chair in their guest bedroom. Thankfully, she remembered to pick up the notes and drop them in the trash before the party last night.

She reaches for her phone when it chirps, thankful for a distraction.

CAN YOU SAY POWER COUPLE??

Georgina clicks on the link from Annette, her publicist, and squints as images of her and Lance fill the screen. It's a promotional video for *Trending in Tennessee.* Maren Morris's song "Bones" blares in the background as Lance climbs ladders and swings hammers, followed by Georgina fluffing pillows and staging shelves. The solo moments culminate with them slow dancing together in a half-finished room. She frowns. Under normal circumstances she would love it, but seeing everything so perfectly edited feels wrong as her mind drifts back to the blood in the bathroom.

She shoves the thoughts away and slips on a robe, then pads toward the kitchen. Lance is already there, seated in the breakfast nook and slumped over his laptop. They're both early risers, even when they're out late.

"Hey," he says, glancing up when he sees her.

"Morning," she mumbles.

"Too much champagne?"

She smiles weakly as she measures out coffee beans. "Apparently."

His fingers click against the keyboard. "There was a lot to celebrate."

"Did you have fun?" she asks, raising her voice over the coffee grinder.

"Yeah," he mumbles when she finishes.

Her mood lifts a little when their eyes meet. He's even more handsome in the mornings, when his face is still relaxed. By the end of most days, his entire body is tense—one of the side effects of being on camera all the time.

"How was my speech?" she asks, hoping it wasn't terrible. She can barely even remember it now, thanks to too many mixed emotions combined with alcohol.

"It was fine. You sounded nervous, but you got through it."

Her eyes widen. "It was bad?"

He yawns. "I said it was fine, babe." A ray of sunlight slices across his bare, muscled chest as his eyes narrow at something on the screen.

Insecurity fills her as she finishes the coffee. "I guess I was pretty nervous. Being compared to Joanna Gaines freaks me out a little," she admits, joining him in the nook. Georgina has loved her for as long as she can remember, but those are some pretty fabulous shoes to fill.

"Yeah, I get it." Lance sips as he scrolls. "And, like, is it even that great of a compliment?"

Her mouth falls open. "What? How is that not a compliment—"

"Calm down, G. I know it's a compliment." He smirks at the offended look on her face. "I'm just saying the Gaineses are kind of boring. That's all. All perfect and neutral and blah." He shrugs. "I'll go with it, obviously, but I don't really want to be a middle-aged dude with a million kids who only uses shiplap and white paint."

Her brows raise at the sudden condescension in his voice, but she wonders if it's just a little jealousy. UpScale is a big network, and Lance's show is popular, but he's not in the same stratosphere of fame as the Gaineses. Georgina isn't, either—which is why the comparison is so exciting.

"I don't think they're boring," she says, keeping her voice light. "They both seem nice and down to earth, and Joanna—"

"I know, I know. She decorates houses and writes recipes and pops out kids," he mutters, covering another yawn. "I just don't get why people love them so much. They don't take any risks. UpScale doesn't either."

Georgina's annoyance rises sharply, but she hides it behind her coffee cup. He keeps bringing up the Gaines's children like they're the worst thing in the world, and she doesn't understand why. They seem cute and well-adjusted, especially considering how famous their parents are.

"Don't get all sensitive about it, babe." His voice softens when he catches the disappointed look on her face. "I know it's a big deal for you—for us. I'm just . . ." He sighs as his eyes drift to the screen again. "Busy."

She nods, but her annoyance lingers. She knows he's busy, but he doesn't seem to notice that she has a lot on her mind, too.

"Are you hungry?" she asks, deciding not to push the subject. "I can make breakfast—"

"I need to head out soon, unfortunately." He sighs. "No days off until Gulch is done."

"Oh." A desperate, sinking feeling hits her as he downs his coffee and snaps his laptop shut.

"I had a miscarriage," she says softly when he starts to rise.

"*What?*"

Her declaration startles them both.

"I . . . had a miscarriage," she repeats as he falls back into his chair. She didn't want to say anything until the moment was right, but the words slipped out before she could stop them. "Yesterday."

"You were pregnant?"

Regret fills her as she nods. "I was only a few weeks along," she explains as confusion shadows his face. Her bizarre appetite and aching fatigue are what prompted her to call her doctor, and he's the one who suggested a blood test. She'll never forget sitting in that office, her heeled feet dangling over the edge of the examination table as she listened to the stunning results.

"How, though?" Lance demands. Confusion shadows his face. "I thought you were on birth control."

"I am," she says, turning defensive. She never forgets to take it, but last month was an exhausting whirlwind of events, so she must've slipped up. "I was going to tell you last night," she adds, setting her cup down, afraid it might slip from her shaking fingers. "After the party."

His face softens, but his shoulders are still stiff. "So . . . are you, like, okay? Do I need to take you to the hospital or something?"

"No. I'm fine—"

"Are you sure?"

She nods, and thankfully—finally—he pulls her close. She's not typically such a touchy person, but her emotions feel like waves, and she wants an anchor. She feels steadier until he frowns down at her.

"The timing wasn't good, was it?"

She blinks at the question. It hurts, but the relief in his eyes hurts even more. "Would you have been happy?" she asks, suddenly wondering. She had assumed he would be, after the shock wore off, but maybe she was wrong? She waits as he fumbles for an answer.

"We'd have to figure out a lot of stuff. . . ."

His words land with a thud in her heart.

He curses softly. "I'm sorry, G, I know it's terrible timing with this, too, but I really have to go." His eyes turn apologetic as he rises. "We'll talk tonight."

Georgina sings along with a moody Adele song, her voice competing with the soft crackle of bacon grease. Maybe Lance didn't want breakfast, but she does. Specifically, she wants ricotta pancakes, eggs with cream cheese and chives, and an unladylike pile of smoked sausage, but a sad little package of turkey bacon had been the only thing in her neglected fridge, so she settled for that.

She catches a glimpse of her reflection against the gleaming glass of the microwave and frowns. Her mounting stress is written across her face, and Lance's abrupt exit didn't help.

"I am loved. I am at ease. My feelings are valid," she mutters, channeling her inner Alvin to stave off some anxiety, but it doesn't work. She digs out her laptop instead. Her mother is the one who taught her that work is the best way to chase away empty feelings, and Georgina has used that strategy for as long as she can remember.

She relaxes slightly as she moves from one image to the next on Pinterest, starting with a collage of summer color palettes, but her uneasiness returns when she eventually ends up on her "I Do" board. She scowls at all the happy couples. She and Lance agreed that they should get engaged and buy a house in the next year, but he hasn't given her any clues about when he might finally propose other than "when things settle down."

She finally glances at her phone again, her anxiety growing. She *needs* to talk to him, even if it's just for a minute. His eyes seemed so far away when he said good-bye.

> Do you want to go out tonight? Or should I cook?

She distracts herself with a few emails while she waits for a reply, but an hour drags by, so she texts him again.

> How's filming going?

She cleans the entire apartment next, glancing at her phone between every other scrub. Lance pays someone to clean and prep their meals each week, which is nice, but those are her favorite forms of stress relief, and she misses them. Once that's done, she forces herself to take a nap but wakes up forty minutes later and immediately starts digging through the sheets, searching for her phone. Desperation rising, she sends one more text.

> Call me, please.

Her phone finally pings.

> Still filming. He'll have a break in twenty minutes–C

Georgina's mood dips further when she realizes it's from Corrine. When Lance finally does call, forty-five minutes later, his voice is sharp.

"What's going on, Georgina? Is something wrong?"

She winces. He only uses her full name when he's annoyed. "Nothing's wrong. I just . . . missed you."

"I told you I was filming."

Embarrassment fills her. *Say you missed me, too,* she pleads silently, but he doesn't. "I know," she murmurs. "I just thought you'd have a break sooner. Sorry."

"It's fine. . . ." He tries but fails to hide his annoyance. "So, you're okay?"

Georgina's breath catches in her throat. The truth is, she isn't okay, but she doesn't know why. She was barely pregnant, right? Why does it matter so much? "Yes, I'm fine," she repeats, trying to ignore the fact that Lance's reaction hurt as much as the actual miscarriage. "I—" She falls silent when Savannah's number flashes across the top of her screen, surprising her. They haven't talked since their last fight.

"G?" Lance's voice turns impatient again.

"Sorry," she says quickly, declining Savannah's call. "Do you want to go out to dinner tonight?" She waits as another voice fills the background on Lance's end, followed by some commotion. "I kind of feel like just getting take-out," she continues, "but whatever you want—"

"I'll call you back."

"Okay—"

She sighs as he hangs up and pulls the blanket up to her chin. Of course he's annoyed with her—he *said* he would be filming all day.

She drags herself out of bed to find the little bottle of Adderall tucked behind his arsenal of hair products, refusing to wallow, but she gets an uneasy feeling when she twists open

20

the lid. For one thing, she's not entirely sure how Lance gets them without a prescription, and for another, it would be *terrible* for her image if people ever found out. She can already imagine the comments.

"Looks like Georgina Havoc isn't so perfect after all!"

"I knew she was totally fake."

"So that's how she does it all—"

Georgina shoves the imaginary voices out of her mind and washes the tiny orange pill down with water. She uses them sparingly, anyway—usually just to get through stressful travel arrangements or exhausting days—and she has enough real worries without inventing more.

Everything is going to be fine, she tells herself when she slips out the front door twenty minutes later. She hates running, but it's better than waiting around for Lance like a desperate little Pomeranian. Her mother used to do that sometimes, first with her father, then with the boyfriends that followed, and Georgina swore she'd never do the same.

The pop music blasting in her ears repeats the same positive mantras as she runs—*get it, girl; be happy; life is good*—but the pit in her stomach deepens with every mile. When she returns to the apartment an hour later, her phone finally chirps.

I need some space tonight.

Anxiety spills over her like ice water as she reads the words again. She tries calling him, but he doesn't answer. Her fingers shake as she types back.

What do you mean?

When he doesn't reply, a tidal wave of panic rises in her chest.

I just had a miscarriage, Lance. I thought we were going to talk about it?

She calls again, but he ignores that, too, so she grabs her keys. She's Georgina Havoc. He's Lance Broussard. This is a misunderstanding. They can fix this. They *have* to fix it. She texts him again.

Please pick up your phone.

She drives to his condo, but the windows are dark. She frowns as a security camera swivels in her direction. She's never loved the fact that Lance didn't sell his bachelor pad after he moved into her apartment, but it is closer to the UpScale studio, and it's his style personified, with tall tan walls, angled furniture, and bold modern art, so she learned to live with it. She drives by the Gulch project next, but his Audi is nowhere in sight. Tears spring into her eyes.

It crosses her mind that she should probably go home and get a grip, but her mind begs her to go anywhere except the empty apartment, so she drives in the darkness, leaving the city and suburbs behind. At some point, her Lexus reminds her that the gas tank is running low, so she snaps out of her trance and parks on the side of a wooded gravel road. She almost gets out, but she and Savannah have watched too many crime dramas. She locks the doors instead and tries to calm down.

Her first panic attack happened when she was ten, at her first tennis match. Her mother had been screaming at her from the stands, trying to remind her of everything she had learned at her expensive lessons while her father watched helplessly, but Georgina still couldn't manage to serve the ball a single time, thanks to her dizzying nerves. Someone eventually led her away, and she sat down on the cool grass while everyone stared. After that disastrous match, Savannah practiced with her for so long that Georgina never missed another serve again.

She exhales. She needs to call Savannah back and make

amends, but her mind is too busy replaying every recent moment with Lance. She wishes she had never said anything about the baby.

"Please don't let me lose Lance, too," she mutters, shooting up another desperate prayer.

She jumps when her phone chirps.

We just need to hit pause, Georgina.

The knot in her stomach tightens. Her fingers fly over the keys.

We don't have to talk about the baby, Lance.
We can just go back to normal. I know it
wasn't part of the plan. I just needed to tell
someone.

They've always had that in common—a love for plans, control, order—so maybe that's the issue. Is he just reeling from the shock? She waits, her hope rising as he types back, but his next message is the same.

I just need time to process this.

She stares at the words and sighs in frustration. Does this "pause" really have to be right now? When she already feels so alone?

We can't process it together?

When he doesn't answer, her sorrow turns to anger.

Lance's sudden silence reminds her of her quick-to-flee father, and he has to realize that, since he's one of the only people in the world who knows about her conflict-filled childhood. *Why is this happening?* she wonders silently. Is God abandoning her, too? How could everything fall apart so fast? More anger fills her until guilt pulls at her heart.

Did God really abandon her, or did she abandon Him first?

As Georgina stares up at the deep darkness, tears touch her eyes. She never paid much attention to church growing up since their attendance was too sporadic to make sense of all the weird songs and sermons, but she's always believed in God, and she used to pray when she was younger. Shame fills her as she realizes God gave her everything she wanted and more, and she still let distractions and doubts creep in along the way.

"I'm sorry," she whispers, meaning it.

2

"**Georgina!**" **Benson Barnes yells,** banging on the door of her apartment. "Let me in!"

"It's unlocked!" Annette Davish-Barnes yells back as Benson barges through it.

Benson joins them in the kitchen, then turns to Annette. "How'd you get here before me? I thought you'd still be doing your hair."

Annette rolls her eyes as he slides into the breakfast nook beside her. "I spend less time on my hair than you do."

Benson scoffs, but he throws her a tiny teasing smile, and she smiles back. They were married when Georgina hired them three years ago—Benson as her agent, Annette as her publicist—but they divorced soon after. Somehow they manage to keep their working relationship relatively smooth, but Georgina secretly hopes they might get back together one day. They remind her of an older Bridget Jones and Mark Darcy, minus the British accents.

Benson beams as Georgina hands him his own warm French breakfast muffin. She knows those are his favorite. "You are truly a gem, Georgina Havoc," he says, taking it gratefully. "I tell you what, if Lance Broussard was here, I'd challenge him to fisticuffs—"

"Shh, don't bring him up until we absolutely have to," Annette says, catching the crushed look on Georgina's face. Benson falls silent as she joins them at the table.

Eight days have passed since the pause without a word from Lance, and her emotions are unraveling. She can't even shower properly. She just stands under the water with her forehead pressed against the hard, cold tile, trying to make sense of his silence. When the days dragged on, she had wondered if maybe he was in an accident or something, but Corrine assured her he's alive and well—and apparently totally unavailable.

"It's fine," Georgina says, picking at the cinnamon topping on her muffin. She feels like baking everything she can think of, but then she doesn't feel like eating any of it. It's a strange form of self-torture.

"Is Talia coming, too?" Benson asks, glancing at the door.

"Here!" Talia Jackson's warm voice sings from Georgina's computer, and he startles. Her smile is easy, but she's one of the sharpest attorneys in Nashville and can be terrifying when she wants to be.

"Sorry," Talia adds, turning on her screen as her son races by in the background. "No babysitter today."

"Don't apologize, Tal," Benson says between bites of muffin. "The gang's all here. That's what matters."

Talia and Annette nod in agreement, but Georgina's mood darkens as the gravity of the situation sinks in. You know it's bad when your agent, publicist, and lawyer are gathered around your breakfast table.

"So, our first order of business . . ." Benson lowers his glasses to study Georgina. "How are you holding up, Gigi? You should put these in your cookbook, by the way, they're phenomenal—Oh!" He nearly drops the muffin when Georgina bursts into tears. "What's wrong—"

"Read the room, Benson!" Annette snaps, handing her a nap-

26

kin. "She was already stressed out about the cookbook, and now this—"

"Sorry," Georgina says, blowing her nose and meeting Benson's startled eyes. She can't stop the tears once they start. "It's not your fault. I'm just a mess right now—"

"It's fine, honey. You're allowed to be a mess," Annette says gently, patting her hand. "None of us saw this coming. But, y'all, can we please just take a moment and appreciate the fact that this apartment is spotless, and she made muffins? That's what we love about you, Georgina. You practice what you preach."

Georgina laughs through her tears. "Thanks." Considering that she can barely drag herself out of bed most of the time, it's a nice compliment.

Benson makes his voice extra gentle. "Gigi, cry as much as you need to, but we must soldier on. Your time is too precious to waste. And we're all very expensive, remember?" he adds, making her laugh again, which is nice after so much crying.

"Any new legal stuff we should know about, Tal?" he asks while Georgina pulls herself together.

"No, not really. I did receive a very annoying call from Mark Malonetti this morning—"

"You did?" Georgina asks, straightening. Mark is Lance's lawyer. "What did he want?"

"He called to remind me about *discretion*," she explains with a scowl. "I guess he didn't like your Instagram post about taking time for self-care. He thinks people will read something into it."

Disappointment fills Georgina. And annoyance. Navigating social media in the middle of this has been a nightmare.

"I kindly reminded him that Lance still hasn't posted *anything* yet, which looks way more suspicious, in my opinion—"

"That's one of the strangest parts of this mess," Annette interjects. "Ty would never tell him to do that, so he must be going rogue." Ty is Lance's publicist, and according to Annette's sources, he's having an even worse week than Georgina, thanks to Lance's sudden unpredictability.

"What about Corrine?" Annette asks with a hopeful look. "Would she give you any intel?"

"Nope," Georgina mutters, lifting her phone to show her their last text exchange. "Already tried that."

> Per the NDA, I respectfully request that you direct all further questions to Mr. Malonetti. I'm sorry, Georgina. Take care.

Annette's eyes flash. "She seriously can't give you anything to work with? Woman to woman? I thought Corrine was a decent human being—"

"She really can't, though," Talia says, aiming a sympathetic look at Georgina. The non-disclosure agreement she and Lance signed was iron-clad when it came to "breakups, separation, or divorce," so not even Corrine can utter the details of their "pause" until they agree on a public statement. Georgina hadn't been enthused by the idea when Lance suggested the NDA, but he insisted it was standard practice, and Talia agreed.

"It's just so out of character for him," Annette mutters, shaking her head. "He's usually so strategic."

Georgina frowns at the troubled look on her face. Annette used to say that they made her job too easy, but Georgina doubts she feels that way now.

"Maybe he's having an early midlife crisis," Annette suggests, glancing at Benson. "He wouldn't be the first."

"I don't know." Georgina sighs miserably. "I hope it's just stress or something."

Benson nods, but Georgina can see Annette's skepticism when their eyes meet. She probably senses there's more to the story, but Georgina can't tell her about the baby right now or she'll start crying all over again.

"My turn, ladies," Benson interjects dramatically. "And, unfortunately, I have a bomb to drop. About UpScale—"

"Seriously, Benny?" Annette glares at him. "That's how you announce it?"

"What? There's no easy way to do it."

"No transition at all? You can't ease her into it?"

"I would if I could—"

"Just tell me," Georgina begs, her heart racing again. So far, all she's heard about UpScale is that they're anxiously waiting for Lance to snap back to his senses, too, but Benson's tense face suggests there's more to it.

"I talked to a few of my little birdies this morning . . . and . . ."

"What?" Georgina demands shrilly.

"If you don't get back together, they're going to drop one of you."

Georgina's stomach falls so fast she almost feels sick. "What?"

"They were banking on your shows merging into one brand, not two competing ones," he explains with a panicked look over what's left of his muffin. "If that doesn't happen, they're going gladiator, Gigi. They're going to make you fight for a spot."

Georgina's stomach drops farther as he frantically smooths his beard—another subtle sign of serious distress.

"And I hate to say this, but he's been at the network longer than you have. And we lost Poppy last year. She's barefoot and pregnant now."

Georgina briefly turns her face away, willing her tears not to fall, but Benson's comment reminds her that she's still not married—and apparently, she won't be anytime soon—and, more importantly, she's never carried a show on her own before. Poppy had been the more popular co-host, and Lance has his own dedicated following, so the doubts creep in fast, along with the unpleasant reminder that Georgina's fame only rocketed to new heights *after* she and Lance became an item. If it really does become a competition, Benson is right. The odds aren't in her favor.

"Don't go there, Georgina," Annette says soothingly, sensing her panic. "We're not going down without a fight—"

"Right, of course not," Benson cuts in again. "But wouldn't it be wonderful if we just resolve the issue? Lovers have spats all the time. Maybe we should plan a little getaway for you two? Some time to clear your heads—"

"No," Annette says firmly. "Lance is the one who asked for the pause, whatever that means, so he needs to be the one to hit play again. Georgina cannot make the next move. She'll look desperate—"

"I understand, Annie, but we *are* desperate. Gigi was always a package deal to UpScale—"

"Do you even hear yourself right now?" Annette shakes her head in disgust. "You sound like you don't believe in her at all."

"I'm just saying—"

"It's fine," Georgina interjects sharply, silencing them both. Even as her heart races, she's reminded why she hired them. Benson is refreshingly unfiltered—sometimes brutally so—while Annette's the ultimate cheerleader. They keep her humbled and motivated at the same time.

"I'm not saying she should throw herself at him," Benson continues defensively. "I just think that if we can resolve the conflict, we should."

"And if we can't, then Georgina will just have to destroy him," Annette concludes matter-of-factly.

Benson sighs in exasperation. "You're always looking for a fight, aren't you?"

"And you're always ready to fold—"

"What do you think, Georgina?" Talia interjects, surprising everyone. Her dark eyes are on Georgina as Benson and Annette's faces swivel to the screen. "What do *you* want to do?"

Georgina feels torn down the middle. Clearly, Annette thinks she should just move on, and maybe she should since she *hates* how easily Lance flipped her life upside down. She had thought they were finally settling into the happy ending part, but he reminded her of how risky love really is.

Still, the thought of throwing the last three years away feels like jumping into the deep unknown, and that scares her even more. Like Benson, she's still holding out some hope that she and Lance can salvage this somehow.

"I want to resolve it if we can," she answers.

Talia nods along with her, and Benson sighs with relief, but Georgina glances at Annette and sees a flicker of disappointment.

"I respect that," Annette finally mumbles. "We just need to tread carefully. We can't let you turn into the desperate ex-girlfriend. You've worked way too hard for that."

"I agree," Benson says firmly. "That's why there are only two acceptable options. Georgina and Lance smooth this over, and we all get the happy ending we wanted. Or . . ." His eyes take on a new intensity as they meet Georgina's. "Gigi gets the show and everything that comes with it."

3

"Dang." **Poppy looks up** from the stack of papers in her lap. "Benson came up with all this?"

"Annette too," Georgina says, recalling their last frenzied work session. Another ten days have passed since the pause, and despite Georgina's gentlest efforts to communicate, Lance still hasn't reciprocated, so Benson announced their first act of war last week—crafting a pilot for a new solo show.

"I'm super impressed," Poppy says, thumbing through the pages. They're inside her boho bungalow on the outskirts of Nashville, Georgina's frequent refuge for the last week. Poppy is curled up like a cat on Jared's favorite beanbag, while Georgina sits on the floor.

Three-year-old Olivia hands her a miniature rocking chair. "That goes in the baby room," she prods when Georgina doesn't immediately place it in the dollhouse. Poppy got her started on interior design early with a fancy Tudor-style dollhouse, complete with plush carpet and patterned wallpaper.

Olivia gives Georgina an approving grin when she finally sets the wooden rocker near an equally tiny crib. Her fiery hair, big vocabulary, and perfect little teeth are Georgina's favorite things about her.

"Benny and Annette really are the dream team, aren't they?"

Poppy murmurs, still skimming. "Why can't they just fall in love again already?"

"Annette says they work too much."

"That's sad. Who came up with the name of the show?"

"Me."

Poppy smiles. "That makes me love it even more. *Georgina Rebuilds.* I would watch the heck out of that. Did you pick the property, or was that UpScale?"

"Also me." She went with a pair of neglected cottages in the middle of Tarragon, Tennessee, instead of a typical Nashville renovation. Benson agreed it was the way to go.

"Everyone's going to be expecting another glam-girl reno in the suburbs, so you've got to dazzle them with something new, Gigi," he urged when they were flipping through endless homeowner applications. *"It can't be the same sleek, shiny thing we're all used to. Leave that to Lance."*

Another reason she wants the cottages is because Tarragon is a hidden little gem. She and Savannah got shipped off to Bible camp there one summer—their father's idea when their mother stopped taking them to church—and Tarragon was one of the most surprisingly beautiful places she's ever seen in her life.

Poppy reads the pilot aloud. "'When beloved designer Georgina Havoc finds herself newly single, it's time for her to pick up the pieces and rebuild! Viewers will watch as she reimagines the future, renovates her love life, and rescues neglected houses in the heart of Tennessee—'"

"Okay, we get it, Poppy—"

"'With help from a few zany characters, Georgina will stand on her own two feet and build a different kind of happy ending—'"

"Stop," Georgina begs, her embarrassment growing.

"What? You don't like it? It's so good, Georgie! Y'all spun that like a DJ."

"No, it's not that—"

"And you know that goober is going to go all out to keep his show, so you have to go hard."

Georgina glances at Olivia, who's listening closely like always, hence Poppy's use of "goober" and not something a little spicier.

"It's just . . . weird." She doesn't mind seeing it on paper but hearing it out loud feels too real.

"What did UpScale say about it?"

"Um." Georgina hesitates. Thankfully, they agreed to most of her proposal, but they had one big, complicated condition—which is the reason she's in Poppy's living room right now. Georgina's almost ready to ask her the question she's been dreading, but her nerves suddenly steer her in a different direction.

"According to Benson, they're pretty annoyed with Lance, too. I guess he's ghosting them."

Poppy's face darkens. "They should be mad. The silent treatment isn't okay. Like, what's his therapist doing right now? Is she on vacation or something? Did Lance just randomly forget that communication is essential to all healthy relationships?"

"Oh, he's definitely communicating *something*."

"*Intentional silence is a response, Georgina,*" Alvin's voice reminds her. "*And it communicates just as much as words. Listen closely.*"

Poppy frowns at the miserable look on her face. "You don't deserve this, Georgie—"

"Mommy, when are you going to stop talking?"

"Excuse me?"

"It's not your turn to play with Goji," Olivia says, with an exasperated look. "Georgie" is still too hard for her to say, so she unknowingly renamed Georgina after the bright orange-red berries she eats at snack time. "Be patient," she adds as Georgina fights back a smile.

Poppy's mouth opens, then closes, but Georgina saves her from further negotiations by focusing on the dollhouse again. "We need to put everyone to bed," Georgina suggests, making the mommy figurine carry the quarter-size baby over to the crib, much to Olivia's delight. "They've been busy rearranging their furniture all day."

Jared sticks his head into the playroom a few minutes later and offers Olivia the chance to water Poppy's impressive collection of houseplants, so Olivia happily grabs his hand and books it out of there.

"Sassy little thing," Poppy mutters, watching her go.

"Learning from the best."

Poppy smiles, but Georgina catches the familiar flicker of doubt in her eyes. She's a fantastic mom, but she's always been hard on herself, whether it's about Olivia's tantrums or her never-clean house or carving out time to talk to Jared without Olivia chattering in the background. Georgina has told her a million times that she's doing a good job—because she is—but Poppy loves them so much that she's always trying to do better.

"Are you sure you're really okay, Georgie? Losing a baby is—" When Georgina stiffens, Poppy falls silent. "Sorry. We don't have to talk about it. I just want you to know that you can feel whatever you're feeling."

Georgina nods but looks down, hiding her teary eyes. "I just want Lance to say something," she finally admits. Anything would be better than silence. "Maybe he is grieving in his own weird way."

Poppy's brows scrunch skeptically.

"He's said he wants kids," Georgina says, sounding more defensive than she means to.

"You know what? Jared has a cute single friend. I'm going to set you up with—"

"No," Georgina says firmly, stopping Poppy before she can

start scheming. "I don't even want to think about going on a date right now."

"It doesn't have to be *now*, but—"

"No, Poppy. Let me be single for five minutes." Her stomach churns at the thought of dating again, especially as her thirtieth birthday looms on the horizon. She thought she would be settled into the wedding-and-babies part of her life by then.

Poppy holds up her phone screen. "He's cute, right?"

Georgina groans at the photo of a smiling man dressed in plaid. "Cute isn't good enough. He's probably a lumberjack or something."

Poppy snorts. "I'm going to tell Jared you said that."

Georgina shrugs tiredly. As lovable as Jared McCrae is, he's not remotely her type. He rarely uses more than four words at a time, and his favorite food is elk. She didn't even know forestry officer was a profession before she met him.

"It's good to branch out."

Georgina throws her a withering look. She's genuinely happy for Poppy, but she and Jared are more like the exception than the rule. While Georgina's been fretting over relationships since high school, Poppy met Jared at a church thing when she was twenty-three and married him six months later in the middle of the woods. Georgina baked the lavender and lemon curd cake. A lot of people had doubts the marriage would last back then—including Georgina—but they are undeniably in love.

"I just want to focus on the show," she says when Poppy still looks determined. She has to keep her career intact, even if her heart isn't. Because if she loses the show, too, she'll lose everything—which is why she finally musters up the courage to tell Poppy what's on her mind. "I do need your help with something, though."

"Of course! Anything you need."

"With the pilot . . ." Georgina ignores the surprised look on her face and forces the rest out, relaying the network's one condition. "UpScale wants you to come, too." She tries to keep her voice light, but her confidence slips as she explains the reason. "That way, if they don't pick me, they can still use it. They'll turn it into a *Nail Breakers* reunion, and then . . . I'll just go from there."

Poppy's face falls.

"Obviously, though, that's not the only reason I want you to come with me. The fans love you more than me," Georgina adds as Poppy smiles weakly. "And I love you, too. . . ."

An awkward silence follows, and she wishes Poppy would say something, but her eyes drift from Georgina's and settle on Olivia's abandoned dollhouse. Georgina hears the softest, saddest sigh.

Georgina's heart sinks, but she understands. Before Poppy left *Nail Breakers*, Georgina had watched her struggle to host the show and be a mom at the same time. The result was complicated, ever-changing schedules, daily exhaustion, tension with Jared, and more than a few tearful conversations about what she might regret more—losing momentum in her career or missing most of Olivia's babyhood. And now Georgina's asking her to do that all over again, and with another baby on the way. Her guilt intensifies as her eyes move to Poppy's bump.

"They won't let you do the pilot without me?"

Georgina shakes her head sadly. "I'm sorry, Pop. It was either me asking you, or Benson crying over the phone."

Poppy finally laughs. "That's not fair. You know I can't say no to crying Benson."

"I know," Georgina says with an apologetic smile. "Which is why I wanted to ask you myself. Because I want you to say no if you want to."

Poppy smiles gratefully, but it's followed by another torn sigh. "How long would it be?"

"A month."

Disappointment flickers across Poppy's face. Georgina knows it's a long time apart from Jared and Olivia.

"How far is it from Nashville?"

"Two hours," Georgina answers as Poppy's brows crease. "No pressure, though, okay? You'll still be the world's greatest friend if you say no—"

"When would it start?"

Georgina braces herself to break more bad news. "June." Poppy doesn't say anything, but "yikes" is written across her face. The terrible timeline means she'll be nearly eight months pregnant when the show wraps up, and her pregnancy with Olivia was miserable toward the end.

"I don't know, Georgie." Poppy's eyes linger over the abandoned dollhouse as disappointment fills Georgina. "I don't want to let you down. . . ."

"I totally get it."

"I'll pray about it, though, okay? And I'll talk to Jared. Just give me a couple days."

Cautious hope fills Georgina because Poppy takes her praying pretty seriously, so it's a good sign. Georgina also feels a tiny sting of shame. Poppy has brought up faith more than once over the course of their friendship. Georgina always evades the topic, preferring to wade in shallow, safer waters, but God's been on her mind ever since that dream-shattering night in the bathroom, and she's trying to keep the lines of communication open.

"I'll pray, too," she says as Poppy's lips lift into a surprised smile.

4

"Five bucks says you can't hit the tiny one."

Cassidy's eyes move from the row of targets he just decimated to a red dot in the distance.

"I set it up just for you," Eddy adds, pulling on his ear protection again. "The grand finale."

Cassidy's confidence wavers a bit, especially since it's an unusually breezy morning for mid-June, but he positions the rifle against his shoulder and makes a few careful adjustments. It's one of his favorites—a Savage Model 10. He hasn't shot something that far away in a long time, but his pride kicks in as Eddy peers over his shoulder.

"Come on, Cass. We're not getting any younger—"

He presses the trigger.

The burst of the bullet rings across the range, but Cassidy barely hears it, too focused on catching the soft ting of metal on metal. When he hears it a moment later, Eddy grabs his binoculars.

"Center right," he grumbles.

Cassidy grins, surprised but pleased. His father had liked the Model 10, too. He would have given Cassidy a hard time for his fancy custom scope, but then probably gone out and bought one for himself.

Eddy digs a wrinkled five-dollar bill out of his pocket. "Here you go, Captain America."

Cassidy waves the money away. "That'll teach you not to gamble."

Eddy smirks. "I knew better." Eddy Alvarez is sort of a cross between a wise grandfather-type and a tattooed drinking buddy, minus the drinking. He also used to be an Army chaplain, which is why Pastor Boggs paired them up at Alcoholics Anonymous two years ago. It was a sobriety-check match made in heaven.

Cassidy packs up while Eddy waits on a bench, Cassidy's thoughts swirling like the gray clouds overhead. In a way, that shot is sort of like his life right now—not totally on target but getting close. He didn't make any new plans after Melody died five years ago, since most of his dreams died with her, but that's been changing little by little, and it finally feels like he's back on course.

"Cass," Eddy mutters, getting his attention again. "We got some company."

Cassidy turns as footsteps approach, then groans inwardly. He and Eddy usually have the range all to themselves on Wednesday mornings, but not lately. "Dagnabit," he mutters when he sees the familiar faces coming toward them.

Eddy fights back a laugh. "No good deed goes unpunished, does it?"

"Apparently not."

They both straighten and smile when two young women pass by with Eddy's nineteen-year-old son, Gus, who looks positively thrilled by the arrangement. Unfortunately for him, the women's eyes are firmly fixed on Cassidy.

"How about this stall?" one of them says, choosing the stall closest to his. "Oh, hey, y'all," she says, glancing coyly at Cassidy in a way that would seem casual and coincidental if she hadn't tried it three other times already.

"Morning!" Eddy says, barely hiding his amusement. "Nice seeing y'all again. Getting in more practice?"

The woman nods and throws Cassidy a hopeful look.

He forces a small smile but keeps quiet. Clearly, he led the poor girl on when he helped her load a gun a few weeks ago, because she's become a permanent fixture at the range ever since. Sometimes she's alone, but other times her friend comes along for moral support. He expertly avoids their eyes as Gus sets up a target.

"Try more donuts and less of those crazy exercises," Eddy whispers, rising from the bench. "That's my secret."

Cassidy fights back a laugh and follows him toward the indoor range. Eddy always gives him crap about his rigid fitness routine.

The smell of propellant and stale coffee hits Cassidy's nose as Eddy opens the door. He much prefers the sunny outdoor range to the indoor one, where mounted animals cover every inch of free wall space and watch them shoot with cold, glassy eyes, but he's just thankful for the escape.

"What would Renata Woodard think of your little fan club?"

Cassidy's mood instantly darkens at the mention of Renata's name, but Eddy is oblivious. Cassidy's brother, Sawyer, is the only person he ever told about his drunken, grief-fueled kiss with Renata four years ago—out of his own embarrassment, and to spare her some, too—but regret hits him hard every time he thinks about it.

"She's got some competition."

When Cassidy shoots him a tired look, Eddy finally shuts up and changes the subject.

"You been a good boy this week?"

"Yep."

"That so?"

"Mm-hmm. Pastor Boggs should give me your job."

Eddy smiles. "Are you still reading all those fancy seminary books he gave you?"

"Mm-hmm."

"We'll see about that." Eddy scratches his patchy beard and ponders his endless trivia questions. Most people probably wouldn't guess it by looking at him, but Eddy Alvarez knows his Bible. He's the one who named Cassidy's return to Tarragon "the Job years," after the Bible's most famous sufferer. Cassidy didn't know Job's story back then, but he eventually figured out the connection. Job had it worse, but Cassidy was a runner-up when he lost his wife, father, career, and self-control in one fell swoop.

"All right, I got one," Eddy says, flipping on the lights. "Who's King Asa?"

"He's the guy with the bad feet. In Chronicles. The first one, I think. A king of Judah."

"Anything else?"

"Yeah, he was actually a pretty good king. Busted up a bunch of idols, ousted some tyrants, beat a couple big armies." Cassidy frowns, recalling another part of the story where a prophet criticized Asa for forgetting to consult God about a certain military strategy. It seemed like a fairly small thing to Cassidy, especially since Asa seemed to have it mostly under control, but that's a theme he's been noticing as he reads—that God wants people to rely on Him all the time, not just in the make-it-or-break-it moments.

"You're the only mentee I got who actually reads his Bible, and it shows. The rest of 'em give me miles of excuses."

Cassidy nods, familiar with the excuses himself since he used to have them, too. He thought he was Christian even though he didn't pay any attention to God until he went to war, and then it still took a few more years before Melody's most passionate prayer was answered and God finally saved him from his pride.

"You're coming up on three years sober quick," Eddy adds, reminding him of just how far he's come—a bittersweet realization, since it also reminds him of how far he fell.

"You gonna throw me a party?"

"I'll leave that to your mama. How's she doing, by the way? Denise said she was sick again."

Cassidy frowns as his mother comes to mind. Despite a lifelong battle with lupus, Goldie Stokes loves living in her way-too-big Victorian and doing everything by herself—an arrangement that doesn't work as well as it used to. Another nasty cold knocked her off her feet last week, but she's already trying to get back in the Harp House kitchen.

"She could be better, but she insists on her own way."

Eddy's mouth turns up. "Hmm, I don't know anyone stubborn like that."

Cassidy smiles weakly, but guilt fills him as it sinks in that he's about to turn his mother's happy world upside down. She's already been through enough.

"Just keep doing what you're doing, Cass," Eddy says, reading the troubled look on his face. "Especially now, with the big changes coming. You gotta stay sharp. You know that already."

Cassidy nods somberly. He and Eddy joke around, but they both know how serious Cassidy's sobriety is. He has to stay out of that deep, dark pit where he almost lost himself, no matter how much he wants to crawl back in sometimes. "I will." He's determined to do it for himself, and his mother, and his brother, and Eddy, and all the rest. And Melody, of course. And God, most of all. He's given Cassidy more chances than he can count, and Cassidy wants to make the most of them.

"How's the grand old house these days?" Eddy asks, lightening the mood a little.

There's a lot he could say about the Harp House—the farm is a mess, thanks to a scatter of unpredictable storms, and the cheap little rental cabins popping up across the plateau are bad for business—but he goes with a simple "busy" and leaves it at that.

"How'd Gavin take the news?"

"He's not too happy with me at the moment." Cassidy can't really blame him, either. The Harp House has been struggling in recent years, like most places in Tarragon, but right about now is when people start booking it for vacations and wedding parties and all the other social events Cassidy tries his best to avoid. Him leaving means Gavin has to run the house in the middle of the busy season *and* start looking for his replacement at the same time.

"Gav's a big boy. He'll figure it out."

Cassidy nods, but guilt gnaws at him. Melody's parents are upset with him, too. Dale had muttered something and handed the phone over to Donna when Cassidy told him the news, which means he didn't have anything nice to say.

"When do you leave?" Eddy asks, pulling him back to the present. "Did they give you a date yet?"

"Sometime in August," Cassidy answers, both dreading and dreaming of his departure as the summer days slip by.

"I hear El Salvador's real pretty in the fall. Especially the coke fields."

Cassidy laughs. "They don't grow it down there. It's the transit spot." He's been studying up on it ever since he accepted the job. He did a special operation in Guatemala years ago, but the situation going on in El Salvador is a whole different kind of beast. Overseas private security contract work wasn't his first choice—he searched high and low for something closer to home with no luck—but his anticipation is building. It's an opportunity he never thought he'd get again after he left the military.

"You're making the right move, Cass," Eddy says right when

the guilt creeps back in. He's good at that sort of thing—pulling up what's under the surface in an easy kind of way. He doesn't use too many words, either. Just enough to make you feel better.

"You just stay faithful, and God will sort out the rest."

5

Shania Twain's voice blasts through the Lexus as Georgina and Poppy cruise to Tarragon. Poppy is the playlist queen, so it's the perfect mix of pop and country for their rural road trip.

"What's this place called again?" Poppy asks after a passionate solo.

Georgina frowns. "Tarragon?"

"No, like this whole area." Poppy motions out the window. "It has a special name, right?"

"Oh. The Cumberland Plateau?"

"Yes, that's it." Poppy admires the forested hills and valleys. "It's crazy gorgeous."

Georgina nods. She knows more about the geography than she ever wanted to, thanks to Benson, who had included every possible selling point in the pilot.

"I could totally live out here," Poppy adds as they glide by another stunning view of water, cliffs, and endless oak trees.

Georgina glances out her window. "I couldn't." It's as beautiful as she remembers, especially now that the sun is breaking through the clouds, but it's way too remote for her taste. She needs people and distractions. Sleeping alone in the apartment for the last month has been awful. "It has a cute history, though," she says, trying to remember the story she learned at camp. "French settlers came in and named everything after herbs or something like that."

"Um, hello, cookbook inspiration?"

Georgina smiles sadly. "Maybe . . ." There's a pile of emails in her inbox, but she's barely had a chance to look at any of them lately, too busy finalizing things with UpScale. They arranged a decent crew for the project, but they also shortened the timeline. Instead of twelve weeks to pull off an amazing transformation, she only has eight.

"'Olivia says she can watch three cartoons before bed instead of two, is that true?'" Poppy mutters, reading a text message aloud. She shakes her head tiredly and types back. "No, Jared, our daughter is clearly playing you like a fiddle. And it's only day one, dude."

Georgina laughs. Poppy is helping her stay sane, like always. When she announced she would join Georgina in Tarragon, Georgina abandoned the Nutella frosting she was in the middle of eating and dropped to her knees. *Thank you, thank you, thank you,* she had thought, stunned and grateful. After so many weeks of confusion and disappointment, she needed some good news, even if it came with a little bit of guilt. She watched as Poppy scooped up Olivia for the longest, tightest hug in all of Tennessee when they said good-bye this morning. Olivia looked surprisingly calm, but Poppy couldn't hide her tears.

"Hold up. You're not texting him, right?" Poppy asks, pulling her back to the present.

"Who?"

Poppy scowls. "Mister-I-don't-communicate-with-my-girlfriend-for-almost-a-month-and-then-expect-her-to-drop-everything-and-talk-to-me. That guy."

Georgina frowns, her emotions churning at the mention of Lance. "No. Why?"

Poppy glares at the screen above the center console. "He's texting you." She points as his name flashes across it.

Part of Georgina wants to scramble for her phone, but she's getting a little better at fighting that urge. She feigns nonchalance. "I promise I'm not talking to him. I've been ignoring his messages."

"Good." Poppy's eyes turn as fiery as her hair in the summer sun. "He should stay on ice forever as far as I'm concerned. 'Hey, G, let's just ignore your feelings and pause until I feel like talking again, sound good?'" She mocks his low voice. "I can't even believe him, honestly. The absolute audacity . . ."

Georgina nods along with Poppy's complaints, but she secretly would've taken his calls if Annette hadn't insisted she give him a taste of his own medicine.

"Oh no." Georgina sighs as her mother's number flashes across the screen next. "I have to take this," she says, reluctantly turning down Shania. "Hi, Mom. You're on speakerphone. I'm driving. Poppy's here." Georgina gets all the information out fast. Her mother loves Poppy, but that doesn't mean she won't say something awful about her behind her back. Her criticism is usually about Poppy dropping her career to be a full-time mom, or that she lets Olivia wear ridiculously mismatched outfits.

"Finally," her mother says with a huff. "Hello, Poppy," she adds sweetly.

"Hi, Faye! How are you?"

Her mother actually had been there when Georgina met Poppy at the Nashville Farmer's Market seven years ago. Georgina just wanted vanilla-infused honey, but Poppy was selling adorable little embroidery hoops, and her bubbly personality sucked Georgina in. Their conversations slowly morphed from a weekly thing to daily texts to an official best friend status in a matter of months. Georgina's mother complained Poppy was "way too much" back then, but Poppy won her over eventually.

Georgina listens as they chitchat. Her mother dominates most of the conversation with updates about work, her gossipy garden club, and Nova, her spoiled Labradoodle—the three things she lives for, besides Georgina.

"Other than that, I've just been waiting for Georgina to return my calls. . . ."

Georgina scowls at her mother's wounded tone. She feels bad about letting their communication dwindle, but she had no choice, thanks to Lance.

"I called you every day last week—"

"And I texted you." Georgina also sent her a bouquet bursting with pink peonies and roses for Mother's Day—her mother's favorite combination—but that went unacknowledged, too. "I've been busy."

"With what?"

"My show."

"I thought it was delayed?"

Georgina freezes, realizing she slipped up. *Trending in Tennessee* is technically delayed, according to UpScale, but Georgina still hasn't told her mother the real reason why. "Um, yeah, it is, but Poppy and I are doing a reunion thingy, remember? I told you about it—"

"Will Lance be part of it, too?"

Georgina exchanges wide-eyed glances with Poppy. "No, this is separate."

"So, what's he doing? I haven't heard from him in ages."

Me neither, Georgina thinks bitterly. "He's busy with a project," she lies, keeping her voice light as a feather. "In Nashville—"

"Y'all were in the magazines at the grocery store again," her mother adds. She adores Lance and always gets a kick out of the tabloids' obsession with them. "Something hilarious about how you're not speaking to each other—"

"You know how they are, Mom," Georgina interrupts, her voice coming out sharper than she wants it to. The rumors are already circulating despite Annette's valiant attempts to beat them back with careful press statements about busy schedules. "Lance is fine. We're . . . fine."

Poppy frowns.

"Did you need something?"

"No," her mother says indignantly. "I just wanted to check on my beautiful daughter. Is that okay?"

Georgina throws Poppy a skeptical look, which Poppy returns. The strain in her mother's voice suggests there's another reason for the call.

"Have you talked to Savannah lately?"

Guilt pricks at Georgina as she remembers the declined call. "No." She's been so busy with the pilot that she forgot to call her back. "Why? Is she okay?"

"I think she's in a cult."

Georgina and Poppy raise their eyebrows in unison.

"Come again?" Georgina says when the shock wears off. "Our Savannah?"

"Yes. I'm worried."

Georgina's confusion grows as she tries to reconcile her mother's words with her pink-haired, party-loving sister. "Like, how? What's she doing?"

"I don't think she's doing *anything*. That's the problem. I ask about her classes or getting a job, and all she says is that she's working on her mental health. I asked her what that means and apparently it's just moping around all day and listening to some Baptist preacher on the internet scream about God. Your father probably has something to do with it," her mother adds dramatically.

Embarrassment fills Georgina as she glances at Poppy, but she just looks puzzled.

"Georgina? Did you hear me?"

"Yes, I'm just processing. . . ." She scowls mid-sentence, realizing she sounds like Lance. "Um, yeah, that is definitely weird for Savannah, but it doesn't sound too culty. Maybe she's just going through a rough time?"

"When is she not?"

Georgina's heart sinks. Her mother's never been the warmest, fuzziest person in the world, but there's no compassion for Savannah in her voice anymore—just exhaustion. Shame fills Georgina as she realizes she feels the same way most of the time.

Her mind drifts back to their last conversation. Savannah was in the middle of some money drama with a roommate, and Georgina didn't offer to help, which surprised them both. There's almost always something going on in Savannah's life, whether it's a feud with their mother, drama with friends, or another lost job. Georgina usually runs to her rescue, but that day Alvin's voice was louder than usual and reminded her that she needs to set boundaries with her sister, too, no matter how uncomfortable it feels. Unsurprisingly, Savannah didn't take it well.

"It's not just the religion thing, Georgina. I do think she's getting in too deep—but you know how Savannah is. This is just her latest little *thing*. She'll distract herself for a while, and then she'll come crashing back to earth, and that's the part I'm worried about. It won't be pretty."

Georgina suddenly understands. She's observed the pattern her mother's describing whenever Savannah gets a new boyfriend or hobby. Her sister floats around in a happy daze until the eventual blowup, and then Georgina or her mother have to help her pick up the pieces.

"Can you please call her?" her mother pleads as they pass the sun-faded *Welcome to Tarragon Valley* sign.

Georgina sighs but doesn't protest. Her life is already falling apart, so she might as well throw Savannah's weirdness on top of the rubble, too.

"Georgina?" her mother presses.

"Yes," she snaps, but her voice softens when her mother sighs in relief. Unfortunately, Savannah doesn't listen to *anyone*, including Georgina, but her mother sounds too hopeful for Georgina to remind her of that. "I'll try."

"Wow. I admit, I didn't see Savannah-joined-a-cult coming," Poppy says when Georgina finally ends the call moments later. "Faye caught me way off guard with that one."

Georgina laughs. "Right? Big if true."

"You gotta love her, though. Never a dull moment with the original boss babe."

Georgina nods tiredly. She complains about her mother often, but Poppy always tries to shift the focus to her better qualities, like the fact that she singlehandedly held Georgina and Savannah's lives together when their father called it quits, or that she clawed her way to the top of the marketing firm where she works. Faye Wright passed down her control-freak tendencies to Georgina, but she also gave her a special kind of determination to go with it.

"People aren't all good or all bad, Georgina," Alvin said once, during one of her many Mom-centered sessions. *"That would be simpler, but we're all a mix of both. Adjust your expectations accordingly."*

"Hey, isn't that the camp you went to?" Poppy asks, pointing toward a wooded lake in the distance.

Surprise fills Georgina, followed by a burst of nostalgia as they pass another sun-bleached sign. "That's it." Lake Chervil is just as serene as she remembers. She's stared at pretty much every shade of blue known to man—most people want blue or white or beige on their walls—but she still can't describe this lake. It's clean-blue meets deep-blue meets glass-blue. Savannah used to swim in it every chance she got, but Georgina could never work up the courage to jump in.

The stunning scenery was one of the few upsides of her and Savannah having to spend a summer in Tarragon. Georgina's mind flits back to her mother's strange announcement. "Baptists are just like normal Christians, right?" If Savannah really is getting into something weird, she wants to be prepared.

"Yeah, they believe all the usual Christian things. Jesus is God, He saves you from your sin if you believe in Him, you go to heaven, et cetera, et cetera."

"Is that what you believe, too?"

"Yeah," Poppy says, keeping her voice light, even though she looks unsure of what Georgina's reaction might be. "I've felt God's presence before," she adds. "And it just makes sense to me. Like, how God is perfect and holy, but He also forgives us, and then how we change—"

Georgina nods along with her, but she has only a vague idea of what Poppy's talking about. That dreaded summer camp with Savannah was where she learned most of what she knows about God, and it was mostly cheesy icebreakers and obstacle courses with a little Jesus talk sprinkled in.

"What do you believe, Georgie?"

Georgina knew the question was coming, but she's still not ready for it. The topic has been on her mind a lot over the past few weeks, but it still feels like a puzzle full of missing pieces. "I believe that, too. . . ."

Poppy patiently waits for her to elaborate, but Georgina's not sure how to put her hesitation into words. Her mother always made religion seem pointless, and she had a decent reason to, given her father's flaky faith. He'd get adamant about church attendance from time to time—after his mom died, or when he crashed his beloved 1982 Alfa Romeo—but it never lasted long or changed anything. He still drank too much and took the bait whenever Georgina's mother picked a fight.

"Are you hungry?" she suddenly asks, changing the subject to her growling stomach as they pass a sign tempting them with food. Thankfully, when Poppy's pregnant, the answer to that question is almost always yes.

They slip in and out of a fifties-style diner twenty minutes later, and Georgina attempts to eat and drive, but spearing lettuce in a Caesar salad while keeping a hand on the steering wheel proves to be more challenging than she thought.

"This is probably just her latest little thing. She'll distract herself for a while, and then she'll come crashing back to earth, and that's the part I'm worried about."

Georgina winces as her mother's words return. Is that what she's doing, too? Distracting herself with a new "thing" in Tarragon while her life falls apart?

"Oh my gosh, Georgie, look at this place."

Georgina glances over as Poppy holds up her phone.

"It's called the Harp House, and it's *so* pretty," she says, scrolling fast. "Oh, shoot, it's booked—"

"Crap," Georgina mutters when her fork falls, and she struggles to reach it. Her anxieties bubble up again. What if it's really over with Lance? Part of her is still holding out a tiny flame of hope for a happy ending, but it's fading fast. And what if UpScale doesn't choose her and her career ends? Will it be a meteoric crash, like her mother described? Or—

"Georgie!"

Georgina straightens as Poppy screams her name.

"Swerve!" she yells as Georgina jerks the steering wheel at the last second. The car veers into the next lane, barely missing a man standing right in the middle of the road, while what's left of her salad goes flying and splatters Poppy's face with dressing.

"Oh my gosh . . . oh my gosh . . ." Poppy says, clutching her heart with one hand and wiping her cheek with the other. "You almost hit that guy, Georgie!"

It all happens so fast that Georgina's too panicked to slow down or stop, but she looks back long enough to see him turn into a speck in her rearview mirror.

Cassidy's heart is beating so fast it feels like it might burst. He's had some close calls in his life, but that was one of the closest. A white Lexus going full speed just missed him by centimeters before it zoomed off. He mutters a prayer of gratitude.

When his heart resumes a semi-normal pace again, he turns his attention back to Eddy's fawn. Cassidy frowns at the poor creature as he lifts it. Dead deer are usually battered and wide-eyed with shock, but this little guy is in remarkably good shape, with just one battle scar on his side, and dark, calm eyes under his budding antlers.

"Well done, sir," Cassidy mutters, gently setting him in the truck bed. He looked death right in the face and didn't flinch. Cassidy tosses his gloves aside and texts Eddy.

Tell Denise I've got her new buddy.

Eddy's wife stuffs everything, from tiny field mice to fancy yellow-eyed owls that she orders out of catalogs, and apparently she just had to have the fawn when she spotted him earlier that morning. Unfortunately for Cassidy, he owed Eddy too many favors to say no.

He climbs in the truck again and heads toward the Harp House but keeps an eye out for the fancy Lexus, partly irritated but also concerned. There's a hundred different ways to get lost in the winding backroads and not that many people around to help. He eventually passes by Kit Vanover's orchard and hits the brakes hard as surprise fills him. It's about the last place he expected to see the Lexus, but there it is, parked outside the bigger cottage with the trunk open, revealing a tower of luggage.

Cassidy frowns. He met the married couple Kit sold the property to two years ago—a woman with a sharp, pointy face and her impatient-looking husband. They told him they wanted to turn the cottages into rentals, but they haven't been back to Tarragon since, and they drove one of those funny little Volkswagen Beetles, not a Lexus. His curiosity grows as he parks in the driveway and starts walking toward the rickety porch. A woman's voice travels through the open door, but it fades as his boots creak against the first step.

Quick, light footsteps follow. "Who are you?"

Cassidy is momentarily stunned as he comes eye-to-eye with the woman who almost killed him. She looks just as surprised as he does.

"Are you with the crew?"

His tongue is temporarily tied as she waits for an answer. Dark, wildly curly hair grazes her shoulders, and curling bangs touch her eyebrows. She's wearing a black shirt tucked into tight, high-waisted jeans to show off a tiny waist and not-so-tiny hips, while turquoise jewelry glitters on her ears and wrists. The step she's standing on makes them almost the same height, and her brown eyes are suspicious as they meet his.

"Pardon?" he says, finally getting a word out.

She glances at his truck, then back at him with an impatient look. "Did UpScale send you?"

He has no idea what she's talking about, so he returns her impatience with some of his own. "No. I'm the guy you almost ran over on the highway."

Color splashes across her face. "Oh."

"Let me guess," he adds, his irritation returning briefly as he relives the harrowing moment. "You were on your phone?"

Some of her embarrassment fades as her pretty eyes narrow. "No, I wasn't, actually." She puts her hands on her hips in a challenging sort of way that probably isn't supposed to be cute, but it is. "I just wasn't expecting someone to be hanging out in the middle of the road."

He frowns. It's a fair point. *Thanks, Eddy*, he thinks.

"Are you a cop or something?" Her posture is still defiant, but he catches a little bit of fear in her voice this time, so he softens his tone.

"No, I'm not. I just thought maybe y'all were lost or something."

She relaxes a tiny bit. "Oh. No."

His confusion returns as he glances behind her, at Kit's run-down cottage.

"I was just a little distracted earlier—on the road—sorry—" Her apology comes out in an awkward rush, but her eyes are sincere under those long lashes. "I should've stopped."

What's left of his annoyance fades—mainly because he's pretty distracted now, too. "It's all right. I'm wide awake, thanks to you."

She offers him a small smile—the first one since he arrived—and it makes her even prettier.

"I'm Georgina, by the way," she says, beating him to a proper introduction as she offers up her hand. Her grip is surprisingly strong as he shakes it, and her painted fingernails match her jewelry.

"Cassidy," he says as predictable surprise flickers across her face. "I know, I know."

"What?"

"My name. I don't know what possessed my mother."

"Oh." She laughs as her cheeks turn that cute shade of pink

again. "It's not bad, though. I mean, yeah, you don't meet that many men named Cassidy. Or any. I don't, at least. . . ." She trails off and turns her head to one side, probably to hide the blooming color in her face. "Anyway." She recovers quickly. "I have a super weird last name, so I get it."

"How weird?"

"Havoc."

His brows raise. "*Havoc*? Like . . . chaos? Destruction? That kind of havoc?"

She laughs again. "Yep. That's me. Georgina Havoc."

"Wow. You don't meet that many women with such a foreboding last name. I don't, at least," he teases.

As her laughter starts up again, he realizes they're officially flirting now, and he doesn't mind one bit. She doesn't seem to, either. "So, are you—"

"Georgie! Are you out here? The whole roof on this thing is a hot mess—"

Cassidy turns toward the front door as a pregnant woman bolts through it. She's talking so fast that Cassidy can barely keep up, but she halts mid-sentence when she sees him.

"Oh . . ." She looks at Georgina with wide, curious eyes. "Who's this?"

"Um . . . Cassidy. Something." Georgina turns to him with a much more businesslike expression than before, but it melts away when her eyes meet his. "What's your last name? Since you already made fun of mine."

He smiles at her playful tone. "Stokes."

Her brows lift with surprise, but he's not sure why. "Okay, then. Cassidy Stokes meet Poppy McCrae," she says, hopping up another step and joining Poppy by the door. "Cassidy is the guy I almost hit on the highway."

Poppy's mouth falls open at her matter-of-fact tone. "Oh my gosh, you are? Are you okay? We were totally going to stop—"

"He's obviously fine, Poppy," Georgina interjects defensively. "Look at him."

Poppy does look at him before turning back to Georgina with a face he can't figure out. Georgina looks confused, too, until color touches her cheeks.

"I am fine," he adds, interrupting their bizarre facial expressions. "No harm done."

Poppy finally tears her eyes off Georgina's. "Seriously, though, we are so sorry! That was crazy. The roads around here are just so long, you know?"

He smiles at the odd comment. "Where y'all from?"

"Nashville," Poppy answers cheerfully, confirming his suspicions. They're clearly city girls, so what on earth are they doing with Kit's cottages?

His eyes travel to the tower of luggage again. "Are y'all staying here?"

They both look surprised for a moment until they vigorously shake their heads. "No way. We're just renovating them. It's for a show. Don't tell anyone, though." Poppy puts a finger to her lips. "The producers are weird about that. They don't want crazy fans showing up."

He frowns. "Okay . . ." She's speaking a language he doesn't understand. Producers? Crazy fans? Secret renovations? Suddenly, he remembers the buyers. "Did the Seelys hire you?"

Poppy looks confused. "Who?"

"Our clients, Poppy," Georgina says, throwing her an exasperated look before answering his question. "Yes, the Seelys applied to be on the show, so we technically work for them, but also for the network." She smiles at the perplexed look on his face. "It's a whole complicated thing."

"Y'all are famous, then?"

Poppy grins as Georgina blushes. "Georgina's the next Joanna Gaines, actually."

"No, I'm just—"

"You should look up *Nail Breakers*," Poppy suggests.

"No, you shouldn't. He's not in our target audience, Poppy," Georgina says quickly, but Cassidy's curiosity is piqued. He has seen those sort of design shows before, where pretty, peppy people come in and paint the walls and throw in a bunch of expensive furniture. Melody had liked to binge-watch them sometimes, and he was secretly entertained, too.

"Do you live around here, Cassidy?" Poppy asks, capturing his attention again.

"Yep. Born and raised."

She smiles at Georgina like that's the most adorable thing she's ever heard before turning back to him. "Perfect, then you'll know. We're looking for a bed-and-breakfast type of deal, or, just, like, literally anything close by. All the hotels are a million miles away."

He's surprised. And concerned. "Y'all don't have a place to stay?"

"No, we do," Georgina says quickly, throwing Poppy another exasperated look. "Poppy just doesn't like it—"

"I'll pay for it myself, Georgie."

"For a *month*? That's ridiculous."

"Not when you're grumpy and pregnant!"

They go back and forth for a while until Georgina finally explains their arrangements to Cassidy, which sound far from ideal. Apparently, their fancy television network put them up in a cheap rental in Crossville. It's bigger than Tarragon, but it's an hour commute both ways.

Georgina's face softens when Poppy stretches wearily. "I already checked, Pop. There's nothing closer."

"There's seriously *nothing*?" Poppy asks, turning to him again with hopeful eyes. "Like, no little off-the-beaten-path places? No Airbnbs?"

He shakes his head sadly. Tarragon really is small—much smaller than she must've realized. "How long are y'all sticking around?"

"Two months," Georgina replies, surprising him. For some reason, he thought their timeline would be longer, since fixing up houses isn't some easy thing, and it's probably even more of a mess when you add a bunch of camera people.

"Sorry, I mean, that's how long *I'll* be here," she adds, correcting herself. "Poppy has to get back to her family in a few weeks."

Cassidy nods, but his thoughts play back her answer as her eyes meet his again. The way she said it suggests she doesn't have a family to go home to.

"It's okay," she says quickly as he ponders their problem. "We'll be fine—"

"Here, how about this." He pulls his phone out of his pocket. "Why don't you give me your number?"

Her eyes widen.

"So I can call you if something opens up?" he adds quickly, keeping his voice casual. The Harp House is booked through the next two and a half weeks, but he can still ask around a few other places.

"Oh. Sure, yeah." Georgina nods and matches his casual attitude, but she seems frozen in place as he offers her the phone.

"Give him your number," Poppy finally mutters.

Georgina shoots her a murderous look before taking it. There's an awkward silence as her fingers fly over the screen.

"Thanks," he says when she hands it back a moment later.

"Seriously, though, it's not a big deal—"

"I'll text you, so you have my number, too."

She falls silent as Poppy's tense face swivels between them as he types, like he's in the middle of defusing a bomb. "There," he says a moment later, pressing send. He throws Georgina a final smile. "You can holler if you need anything."

"What did he say?" Poppy demands when Georgina doesn't immediately share the contents of Cassidy's text. When he drove off a few minutes earlier, the two of them raced inside the cottage to hunt for Georgina's phone. Georgina got to it first, but just barely. Poppy moves like a turtle when she's pregnant, but she put on an impressive burst of speed.

"Spill it, Georgie!"

"Calm down, it's just a smiley face—"

Poppy gasps. "Oh my gosh, which one? The normal one, or one with the happy eyes?"

"Just the normal one," Georgina says dismissively, quickly pocketing her phone and hiding her smile. He also sent a car emoji and the grinning face with the little sweat droplet, but she doesn't mention that since Poppy's ready to psychoanalyze him. Georgina is, too, but she's not about to admit it.

Thankfully, the cottages temporarily distract them as they make their way through. The larger one has a standard layout with combined living and dining areas leading to a galley-style kitchen and a nook-sized sunroom, plus a tiny bedroom and even tinier bathroom. The second, smaller cottage is just a room with a bathroom, but it does have a decent-sized porch.

Georgina grabs her planner and writes down the various flaws as they walk and talk—chipped paint, hideous wallpaper, unforgivable wood paneling, stained carpet, broken windows patched together with plywood and duct tape—the list goes on. When a faint, sickly sweet smell of rot hits her nose, she looks up and immediately spots the culprit. Coppery water stains cover the kitchen's flaky ceiling like dark, splotchy clouds.

"Ew," Poppy says, noticing too. "That rocking chair is cute, though."

Georgina nods. She wasn't expecting any furnishings, but there are some dusty, delicate curtains on one of the windows and a very fragile-looking rocking chair in a corner of the living room.

"I thought you said they were just needs-a-little-love-and-paint bad." Poppy dodges a drop of water from the ceiling. "This is more like termites-and-lead-paint bad—"

"They're somewhere in the middle," Georgina insists, but doubt fills her as she surveys the neglected room. Now that they're here, she's second-guessing her choice. She had wanted a property that would make for a big transformation, but her time and budget are already tight even without water damage.

"At least they're super tiny," Poppy says, finding the silver lining. "Have you met the Seely people yet?"

Georgina nods and fills her in on their clients, Curt and Monica Seely. Monica is obsessed with UpScale shows, which is why they applied, but Curt doesn't want to do more than a standard before-and-after reaction.

Poppy cheers at the news. "I love it when they just let us do our thing."

"Me too." Minimal client involvement means they can branch out beyond open-concept layouts and shades of beige.

"And hopefully we can finish super fast," Poppy adds as she lowers herself into the ancient rocking chair. Georgina prays it's sturdier than it looks.

"So . . ."

Georgina frowns at the serious look on her face. "What?" Her concerns rise as Poppy laces her fingers over her bump. "What's wrong?"

"Are we finally going to talk about the guy you were flirting with?"

Georgina nearly drops her pen. "What? No—"

"That was a rhetorical question. Of course we're going to talk about it."

"No, Poppy—"

"The sparks were flying so fast I had to duck."

"Maybe in your imagination."

"Y'all were flirting, Georgie, clear as day."

"We were literally talking about how I almost killed him," Georgina interrupts shrilly. "Remember that? Good times. Very romantic."

Poppy wiggles her eyebrows. "He didn't seem to mind."

Georgina turns to hide her warming face. "It doesn't matter if he minds or not, I'm not interested."

"Aren't you supposed to be rebuilding your love life? Pretty sure I read that in the pilot." Poppy grins as Georgina's face flames. "What better place to start—"

"Seriously, Poppy, stop," Georgina snaps, her frustration spilling over. She understood why Annette insisted she include that part—viewers need to see her as happy and moving on— but she's far from ready to "rebuild" anything with anyone. "I'm still technically in a pause, anyway," she adds miserably as sympathy softens Poppy's face.

"Talia's going to get that part sorted out."

Georgina nods, but her emotions war within her as she thinks about officially ending it with Lance. The thought is freeing and terrible at the same time.

"I *never* thought I would think Cassidy is a hot name," Poppy muses, drawing another scowl from Georgina. "His mother took a big risk, but it paid off."

"Do I need to call Jared? Are you going to be okay?"

She giggles. "Oh, come on. You have to admit it works for him."

Georgina shakes her head wearily, but unfortunately, Poppy

is right—it does work for him, just like everything else. Every Cassidy she's ever known has been tiny, peppy, and female, but this new Cassidy is all height, muscles, and dark, windblown hair. Along with the most dangerously disarming smile she's ever seen.

"He was also totally into you—"

Georgina hurries out the door before Poppy can finish, leaving her behind to study the exteriors on her own. As she trudges along the gravel path between the two houses, she looks for flaws and finds plenty—rotting wood, prickly weeds, and an abandoned pile of rusted metal—but none of this keeps her mind off the mysterious Cassidy Stokes for very long. The way he looked at her sent her heart racing, and that seemed to be on purpose. Lance comes to mind next, and she feels a twinge of guilt, which frustrates her even more. Why should she feel guilty when he ghosted her for weeks? She shoves the mishmash of feelings away and returns to the porch again.

"I got a signal for three seconds!" Poppy announces triumphantly.

Georgina's phone buzzes in her pocket.

"How does it look out there?" Poppy asks, surveying the landscape. "Easy fixes or a headache?"

"Not a total disaster . . ." The words fade on her lips as she reads a new message.

Mom said you're in tarragon???

"What?" Poppy demands, hurtling toward her. "Is it Cassidy? What did he say?"

"No, crazy person!" Georgina pulls her phone away before Poppy can snatch it. "It's just Savannah."

"Oh." Disappointment shadows her face. "Are you going to

ask her how cult life is going? Does she have to wear a denim skirt?"

Georgina laughs, but she's already dreading having that bizarre conversation. "At some point. Anyway, we should go. I want to shower before the circus comes to town." The rest of the UpScale crew should arrive in Crossville shortly after they do.

Poppy sighs glumly.

"I know it sucks, but the sooner we get there, the sooner you can FaceTime Olivia."

Poppy's angst fades and Georgina smiles knowingly.

"Fine," she mutters. "Let's go."

Georgina hands her the keys while she runs back inside the main cottage to lock up, but she pauses in the living room for a moment and lets her mind run wild with possibilities. She designs better when she has time alone in the space, before tools and camera people and a million different visions and voices clamor for her attention. Her thoughts move between colors and styles, trying to merge the dust-covered reality with her imagination, but it's harder than usual. She thinks of everything except the task before her—Lance, Upscale, her mother, Savannah. She suddenly scowls.

Cassidy Stokes is on her mind, too.

"Come on, Joanna!" Poppy yells from the car. "You need your beauty sleep for tomorrow!"

Georgina prays for inspiration as she heads for the door, but her mood sinks as they drive. The sad truth is she's not like Joanna Gaines, no matter how much anyone says otherwise. JoJo would know how to pull this mess together, but Georgina has no idea where to even begin.

6

Goldie Stokes's house smells like Jubilee kitchen wax and cedar oil when Cassidy arrives—two clues that she's been up cleaning when she's supposed to be resting. The final clue is the sound of pie plates clanking in the kitchen. He follows the sound, his concern growing, when Lila Briar suddenly rounds the corner with a plastic bucket in one hand and a mop in the other.

"Cassidy!" She jumps and clutches the bucket to her heart as he halts. "Goldie didn't say you were coming over today."

"Sorry." He's relieved to see Lila is the one cleaning instead of his mother. "I wanted to surprise her." Drop-in visits are better because she can't fuss about him coming. They both turn toward the kitchen as more dishes clatter.

"She's been busy in there," Lila says with a hint of concern.

He enters the kitchen and finds his mother dressed in what most folks would wear to church, with her hair in curlers. It's barely nine o'clock on Saturday morning, but her favorite apron is tied around her waist, and six floured pie pans crowd her countertop.

She smiles when she sees him in the doorway. "Well, hello!" She's a tall woman, but he still leans down so she can kiss his cheek. "Been a while since I've seen you," she adds.

"I wanted to let you rest," he says wearily, settling into a chair. She looks better than she did a week ago, but her steps are slow. She always used to joke about being old since she had Cassidy and Sawyer later than other ladies in Tarragon had their children, but Cassidy never thought of her like that. Even now, her bright smile contradicts her tired eyes.

"Are you feeling better?"

"Oh yes, a million times better. Dr. Rope gave me some new pills, and they did the trick. I really don't think it was pneumonia, though. He was being a little bit dramatic."

Cassidy smiles at the stubborn skepticism in her voice. According to her, Dr. Rope has never made a correct diagnosis in his entire life. "Would he approve of all this?" Cassidy motions to the arsenal of ingredients on the island—melted butter, two dozen eggs, heavy whipping cream, three canisters of flour, an unopened bag of cane sugar, lemons, cocoa power, and a pile of European pears, just to name a few. The air already smells like Crisco and cinnamon—his mother's signature scent.

"Why wouldn't he? I've got my stool right here." She nods at the wooden stool Cassidy's father made decades ago so that she could sit at the perfect height while she worked in the kitchen. "And Lila's going to clean up after me. Did you say hello to her when you came in?"

"I did."

"Good. You should invite her to the Cornbread Festival. Unless Renata already snatched you up?"

Cassidy doesn't say anything. First, because the Cornbread Festival is still weeks away and no one else is thinking about it yet, and second, because he knows better. Even if he just nods along absently, she'll tell Lila it's a date.

"No reason you should go alone."

Cassidy stays silent. He likes Lila, but not in the way his mother wants him to. She's a Christian, cute, easy to talk to, and the hardest-working woman he's ever met, but the spark just isn't there. With him, anyway. Gavin might feel differently, but Cassidy hasn't broached that subject yet.

"Paula Deaton told me they're bringing in singers from Chattanooga," his mother continues, measuring out flour. "Real professionals."

Cassidy takes all the hints with a stony expression.

"I hope they do the boat rides this year. I don't know why they ever stopped those in the first place. Those were popular with the young people."

He sighs internally. He wonders if Lila can hear his mother from the dining room.

She chatters on like a saleswoman, but his eyes fall on a new work-in-progress scrapbook on the cluttered breakfast table. Little American flag stickers and baseballs make a tidy border, while a picture of his much-younger parents takes up most of the page. His father's eyes are hidden behind sunglasses, but his smile is bigger than they could usually catch on camera.

Cassidy almost turns the page but stops himself, remembering that there's probably pictures of Melody, too. Her playing softball or cheerleading or smiling with a cherry-red snow cone in her hands or sticking her tongue out behind Cassidy's back. His mother's favorite photographs flash before his eyes without him even having to see them. Unlike him, she loves old photographs, no matter how much they make her cry.

"How's Renata?" she asks, switching tactics. She doesn't like Renata nearly as much as she likes Lila, but Cassidy's bachelor status bothers her enough that she's willing to compromise.

"Fine," he lies. The truth is Renata's not fine. She's miffed at him for ignoring her texts, but she tried to pull another "let's talk about our real feelings for each other" conversation two weekends ago after drinking cosmos with her beauty pageant friends, so he's been keeping his distance.

"You're awful quiet this morning, aren't you? Something on your mind?"

He looks up in surprise and meets her hazel eyes. He knows he should tell her about his new job—she'll understand more than most people, given his father's line of work—but the concerned look on her face stops him.

"Ardy told me the hens are sick again," she adds as Cassidy relaxes again. She thinks he's fretting about the Harp House.

"I know Gavin wants them all natural and such, but those puny little birds are costing y'all a fortune, Cass. Just tell him to bite the bullet and give them an antibiotic. It ain't the end of the world."

Cassidy smiles. The entire Harp family would throw a fit over that suggestion. "Don't let Gavin catch you talking like that."

She shakes her head. "I'll tell him myself tonight. I'm going over there to work on a new menu."

He sighs wearily, but she pretends not to notice. She lives to feed people, and she's by far the best cook they have, but they both know it takes a toll on her.

"What are all the pies for?" he asks, changing the subject. She loves baking almost as much as matchmaking.

"The deacons decided to do a pie contest instead of my caramel apples this year." There's a soft twinge of betrayal in her voice as she settles onto her stool again and reaches for a peeler.

Cassidy studies her elaborate setup. "Can you enter more than one?"

"No, just one, but I'm testing out a few different flavors."

"Oh. Well, that'll give you a nice break, won't it? You can just make one pie instead of all those apples."

"Don't be silly, boy. I'm still making the apples. It's a tradition."

"Deacons be darned?"

She ignores him, but he sees a small smile on her lips as she consults a worn-out recipe card. A memory of her famous caramel apples covering a long, plastic-covered table comes to mind. Perfect, impaled apples as far as the eye could see decorated with every kind of candy. Apples from Kit's orchard.

"You've got some new neighbors, by the way."

She drags her eyes off the card. "Come again?"

"Two girls from Nashville are fixing up Kit's house. I met them yesterday. Poppy. And Georgina," he says, letting the unusual name roll off his tongue. It sounds like a dessert.

Her mouth falls open. "What on earth?"

"They're gonna put Kit's cottages on one of those design shows."

"They're gonna do what now?"

"You know what I'm talking about, Mama. Where they go into ugly places and make 'em real fancy—"

She listens closely as he recounts the conversation from the day before as best he can.

"Well, I'll be." She shakes her head and rolls out a long piece of dough. "I always wondered about those shows. Seems like they have to do shoddy work to get them done so fast, don't you think?"

"I don't know, but they're gonna need a lot of help. Kit's place is in rough shape—"

Lila suddenly bolts through the kitchen and throws Goldie an apologetic look as she hurries to the sunroom with her phone pressed against her ear. Cassidy can tell from the tense look on her face that it's something involving Julie.

"Poor Lila," his mother says as she disappears behind the screen door. "Julie's being difficult today."

Cassidy thought he and Sawyer had been a handful, but Lila seems to have it harder with her fifteen-year-old daughter. Julie's absolutely merciless when it comes to her mother.

Cassidy's heard her talk Lila into circles so many times, saying one thing, then saying something different, all before bursting into big, pitiful tears when Lila finally snaps. He's considered hiring Julie at the Harp House so Lila can keep an eye on her while she cleans, but he's not sure if Gavin can handle the extra hassle. Especially now.

"Are the television gals your age?" his mother asks, unknowingly drawing his thoughts back to Georgina.

"I think so." She seemed young with her long lashes and bangs, but there was also a kind of determination in her eyes that made her seem more confident than most women. "Maybe a little younger."

Lila reappears with her phone tucked away in the waistline of her leggings. "Sorry, Goldie," she says, her shoulders slumping.

"Everything okay, honey?"

She shrugs tiredly. "Oh, Julie's just about to lose her job at the car wash. Some drama with the manager's daughter." She sighs. "I'll finish up here and then—"

"No, go take care of your business, Lila," his mother insists. "You can catch up later."

Lila hesitates, but then she nods gratefully. "Thanks."

Cassidy lowers his voice as Lila gathers up her cleaning supplies in the next room. "Don't you dare clean all this up," he whispers, motioning to the cluttered kitchen. "I'll come by and do it later."

She laughs like that's the silliest thing she's ever heard. "I'm better off just leaving it till tomorrow, then."

He throws her a pleading look. "Please just rest, all right? The more you rest now, the less you have to later—"

"I'm fine," she says with a huff, carefully rising from her stool to peer into her full-to-bursting fridge. "I have some food for you. You too, Lila," she calls. "Oh, and maybe the television gals would like something home-cooked." Her eyes twinkle as she looks back at him. "You and Lila can take it to them."

He scowls.

"Take what to who?" Lila asks.

"Some young ladies moved into Kit's house!" his mother announces, which only confuses Lila further until Cassidy explains the strange circumstances again.

"Those names do sound familiar," Lila says, mulling over his description while Goldie loads them up with baskets of Tupperware. "Julie likes all those shows."

"You go sort her out, Lila," Cassidy says, freeing her from his mother's scheme. "I can handle the food."

"I don't even know how I'm still hungry. I literally just ate three protein bars."

Georgina barely hears Poppy's mutterings. She's too busy fighting with what's left of the Scotch tape and scanning the wall for another blank space.

She's hardly made a dent in the pile of pictures by her feet, but the wall is already crowded with all things cottage-themed— wildflowers, baskets of strawberries, ruffly white dresses, moss-covered stones, vintage teacups—whatever Georgina could pull from the magazines she never throws away. She added a couple unexpected things, too, like an old revolver, speckled eggs, and a fog-shrouded moon, but the match of creativity doesn't strike. Suddenly, a loud grumbling sound captures her attention.

"Sorry, that was obnoxious," Poppy says, covering her stomach when it gurgles again. "Have you heard from UpScale?" she asks hopefully. "Are they getting close?"

"Nothing since this morning."

Poppy nods from the rocking chair she claimed yesterday, but Georgina catches a tiny frown on her lips. It's bad when not even Poppy can hide her misery. Georgina shoved open every window in the sweltering cottage, but it doesn't keep the sweat from rolling down their faces.

"Don't come near me, by the way," Poppy adds, grimacing as she lifts her arm and sniffs. "I smell like a trash can. I'm officially giving up on natural deodorant. I need the chemicals."

Georgina smiles weakly. She's pretty sweaty and frazzled herself—and guilt-ridden, too. Poppy's feet are squished and swollen inside flimsy flip-flops, and she already ate through most of their snack supply.

"Maybe we should go with a garden party vibe," Poppy suggests, ripping out an *Alice in Wonderland*–themed fashion shoot and holding it up for Georgina's approval.

"Cute, but that's been done a million times."

"Okay, how about log cabin chic?"

Georgina shakes her head. "Too predictable."

"Super glam spy bunker?"

"It needs to make sense with the house vibe, Pop. It's too cozy for that."

Poppy scowls at Georgina first, then at the challenging little house. "Well, it would help to get Damien in here so we could finally figure out a space plan."

Georgina catches the whine in Poppy's usually cheery voice and her irritation simmers all over again as she thinks about the last twelve, chaos-filled hours. They were supposed to meet Damien today—Georgina's favorite contractor—but right around the time she and Poppy arrived at the rental in Crossville last night, she got a call from UpScale letting her know the crew forgot some important sound equipment and had to turn around.

Georgina had forced herself to stay calm and cool for Poppy's sake, since she was in the middle of her long-awaited FaceTime with Jared and Olivia. Georgina unpacked their things and listened, amused, as Poppy struggled to answer a hilarious stream of questions about baby hippos on Noah's ark. When Olivia finally ran out of steam half an hour later, Poppy snuggled into one of the too-stiff twin beds, and Georgina tiredly hit the lights.

Can something go right, please? she asked silently when she tucked herself into the empty bed. She's trying to pray more consistently instead of just sending up random, desperate flares, but it doesn't seem to make much of a difference. The pressure is mounting, and her dreams were as dark and strange as ever, moving between a blue wave, a black tornado, and a blinding light, and she woke up abruptly with Savannah on her mind. She groped around for her phone and texted Savannah again, but she still hasn't heard anything back. The memory prompts her to pray now, too.

God, please let Sav be okay—

Georgina curses softly when three clippings suddenly fall off the wall at the same time.

"Are you good, Georgie? I feel like you're having *A Beautiful Mind* moment."

"I'm fine," she snaps, not in the mood for Poppy's jokes. "I'm just—"

They scream in unison as a plate-sized moth with whishing wings darts by Georgina's shoulder, making her bolt toward the kitchen. Poppy leaps up and follows, still screaming, as Georgina grabs a magazine and tries to shoo the fuzzy beast through one of the windows.

"That thing was as big as your face!" Poppy shrieks, slamming the window shut as soon as the massive bug floats away.

Georgina hurries to shut the rest of the windows while Poppy swats at more imaginary insects. Georgina had forgotten until now that Tarragon has the absolute worst bugs. Memories of synchronized screaming come to mind as she recalls the nights

she, Savannah, and a handful of other horrified female camp-
ers spent inside the millipede-infested cabin at Lake Chervil.
The flashback reminds her of Savannah yet again, but Poppy's
pitiful face captures her full attention.

"Do you totally regret coming with me?" Georgina braces
herself for the worst.

"No," Poppy says quickly, and she almost sounds like she
means it. "You need to make it up to me, though. Now."

"How?"

She covers her stomach as another rumble fills the cottage.
"Food."

Cassidy slows his truck as he reaches the cottages, wondering if Poppy and Georgina are there yet or still in Crossville.
There's no sign of the Lexus, or any other car for that matter,
so he almost turns around, but some movement on the porch
catches his eye. He squints and sees it's Poppy waving her phone
around, searching for a signal.

"Cassidy!" She waves wildly as he pulls in the driveway. "Hi!"

He smiles at the ecstatic look on her face as he joins her on
the porch. No one's ever looked so happy to see him. "Y'all
doing okay?"

"Honestly, I've been better. Way better. Here, come in." She
pushes open the heavy front door. "It's marginally cooler in
here. Oh, um, maybe not, actually." She wipes the sweat from
her forehead. "Sorry. I can't tell anymore."

Alarm fills him as he follows her inside. The last time he
was here, it was cluttered but clean, with cherry preserves on
every surface and Kit Vanover frantically boiling more like her
life depended on it. He smiles, remembering her many quirks.
She was always swimming in fruit in the summers, even after
she sold most of it to the Harp House. As he surveys the house

now, he realizes all the charm is gone. There's also no sign of Georgina, which fills him with surprising disappointment, but he pushes it away.

"How was Crossville?" he asks, wondering if that's where she might be.

"Also terrible." Poppy sighs lightly. "But it's fine."

When something flutters to the ground, his eyes move to the wall behind her. Someone stuck a bunch of pictures to it, but they're floating down like butterflies in the humidity. "Y'all have been busy over there."

Poppy turns. "Oh! That's Georgina's vision board."

"Huh." He studies it more closely, looking for some kind of pattern, but it's more like a wild art piece, with the fantastical mixing together with the mundane. "Interesting."

Poppy's curious eyes slide to the basket in his hands, and he remembers his original mission. "My mother sent food," he explains, handing it over.

"Wait, your mother? She lives around here, too? Oh my gosh, that's the cutest thing I've ever heard." She eagerly takes the basket and peeks inside as a huge smile breaks across her face. "Tell her she just saved my life," she says, pulling out a container full of fig-and-pecan pie and setting it on the flaking linoleum countertop. Her eyes are ravenous, but she suddenly halts. "You don't happen to have, like, silverware, do you?"

He frowns, not expecting that request. "How about a pocket-knife?"

She sets the container down again with a disappointed look.

"If you need to eat, go on and eat. Don't hold back on my account."

She looks surprised, then embarrassed, then relieved, all in about ten seconds or less. "Are you sure? I don't want to weird you out—"

"Oh, wait, hang on a second." He goes back out to his truck.

It takes a little digging, but he finds a lone plastic-wrapped fork and spoon in the glovebox. "Here you go," he says, returning with it and dropping it by the pie. "Divine providence."

"I could seriously cry right now."

She looks like she means it, but thankfully, she doesn't. Instead, she cuts off a crooked piece of pie with the flimsy fork. "I have to eat all the time when I'm pregnant," she explains between dainty bites. "Georgina went to town to get some snacks and stuff."

"Ah." Amusement fills him as he tries to imagine her cruising down Tarragon's quiet, postcard-style Main Street in her Lexus, no doubt causing a stir. "Well, if y'all want something closer, you can always get food at the Harp House."

"That's the fancy mansion place, right?"

He nods.

"I didn't know they had food! Is it like a restaurant or something?"

"No, just tell them I sent you."

When confusion clouds her face, he adds the missing piece. "I work there."

Her mouth falls open. "Oh my gosh, you do? What do you do there?"

"Agricultural operations."

Her brows scrunch. "Is that like . . . farming?"

He smiles. "Kind of." There's more to it than that—his role at the Harp House has always been a strange mishmash of responsibilities, thanks to his marriage to Melody—but Poppy seems thrilled by his answer, so he leaves it at that. "When do y'all start your show?"

An unexpected scowl shadows her face. "Today, actually, but the crew forgot a bunch of stuff. It's fine, though," she adds quickly, trying to hide some of her frustration. "We'll figure it out."

An idea strikes Cassidy as her scowl fades and she sighs tiredly, but he needs to think on it a bit—and pray, too. There are plenty of reasons to mind his own business, but Poppy's sad, sweaty face tugs at his heart, along with Georgina Havoc's brown eyes.

"Let me see what I can do."

7

Georgina's on her way back to the cottages with Poppy's snacks in tow when her phone buzzes from the cupholder. She grabs it, hoping it's Savannah, but her heart skips a beat when she sees Lance's name instead. Poppy's disembodied voice warns her not to give in, but her willpower slides and she finally opens his messages. Doubt hits her hard as she reads through a pileup of pleas to talk—and a tiny part of her wonders if she should've taken his calls—but his most recent message vaporizes any regret.

Last opportunity, G.

She stares at it until the Lexus starts to drift and she corrects course again. *Or what, Lance?* She demands, her anger bubbling. He'll cut her out of his life *again*? What's he going to do that's worse than he's already done? She's tempted to unload her fury in a message of her own, but Alvin's calm voice reminds her that unlimited anger has unlimited consequences, so she keeps her reply as cold and clipped as possible.

Talk to Talia. I'm not available right now.

Surprise fills her when he replies almost instantly.

Too busy with your new show?

Shock washes over her. Not because he knows about the show, since there was no way to keep it totally under wraps, despite Benson's best efforts. The reason she's shocked and shaking right now is because she's finally figured out why Lance wants to talk all of a sudden, and it's not because of her, or the miscarriage. It's because she's moving on.

Can we please just talk? I miss you.

Georgina swallows back a bitter taste. Lance seemed like her perfect match in so many ways, but he's clouding her mind with so much confusion.

From the moment they met three years ago, it seemed like they were meant to be together. She was the new girl at Up-Scale, shyly weaving her way through a party at a producer's house when he invited her to join him on the tennis court in the host's backyard.

"*I read your bio,*" he said, with a wink that made her heart flip. "*I'm ready for some real competition around here.*"

He was the network's most popular designer before Georgina and Poppy came along, so the fact that he even noticed her at all stunned her. She recovered long enough to hit a few tennis balls back in his direction—an impressive feat considering she was barefoot, thanks to her kicked-off heels—but her surprise returned full-force when he met her by the net and kissed her.

The unwanted memory is interrupted by an incoming call.

"Hello?" she answers, hoping it's finally someone from the crew.

"Hey, Georgina. It's Cassidy."

Butterflies flutter in her stomach. Even his phone voice is hot, thanks to the light southern accent.

"We met yesterday," he explains, as if she needs the reminder.

She's thought about their brief encounter more times than the actual project.

"Hi," she says, then adds, "How are you?" when he doesn't immediately fill the silence.

"Uh, pretty good. You?"

"Great!" Her voice comes out higher than usual as her nerves and curiosity mingle together.

"Good."

He sounds a little awkward, too, which makes her feel better until she remembers Poppy's commentary. It occurs to her that he might be about to ask her out, and she has no idea if she wants him to or not.

"Anyway, the reason I'm calling is . . ."

She holds her breath.

"There's a room at the Harp House if you and Poppy want it. It just opened up."

Surprise and disappointment collide. "Oh."

He plows ahead in an extra-professional tone and tells her all the details—amenities, policies, and pricing. "I work there," he adds, surprising her again.

Her confusion grows. That makes more sense but also doesn't, since he doesn't exactly seem like the hospitality type.

"If y'all are interested, you can check in today."

Georgina frowns. On the one hand, it's an absurdly good upgrade from their current situation. On the other, she probably doesn't need to be in closer proximity to a hot, hospitable cowboy. "Um, can I call you right back? I'll talk to Poppy."

"Sure thing."

The torn feeling doesn't fade as she hangs up. When she pulls up to the cottage a moment later, Poppy's waiting for her on the porch with her sweat-damp hair piled on top of her head. Unsurprisingly, once Georgina relays the message, she doesn't hesitate.

"Yes!" she screams, doing a happy dance. "Let's go, start packing up—"

"Hold on, Poppy."

"What? Why? Oh my gosh, wait a second. . . ." She smiles wider. "I bet a million dollars he pulled some strings for us! Also, he looked totally sad when he realized you weren't here, just FYI—"

"What?" Georgina interjects, confused. "What are you talking about?"

Poppy happily fills her in on his visit, but Georgina's sure she's exaggerating his "disappointment" in her typical Poppy way.

"He's *so* cute, Georgie! He works on a farm, and his mom made us the nicest little basket of food—"

"His mom?" Georgina's head spins from all the new information. She never knew so much could happen during one emergency snack run.

"I guess she lives around here? That's what he said."

Georgina surveys the landscape, wondering what on earth she's talking about. The orchard goes on for miles, then there's a distant little pond, more trees, and farmland. Suddenly, she spots one lone house on the horizon—a yellow Victorian—and feels a jolt of surprise. "Oh my gosh."

"What?" Poppy asks, following her gaze.

Georgina can't take her eyes off the house as a hazy memory sharpens in her mind. "I've been in that house before."

"What?"

"I think I know who he is."

"Who?"

"Cassidy," Georgina snaps, pulled between the forgotten yellow house and Poppy's puzzled face.

"You know Cassidy?"

"No, not him. Sorry." She realizes she's not making much

sense, but the past is mingling with the present. "I think Savannah was friends with his brother. At summer camp."

Poppy gasps.

When Cassidy told Georgina his last name, she had thought it sounded vaguely familiar, and now she knows why.

"Is his brother as good-looking as he is?"

"We were, like, fourteen, Poppy. I can't remember," she lies. Sawyer Stokes was cute enough that Savannah had followed him around all summer with heart-shaped eyes. That's why she roped Georgina into helping his mother's Bible study friends sort through pecans—one of the most boring ways to earn their mandatory "service" hours.

Savannah and Sawyer had droned on about their favorite comic books while the older ladies picked through most of the pecans, so Georgina entertained herself with the photographs over the dining table. Almost all of them included an impossibly handsome young man dressed up in military uniforms, ranging from dusty fatigues to the starched, fancy kind. It was almost like a shrine.

"*My brother is in Afghanistan*," Sawyer said when he noticed Georgina's eyes moving from frame to frame to frame. "*Mama isn't taking it well*," he whispered jokingly.

Georgina frowns as her memory falters. What was her name? Gloria? Glenda? Georgina can't remember now.

"That's totally a sign!" Poppy teases. "Y'all were meant to be together."

Cassidy's eyes are on the piece of paper in front of him, but his mind is in El Salvador. He's never been much of a list person, but he's got about a hundred loose ends to tie up between his mother, the Harp House, and the mission, so he finally busted out a notepad and dumped everything on paper. Melody was the more organized one, but even she would applaud his chicken-scratch efforts.

All of a sudden, the door swings open and Gavin barges in, dressed in his usual preppy uniform of a pressed button-down with slacks. His forehead is lightly sunburned from too many summer weddings. Melody was the only Harp who didn't melt in the sun.

"I wondered if you were hiding in here."

"I'm not hiding," Cassidy says coolly as he approaches his desk—formerly Cassidy's father-in-law's desk.

Cassidy slid into Dale Harp's role on the farm side, while Gavin ended up taking over his mother's responsibilities as the event coordinator—a job that required more socializing than Cassidy could muster. They're quite the odd couple, but they've somehow managed to keep the house standing since Dale and Donna retired, which has been no easy feat.

He forces himself to smile despite Gavin's unhappy expression. "How's it going—"

"Did you cancel the Connelly reservation?"

Cassidy's smile fades. It didn't take long for that message to travel. "No, I just asked them to push it back a few days and take the Ballad Room instead. They didn't mind." He also offered Rick Connelly a big discount to sweeten the deal, but he doesn't mention that part. Gavin's face is already red enough.

"Why?" he demands.

Cassidy is about to explain Georgina's situation, but Sawyer comes to the rescue. "It's a long story, Gav," he says, reaching for his buzzing phone. "I'll fill you in later," he adds, hoping his last-minute finagling works.

Gavin ignores the dismissal. "Philip also said something about you wanting to hire Julie Briar. What kind of bright idea is that?"

"Just consider it a favor to Lila."

Gavin's eyes narrow as Cassidy smirks. He's almost certain Gavin likes her, but he's always been shy about that sort of thing, so Cassidy doesn't push the subject.

"We'll talk about it later," he says, more firmly this time. Gavin trudges to the door and shuts it harder than necessary.

"Yo," Sawyer says when Cassidy finally answers. A video game blares in the background. "What's up?"

Cassidy tries to let the conversation flow naturally with their usual updates and jokes and not just rush straight to his request, but his eyes drift to the long-ago-emptied liquor cabinet. He lets the temptation pass but takes note of what inspired the impulse. Pressure, mostly, and having to ask for help. He hates that more than anything.

"Sawyer," Cassidy says, finally cutting him off mid-rant about the Florida traffic. "I need to tell you something." When the line goes quiet, he tells him about the mission in El Salvador and steels himself for another round of guilt.

"No way, dude. Congrats. That's awesome."

Cassidy exhales. Sawyer's response is exactly what he needed it to be. "Thanks." He wishes he could tell their father, since he would've been thrilled—and he would have had plenty of advice, too, whether Cassidy wanted it or not—but Sawyer's the next best thing. His brother knows enough about the ins and outs of military conflicts to understand how private security contracting works.

"The terrorists keep blowing up American gas lines, and then they take a bunch of hostages whenever anyone tries to fix them. They've killed most of them," Cassidy adds sadly, wishing he could get there sooner. "And they're harassing the local folks to make them move their drugs. Sometimes little kids—"

"Time to take 'em out," Sawyer growls.

Cassidy would love nothing more, but he's a civilian now, which means he'll have to leave that part to someone else. He and a couple other former military men just have to ensure someone can safely fix the gas lines, which will maybe blow up a few drug dens along the way if they're lucky.

"Nah, for real, though, Cass, that's awesome. It's like James Bond or something. Right up your alley."

Cassidy smiles weakly, thankful that Sawyer understands. Despite its size, the Harp House feels pretty small sometimes, and, even more than that, he just wants to find his purpose again. Dinner parties and weddings are all well and good, but it's always been hard to enjoy them when he knows other people are suffering and he could help.

"What about Mom, though?" Sawyer asks, beating him to the next subject. "She can't live out there all by herself."

"That's what I wanted to talk to you about." Cassidy holds his breath as silence eclipses the line. "It would make sense for her to live with you and Rachel."

There's some sudden fumbling on Sawyer's end.

"Y'all got that little guest house thing, so you won't be stepping over each other. And she'll want to be around her grandchildren when you finally give her some—"

"Woah, slow down. Don't give Rachel any ideas."

Cassidy laughs, but his hopes teeter on his next question. "Do you think she might be open to the idea? Seems like she and Mom get along pretty well. . . ." Rachel is a pint-sized Realtor with an overwhelming love for babies and old people, but she and Sawyer are technically still newlyweds, so she might not want her mother-in-law around just yet.

"Rach? Oh, yeah, she loves Mom. They're buddies."

"See, look at that—"

"Is *Mom* open to it?"

Cassidy frowns. "I haven't asked her. I haven't told her about the job yet, either," he confesses as Sawyer groans. "I just want to get more stuff figured out first—"

"I don't know if either of us can convince her to move, Cass." Not even their father had been able to do that when he was still traveling around the world. She could've followed him, but she had stubbornly stayed put, citing the need for friends and stability despite criticism from more traditional Tarragonians. Cassidy and Sawyer were miffed about it growing up—exotic military bases sounded infinitely cooler than Tarragon—but Cassidy's thankful in hindsight. If they'd moved around all the time, he probably would never have met Melody.

"Even when Dad died," Sawyer continues, "she still wasn't budging."

"I know, but it's different now." When their father died a year after Mel, she had taken it remarkably well—probably for Cassidy's sake—but she was in better health back then. Those days are gone, and they're not coming back. "She's tired all the time and getting sick more often—"

"I hear ya, man. Something has to change—"

"And I think she'd prefer Florida over El Salvador."

Sawyer laughs, but the silence returns, so Cassidy delivers his final pitch. "She'll be happy with you and Rachel, Sawyer. The weather's easy, she'll have her own little apartment, no stairs to climb, Rachel to talk to, stuff to do at your church—"

"She's gonna miss her Golden Boy, though."

Cassidy smiles at the good-natured jab. Between his smart mouth and endless fights, teenage Sawyer had kept their mother busy, but they've given their mother an equal amount of grief over the years—although no one would ever know it by the way she talks about them. Suddenly, the guilt creeps back in.

"Do you think I'm being selfish? Doing this to her? Between Dad and Melody—"

"No." His brother's answer is quick but firm. "You're just moving on. It's good."

Sawyer's words steel him, but the uneasiness lingers. Cassidy doesn't *have* to take the job—and there's a decent number of reasons why he shouldn't—but he's been living other people's dreams ever since his shattered, and he's done that long enough.

"Maybe you and Rachel can come to Tarragon for a couple days," he suggests, bringing the conversation back to their mother. "Then we could all sit down and talk about it. Maybe next week?"

"*Next week?* It's my busy season, Cass—"

"I know, but you owe me. Think of all the times I beat up Dylan Hayes for you."

"What? Nah, we worked on that together. You can't take sole credit."

"Just come up for a couple days. We can make it quick—" Cassidy falls silent as his phone buzzes against his ear. He has a call waiting. "Hey, Sawyer, sorry. I'll call you back."

Sawyer mutters something that Cassidy doesn't catch as he ends the call. He's in too much of a rush to answer Georgina. "Hello?"

"Hi again. It's me."

He smiles at the more relaxed greeting. "Hi."

"So I talked to Poppy . . ."

He can hear the hesitation in her voice—probably because he feels it, too—but there's also a touch of hopefulness. "And?"

"We're going to take you up on that offer."

***

The sun is slipping under the horizon when Georgina finally returns from Crossville with their luggage, and somehow the Harp House is even more stunning in the fading light than it was when she dropped off Poppy hours earlier.

It's a true historic Italianate mansion, with tall columns, arched windows, and a sweeping balcony, and it has been featured in a dozen magazines since the Harp family renovated it in 1982—an interesting factoid Georgina learned from the internet earlier that afternoon. The estate is tucked behind a row of weeping willows and sculpted gardenias, and it boasts eleven bedrooms, multiple sitting rooms, a chef's kitchen, two dining rooms, a billiards room, and a formal library, and she'd marvel at it longer if she wasn't utterly exhausted.

She's about to hoist the bags out of the trunk when a young man with sunny blond hair and a peeling forehead sprints down the porch ramp with a luggage cart.

"Let me get those for you, ma'am."

Georgina happily relinquishes control. Between her overpacked bags and Poppy's giant body pillow, it's a lot to carry, but he expertly loads them on the spindly cart. "Thank you."

"Of course. Valet service? You're in the Cadence Room."

She hands over her keys and follows him through the ornate front door. A woman reading on the porch looks up from her book long enough to smile.

"Elevator is this way, stairs that way," the young man says, briskly rolling the luggage over various bumps and dips in the hardwood floors. Amazingly, it doesn't topple as she trails after him. "What brings y'all to Tarragon?"

"Um . . ." She's momentarily distracted by the inside of the house. Warm woods, black and white marble, high ceilings, arched doorways, romantic draperies, timeless furniture—it's a designer's dream. "A work project," she finally answers, tearing her eyes off the décor to meet his curious gaze.

His eyes narrow slightly as he looks her over, but she has no idea why.

"I can take it from here," she says when they reach the elevator. He helps her wheel the luggage inside the tiny space.

"Enjoy your stay," he says with another strange look as the doors close. A moment later, she's hurtled upward so fast her stomach flutters.

It's a minutes-long struggle, but when the door opens again, she manages to squeeze around the cart and heave it down a narrow hallway, searching for the Cadence Room among other music-themed possibilities. When she joins Poppy inside their suite a moment later, it's like she's standing inside a page of *Southern Style*, with two grand-looking queen beds covered in colorful quilts and the perfect mix of old and new furniture.

"You never have to make that drive again," Poppy says happily, helping her drag the cart inside before flopping on a bed and curling up like a kitten. She's freshly showered and dressed in leggings and one of Jared's giant T-shirts. "How's it feel?"

"Good," Georgina says, stretching her knot-filled back. She'll have to unload the luggage later because the other heavenly-looking bed is calling her name.

"I got you some dinner. It's on that little desk over there. They had espresso, too. The good kind."

Georgina opens a box on the hand-painted secretary desk and finds a colorful chicken orzo salad and the prettiest little lemon bar she's ever seen. She sips the espresso and raises an eyebrow. It *is* the good kind.

"The food is amazing," Poppy says, snuggling in deeper. "The whole place is amazing, actually. I feel bad for the rest of the crew." Her voice is muffled by the pillows as she burrows in deeper.

Georgina fishes her phone out of her purse to check for an update since she hasn't heard from anyone at UpScale all day, but she's greeted by a message from Benson instead.

Emergency, Gigi. Call me ASAP.

91

Her fatigue evaporates as a million terrible possibilities come to mind. She almost calls him right then and there, but Poppy's soft snores fill the room. Georgina understands. It has been a *long* forty-eight hours.

She grabs the espresso and her workbag and carefully closes the door behind her. She takes the stairs instead of the rocket-like elevator, searching for anywhere private. The woman is still outside reading her book under a row of string lights, so Georgina finds a little nook off the parlor.

Benson picks up on the first ring.

"Hi, Gigi. Annette's here, too."

"Hi, babe," Annette says, trying to sound cheerful, but Georgina can hear the stress in her voice. "Sorry to bother you—"

"Is this about Lance? Or UpScale?" Georgina wants to cut right to the chase. She's hoping it's the former and not the latter, or something else entirely—anything but the news that UpScale is pulling the plug on her pilot or something equally catastrophic.

"Both," Benson answers in a panicked voice. "Lance took your contractor."

Georgina's stomach drops. "What?"

"Damien pulled out of the project this afternoon."

Her panic rises. "Why—"

"Because Lance Broussard is an awful human being!" Annette interjects furiously. "He's throwing his weight around the network and intimidating people. That's why they're scrambling—"

Georgina's anger surges as Annette's words sink in. Apparently, yesterday's delay wasn't about sound equipment after all. It was about Lance getting back at her. The worst feeling in the world comes next, and it makes her drop into the closest chair.

"I'm talking to Brigitte right now," Benson says soothingly, sensing her despair. "She's looking for a replacement—"

"Brigitte Sweetser?" Georgina interrupts.

"Yes?"

Her mood plummets further—something she didn't even know was possible. "I thought I was getting Leilani?"

"No, we got Brigitte. I told you that?"

Georgina exhales slowly. Not only is she not getting her go-to contractor, but she's also not getting her favorite producer, either. Benson *didn't* tell her that, but she's not surprised by the miscommunication. The entire process has been a rushed nightmare, thanks to Lance.

"What's wrong with Brigitte?" Benson demands. "We love a ruthless woman in a fanny pack."

Georgina can't even laugh. Her throat feels like it's closing in. "So . . . I need to find my own contractor?" she asks, finally forcing a few words out. "Is that what you're telling me?"

"Yes, but mostly just for the permits. Besides that, it's just knocking down walls, right? Brigitte's looking, too."

Georgina hangs her head in exasperation. A good contractor does much more than permits—and she's going to need a phenomenal one to stay on their crazy timeline—but she can't blame Benson for being clueless. This is way outside of his wheelhouse.

"Okay," she says hopelessly. "I guess I'll just figure it out."

"You got this, Gigi," Annette insists, but Georgina ends the call, not in the mood for a pep talk. She almost calls Lance but stops herself at the last second, since that's probably what he wants. She observed a familiar pattern with her parents—one would poke and prod until the other would finally give in.

As she scours the internet for a contractor, she suddenly wishes she had another little orange pill to go with what's left of her espresso. "No," she mutters, surprised by the strength of the craving. Thankfully, a new text message steals her attention.

Mom is completely losing her mind

Georgina's eyes narrow as she reads Savannah's terribly timed complaint. They used to have a family group chat, but it dissolved into an endless stream of passive-aggressive jabs between Savannah and her mother. Georgina tries not to pick a side in their ongoing battle, but tonight she's too tired to feign neutrality.

She's just worried about you. I am too.

Georgina waits as the little typing-in-process dots appear, bracing herself for a rant, but a minute passes and the dots disappear, so Georgina sends a message of her own.

I love you, Sav.

An unexpected tear falls and fades into her jeans. Being back in Tarragon reminds her of just how much she misses her sister, even with her tiresome antics. Their summer fun in Nashville with their friends was stolen away, but there was something healing about Lake Chervil, even with its giant bugs and silly games.

She and Savannah would spend hours every night talking in their damp little cabin when the other girls fell asleep, whispering about the boys they liked and the careers they wanted and how annoying their parents were. Georgina frowns as she remembers more. They used to talk about God sometimes, too.

"Hey."

Georgina turns sharply at the sound of an increasingly familiar voice. "Hey," she says back, sitting up straighter as Cassidy Stokes smiles at her from the arched doorway. She's been secretly hoping she might run into him again, but now isn't ideal.

"How's it going?"

"Good," she lies. Worries about her unimpressive ponytail

and barely-there makeup pop into her head before she can stop them. "Just getting some work done," she adds, avoiding his eyes until she gets her nerves in check. "This is a top-notch nook, by the way. The whole house is great, actually. I don't think you'll be able to drag Poppy out of here."

He smiles. "I'm glad it worked out. Seemed like she was struggling a little bit."

"Yeah . . ." she mumbles, discreetly noting his clothes, which are basically the same ones he was wearing yesterday—jeans and a T-shirt straining against his muscled arms. "What do you do here again?" Considering he can pull discounted, months-long reservations out of thin air, his role seems too important for jeans, no matter how good he looks in them.

"I run the farm side of things."

"Oh, right. Poppy mentioned a farm. . . ." She forgot that detail since Poppy was mostly focused on his hotness, which Georgina is currently trying to ignore—and failing miserably. Everything about him is naturally rugged, with his wild hair, tanned skin, and easy, slightly slanted smile. No man should be so effortlessly attractive. He should have to try harder.

"Yep. We've got a vineyard, too," he adds. "It butts up to Kit's orchard."

Don't think about his butt. "That's cool," she mutters, embarrassed to realize his presence has reduced her maturity to that of a teenager.

"How's your show thing going?"

She smiles. The way he says it—like it's just some kind of normal, mundane task—is weirdly refreshing. "Fine, aside from a couple delays. Normal stuff." Not normal at all actually, since her saboteur ex-boyfriend just stole her contractor, but Georgina spares him those details. "Is it okay to work in here?" she asks, changing the subject. "I didn't ask anyone."

"You can work wherever you like. You don't have to ask."

"Thanks."

A brief, awkward moment passes as he seems like he's about to say something else but second-guesses it. "Actually . . . follow me."

The command surprises her, but she grabs her stuff and follows him down a long hallway. They stop outside a heavy-looking door moments later.

"Another upgrade for you," Cassidy explains, opening the door and revealing the quintessential gentlemen's club–style office. Everything is overstuffed, leather brown, deep green, or gray-streaked. And it is *so* quiet.

Georgina stares. "I didn't know farmers had offices like this."

He laughs. "Only the really good ones."

"Are you sure you don't mind?" she asks, glancing around. It's beautiful, like the rest of the house, but she feels completely out of place in it.

"Yep," he says. "I don't use it that much."

She frowns. It does have a very untouched feeling, despite the deep colors and warm light coming from a heavy lamp hanging overhead. No pictures, no degrees, no clues about his past or present—and nothing military-ish, either. Suddenly, she remembers the yellow Victorian and questions her memory. Maybe she's got the wrong Stokes?

"Any decorating tips?" he asks, noticing her scrutiny.

"Um . . ." She forces her thoughts back to the present. "A plant would be good. Or, like, five. Something alive."

He smiles as she carefully sets her laptop on the massive desk in the middle of the room. It's an executive-style one that looks like it weighs five hundred pounds.

"You're not gonna hurt anything, Georgina."

Her stomach flutters again. That's the first time he's ever said her name like that, and it sounds so familiar, even though there's no reason it should. "Thanks."

The oversized chair swallows her up, but he uses his giant booted foot to press a pedal, slowly raising her up until she can survey the whole desk. She throws him an embarrassed but grateful smile as she rises.

"You're very nice," she blurts out, feeling like she should probably acknowledge that, given how much he's helped her and Poppy, but she regrets it when his lips slant into an amused smile.

"Isn't everyone nice to you?"

There's just a touch of flirtation in his voice, but it's enough to make her skin warm. She sighs lightly when Lance suddenly comes to mind. "No," she says sadly. "Not everyone."

He looks genuinely surprised. "Well, some people are just stupid." He shrugs. "What are you gonna do?"

She laughs at his matter-of-fact tone, but the current of electricity between them crackles as he says good-night and slips out the door with another smile. As she tries to settle in to the overwhelming quiet, her eyes drift down to a piece of paper tucked under the desk glass.

Count it all joy, my brothers, when you meet trials of various kinds, for you know that the testing of your faith produces steadfastness. And let steadfastness have its full effect, that you may be perfect and complete, lacking in nothing.

She frowns. The handwriting is neat but it all blends together, like someone wrote it in a hurry.

If any of you lacks wisdom, let him ask God, who gives generously

To all without reproach, and it will be given him. But let him ask in faith, with no doubting, for the one who doubts is like a wave of the sea that is driven and tossed by the wind.

Georgina's heart feels heavy as she rereads the wave part. Driven and tossed—that's what she's feeling right now. Maybe she's felt it her entire life, but now it's just building into a storm that she can't outswim. She reads it again slower, searching for the answer.

Ask God. Ask in faith. No doubting.

She startles as her phone chirps and Savannah finally writes back.

I need help

8

"Are you kidding me?" Georgina gripes as she and Poppy pull up in front of the cottages. There's not a single UpScale van in sight. "Brigitte makes us rush around all morning, and they're not even here yet—"

"Goosfraba," Poppy says calmly, quoting Jack Nicholson in *Anger Management*, which, unsurprisingly, does not help. "They'll be here soon."

Georgina's irritation with Brigitte Sweetser has been simmering. She called Georgina early that morning to announce that she'd finally found a contractor, and everyone needed to be at the cottage at seven o'clock sharp, so Georgina and Poppy had dutifully dragged themselves out of their cloudlike beds in the Harp House and miraculously arrived on time—for nothing.

"This whole thing is such a mess, Poppy," Georgina laments, recalling the last three chaotic days as the crew finally arrived in Tarragon and started setting up. The Seelys showed up, too, for their initial walk-through, and they were much more opinionated than they first let on. Georgina and Poppy fielded three hours of impossible requests for a sauna and skylights—never mind their shoestring budget. Georgina also had to deliver the news that they only have enough time to renovate the larger cottage, which led to a long, uncomfortable silence from Curt Seely.

Brigitte eventually declared they had enough walk-through footage and sent the Seelys on their way, but now Georgina has a nagging feeling she might not be able to make them happy, and she needs to. If the big reveal falls flat, it'll ruin the entire pilot.

On top of all that, Savannah hasn't responded to any of her calls or texts since her plea for help, an annoyingly familiar Havoc family song-and-dance. It's not Sav's first time sending bizarre messages and then going silent while Georgina panics, and it surely won't be the last.

"It is indeed a hot mess," Poppy agrees, happily hopping out of the Lexus. "But that's what we do, Georgie. We make messy things cute. Let's go."

Georgina reluctantly trudges after her, grumbling as she steps over thorny weeds and rocks in her designer flats.

"At least we have a contractor now," Poppy adds cheerfully.

Georgina nods, but she can't help but feel anxious about that, too. They've already had one contractor fall through because of the distance, followed by another who didn't want to be on camera. Her irritation with Lance spikes as they step inside the cottage and survey the dusty jumble of cords and equipment. The tired floors creak under her footsteps as Georgina turns on a fan.

"Yay!" Poppy cheers, pointing out the window. "They're here!"

Georgina joins her by the grubby glass as three UpScale vans fly up the gravel road.

"Morning!" Poppy sings, greeting the crew.

"Morning," Brigitte says flatly, filing in last.

"Where's the contractor?" Georgina asks, looking for a new face in a crowd of familiar ones.

"He'll be here soon," Brigitte says dismissively, freeing her phone from the fanny pack she's never been seen without. "We have some reshoots, anyway. The inspiration scenes fell flat," she adds with an unimpressed look at Georgina. "You were all over the place yesterday."

Georgina throws her a look right back, but Poppy gives her a gentle nudge. Brigitte's undeniably talented—Georgina had watched as she stealthily fought her way up from an assistant role to head producer when no one thought she could—but she's *so* cold. Not even Poppy can make her crack a smile most of the time.

"What could we do better, Bridge?" Poppy asks, ignoring Brigitte's well-known distaste for nicknames.

"Y'all just need to focus on one big element. Georgina has too much going on over here." She points at what's left of Georgina's vision board, which isn't much, thanks to the heat and constant movement in and out of the house. A few of her favorite images got trampled along the way.

"And then there's the bigger issue," Brigitte continues, her gray eyes darting around the room. "Obviously, the cottage is going to look better when you're done with it, but how will *Georgina* transform along the way? We still need to answer that question."

Her irritation grows, but Brigitte has a point. Her own personal growth is supposed to be a major element of the pilot, so she needs to find a way to work that in—once she figures out what it is. She doesn't feel particularly "transformed" at the moment.

"Do we know anything about the previous owner?" Brigitte asks, studying Georgina's battered vision board again. "Something we can use to build the story?"

Georgina shakes her head, but Cassidy suddenly comes to mind, along with a slight mood lift. "I can ask someone, though," she says, thankful for another reason to talk to him, even though they've been finding plenty since that night in his office. She's always in a hurry whenever their paths cross, so their conversations are brief, but he seems as pleased to see her as she is to see him.

Brigitte is summoned away moments later, leaving Georgina and Poppy stranded in the middle of the mess as the crew mounts more cameras and Poppy gets fitted for a new microphone that can wrap around her bump.

Georgina busies herself with a tentative demolition plan as the minutes pass. She doesn't know much about the construction side of things, but she's watched enough experts to guess which walls and beams might be necessary versus which ones might be dispensable. She moves to the dilapidated porch and tries to reimagine it next, but Poppy's voice fights for her focus.

"Georgie . . . the orchard!"

"Hmm?"

"The orchard," Poppy repeats excitedly when Georgina finally looks up from her sketch. "That's the inspiration!" Poppy points toward the magnificent view of fruit trees and rolling hills, and Georgina finally understands.

"Yes . . ."

"Fruit-inspired hues with a rustic touch? Something like that?"

Georgina gasps. "That's brilliant, Poppy!"

She laughs. "Don't sound so surprised. I'm good at this, remember?"

Georgina smiles as relief fills her, followed by a jolt of familiar creativity. "You're the best."

Poppy smiles back, but there's a touch of sadness to it. She knows how much Georgina misses her. And Georgina knows how much she misses Jared and Olivia.

"I'm seeing sage greens and something warm," Georgina says, distracting them. "Maybe different shades of apple?"

"Yes! And we have to put robin's-egg blue somewhere. Not a lot, obviously. Just a pop. It's the perfect space for that."

Georgina nods. "And plaids, but the feminine kind."

"I'm so here for a pink plaid! And I want a million dainty dishes inside one of those massive hutch things—"

"Ray, I need somebody now."

They both fall silent when Brigitte's sharp voice cuts through their ideas. She's pacing the driveway, so they quickly hush up to hear the rest.

"No, it's *not* just a cosmetic job. That's what I'm saying. There's water damage, and we need to move walls. We can't pull this off without him." They can't hear the rest as she walks toward the trees—one of the few random places to get a decent cell signal, to everyone's intense annoyance.

Georgina shoots Poppy a worried look and whispers, "If this contractor backs out, too, I'm going to scream."

"Brigitte will figure it out," Poppy insists, but she looks worried, too.

"Is there an issue?" Georgina asks when Brigitte joins them a few minutes later. Her expression is smooth, but there's a hint of redness in her cheeks.

"The contractor had a conflict come up," she announces without emotion. "It's fine," she adds when she sees the devastated look on Georgina's face. "I'm working on an alternative."

Georgina doesn't scream, but she does sigh. Poppy's face falls ever so slightly, too. She's probably worrying about being apart from Olivia even longer, which is a real possibility since they've already lost three days.

"I literally can't believe this," Georgina mutters when Brigitte hurries off, her fanny pack bouncing with each step. "Thank you so much, Lance," she adds bitterly. She still hasn't contacted him yet, per Annette's instructions, but she's tempted to finally break her silence. "I'm really starting to hate him—"

"Go get some food, Georgie," Poppy interjects gently, turning motherly, which is sweet and annoying at the same time. "You didn't eat enough breakfast."

"I'm fine—"

"No, just go. Sneak away while you can because you know it only gets crazier from here. Retreat and regroup. I'll keep an eye on everything."

Georgina doesn't move for a moment, torn between wanting to stay and complain or just quash the project altogether, but Poppy is right. Food always helps. Especially good food, instead of UpScale's wilted catering.

"Bring me something, too!"

Georgina slides inside her Lexus minutes later and blasts the air conditioner but shuts off the music, trying to savor the rare silence, but it fills her with sorrow as she navigates the winding wooded roads. She's been having more dreams than usual— mostly just stressful, nonsensical things, like she's being chased by fireworks or floating in too-blue water—but last night she dreamed about the baby.

God suddenly comes to mind, along with a surprising sense of peace. He does seem a little closer in the quieter moments, so she repeats her usual prayer requests—for Savannah to be safe, for their mother to be calm, for Poppy to stay focused, for the show to be a success . . .

As her mind retraces the morning's events, she suddenly feels bad about taking her frustration out on Brigitte. Brigitte has plenty of quirks, but she doesn't *have* to help Georgina. She could've pulled a Damien and found a reason to stay in Nashville, but here she is, hours away from her boyfriend and her beloved chihuahua, pouring just as much energy into the project as Georgina and Poppy.

She reaches for her phone, intending to send Brigitte a quick thank-you, but a jolt of anger derails her plan. She dictates a text to Lance instead.

"You're the one who wanted this, Lance." Her voice wavers with hurt. "The least you can do is get out of the way while I put my life back together—" She curses softly when an incoming call erases the half-formed message.

"It's about time," she says coolly, answering it.

"Wow, okay." Her sister's voice fills the Lexus. "Pretty sure you're the one who ghosted me first."

"I didn't ghost you, Savannah. I was busy. And my life is currently falling apart—"

"What? How?"

Georgina hesitates, but the bizarre bond of sisterhood makes her temporarily set aside her pride. She spills her guts to Savannah after months of keeping secrets from everyone else. The miscarriage, the stupid pause, the current shamble-y state of her new show—all of it. Savannah is silent as the truth pours out like water from a faucet.

"Wow . . ." Savannah says minutes later, still in shock. "I'm so sorry, Georgie." Her voice is filled with rare, genuine concern, and it touches Georgina's heart. "That seriously sucks, but I always kind of thought Lance was a loser. His energy was just way off, and you can do better—"

Georgina bites her tongue as Sav rants on and ruins the moment. When it comes to men, "loser" is Savannah's favorite category, but Georgina forces herself not to retort.

"Isn't Poppy having her baby soon?"

"Yeah, in August. Why?"

"So, are you, like . . . okay? With what happened? With the . . ." Savannah trails off mid-sentence, and Georgina finally realizes why. She's trying to ask about the miscarriage.

"I'm fine," Georgina says flatly, not wanting to talk about it. Savannah fumbles for something else to say but ultimately goes with another sincere "that sucks" as Georgina smiles. Savannah's familiar voice is comforting in its own way, even without pretty words.

"What's Tarragon like these days?" she asks, changing the subject.

"The same, basically." Aside from the presence of Cassidy Stokes—a detail she's leaving out for now. She almost asks about Sawyer Stokes, curious if they stayed in touch or not, but Savannah beats her to the next question.

"Did you see the camp?"

"Yep."

Savannah tries to pull her into more memories, but Georgina reluctantly pushes them both back to the present.

"How are you, Sav? You freaked me out with that text on Saturday."

"Yeah . . ." Her voice suddenly turns sheepish. "Sorry about that."

"What happened?"

"Nothing. I was just having a weak moment."

"About?"

"Life."

Georgina frowns at the sudden vagueness. "Like, school stuff? Is the semester over?"

"Yeah, it's over. And I don't know if I'll go back, honestly. I think it's kind of stupid. I don't need a degree to make art."

Georgina's annoyance rises steadily as she listens to her sister's complaints. Savannah has already spent tens of thousands of dollars of their mother's savings to attend a private art school in Sewanee, and now she's going to quit? Georgina had seen it coming, though. Their mother was much more passionate about the degree than Sav ever was.

"How's Jack? Jackson?" Georgina asks, wondering if Savannah's on-and-off-again boyfriend is the problem. "Is that his name?"

"Jack. He's fine," she says lifelessly. "We don't really talk anymore."

"Oh." Guilt pricks Georgina as she realizes just how long she let their communication slide. "So, nothing specific caused the weak moment?"

"Nope. Just life, like I said."

"Tell me, Sav." Even through the phone, she can tell when she's hiding something.

"Let it go already—"

"Tell me!"

"No!"

"Why not?"

"Reasons."

Georgina groans. "This is *so* annoying, Savannah, after I literally just told you everything, which I'm never going to do again if you can't even—"

"Fine! I'm in a rehab, okay?" Savannah finally snaps, cutting her off. "In Franklin. Do not tell Mom, or I will kill you. I mean that."

Silence fills the line for a moment. Georgina is too stunned to respond. "What? What kind of rehab—"

"It's like a recovery place. In a hospital. I checked myself in after I texted you. Just for, like, a week," she adds defensively.

"*You* did?"

"Yeah."

Georgina's mind immediately goes to the worst possibility. She knows Savannah used to do a medley of drugs with a particular group of friends a few years ago, but Savannah had insisted it wasn't an ongoing thing. Now Georgina's not so sure that's true.

"It's just my stupid medication. They messed it up again."

Georgina's shock slowly fades to relief as she realizes she's talking about her antidepressant medication. Their mother urged her to start taking it in high school after a doctor mentioned it could help with her social anxiety, and Savannah has been on something ever since.

"The Zoloft randomly stopped working," Savannah continues. "So they put me on Effexor, and it literally almost killed me, Georgie."

Georgina's eyes widen as Savannah describes a nightmarish episode of days-long insomnia.

"I was so tired it hurt. Like my brain was banging against my skull. And then I was thinking about shooting myself all the time—"

"Oh my gosh, Savannah!" Georgina is trying to stay calm and listen, but that last part is too horrifying. "That's so scary."

"I know. That's why I came here. It was freaking me out."

Georgina exhales as her heart slows down again. "So . . . are you okay now?"

"Yeah, except they want to put me back on the Zoloft again, even though it doesn't do anything." She groans. "I don't want to take this stuff anymore, Georgie. I just want someone to fix it."

"You need to listen to them, Sav. Your body is probably all confused, so you need to take it slow."

"I get that, but I'm the one paying for the treatment, so I should get some say."

"How are you paying for it?" Georgina interjects as it dawns on her that rehab has to be expensive, and Savannah doesn't have a steady income most of the time. She gets by with loans from Georgina and their mother.

"Savannah?" she asks when the silence lingers. "Are you still there—"

"Dad," she answers glumly.

"*Dad?*"

"I know," Savannah says bitterly. "Worst moment of my life."

That's the most shocking revelation so far. As far as Georgina knows, Savannah hasn't talked to their father since they had a screaming match in Savannah's apartment about her dropping out of community college years ago. Savannah laughed sarcastically when he said he was upset about her "wasted potential," and that sent them both over the edge.

"*What an absolute joke,*" Savannah had seethed after he slammed the door behind him. "*Why doesn't he worry about his own potential? He wouldn't know mine if it slapped him in the face.*"

Georgina had stayed silent. She didn't want Savannah to drop out either, but she wasn't surprised by her sister's reaction. Their father only seems to care when it's convenient, and sometimes that's worse than not caring at all.

"It sucked to ask him," Savannah continues, her voice calling Georgina back to their conversation. "But I knew he wouldn't tell Mom, so I was like, whatever, I have to do it." Their father avoids their mother as much as Savannah avoids him.

"What did he say?"

"Nothing, thank goodness. He just sent the money."

Georgina fights back some bitterness of her own. She doesn't have high expectations for their father by any means, but she would've thought he could've at least mustered up a word or two. As usual, she was wrong. "Well, I'm glad you're getting some help. That's smart."

"I hate it here."

Georgina smiles weakly at her miserable tone. "I don't think rehab is supposed to be fun."

"It's not. I literally can't do anything except sit around—"

"Why does Mom think you're joining a cult?" Georgina interjects, suddenly remembering that bizarre detail.

"*What*? Is that what she said?" Savannah groans in exasperation. "That woman needs to lay off the Xanax. She's reaching new levels of ridiculousness. I literally just heard a preacher on the radio, and he helped when I was on the Effexor, so I found his stuff on YouTube. I was listening to it a couple times when she called, so I told her about it, therefore . . . I'm in a cult? I don't even know, I guess it's a super slippery slope, Georgie. Watch out."

Georgina laughs as relief washes over her, but her curiosity remains. It sounds less weird than their mother suggested, but it's still unusual for Savannah to care about what preachers have to say. "What's his name? The radio guy?"

"S. M. Lockridge. I actually just found out he's dead, which is super sad—" Savannah cuts off when a woman's voice fills the background. "Crap, they're coming to take my phone. I'll call you when I get it back. And I mean it, do not say a single word to Mom, for her own sake," she growls. "Love you. Bye."

As she hangs up and the silence takes over again, Georgina parks at the Harp House and does a long, Alvin-esque exhale. She feels relieved and helpless at the same time. It seems like God is on Savannah's mind, too, which is comforting yet a little worrisome, given her sister's current mental state. Is Savannah just desperate and reaching out for something? Is Georgina doing the same thing?

Her feelings war within her, but a glance at the clock propels her out of the car and she hurries inside the Harp House. A young man throws her a polite smile. His name is Philip, but Poppy calls him "the baby butler" because of his pimpled face and formal manners. There's a teenage girl with him. Julie, Georgina remembers, as the girl turns painfully shy. Her mother, Lila, cleans their room, and she had mentioned Julie watched *Nail Breakers* religiously, so Georgina made a mental note to go over with Poppy and say hello sometime. She prefers timid fans over the aggressive ones.

"Good morning, Miss Havoc," Philip calls out as Georgina passes by. "It's all about the personal touch, Julie," she hears him whisper. "Making sure the guests feel seen and whatnot."

When Julie throws him a withering look, Georgina hides her amusement and makes her way to the dining room, marveling at the details as she walks. The Harp House is a seamless operation, whether hosting events or simply checking visitors in and out. She also learned that the man who wheeled in their luggage is named Gavin Harp, and he's involved in pretty much everything. Based on the people-watching they've done thus far, she and Poppy have determined that he likes Lila, and there's a pretty decent chance she likes him, too. They're silently rooting for them.

"*I'm getting total* Titanic *vibes, minus the tragedy,*" Poppy had mused over breakfast yesterday, discreetly watching them. "*He's like a young Leonardo DiCaprio if you squint, and Lila's got that more mature Kate Winslet look—*"

Georgina had to shush her when other guests walked by. "*Poppy! Do you ever stop matchmaking?*"

"*I can't. It's my spiritual gift.*"

Besides Gavin and Lila, there's a small fleet of servers, part-time cooks, an aging handyman, two chatty gardeners, the cleaning crew, and Cassidy, of course—whose truck she happened to notice in the parking lot when she pulled in. She ignores the anticipation fluttering in her stomach as she enters the dining room, which is arguably the best room in the entire house.

A sleek, simple table for twelve shines under a crystal chandelier. It's always decorated with white hydrangeas, and it feels twice as large thanks to a towering mirror hanging over the marble fireplace. But Georgina's absolute favorite detail is the weeping willow wallpaper dotted with blue clouds and tiny pink magnolia clusters. She expects the usual buffet-style spread, but it's bare besides the gleaming espresso machine.

She ponders a new plan, but she gets lost somewhere along the way and ends up with too many doors to choose from.

"It's not up for debate, Mama."

Georgina halts when she hears Cassidy's voice.

"You need to cut back," he adds firmly. "Or you need some help in here."

"No, I don't," a woman says stubbornly.

"Yes, you do."

"Y'all are already stretched thin, Cassidy. You'll have to find someone and train them and all that, and I don't want to add anything else to your plate."

"You think I care about that more than I care about you?"

When the woman falls silent, Georgina's about to retreat, but a server suddenly barrels through the door. She catches Cassidy's eye through the doorway.

"Georgina?"

Her eyes widen. She can't run away now, so she awkwardly shuffles inside the room, which turns out to be the kitchen—a room she's been secretly wanting to see, but not under such embarrassing circumstances. Unsurprisingly, it's just as gorgeous as the rest of the house, with white brick walls, curved cabinets, gold-flecked marble countertops, and a gleaming dual fuel range.

"Hey. Sorry," she adds, blushing at the surprised look on his face. His mother is looking at her, too. Her hair is mostly silver, but a few dark strands still match Cassidy's, and their brows raise in the exact same way.

"I was just looking for food. For me. And Poppy," she adds unnecessarily.

"Oh. You just missed it," Cassidy says, nodding at the rolled-away cart. "But I gotcha covered. Mama, this is Georgina Havoc," he adds before opening the massive fridge. "She's the one fixing up Kit's house."

Georgina's nerves rise as the woman's face breaks into a smile. She was right after all—it's the same chatty woman who welcomed her and Savannah inside the yellow Victorian all those years ago.

"It's so nice to finally meet you! I'm Goldie."

Georgina smiles back as she finally remembers her name. It's fitting given her bright smile and butter-colored apron.

"It's nice to meet you, too. And thank you for the food the other day," she adds, recalling the fig-and-pecan pie that saved Poppy's sanity. "We—"

"Why do you look so familiar to me, honey?"

Georgina stiffens. Surely she doesn't remember her from all those years ago? She was all braces and frizzy hair and shyness back then, and she prefers to keep that version of herself safely stowed in the past.

"Maybe you saw her on TV," Cassidy suggests, smiling over his shoulder. "Georgina, do you want crepes or the egg muffuletta?"

Georgina sighs inwardly. Not only is he built like a Greek statue, but he also knows how to correctly pronounce *muffuletta* with his cute southern accent? She never knew such men existed.

"Umm . . . crepes. Please," she says, too tongue-tied to attempt saying it herself. "Actually, I'll take one of each." She can't forget to feed Poppy. Suddenly, Brigitte comes to mind, too. "Can I have one more, too? Possibly? I'll pay extra—"

He shakes his head. "Here you go," he says, handing her three heavy, neatly labeled boxes. "We keep a few extras for the servers. There's plenty," he adds when she hesitates.

"Thank you—"

"You'll have to join us for Sunday dinner sometime, Georgina," Goldie chimes in excitedly, glancing between them. "It's a tradition," she adds when Cassidy gives her a funny look. "I have all the new neighbors over."

"Oh, that sounds nice," she says, even though it actually sounds terribly awkward since she and Cassidy can barely keep their eyes off each other when they're together. "Shoot." She glances at the closest clock and starts her escape. "I've got to run."

"I gotta go, too, actually," Cassidy interjects, surprising them both. "I'll walk you out."

Georgina's nerves bubble up as he grabs keys off the counter and gives Goldie a quick, adorable kiss on the cheek, then hurries over to get the door.

"Thank you," Georgina murmurs, walking through it.

"Yep."

"Sorry for barging in there, by the way," she adds when the door closes behind them. "Your mom was probably like, 'Wow, who is this weirdo?'"

"Nah, you're good. It was a nice surprise," he says with a smile that makes her stomach do a somersault. Suddenly, his eyes drift downward, and Georgina realizes she's clutching the boxed lunches much tighter than necessary.

"Do you want me to carry something?"

"No, I got it." She tries to relax a little, but his manners and muscles make it difficult.

She follows his lead and a few moments later he opens another door leading to the back portion of the wraparound porch. A cobblestone path weaves to the gravel parking lot where her car shines in the late-morning sun.

As they walk to it, she suddenly remembers Brigitte's question. "Hey, you don't happen to know anything about the cottages, do you? Like, who used to own them?"

"Kit? Yeah, I knew her. Why?"

She relays Brigitte's critique.

He rubs his stubbled chin. "Kit could be an inspirational character, I suppose. She was a midwife. That's why there are two cottages. The bigger one was hers, and the small one was for the mothers. She retired and moved in with her daughter. In Vermont, I think?"

She smiles. "Cute. I like it. What about the orchard? Know anything special about that?"

"Not really. It's been around for as long as I can remember."

Georgina nods along, but she really wants to ask questions about *his* life more than anything. Like, what was it like growing up in a place like Tarragon? And how does one go from being G. I. Joe to being a mysterious farmer with Bible verses on his fancy desk?

"I do know Kit quit some kind of nursing job before she moved out here," he adds, his brows scrunched like he's racking his brain for information. "Maybe that helps? Y'all could talk about swapping out the stressful for the simple, or something like that?"

"Did you just come up with that on the fly?"

He laughs as they approach her car. "I guess I should've been in show business all this time."

"Maybe. Except I literally can't think of anything more stressful than delivering babies. I would pass out."

He smiles as they reach her car. "Yeah, it wouldn't be my first choice. She didn't get a whole lot of business out here, though. Maybe that's how she managed it." He waits as Georgina digs around for the keys in her purse, but her fingers fumble under the weight of his presence. "So, did your show officially start, then? The filming and all that?"

"Sort of," she says, still searching through the abyss of her bag. She knows better than to just toss things in, but she did it anyway. "We still need a contractor. Usually, you *start* with one of those, but . . ."

He frowns as her search continues. "Just someone who does construction? That kind of contractor?"

"Basically, yeah." She blows a stray curl out of her eyes. "I mean, it would be great if they're good on camera, but I can't be that picky right now—" She falls silent when he finally takes the boxes, and their hands brush in the process.

"Thanks," she murmurs, finding the keys a moment later.

"Yep. So you need—"

"Cassidy!"

Georgina jumps at the sound of a high, happy voice as Cassidy whips around. A woman is walking in their direction, and the closer she gets, the more Georgina dies inside. She's beauty-queen stunning, with bouncy blond hair and mega-white teeth that probably glow in the dark. Her pale pink dress matches her sky-high heels, and they don't faze her one bit as she glides over the gravel, gunning for Cassidy.

"Sorry." His face turns tense as he hands Georgina the boxes again. "I'll, uh . . . catch up with you later."

Georgina nods, but her good mood evaporates when his apologetic eyes meet hers.

"Sorry about the contractor," he adds. "I hope y'all find someone good."

"Thanks," she mumbles, trying to ignore the sting of disappointment as he hurries to meet the woman halfway. "Me too."

"Who was that?" Renata demands, peering over Cassidy's shoulder as Georgina gets inside her car.

"A guest," he says shortly as the Lexus peels out of the parking lot.

Renata's eyes narrow. "The design show girl?"

He frowns as dust flies by his head. "Yeah." Georgina's going way faster than she needs to, and he thinks he knows why.

"Gavin said y'all have been talking a lot. . . ."

Cassidy ignores the suspicion in Renata's voice and tries to ignore his disappointment, too. He was enjoying Georgina's company more than he should've been, anyway. He's asked himself more than once what exactly he's doing flirting with a perfect stranger a couple months before he leaves for another country, but all he knows is he likes being around her, and the feeling seemed to be mutual. Until about two minutes ago.

"What are you doing here, Ren?" he asks, focusing on her instead in the hopes she'll forget about Georgina.

"I'm not here to see *you*," she snipes, but her eyes give her away. "I'm talking to Gavin about Emmeline's shower. You're coming, right?"

"To a baby shower?"

"Yes?" She looks at him like he's as dense as copper. "The first part is for couples, and then y'all can go golf or shoot or grunt or whatever it is you do together."

He smiles reluctantly. Renata's always been funny. She and Melody used to laugh so hard that mascara would run down their cheeks. "I'm gonna pass, but tell Emme I'll get something for the baby."

Annoyance flashes across Renata's face—something he's been seeing more of lately—but he doesn't waver. She needs to get used to the extra distance he's putting between them.

"Anyway, have fun with Gav," he says, starting to leave.

"Thanks. He's been a real treat these days."

"He gets like that when we're busy."

"Or is it because you're trying to quit on him?"

Cassidy halts. His shoulders stiffen. "Come again?"

She feigns innocence. "I said, is Gavin acting up because you're walking out on the Harps?"

Shock fills Cassidy. And annoyance. No one is supposed to know about that except Gavin, the Harps, and Eddy. His mother is next on the list. "What are you talking about, Renata?"

"I'm talking about the job you're supposedly taking in some awful war-torn country," she says, tears brimming in her eyes right on cue. "And I'm waiting for you to tell me that's ridiculous, because it is—"

"Who told you?"

"You know I hear everything, Cassidy."

He scowls.

"Yes or no? Are you really trying to leave again?"

"I'm . . ." His mind moves between a few different strategies, trying to determine which one will do the least amount of damage, but they're all bad. "Yeah," he says finally as her tears fall. "I'm leaving."

"Oh, Cassidy! Why? How can you do that to Dale and Donna? To Goldie? That's not right and you know it. You made a promise to Melody—"

"Don't," he says sharply, and thankfully she quiets down again. He cares about Renata—they've known each other since they were kids, and Melody loved her like a sister—but he's not going to let her use his dead wife against him anymore. "I know what Mel would want better than anybody."

Renata throws him a wounded look, but the look on his face keeps her silent. Dale and Donna already tried the same guilt trip. Melody's memory is the most precious thing on the planet to Cassidy, but they can't use it to keep him here forever, no matter how good their intentions might be.

"We'll talk later," he says flatly, when Renata looks like she's going to start back up again. "And keep that quiet, Ren. I don't want my mother hearing about it from somebody else."

She gasps. "You haven't told Goldie yet?"

His mood darkens even more as he realizes his blunder. He wanted to have more ducks in a row before that conversation, but now he knows he can't wait much longer. Renata Woodard has never kept a secret in her life.

9

"You *have* to buy this dress, Georgie."

Georgina doesn't look up from her phone.

"You can wear it to Sunday dinner!" Poppy adds gleefully.

Georgina still doesn't look up.

"Georgie?"

She and Poppy are inside a cute secondhand shop on Tarragon's historic little Main Street, working on a new scene for the pilot. Brigitte's been keeping them busy with "extra" scenes while she sorts out their new contractor named Tom, a precious but elderly man who makes everyone nervous whenever he climbs a ladder. Spending the morning shopping with Poppy is one of the better parts of the last two weeks they've spent in Tarragon so far, but her good mood crashes as she rereads Lance's latest Instagram post.

"What's wrong?" Poppy asks, finally lowering the dress.

Most of his posts since the pause have been his usual modern aesthetic, with perfectly vanilla captions sprinkled in with a few brand promotions, but this one is different. It's an artistic little grenade—and he knows it.

"Why does your face look all tight?"

"Because of this," Georgina snaps, thrusting the phone at her. She watches as Poppy's eyes narrow on his solemn selfie and the bizarre, rambling paragraph all about hitting the pause button on life, followed by a Rumi quote.

"*You have to keep breaking your heart until it opens.*"

"Yikes," Poppy finally mutters, breaking the long silence. "That's bad."

Georgina grabs the phone again. "He can't make *any* part of this process easy," she says bitterly. It's extra infuriating since she's been working hard to keep her own social media as vague and cheerful as possible, per UpScale's instructions.

There was finally a lull in the tabloids about their "separate" lives after weeks of dramatic speculation, but now the rumors will fly all over again—by Lance's design. She scrolls through the comments, which confirm her fears.

> Guys, this is totally a breakup selfie.

> BRB gonna go check on Georgina

> noooooooo!

> Chip and JoJo would never break our hearts like this.

> WHAT ABOUT YOUR NEW SHOW?

Poppy frowns at the devastated look on Georgina's face. "Does this mean you're officially broken up?"

Poppy sounds hopeful, but Georgina fights the urge to throw her phone against the wall. She has no idea how to answer that question, which just adds more fuel to her fury.

"I can't believe him." She wants to comment on it herself and tell the world that this was all Lance's stupid idea, not hers. "I should be able to make my own statement if he's allowed to do this."

"Call Talia! Isn't he breaking the rules?"

Georgina thinks it over for a moment, then sighs miserably.

"No, he's too smart for that. He didn't actually mention the breakup—"

"He's not *that* smart."

Georgina dabs away a humiliating tear rolling down her cheek. She wants to agree with Poppy, but they both know Lance is smart. He reads all the latest self-help books and plays chess, and he can rattle off his ten favorite fashion designers, dead or alive. He's also determined and ambitious and fun, and he made her happy until he ruined everything. As his perfect contemplative face stares back at her from the screen, she hates him and misses him at the same time.

She types a message to Talia before she can talk herself out of it.

Please set up a meeting with Lance. The pause is over.

"Anyway," Poppy says, trying to distract her from her rattled emotions. "Lance sucks, per usual, and you have to wear this dress tonight."

Georgina throws her an exasperated look. She's acting like dinner at Goldie's house is the Met Gala, but Georgina's been dreading it ever since Goldie repeated her invitation at the Harp House last night. Poppy said yes before Georgina could stop her.

"You're giving up too easily, Georgie. You and Cassidy were totally vibing—"

"Yeah, which is gross, since he has a girlfriend." Her mood sinks every time she thinks about that awful moment in the parking lot when he practically ran toward the beautiful blonde. He's been easy to avoid thanks to their weird schedules, but he's glanced in her direction more than once.

"You don't know if she was his girlfriend or not," Poppy says tersely, holding out the dress again. "She could've been his sister or something."

"She wasn't—"

"Ladies, can we get back to filming, please?"

They both turn and meet the weary gaze of Nathan, the head cameraman. He was given the unfortunate job of filming them while they shop, when it's especially hard for them to stay on task. "Brigitte wants the off-site stuff done today."

"Of course! One second." Poppy flashes him her sweetest smile, then lowers her voice. "Just buy it and wear it, okay?" she growls.

Georgina finally snatches the dress from her, and her mood lifts a tiny bit. It's light and summery and patterned with tiny pink-orange peaches. "Fine," she grumbles, throwing it in their basket. "I'll buy it, but I'm not wearing it for him."

"Let's roll!"

The next hour is easy enough as they talk and walk around the store, pretending to pick out a bunch of fabulous vintage items they pulled earlier that day with the help of the sweet shopkeeper named Alice. She opened the store on a Sunday just for them. Brass candlesticks, simple oval mirrors, gilded frames, and a tattered chair with good bones—it's a surprisingly good haul for such a quaint little shop. They usually use furniture from UpScale's advertising partners, but the time and distance is too complicated for that. Georgina doesn't mind, though. She prefers secondhand things, but the fun comes to an abrupt halt when Poppy suddenly runs toward the bathroom.

"What just happened?" Nathan asks, poking his head over the camera as Poppy slams the door behind her. "Is she okay?"

Georgina hurries after her. "Poppy? Are you all right—" Georgina cuts off as Poppy vomits. "Oh no." There's a pause followed by more puking. Georgina winces. "Do you need help?"

"I just need . . . water," Poppy whimpers, flushing the toilet. "Or food. I don't know. Something."

Georgina searches for Alice, who reappears with a can of diet ginger ale and a package of brown sugar Pop-Tarts. Georgina hands them to Poppy through the cracked door.

"Thanks," she mutters, quickly shutting it again.

Nathan suppresses a sigh as the minutes pass. "I guess we're taking a break," he finally says grumpily, dismissing the rest of the crew.

They scatter, but Georgina lingers near the bathroom, waiting for Poppy. She peruses a book display and flips through one with a green and gold spine.

There is but one good; that is God. Everything else is good when it looks to Him and bad when it turns from Him.

She glances at the cover and frowns. The title seems odd for a book about God—*The Great Divorce*—but that sentence intrigues her enough to add it to their pile of purchases. Even if she doesn't get around to reading it, it'll look good on a coffee table. Her phone chirps.

> Apparently, Lance is out of the country?? That's what Malonetti said.

Georgina stares at the message from Talia as shock spills over her. She pulls up his selfie again and studies it more closely. Her eyes narrow skeptically, but then she spots a sliver of a palm tree behind his head. Anger fills her.

> Did he say when he'll be back?

> "an indeterminate amount of time." I'll figure it out.

Georgina's anger lingers. He really left the country without telling her? That's a hurtful new low. Her mind races to another upsetting possibility—is he doing something international for his solo show? That's been a dream of his for the last couple years, but UpScale wasn't interested. Maybe they finally gave in?

"Sorry," Poppy mutters, remerging from the bathroom with a pale, puffy face. "Morning sickness came late today."

Georgina forces herself to look calm for Poppy's sake. It doesn't seem like the right time to announce Lance's latest curveball. "We can just be done for today, Pop."

"What? No! I'm fine. Let's just finish. Where the heck is everyone?"

Georgina begs her to take a longer break, but she refuses, so they forge ahead and film a scene at a nearby café. Brigitte wants them to go over potential color palettes and fret about the water damage, but Poppy almost pukes again when someone pulls a quiche out of the microwave, so Nathan calls it quits for the day with a defeated look. Georgina is filled with guilt as Poppy's face flames with embarrassment.

Once they're freed from their microphones and safely inside the Lexus, Poppy covers her mascara-streaked eyes with her hands and sobs.

"I'm so sorry, Georgie."

Georgina's heart sinks. She could tell this was coming the moment Poppy stepped out of the bathroom. She puts her hand on her slumped shoulder. "It's okay."

"I can't ruin this for you."

Georgina smiles through tears of her own. Poppy really is the best friend she's ever had. The last two weeks in Tarragon have been harder on her than she'll ever admit—and yet she's still thinking about Georgina.

"I'm just struggling a little—"

"You can go home, Pop. I mean that. Olivia needs you more than me. Jared, too." Georgina glances at Poppy's bump. "And his future elk-eating buddy in there."

Poppy smiles, but her heart is clearly torn. She thinks it over for a moment, then firmly shakes her head. "No. We're doing this."

"Poppy—"

"Don't try to talk me out of it! I don't care if I have to carry a barf bag around. We're freaking doing this, Georgie."

Georgina smiles gratefully.

"But you have to do something for me."

"Anything, obviously."

"Do you promise?"

"I don't know what I'm promising yet—"

"I know. It's a proactive promise." Poppy smiles slyly. "I want you to promise me that you'll keep the promise I'm about to ask you to keep."

Georgina laughs. "Okay . . ."

"Go to the dinner tonight."

Georgina's laughter fades. "Without you?"

Poppy nods.

She groans. "Why, Poppy? There's no point, and I don't want to go without you."

"Please just go," Poppy pleads. "If Cassidy really is a jerk, I'll drop it forever, but just go and confirm, okay? I need closure."

Georgina wants to protest. She dreads the idea of having dinner with Cassidy and Goldie and whomever else might be there, especially without Poppy to lighten the mood, but considering what Poppy's currently putting herself through for Georgina's sake, she doesn't have much leverage.

"Fine," she says, resigning herself to a few hours of misery as Poppy whoops triumphantly. "I'll go."

10

Sorry, Cass. Hospice ministry tonight.

Cassidy sighs as he reads over Pastor Boggs's text. He's learned to have more than one strategy when he feels like drinking, but he's already blown through most of them. He had prayed first, and that helped a little but not enough, so he had tried calling Eddy, but he didn't pick up, and neither did Sawyer. Now Boggs is busy, too.

He reluctantly lowers himself to the floor in his office. It's time for his least favorite tactic, which is one hundred push-ups. The dread of doing them usually makes the craving for alcohol fade, or it wears him out long enough to stop him from doing anything stupid.

You doing okay?

Cassidy types back a quick yes to Boggs, not wanting to worry him. He learned the hard way that Boggs has no problem sending over some poor church elder to check on him, no matter how inconvenient it might be. Derek Boggs is a quiet man, especially for a preacher, but he's not shy about that sort of thing. After Melody died and Cassidy started drinking, he's the one who said enough was enough and rallied the troops—Eddy, Gavin, Goldie, and the most experienced grief counselor he could find—to get Cassidy back on his feet. Cassidy chafed under the scrutiny at first, but Boggs didn't care. He was too determined to save his life.

As Cassidy races through the push-ups, he knows he must be a ridiculous sight, all dressed up and huffing and puffing on the hardwood floor, but he keeps going, willing the desire to fade, but it lingers longer than usual, even as his muscles start to ache. He suspects it has something to do with stress, along with his mother's announcement that she invited Georgina Havoc to dinner tonight. He wants to smooth things over with her, but it seems unlikely, given that she's acting like he's a nasty cold she doesn't want to catch.

He's got about thirty left when his phone starts ringing.

"Hello?" he pants, grateful for a reason to quit as he answers Sawyer's call.

"Why are you breathing so hard? You running from Renata or something?"

Cassidy laughs. "Push-ups," he explains.

"To help fight her off?"

Cassidy laughs harder, but he also feels a twinge of guilt about their ongoing jokes. "Just getting some exercise." Typically, he would just admit he felt like drinking—being blunt about it helps—but the memory of his kiss with Renata is enough to make what's left of the temptation disappear. He *never* wants to make another mistake like that again. "Did you book your flight?" he asks, changing the subject.

"Yep. Friday, baby."

Cassidy cheers. "Is Rachel coming, too?"

"Nah, she couldn't get the time off. She's even busier than I am."

"Too bad. Shouldn't take long, though—" There's a knock

on the door, and Gavin lets himself in before Cassidy can stop him. Cassidy signals for him to wait a minute.

"What time do you land?" Cassidy asks Sawyer as Gavin settles into a chair. He studies a pile of Boggs's books while he waits for Cassidy's undivided attention.

"Early," Sawyer says, clearly already dreading it. "I'll text you."

"Sounds good. I'll see you soon."

Gavin cocks his head when Cassidy hangs up a moment later. "Who's coming on Friday?"

"Sawyer." Cassidy glances at his watch, hoping Gavin will take the hint that he doesn't have much time.

"Oh." Gavin forgets to be annoyed for a second and smiles. Everybody loves Sawyer. "What's the occasion?"

"He's gonna help me break the news about the job to my mother," Cassidy says smoothly, feigning cheerfulness. "Unless Renata beats me to it."

When Gavin's forehead reddens, Cassidy's suspicions are confirmed. His brother-in-law looks as guilty as a convict.

"Any idea how she found out about it, Gav?"

Gavin raises his hands in surrender as Cassidy's tone sharpens. "I know what you're thinking, but it wasn't me. Dad told her."

Cassidy's eyes narrow. His father-in-law just crossed a very thick line.

"I knew it was a bad move," Gavin adds quickly. "I told him not to, but he thought she might be able to get you to stay."

Cassidy's surprise turns to anger. "Well, you were right. That was a big misfire on his part, because now I'm in even more of a hurry to get out of here." For his sake, and Renata's, too, because apparently the Harps aren't willing to let her fairy tale fade, either.

Gavin looks offended and apologetic at the same time. "I

guess I can't really blame you. I know Dad's been giving you a hard time." Guilt slowly shadows his eyes. "Maybe I have too. We just . . ." Gavin doesn't finish the sentence, but the look on his face makes Cassidy's anger fade. Sometimes he forgets that Melody's family loves him. She wasn't the only one.

"What's your deal with Ren, anyway?" Gavin asks, changing the subject as soon as he can. "Did y'all have a falling out? She said you aren't talking to her anymore."

Cassidy sighs. He's been trying to go back to their simpler, platonic friendship for years, but she's the one who refuses. "Have you ever seen a bobcat prowling around looking for a squirrel, Gavin?" he asks, rubbing his temples. "That's the deal. And Renata's the bobcat."

Gavin bursts out laughing, but he quiets down when he sees the miserable look on Cassidy's face.

"I don't want to keep hurting her feelings," he adds, meaning it. "But we just don't go together, no matter how much y'all want us to." He knows it would make for a nice little happy ending for everyone, since Renata is like a second daughter to the Harps, but he also knows what love is, and it's not what he feels whenever Renata Woodard is in the room.

"Dale needs to respect my decision," he continues. "Me leaving Tarragon doesn't mean I'm leaving the family—"

"We know that," Gavin mutters defensively, crossing his arms.

Cassidy's face softens. Sometimes Gavin looks like a little boy again, like he did when Cassidy first met him at one of Melody's softball games. "Then act like it, Gav. I'll always be your brother, whether you like it or not."

Gavin can't force a smile, but there's resignation in his eyes as he rises from the chair and drops a thin stack of papers on his desk.

"You coming to dinner?"

"Not tonight. Gotta prep for some interviews. Those are your copies."

Cassidy studies them and suddenly understands. They're applications for his job.

Gavin slips out the door a moment later, leaving Cassidy to wrestle with his guilt as his eyes fall on the verses he slid under the glass five years ago, a few months after Melody died.

Count it all joy, my brothers, when you meet trials of various kinds, for you know that the testing of your faith produces steadfastness.

He exhales. If someone would've asked him about his "trials" back then, he would've said that he'd had way more than his fair share. He saw some of the worst things the world has to offer when he was at war, but those moments pale in comparison to the day he buried his twenty-seven-year-old wife on a beautiful spring day. To Cassidy, it felt like the ultimate betrayal from the God she'd loved her whole life.

He closes his eyes, reluctantly remembering more. He was drunk when he got the news that his dad died of a stroke less than a year later. They'd had an argument about Cassidy re-enlisting the day before. His father had insisted he quit drinking, get out of Tarragon, and get back to business, but Cassidy had surprised them both and shrugged him off. His father was trying to save his life, too, but he was too bitter to realize it.

The regret that filled him when his mother called him with the news was the heaviest weight he's ever tried to carry, and he thought he might collapse beneath it, but that's where God finally met him. Right in the middle of the wreckage.

He feels pulled toward the empty liquor cabinet again, but it's not as strong this time. Guilt is a powerful trigger, but, by God's grace, it's slowly losing its hold on him.

"You're moving on, Cass."

Contrary to what everyone else says, Melody would've wanted that.

"I am moving on," he repeats quietly. "But I'll never stop loving you."

As sweat drips down her neck, Georgina seriously regrets her decision to walk to Goldie's house. She craved fresh air after hours being cramped in the cottage with the crew, but now that she's a little over halfway to Goldie's, she's realizing the distance was farther than she thought.

"Not your smartest move," she scolds herself as her heels sink into the gravel. Her mood sinks along with them. She hasn't heard from Savannah since their last alarming conversation, which is unnerving but probably a good thing, since she's supposed to be recovering. Lance is also quiet from wherever the heck he is in the world right now, which is *not* a good thing, since Talia's been bombarding him and his lawyer with calls and emails all afternoon. Georgina has been copied on every single one.

Please read the attached wording and respond within three business days, per the terms of the NDA. Mediation is my client's preference, but we have other less peaceable options if necessary.

It was painful to read over the statement and imagine a life without Lance after years of building a perfect one, but Georgina had forced herself to do it. Her future looks nothing like she imagined, but even the unknown is better than false, foolish hope.

Her eyes travel to the sky above, which is gloriously blue with little wispy clouds, and her mind drifts back to Poppy's latest conversation with Jared and Olivia in the Harp House after Poppy was finally done puking her guts out. They have a routine where Jared reads Olivia some kind of children's Bible in his simple, straightforward way, and Poppy listens in. Then they pray.

"*Do you want to pray for anything, Olivia?*" Jared always asks.

Sometimes she responds with an unapologetic no, but she was enthusiastic tonight. "*Thank you, God, for my shows, and for the baby, and for the butterflies and squirrels. Please make more squirrels, God. We need them in our yard—*"

Georgina smiles weakly. Her prayers probably sound just as random when her mind gets tangled with distractions and questions. She skimmed her thrift store find between reshoots today—the formal, British-sounding prose makes some of it hard to follow—but she's slowly figuring out the story. It's about a man on his way to heaven and the conflicted people he meets along the way.

No natural feelings are high or low, holy or unholy, in themselves. They are all holy when God's hand is on the rein. They all go bad when they set up on their own and make themselves into false gods.

She's been mulling over that bit all day. She always thought that some feelings were bad—like sadness, or desire, or cravings—but this weird little book has her rethinking it. Maybe those feelings can be holy, too, if God is involved.

"Whoa!" she yelps in surprise as a zigzagging bumblebee dive-bombs the peaches on her dress—the second one so far. She flails around until the buzzing fades, then bends down to pick a pebble out of her shoe.

She straightens when an engine rumbles behind her.

"Georgina?"

She turns around as Cassidy's truck slowly approaches. His window is rolled down, and he looks as surprised as she does. She glances at the passenger seat. He's also alone.

"Why on earth are you walking?"

"Um . . ." She searches for words, but they don't come as quickly as usual. They haven't been this close since that awful day in the parking lot. "I wanted to."

His eyes move over her glistening face, then down to her high-heeled feet, which, admittedly, hurt. He frowns. "I can drive you the rest of the way—"

"No," she says tersely, keeping her slow pace. "I'm absolutely fine walking."

"Yeah, you look absolutely fine," he says, matching her cool tone.

Heat fills her face. "I am," she repeats, pretending to be unruffled. "Carry on."

"Suit yourself."

She keeps her face as serene as she can as he navigates around her, ignoring his sexy, smirking face in the rearview mirror. "Remember the beauty queen, Georgina," she reminds herself, successfully quashing some of her rogue feelings. "Remember how he literally sprinted toward her . . ."

When she finally arrives on Goldie's petunia-covered porch five minutes later, the door immediately swings open, and Goldie ushers her inside. "Oh my word! Are those little peaches on your dress? You're as pretty as a picture tonight."

"Thank you." Wonderfully competing smells hit Georgina's nose as she enters the elegant old house. Something soft tickles her ankle, and she finds a purring Siamese cat rubbing its chin against the edge of her shoe. A second one scampers across the room.

"Tango and Cash," Goldie says, trying to shoo them away.

"They're cute," she says, petting Tango. "I like cats," she adds when Goldie looks unsure.

"Oh, good. Tango is the biter, so just keep an eye on him."

She nods to a door off the entryway. "You can go on into the dining room. Cassidy's in there."

Georgina straightens as the cat tries to nip her finger. Cassidy is one problem, but Goldie is another. She's a genuinely sweet lady and positively thrilled to see her, so Georgina can't ruin her dinner, no matter how mean she wants to be to her son.

Heart drumming, Georgina obediently enters and finds Cassidy seated at the huge trestle table, and he's wearing a suit instead of his dusty work clothes. She sighs inwardly. This whole ordeal would be easier if he didn't have to look perfectly rugged and pulled together at the same time.

"How was your little stroll?"

"Fine," she snaps, but her face warms as his eyes travel up her curve-hugging dress. She almost didn't wear it, but the fit was too perfect, and, contrary to what she told Poppy, she did put in a little extra effort. There's no reason why she can't look good and get closure at the same time.

Surprise fills her when he stands up and pulls out a chair. "Thank you," she adds stiffly, sitting down.

His eyes meet hers when he settles into his own seat again, but she quickly looks down. Goldie prepared a full southern setting, complete with three spoons and two forks each, all placed in order of use. A long, loaded moment passes between them.

"Is it just us?" she asks, her concern growing as she notes the empty seats.

"I don't know. Were you expecting somebody specific?"

She adjusts one of her forks. "I thought maybe you were bringing your friend."

His face scrunches. "Who?"

"The woman in the parking lot. Tall. Blond. *Very* happy to see you."

"Oh." He frowns. "Renata."

"Pretty name."

His lips slant into a small smile as her tone turns cold. "Yeah, I don't know where she is tonight. I haven't talked to her since then."

Georgina's eyes narrow.

"How's Poppy doing?" he asks, effortlessly changing the subject. "Is she feeling—"

"Cassidy, play something on the radio!" Goldie yells from the kitchen, startling them both. "Music," she adds, which makes him laugh.

"What did she think I was going to pick? The news?"

Georgina smiles reluctantly as he stands up and fiddles with a radio. A mishmash of music and static fills the room.

"Poppy's doing better," she says, answering his question so she can ask her own, but he turns up the volume on a familiar country song.

Her face warms as he sits down again and looks her in the eye. Unlike her, he doesn't seem uncomfortable at all. "How do you and Renata know each other?" she finally asks, crossing her arms. "You seemed—"

"She was good friends with my wife."

Georgina blinks. She must've misheard him, so she waits with a puzzled expression, but all he offers her is a small, sad smile.

"Your . . . wife?"

"Mm-hmm. Melody. She died five years ago."

"Oh." It feels like all the air is leaving her body. "Um . . ." *His wife?* "I am so sorry—"

"It's fine," he says, gently cutting her off. "You don't have to do all that. I didn't want to spring it on you, but there's no real casual way to bring it up."

"Yeah . . ." He's right. She wouldn't have been prepared for that in *any* setting.

"I think there was just some kind of misunderstanding," he

adds, keeping his voice light even as her face flames. "Renata is an old family friend."

Georgina tries to form words, but she can't think of anything. Her shock and relief are still too strong.

"So . . . maybe we can pick up where we left off?"

His question makes her heart race even faster, but Goldie arrives before she can answer it. Cassidy tries to take a platter from her, but she refuses to hand it over.

"Lila just called. She can't make it tonight," she says, setting an heirloom tomato salad near the candlelit centerpiece. "She's sorting out Julie. She apologized about a million times."

"Darn," Georgina says, finally mustering up one coherent word. "Lila seems nice," she adds.

"She's just the sweetest," Goldie agrees, arranging a basket of cloud-shaped rolls.

"Julie, not so much," Cassidy interjects with a joking smile.

"She's fifteen," Goldie explains. "And Lila does it all by herself."

"Oh." Sympathy fills her. "I think most teenage girls are pretty hard on their moms. My sister and I were, anyway."

"Boys, too," Goldie says, shooting Cassidy a look that makes him laugh. "How's Julie doing at the house?"

"Fine so far. Gavin wasn't too enthused about the idea, but they actually get along all right. Philip doesn't let her get away with anything."

Georgina's manners suddenly kick in when Goldie turns toward the kitchen again. "Can I help you with anything?"

"No, you cannot," she says firmly when Georgina starts to rise from her seat. "You just sit right back down and relax." She scurries through the doors again without another word.

Cassidy smiles at the stunned look on Georgina's face. "Sorry, I should've warned you. She's all cute and nice until it comes to her cooking, then she turns into a bulldog. Julie was supposed to help her in the kitchen, but that lasted about two whole minutes."

"At the Harp House?"

He nods. "I'm trying to get her to cut back. For her health."

As they make more small talk, the tension eases, and it occurs to her that they're finally having a semi-normal interaction, even though nothing has been normal between them since the moment they met. And it's nice.

Georgina clears her throat. "So, about where we left off—"

Goldie pushes through the doors again, this time carrying another tray. "Oh my word, I forgot the tea! Go grab it, Cass. I can't believe I left y'all parched in here, and you didn't even say a word."

Cassidy dutifully disappears into the kitchen while Goldie carefully arranges pan-fried chicken and butter-drenched mashed potatoes on the table. She pauses to throw Georgina a smile. "I hope he's behaving himself?"

Georgina nods but her face warms. He's been better behaved than she has over the last few days.

"Good. He—" Goldie pauses when Cassidy returns with a huge ceramic pitcher. Georgina expects him to set it on the table, but he leans in to fill up her glass instead.

"You like sweet tea, right?"

"Mm-hmm." She's actually never liked sweet tea—something other Tennesseans have berated her for her entire life—but right now she's willing to drink gallons of it if it means being this close to him.

"I'll say grace," Goldie offers, once he takes his seat again.

A bittersweetness fills Georgina as Goldie leads a simple prayer. Her father used to pray before meals sometimes. Her mother never prayed, but she bowed her head as a compromise.

"Georgina, I finally figured it out," Goldie says, recapturing her attention after the synchronized amen. "I know why you look so familiar to me."

Georgina's hand hovers over the salad. Is Goldie about to out her as the awkward camper who picked through her pecans all those years ago?

"You were in my favorite magazine! *Bake from Scratch.*"

"Oh!" Georgina says, stifling her relief.

"I marked your babka recipe," Goldie adds, passing her the potatoes. "Do I remember right that you have a cookbook coming out?"

Georgina smiles, but the question stings. "Potentially." Her book was almost a done deal back when she and Lance were dubbed the next big thing, but those talks have ceased since the pause, which means it's probably off the table unless she scrapes out with the show.

"How does somebody get into all that? Television and books and such?" Goldie asks with an admiring look. "You must work very hard."

It's tricky, but she tries her best to describe her weird, winding career path—minus the Lance parts—between bites of Goldie's incredible food, starting with her leaving a terribly dull job at her mother's marketing firm to helping Poppy stage houses for a booming Nashville property manager. From there, they built their blog and dedicated Instagram. Then their on-a-whim pitch to UpScale led to a whirlwind of success.

Goldie listens intently. "And what about your family? Are they in Nashville, too?"

"My mom is. My dad isn't."

Surprise flickers across Goldie's face, but it fades fast. "And you mentioned a sister?"

"Savannah."

"Where does she live?"

"Um . . . Franklin, at the moment." Rehab probably isn't

part of Savannah's preferred biography, so Georgina leaves it out. "She's going to art school." *Except she's dropping out,* she suddenly remembers.

"My goodness, y'all are a creative bunch. Sawyer—that's Cassidy's brother—is the artist in our family. He's in Florida now." Goldie points proudly at a recent wedding picture.

Georgina smiles politely. The family resemblance is still going strong. Apparently, Sawyer has his own construction business now, and he's newly married, but her eyes drift from his picture to the one beside it. It's not the same one she noticed years ago, of a younger, hard-faced Cassidy in military fatigues. He's older in this one, and he's dressed in a formal kind of uniform, with his arm around the waist of a beautiful blond bride.

"Cassidy was a Special Forces Weapons Sergeant," Goldie says, noticing Georgina's interest. "And he was going to teach at Fort Campbell—"

"Don't bore her, Mama," he interjects. "I'm sure Georgina isn't as interested in my life as you are."

Georgina frowns. She wishes that were true, but he couldn't be more wrong. Thankfully, Goldie ignores him and lists out his accomplishments instead, starting with his degrees in agriculture and Spanish, followed by various deployments and tests and boot camps and promotions.

"So, you basically shot people for a living?" Georgina asks, trying to wrap her mind around the acronym-filled military language and his missions in remote parts of the world. "Is that, like, a sniper?"

He nods.

Her eyes widen. "And you actually *liked* it?" She can't imagine why anyone would, but his face lights up at the question.

"I loved it."

Surprise fills her—and disappointment. She wants to press him for a reason, but Goldie changes the subject to Cassidy's father, Clive, also a military man, who had some kind of specialty in "warfare tactics" and "long-range marksmanship." Georgina's head spins when Cassidy starts chiming in with even more enthusiasm.

"I kind of hate guns," she finally blurts out.

He laughs, but his laughter fades at the serious look on her face. "You're just messing with me."

She shakes her head.

"Have you ever even shot one?"

"Nope," she says proudly.

"Then how do you know if you hate them?"

"Because they kill people."

"Wow."

She laughs as he stares at her like she's an alien who just landed in the middle of his mother's dining room.

He shakes his head. "I don't even know where to begin with that."

"Cassidy," Goldie chides. "It's all right, not everyone is an enthusiast."

"I'm not saying she has to be an enthusiast, Mama, but she should at least shoot a gun once in her life." He throws Georgina a challenging look. "You might actually like it—"

"Time for dessert!" Goldie interrupts when Georgina's skeptical eyes lock with his. Goldie springs from the table and heads for the kitchen, leaving them to finish the battle without her.

"How exactly does a Special Forces Weapons Sergeant . . ."

He smirks at the extra careful way she says it.

". . . end up working at the Harp House? Did you retire or something?" He seems too young to "retire" from anything, but she has no clue how it works.

"No. It's called a compassionate discharge. They let me leave because Melody was dying."

It takes a moment for his words to sink in—maybe because

of the strange placement of "compassionate" in the middle of such a sad sentence.

"And she was a Harp," he adds, offering up the last piece of the puzzle. "She wanted to be home when she died."

"Oh . . ." *Melody Harp.* Georgina searches for something to say, but then she remembers he doesn't like the usual platitudes, so she goes with her first thought instead. "That's the best name I've ever heard."

He smiles.

Goldie returns with bread pudding moments later, and it's so good that it renders Georgina temporarily speechless.

"Is this French bread?"

Goldie looks surprised but delighted that Georgina noticed. "It is. That's the Louisiana way. What do you think? I like it because it holds everything together better."

"Do you share any of your recipes, or are they secret? I respect both approaches."

Goldie laughs. "I'm a little more on the secret side, but I'd make an exception for you."

Cassidy raises an eyebrow. "She likes you," he mouths behind his spoon, which makes Georgina smile behind hers. As the evening draws to an end, it dawns on her that she's having fun—actual, relaxed fun—for the first time since Lance turned her world upside down.

"Georgina, I'm sorry, I know you're a strong, independent woman and all that, but I simply cannot let you walk back to Kit's house by yourself," Goldie says an hour later, when candle wax is dangerously close to dripping on her lace tablecloth. "I'd worry myself to death."

Surprise fills Georgina as she peers out the window. More time has passed than she realized because it's pitch-black outside beyond the porch light.

She glances at Cassidy and tries to keep her voice as natural as possible, even though her heart starts drumming. "Maybe I can get a ride with you?"

"Sure."

She exhales, grateful that she doesn't have to wander around in the dark, but also because he sounds a tiny bit nervous, too.

They say good-bye to Goldie a few minutes later—after she loaded Georgina up with a giant container of bread pudding for Poppy—and Georgina's nerves reach an all-time high as Cassidy opens her door and she climbs into his massive truck. She expects it to be dirty, but it's clean and empty and smells like oranges and sunscreen.

"You're not mad at me anymore, then?"

Her head swivels in his direction as he settles into the driver's seat. "About what?"

"Renata."

Color fills her cheeks as he turns the key. "Oh." She turns to look at the starry darkness instead. "No. There was just a little misunderstanding, like you said."

"You don't have a boyfriend?"

Georgina's heart nearly stops as he starts driving. She glances at him, wondering if he feels as weird about that question as she does, but his face is relaxed. Awkward subjects just don't faze this man like they should. "No," she says, the word coming out softer than she meant it to. *I don't think so*, she thinks, remembering the mess.

"That's surprising."

Her heart drums inside her chest. "It's kind of a recent development, actually." She wonders if that might finally catch him off guard.

"Your idea or his?"

"His."

Embarrassment fills her as his expression changes ever so slightly. Did that revelation change his opinion about her?

"That's even more surprising," he finally says, turning on the road to the cottages.

Her stomach flutters as he parks beside her car. It's slowly dawning on her how dangerously close she is to throwing caution to the wind and kissing him. And it seems like he might be thinking the same thing.

No, she commands herself, reminding herself of all the reasons not to as his dark eyes meet hers. She's barely single, they just met, he's a widower, he's obsessed with guns—the list goes on and on. *No, Georgina*, she repeats while her heart screams the opposite. There are a million reasons why it's a bad idea, but none of them are as persuasive as the look on his face.

"Your mom is the best cook I've ever met," she says, bringing up Goldie in order to douse the flames. "And I've met, like, famous chefs and stuff," she adds stupidly, getting flustered as his eyes move over her. "I'm not bragging or anything. I'm just saying . . ."

He looks amused by the sudden change of subject but goes along with it. "Yeah, she is. She reads all the magazines—"

"That's amazing," Georgina gushes, cutting him off as her phone chimes somewhere in the background. She pulls it out of her purse and holds it like a little shield, but new messages from Lance and Savannah throw her off even more.

I didn't tell Damien to drop your project. That was UpScale.

Her stomach drops, but Savannah's message shocks her even more.

i'm coming to tarragon! call me now

"What?" she mutters, reading it again.

"You all right?"

Georgina tears her eyes off the screen. She must look as confused as she feels because his face fills with concern. "Yes. Sorry." She tucks the phone away again and feigns calm, but the interior lights inside his truck are fading, leaving them in the dark.

"I'm technically not single yet," she admits in a last-ditch effort to jolt them both back to their senses. It seems to work because his eyebrows shoot up.

"You're not?"

"I mean, I am, kind of, but it's complicated." She kicks herself for bringing up Lance again—he's the absolute last person she wants to think about right now—but Cassidy waits for an explanation. She does her best to describe the pause and the NDA and their competing pilots without making her life sound like a total train wreck, but his puzzled face fills her with a fresh wave of embarrassment as he mulls it over. She waits, expecting questions or annoyance or *something*, but the only thing she gets is a tiny frown.

"Well, anyway . . ." She places a shaky hand on the door handle, crushed but relieved at the same time. "Thanks for the ride—"

The rest of the sentence never materializes because he kisses her, and she instantly forgets the long list of reasons why he shouldn't as his mouth moves over hers. Her eyes close. It's the *perfect* kiss—gentle enough to draw her out of her racing thoughts but deep enough to make her pulse pound until she finally drags herself away.

"Um . . ." She tries to catch her breath. "What are you doing?"

His frown returns. "Kissing you?"

"Why, though?" she demands, her skin warming at the pleased look on his face. "I just threw a bunch of red flags at you."

"Yeah, I caught all those."

Her eyes widen. "So, what are you doing?"

"I just wanted to."

His simple answer stuns her. For a moment, he looks like he might elaborate, but then he shrugs.

"Yeah, that's it. I like you, and I wanted to kiss you." Uncertainty flickers across his face. "Did you not want me to?"

Her brain hiccups over that first part—"*I like you*"—and the sincerity in his voice as he said it. And then there's the second part. "I . . ." Her face turns even warmer as he waits for her answer.

"If you don't want me to, I won't—"

"No, no, it's not that," she says quickly, cutting him off before he takes kissing off the table. "I just . . ." *Want you to kiss me again*? He made her forget about the world crumbling beneath her feet for a few blissful moments, but reality is sinking in again.

His brows raise as her face turns more serious.

"I just don't want anybody to get hurt," she finally explains, putting her hesitation into words. "Because I like you, too. A lot." A tortured sigh escapes her lips before she can stop it. Her embarrassment reaches an all-time high, but the admission makes his lips lift into a smile. "Are you okay with a no expectations kind of thing? It's fine if you're not, but I just can't do anything serious right now."

She falls silent as he drags a hand through his hair in an adorably frustrated kind of way. *I understand completely*, she wants him to say, but she bites her tongue and waits for his answer.

"I don't have a bunch of expectations, Georgina."

A shadow of sadness touches his eyes when he finally speaks again, and she feels it more deeply than she should, considering he's barely more than a stranger.

"I know things don't always go according to plan," he adds.

She nods. She's figuring that out, too.

11

Georgina's tired eyes flit between the stenciled ceiling and her phone as she waits for Savannah's call. It's a little after one o'clock in the morning, and between her sister's text and kissing Cassidy just a few hours earlier, she's exhausted and electrified at the same time. In normal circumstances, that kiss would be the only thing running through her mind, but Savannah's sporadic updates compete for her attention.

"Finally," Georgina hisses, snatching the buzzing phone before it can wake Poppy. "Where the heck are you, Sav?" she whispers.

"I have no idea."

Her annoyance intensifies. Once she and Cassidy finally tore themselves away from each other in his truck, Georgina had forced herself to focus on stopping Savannah from coming to Tarragon, but it was too late. She was already on her way.

Savannah's laughter bursts in her ear. "Wow. I'm *completely* lost. Whoops."

"Why is that funny, Savannah? You think I can just find you in the middle of Tarragon?"

"I think I'm close to the camp. Maybe."

"Use your GPS."

"My phone's about to die."

Georgina groans silently. She shouldn't be surprised—it would be more unusual if Savannah had a charged phone and a full tank of gas before embarking on a four-hour road trip in the middle of the night—but she's still furious with her sister. "Send me your location before your phone dies," she growls. "I'm coming."

"Okie-dokie."

Georgina curses under her breath as she rises from the bed and throws a T-shirt over her silk pajamas, then slips on Poppy's flip-flops. She wishes she could wake Poppy—she graciously agreed to let Savannah stay in their room until Georgina figures out what the heck is going on—but they stayed up too late talking about the kiss, which had Poppy practically hyperventilating with excitement. Now she's snuggling her favorite body pillow, and Georgina doesn't have the heart to tear them apart, so she sneaks out the door and hurries down the hallway and stairs.

Thankfully, the downstairs parlor is empty, since most people don't sprint through beautiful mansions in the middle of the night to find their wayward sisters. Her phone pings again as she's getting in the Lexus, and she gets a screenshot of a map, followed by a blurry picture of Savannah grinning in the dark.

come quick before I get murdered, pls

Georgina's irritation simmers as she squints at the map. It has crossed her mind that her sister might be on some kind of substance, but Alvin's voice advises her not to go to the worst possibility yet, for her own sanity. At least if Savannah is high on something, she's safe and sitting in her car somewhere. Georgina just has to find her.

As she drives farther from the Harp House and deeper into woods, it crosses her mind that she could call Cassidy and ask for help, but her pride stops her. She already poured out enough of her problems for one night, and she's not sure how much more he can handle, no matter how unshakable he seems.

When almost twenty minutes go by with no sight of Savannah's Mercedes, Georgina tries calling her again, but it goes straight to voicemail.

"Please help me find her," she prays, her desperation growing as she rounds another dark corner and finds more endless trees. Panic pricks her as she second-guesses her next turn. "Please—"

She slams on the brakes as an animal scampers by in the light of her headlights. The sudden jolt forward fills her with more panic, but relief spills over her as her eyes settle on her sister's car in the distance. Savannah waves wildly from the driver's seat.

"Thank you," Georgina mutters, her heart still thudding as she parks. "Thank you, thank you, thank you."

As soon as Georgina is out of the car, Savannah tackles her with a too-tight hug. She doesn't appear to be on drugs, but she does look like she lost another ten pounds off her already-small frame. Georgina can feel the bones through her T-shirt as she hugs her back.

"It took you forever," Savannah says, eventually breaking free. Her barely pink hair hangs limply over her pale face, but her eyes are clear, and her smile is bright.

"What are you doing here, Savannah?"

"What do you mean? You said you needed help!"

Georgina searches for a memory of that, but nothing materializes.

"You said everything was falling apart with Lance jacking around with your crew," Savannah explains earnestly, acting like Georgina is the confused one. "And I can, like, paint or something. Or clean. Whatever you need—"

As she rambles on, Georgina finally remembers the week-old conversation where she poured out her various Lance-related woes. Heat touches her face. Kissing Cassidy made her forget about him completely.

"What's the problem?" Savannah demands when she's quiet for too long. "You didn't want me to come?"

"No, I'm just . . ." *Totally unprepared for this. All of this.* She's about to tell Savannah that she kissed Sawyer Stokes's brother, but she stops herself at the last second. Savannah might freak out even more than Poppy—and not in a happy way.

"Georgie? Hello? Why do you look like you're super high right now?"

"I'm not," Georgina snaps, her face turning warmer. "This just isn't the best time. . . ." She trails off as Savannah's face falls. "Did you bust out of rehab or what, Sav?" she asks, flipping the spotlight back on her. "Is there a manhunt going on that I should know about?"

"No." She crosses her thin arms defensively. "I finished the 'treatment,' which was basically just a prison sentence in a hideous room. You would've hated it so much—"

"Did they get your medication figured out?"

"Just more worthless Zoloft, which I'm not going to take." Georgina frowns.

"Stop, it's fine. I'm just going to do my own thing."

"Savannah—"

"You don't get it, Georgie," she snaps, her dark eyes suddenly flashing. "I've taken this stuff for basically my entire life, and I'm over it, okay? It worked for a while, but now it doesn't," she adds, ignoring the skeptical look on Georgina's face. "I feel good for once. Don't ruin my vibe."

"Okay."

Her eyes darken at the conflicted look on Georgina's face. "I seriously thought you'd be happy to see me—"

"Don't even start," Georgina says, cutting her off before she can deploy a Faye-style guilt trip. "I *am* happy to see you," she adds, meaning it despite the less-than-ideal circumstances. "I just . . ." *Want you to be okay*, she answers silently, sending up another prayer. Savannah sounds convincing, but Georgina suspects it's probably a more delicate situation than her sister is ready to admit.

"I am okay! And, like, seriously, look at this. Look at it!" Savannah points upward at the huge star-streaked sky as the cicadas sing. "I would not be looking at this right now if I was still in that hideous double-mint room."

Georgina smiles weakly.

"I was sitting there, bored out of my mind, until I was finally like, what do I want to do this summer—"

"And you chose Tarragon?"

"No, I chose *you*." Savannah grins. "I missed you," she adds in a sisterly-but-manipulative way that still tugs at Georgina's heart. "Let me help you for once."

Georgina searches for an alternative, but her sister looks determined, so she finally gives in. "Fine," she says as Savannah cheers. "Follow me."

12

"This is one heck of a welcome home party, Cass."

Cassidy wipes away the rain splattering his face. They're on the west side of the farm, where an early-morning thunderstorm hit the hardest. A few heavy clouds linger in the sky. "Just help me, will ya?"

Sawyer sighs as he peers down at the mudhole, where Pete, one of the Harps' beloved steers, is floundering around in a shallow pool of muddy water. Thankfully, he's not going to drown, but he sure is acting like it.

"There's no way we're gonna lift him out of there," he mutters.

"I know," Cassidy snaps, heaving more mud out with his shovel. "That's why we're digging." He can't just stand around and do nothing while Pete panics.

"Digging ain't gonna work, either," Sawyer mumbles, dragging his soaked hair out of his eyes. When Cassidy picked him up from the airport earlier, he looked all crisp and stylish in the clothes Rachel picked out for him, but now, thanks to their failed attempts to coax Pete out, they both look like they've been through a mudslide.

When Cassidy shoots him a final look of warning, he begrudgingly grabs his shovel.

"Are we talking to Mom today? About your grand plan? She looked pretty worn out."

Cassidy frowns. He'd noticed the same thing. "We'll see— Stop it, Pete!" he growls when the steer's wild movements undo some of their progress. The more Pete panics and churns up the water, the deeper the hole gets. In a last-ditch effort, Cassidy leans down to grab him, but Pete flails in the opposite direction.

"We're trying to help you, dummy!" Sawyer yells.

Cassidy curses as more light rain falls. A strong, stubborn steer panicking in the mud is a pitiful sight. He finally hands Sawyer his valuables and lowers himself to the ground so his face is closer to Pete's. Cold mud soaks his clothes, but Cassidy ignores the discomfort and puts his hand out again, slower this time.

"It's okay, buddy," he says softly. "Help is on the way." Pete doesn't recoil this time and lets Cassidy stroke his wet, fuzzy face.

"You must really love that little punk," Sawyer says, grimacing at Cassidy's soaked clothes. "I'd turn him into steaks if I were you."

Cassidy smiles. He'd like to blame Pete, but he had known there was a deepening dip in the ground for weeks. He'd thought about filling it more than once, but he never got around to it, thanks to too many distractions. Now, ol' Pete has to suffer the consequences while they wait for the animal rescue team.

He's not particularly fond of Pete and his troublemaking ways, but Melody was. She's the one who named him when they moved back to Tarragon, and Cassidy thought Pete was a hilarious name for a gangly little calf.

Cassidy smiles as the memory fades. He's been reading a new book Boggs gave him about Bible translations, and a word he learned suddenly pops into his head—*splagchnizomai*. It's the

Hebrew word for "guts," and he can't pronounce it to save his life, but he understands exactly what it means, especially now, with his body pressed against the cold dirt. It reminds him of the most humbling moments of his life.

Apparently, most Bible translations use "heart" to describe God's emotions, but splagchnizomai is the original word, which means God was feeling with His guts, not His heart. It sounds strange, but that's more comforting to Cassidy than the usual things people say about God—that He's all nice and clean, that He's way up above the mess happening down here. Cassidy's felt so many things that go way beyond his heart, like wrenching grief or burning desire. Those are things he feels deep in his gut, and, apparently, God does, too.

"Sawyer?"

"Yeah?"

"Do you think people can have no expectations?"

"Huh? What are you talking about down there?"

Cassidy searches for a way to ask the question without really asking it. "Like . . . you know, going into something new. Can you do it without having expectations?"

"Are you talking about El Salvador?"

"Sure. . . ."

Sawyer ponders it for a moment. "Well, you already got expectations, don't you? You know it's going to be hard and hot and dangerous and all that, but you're also gonna help a bunch of people, so that's why you're gonna suffer through it." He shrugs. "I mean, you gotta have *some* expectations so you know what you're getting into, right? That's how you figure out if it's a good move or not."

Cassidy frowns. "What about in a relationship?"

Sawyer's brows lift. "With a girl?"

Cassidy suddenly wants to retreat, but it's too late now. "Yeah."

"You got a reason for asking?"

Cassidy clears his throat, ready to deploy some expert-level deflection, but he's saved when voices start shouting behind them. The rescue team appears a few moments later, and Pete panics all over again as they wrap the lifters around his body. It takes some slow, careful maneuvering, but they eventually haul him out, and Pete thanks them with a few indignant snorts before someone leads him to safer ground as Cassidy stands up again.

"So, what's next on the agenda?" Sawyer asks, leaning on his shovel. "You need some gutters cleaned? Maybe some toilets scrubbed?"

Cassidy grins and wrings out his shirt.

"Oh, I know. Maybe we should get root canals together—"

"I gotta go help a friend," Cassidy interjects, cutting his whining short. "At Kit's place."

"Who?"

"You don't know her."

"It's a her?"

"Mm-hmm." Cassidy busies himself with the shovels, but his short answer piques Sawyer's curiosity even more.

"I see. And how do you know *her*?"

Cassidy explains the circumstances surrounding Georgina's show as they walk back to the house. He emphasizes some details, like the elderly contractor and thrown-together crew, but he leaves out a few others, like the part where he kissed her five days ago, and they've been stealing every moment together they can ever since.

"Yeesh," Sawyer mutters, scraping the mud off his boots. "Sounds like a big mess."

Cassidy frowns as more thunder rumbles overhead. Georgina Havoc is not the type of woman he ever imagined being drawn to, with her public persona and all the behind-the-scenes drama that comes with it, but he is. She caught and kept his attention from the moment they met.

He knows it was reckless to kiss her—she basically told him so, and Sawyer's candid answer to his question confirmed that there was a reason for the nagging feeling in his stomach. Maybe it's just the bad timing? Or is it actually good timing, since they're both leaving soon? Or maybe it's because no matter how hard she tries to keep things safe and surface-level with small talk and jokes and near-constant kissing, they can both sense something deeper growing between them.

"She just needs a little help," he adds innocently when Sawyer throws him a weary look. "Shouldn't take long."

"I can shower first, right?"

Cassidy nods, planning to do the same. "And wear something nice, too, in case you end up on TV. Gotta make Rachel proud."

"Ready to rumble?"

Georgina smiles weakly as Talia's confident face greets her on her laptop. "I think so." She's waiting inside the smaller cottage, which Brigitte had turned into a catchall space for snacks and extra equipment, plus a little corner she calls her "headquarters," where she can watch the day's footage on a row of giant monitors and bark commands even more efficiently. The room is also outfitted with a ginormous fan and a portable data network that Nathan finally got around to setting up, so it's the perfect place for an unpleasant Zoom conversation. Talia gives Georgina a stealthy thumbs-up as the mediator returns to his screen.

"My apologies, ladies," he says, settling in again. "I forgot to turn off the oven."

"Oh no!" Georgina says, her voice coming out higher than she intended, but she can't help it. Bart Holladay, a middle-aged man with a bowtie and a cat sprawled across his desk, is her quickest ticket out of pause purgatory, so she needs to make a good impression. Lance and Malonetti haven't even joined the call yet, which isn't that surprising, considering they waited until the last possible hour to respond to Talia's emails. Apparently, Lance is still in his mysterious tropical location.

"How y'all doing this morning?" Bart asks, discreetly glancing at his watch. "Are we ready to make some positive progress?"

Georgina nods enthusiastically. The sooner she and Lance can stop the confusing back-and-forth, the better. She sent Benson a screenshot of his bizarre "UpScale-pulled-the-plug-on-Damien" text last week. He responded with a stream of angry emojis.

Lies. My birdies are trustworthy, unlike that
swine. He's pulling something.

Georgina wants to believe that, but Lance planted a tiny but growing seed of doubt in her mind about UpScale. They clearly aren't as excited about her solo show as she is—as seen by the scant resources and using Poppy as a parachute—so he might be telling the truth.

"Now, we just need our other friends to join us," Bart murmurs, glancing at his watch again.

Georgina catches the gleam in Talia's eye as they wait. Bart seems to have more patience than most, but it still doesn't bode well for Lance.

He clears his throat. "I'll just go over a few quick things while we wait—"

Suddenly, something crashes outside, and Georgina hears Poppy yelp. Bart's and Talia's eyes widen as Georgina rushes outside.

"Sorry!" Poppy says when Georgina bursts through the door. "I broke the swing."

Georgina's heart races as she takes in the broken cord of the heavy porch swing, followed by a few splintered pieces of wood, before they travel up to Poppy's bump. "Are you okay?"

"Yeah, my butt barely even touched it."

"Good—"

"I am insulted, though."

Georgina laughs as relief fills her. Poppy is determined to finish her final weeks in Tarragon strong, so the last thing they need is a freak porch swing accident.

"Want me to grab a chair?" Poppy graciously agreed to stand guard and make sure no one interrupts the meeting, so it's the least she can do.

"No, I'm good. Go get 'em, tiger."

Georgina hurries back inside.

"Everything okay over there?" Bart asks as she joins the call again.

Georgina nods. "Yes, sorry about that. Please continue."

Bart carefully scooches the cat off his papers. "I was just saying that my goal today is simply to help you and Mr. Broussard work together." He smiles warmly through the screen. "There's no winning or losing here, and believe it or not, it can actually be fun!"

Talia smiles politely as he delivers that last line with gusto, but Georgina can't force her lips to do the same. She appreciates his passion, but this definitely isn't going be *fun*.

"If we can't achieve our goal today, you'll move on to a more formal process, but I'm optimistic it won't come to that—"

Georgina skims over the documents in front of her, rehearsing what they talked about. Besides deciding on the breakup statement and revising the NDA, they also need to make sure Georgina leaves with as many brand partnerships as possible. UpScale hinted that they'll have to fight over those, too.

When the minutes tick by with no sign of Lance or his lawyer, Talia discreetly texts Georgina.

Is he really going to blow this off?

Georgina keeps her face smooth as she types back.

Maybe.

She's learned not to underestimate his awfulness.

Talia's typing again when Bart suddenly rises from his chair. He forgets to turn off his screen this time, leaving her and Talia to watch the cat knead his mouse pad until he returns a minute later.

"I have news! That was Mr. Malonetti," he says, expertly plopping the cat on the floor again. "Unfortunately, it sounds like he's come down with a stomach virus, so he requested we reschedule this—"

"That is unfortunate," Talia says coolly as Georgina's annoyance simmers. "But it wasn't exactly easy to schedule *this* meeting, and my client is ready to move forward."

Bart frowns at the serious look on her face.

"I'd like to request an in-person meeting in Nashville within three weeks, with an UpScale representative present, as well as an arbiter," Talia suggests, pouncing on her opportunity. "That might give everyone a stronger sense of urgency."

"If you really think that's best—"

"We do. Thank you for your time this morning, Mr. Holladay. I'm sorry it was wasted—"

"Oh no, not at all." Bart waves her words away. "I wish you the best, Miss Havoc. And Mr. Broussard, too. May you find a harmonious resolution," he adds with a slight bow toward the screen. They wait patiently as he struggles to end the call. "Come on, Topsy, let's go—"

Georgina texts Talia when their screens finally go blank.

> Someone's in the right profession.

😂

> Can Lance really draw this out forever, Tal?
> That's what it feels like.

Georgina anxiously waits for her reply.

No. I'm documenting everything, btw. This
made you look cooperative and competent,
and he looks shady. Stay strong! The finish line
is in sight.

Georgina hopes Talia is right. She's finally gaining some momentum with the pilot—and with Cassidy, too—and she doesn't want a stupid technicality with Lance slowing her down.

Poppy's brows raise when Georgina meets her on the porch again. "Is it over already?"

"He didn't show."

Poppy throws her hands up. "Are you kidding me? He's such a—"

They both turn sharply as a twig cracks, followed by a muttered curse.

"Who's that?" Georgina asks Poppy as a woman dressed in black hurries toward the back door of the main cottage.

"Brigitte's new assistant," Poppy answers, watching the woman scamper away. "Isla? Izzy? Something like that."

"Oh, right." Georgina forgot that Brigitte already blew through the first one. Surprisingly, UpScale supplied a replacement at record speed.

"We should head that way, too. Brigitte's ready for demo."

Georgina nods. She's more than ready to destroy some walls, too, thanks to Lance.

160

Bam!

She throws her hammer against the little half-wall between the kitchen and the larger living area an hour later. Nathan's camera hovers nearby, capturing the flimsy plaster and dust flying, but it's slow work between her and tired Tom. Poppy cheers from the sideline, per Jared's request.

Nathan makes some kind of gesture, but Georgina doesn't stop as her mind moves from Lance to her sister, who's been an enigma over the last five days. Lila had converted a dainty sofa into a surprisingly comfy bed, which Sav wasted no time in cluttering up with her clothes and art supplies.

Sometimes she flits around the set, asking Georgina and Poppy a million questions while she helps with random tasks like taping walls or pulling up grody carpet. Other times, like today, she locks herself in their room and blasts her S. M. Lockridge sermons or runs for miles on the wooded path around the Harp House. Georgina reluctantly went through her car during one of her runs, looking for drugs or other clues about her strange state of mind, but all she found was empty fast-food bags, a battered tennis racket, and a pile of rumpled clothes in the backseat.

Poppy finally pressed Savannah about the sermon binge yesterday, asking what she likes and what she's learned, but Savannah turned sheepish under her questioning.

"I don't know. . . ." Sav said, shrugging as Poppy prodded. *"It's just cool to hear someone who loves God so much. Like, you can just tell he really means it. And . . . that's cool."*

Georgina had listened to the passionate preacher a few times, too—it's hard not to, considering Sav's preferred volume level—and she can understand the appeal, even if the subject matter is unfamiliar. Mr. Lockridge has a warm, musical voice, and everything he says sounds like a matter of life and death. Georgina hasn't broached the subject with Savannah

herself since her own relationship with God is still pretty un-
defined.

Bam!

Cassidy swiftly comes to mind as she swings the hammer,
along with annoyance at Savannah and Lance for distracting
her from the most amazing kiss of her life, which has been
followed by an equally impressive second, third, and fourth.

"Miss Havoc?" Tom says timidly.

She ignores him, determined to demolish the wall between
her and her vision as sweat rolls down her back. They haven't
replaced the air conditioners yet, so the cottage is still painfully hot, but she barely notices as her mind wanders back to
Cassidy. The only downside is that the more time they spend
together, the less restraint she has, and the more he seems to
muster—which is wildly frustrating.

Bam!

"Georgina!" Brigitte barks, finally getting her attention.

"What?" she snaps, lifting her safety goggles. "I almost had it."

Tom's eyes widen. "There are people here for you."

"Who?"

He gestures behind the camera, where Cassidy is standing
beside Brigitte. Georgina's heart flips when he smiles, but Poppy
is a few feet behind them, and she's not-very-subtly cocking
her head at another man standing nearby.

"Who the heck is that?" she mouths.

"Georgina?" he says. "*You're* the television star?"

Surprise fills Georgina—and Cassidy—as she instantly recognizes Sawyer Stokes. "Oh my gosh!" She claps a hand over
her mouth. Savannah would die if she saw him now. He's always
been cute, but now he's all grown up. "I literally can't believe it."

"Been a long time, huh?" Sawyer says.

Georgina is speechless as his grinning face brings back a
flood of memories—smoky bonfires, meandering treks through

the woods, Savannah's hopeful eyes darting to his between rounds of silly card games.

"What's Savannah doing these days?" he asks before she can address the puzzled look on Cassidy's face.

"She's, um . . ." *Blaring sermons? Running like a madwoman on the winding dirt roads? Being unusually helpful?* "She's here, actually," Georgina finally answers, settling on that. "In Tarragon."

"No way. She is?" His whole face brightens. "It's like a reunion! If only those goody-goody counselors could see us now," he adds, making her laugh. "Who would've guessed shy little Georgina Havoc would be a celebrity?"

She smiles at the surprised look on his face. "Yeah, except I'm not really a celebrity—"

"Yes, she is," Poppy chimes in as Georgina steals a glance at Cassidy, who's looking at her curiously, and he's not the only one. Georgina can practically see the cogs turning as Brigitte's eyes move between him and Sawyer before her assistant whisks them away to sign a pile of papers.

"So . . ." Brigitte sidles over right on cue. "Sawyer is your childhood friend?"

Georgina nods. "Well, kind of. I met him when I was like fourteen. And he was better friends with my sister—"

"That works," Brigitte mutters, her fingers flying over her iPhone keys. "And Cassidy is his brother?"

"Right." Georgina glances in his direction, and he looks back in a way that warms her skin. Even the woman winding the wire around his waist looks a little overwhelmed.

"Older or younger?" Brigitte asks, demanding Georgina's attention again.

"Older."

"And how do you know him?"

"Um . . ." *I almost ran him over, and now I kiss him every*

163

chance I get? "Through the Harp House. He works there," she adds, fanning herself.

"Any television experience?" Brigitte asks, studying Sawyer closely as he and Cassidy laugh about something.

"I don't think so—"

"That's fine. They seem pretty natural."

Georgina catches a tiny but approving smile—a rare sight coming from Brigitte.

"We should get some scenes with them and your sister," Brigitte suggests as uneasiness fills Georgina. Apparently, she likes Sawyer's "reunion" idea, even though Georgina doesn't. "Do you think you can get Savannah on board?"

"Um . . ." Georgina doubts it. Nathan's already tried to get Savannah on camera more than once, but Savannah turns cold and quiet whenever he tries to capture a candid moment. "I can try—"

"Great, thanks. Nathan!" she suddenly snaps, making Georgina jump as the crew reassembles. "We'll shoot the kitchen first, with Georgina and Cassidy working together. Get some OTFs with Cassidy and Sawyer, too—"

"What's an OTF?" Cassidy asks, joining Georgina again.

"On the fly," Georgina explains as people scurry around them. "It's when they ask you questions about yourself, or the project, or me. It's just unscripted, candid stuff. The viewers like it."

"I like unscripted stuff, too."

She pretends not to notice his flirtatious tone, but a brief moment of eye contact confirms they are on the same page. There will be more kissing at some point—and soon. Neither of them can last very long without it.

The morning zooms by as they tackle the stubborn half-wall Georgina was working on when he walked in. She happily hands over the hammer.

"You want it totally gone?"

"Yes, please."

"As you wish."

She steps back just in time as he tears it down in a few easy blows. He smiles at the surprised look on her face. "What else?"

"Um, hold on." She searches through the cluttered countertop for her notebook. "I thought that was going to take a little longer."

"I think I got it," he says, looking over her shoulder at the sketch in her hands. "You want that wall by the sunroom gone, too, and you're gonna make a loft over there?"

"Yes, exactly. Big enough for two twin beds, so families can stay here, too," she adds, imagining the younger version of herself reading in the new loft space between strolls through the orchard. Hopefully it'll make the Seelys happy—and a few others along the way.

"Good idea," Cassidy says, still studying her sketch.

"Thanks," she says, pleased by the impressed look on his face.

He and Sawyer tear out the faux-wood walls of the sunroom next and kick the debris away with their giant, booted feet. Once that's done, they drag the ancient appliances out of the kitchen, cracking jokes while Nathan follows close behind. Sawyer's presence brings out Cassidy's southern drawl more than usual, and he pretends to be offended when Georgina tells him so.

"Y'all are doing great," Poppy cheers from afar, back in her beloved rocking chair. Tom joins her, and they tap their bottles of water together like champagne flutes.

Brigitte puts Georgina and Cassidy together more than once, and he makes her burst out laughing with his ridiculous commentary.

"And, here, we have the finest mothballs money can buy," Cassidy says in a dramatic voice, kicking aside a dusty packet before ripping out the shelves in the bedroom closet. "Oh, and I'm sure y'all will want to repurpose this somewhere," he adds, handing her the creepiest doll figurine she's ever seen, then laughing when she chucks it across the room. It's not the smoothest filming Georgina's ever done, but it is the most fun, and, for once, Brigitte doesn't make them reshoot anything.

"It's fine, just let them banter," Georgina hears her whisper in between their laughter. "This is good."

"P and G, preview the kitchen," she commands later, after they've finished most of the demolition. "Let's get that knocked out today, too."

Georgina's nerves rise as she prepares her monologue—especially since Cassidy is watching curiously a few feet away. "Hey, y'all," she says to the camera, ignoring his amused smile. "It's time to tackle the kitchen, and we've got big plans that'll pack a punch in this small space."

Poppy takes over. "First, we'll paint the cabinets a rich cream color—"

"Y'all are gonna paint 'em?" Sawyer interjects loudly, surprising everyone—especially Brigitte. Cassidy looks as surprised by his brother's outburst as she is. An awkward silence falls over the set until Georgina finally responds.

"Yes?"

His face darkens. "Don't."

"Why not?"

"Because that's like putting mascara on a pig."

"Lipstick," Cassidy corrects quietly.

"It is?" Georgina watches as Nathan pulls the main camera back, capturing the strange conversation.

"Yeah." Sawyer strides over to knock on one of the cabinets. His knuckles make a light, dull sound on the wood. "Fakes. Somebody skimped on these. Y'all got all these fancy plans for this place, and then you're just gonna slap paint on some cheap wood? No ma'am. You gotta put in something nice."

"That would be nice," she says slowly, glancing at Brigitte. "But we can't."

"Why not?"

"The budget." She had wanted new cabinets—along with new pretty much everything—but the plumbing and roof repairs added up fast.

"Huh? Just go talk to Dave at Sunny Salvage and get the wood from him," Sawyer insists, undeterred. "It's not gonna be more than a few hundred bucks, and then you just need someone to build them—"

"Good idea," Cassidy says, interrupting him. He snaps his fingers. "Hey, Sawyer, you don't happen to know any carpenters, do you?"

Sawyer snorts. "Nah, not me, but there's gotta be somebody else who can do it around here. What about Roy Boyenger?"

"Roy died."

Sawyer's mouth falls open. "He did?"

"Wait, are you a carpenter?" Brigitte butts in.

Sawyer nods. "Yeah, but I'm just visiting for a couple days," he adds quickly. "I gotta head back—"

"Great, that's great." Brigitte grasps for her phone inside the fanny pack. "Sawyer, would you mind chatting with Tom about a couple of plans we've been throwing around? Nathan, make sure you get that conversation, please."

Sawyer looks a little uneasy, but he agrees, and they take a break while Tom talks his ear off, and Brigitte makes a frenzied phone call to Curt Seely about the budget. Georgina observes the drama for a moment, then sidles over to Cassidy, who's waiting in a quieter corner of the room.

"I think Brigitte's going to throw some money at Sawyer," she whispers, watching Brigitte pace around her usual spot on the porch.

"You think so?"

"Yep. You too, maybe."

"I don't mind working for free." He moves a little closer when a crew member squeezes by with a discarded door. "It means I get to see you."

Georgina accidentally-but-not-really presses her side against his when someone else hurries past with a coil of extension cords. "Still, I'll have to make it up to you somehow," she whispers, her lips lightly touching his ear. "Any ideas?"

"I'm sure we can think of something—"

His brows raise as she grabs his hand and pulls him into the bathroom with her. It's so ridiculously tiny that there's barely enough room for both of their bodies at the same time, but it doesn't end up being a problem as they tangle together.

"There's no camera in here, right?" he asks, barely getting the words out because Georgina won't lift her mouth from his.

"No," she mumbles back, still refusing to let him breathe. Typically, she would have a little more self-control, but no man has ever had this effect on her before, not even Lance, and she just wants *more*. More Cassidy. More kissing. More touching. The feeling seems mutual as his hands move everywhere—cupping her face, lacing into her hair, sliding down her back. She inhales sharply when one slinks up her shirt, leaving a trail of heat beneath his fingertips, but then he suddenly pulls back.

She glares up at him. "Stop doing that."

"Doing what?"

"Stopping."

He laughs as she ambushes him again, but his laughter fades when her kisses travel down his throat. She smiles at his sudden intake of breath and plans on traveling lower, but he lifts her mouth back to his.

"I *hate* your self-control," she growls.

"Sorry," he says with a sad sigh. "I guess I'm just too old-fashioned—"

"No!"

He smiles at the tortured look on her face. "If it's any consolation, you're definitely putting me to the test."

She kisses him one more time, unwilling to give up. He accepts the surprise attack with a grin on his lips, but he turns more serious as her tongue dances with his.

"Georgina," he mutters raggedly, pulling away. "We should slow down." When she won't quit, he lets out a frustrated sigh and takes over with a deep, searching kiss that steals her breath away. His hands grip her hips possessively, and she gasps when he gently bites her lower lip. She pines for more, but he shakes his head.

"Nope, that's all you get."

"You don't want more?"

His eyes narrow. "That's what you took away from that?"

She bursts out laughing but claps a hand over her mouth when she remembers there are a dozen people on the other side of the door.

"Of course I *want* to," he mutters, letting out a tortured breath of his own. "But not now. And not in a bathroom."

Georgina's confusion lingers, but the look on his face is so sweetly protective that her frustration fades. "It is a hideous bathroom."

He laughs. "I just think we're getting this a little out of order."

"What? What order? We don't have expectations, remember? So we can't have an order—"

He shushes her when voices pass by the door. She silently waits for an explanation, but insecurity fills her when his mouth slants into a frown.

"There's nothing wrong with you, if that's what you're thinking," he adds, noticing her face fall. "Honestly, I kind of wish there was." His sigh makes her smile. "I just wanna take my time. That's all."

"Why, though?"

"Because we don't have to worry about this part." He motions between their bodies. "We got that figured out pretty fast. And kissing clouds your head. You gotta decide if you really like me, or if you're just using me for my body," he says teasingly.

"Why can't it be both?"

He fights back a laugh this time, but then his face turns sweetly serious again. "Can you just let me set the pace?"

Surprise fills her as his eyes meet hers, and a little bit of discomfort. No man has ever asked her that before. She either had to initiate everything or slow it all down. Cassidy Stokes is entirely new territory.

"I won't disappoint you." The look he gives her makes her want to pounce all over again, but she maintains some self-control.

"Okay . . ."

"Good—"

Their whispering stops when there's a sharp knock on the door. "Yo, is somebody in there?" Sawyer yells as they exchange horrified glances. "I gotta go!"

There's a long, tense silence as their bodies freeze. Georgina's eyes widen when Sawyer wrestles with the doorknob.

"Sawyer," Cassidy finally answers. "It's me."

Georgina breathes again as the wrenching stops.

"You done?"

"Yeah, but . . . there's a leak. A big one. Go find . . ." He glances at Georgina for help.

"Poppy?" she mouths.

"Poppy?" he mouths back, unimpressed. "What's she going to do about it?"

Georgina bites her lip to keep from giggling. "She's slow," she finally whispers. "It'll take her a while to get here, so I can sneak out."

"Cass?" Sawyer prods.

"Uh . . ." Cassidy thinks fast. "Go find Jerry."

"Who the heck is Jerry?" she whispers, confused.

"The plumber," he says to Sawyer as his footsteps fade from the door. "The imaginary plumber," he adds, kissing away her laughter before she escapes. "Now get out of here."

13

Georgina feels frazzled as she enters her room in the Harp House. She had to spend most of the morning waiting around at the cottage, thanks to the early delivery of the gorgeous canopy bed she and Poppy ordered, so her face is spackled with makeup and her clothes are probably way too nice for whatever Cassidy has planned. They're supposed to meet in the parking lot in twenty minutes for a "surprise" outing on the farm before she has to film again.

When a chemical smell hits her nose, she halts mid outfit change. She glances toward the bathroom. "Sav? Are you in there?"

"Yeah!" Savannah yells. "One sec."

The door opens a moment later, and Georgina scowls as she steps inside. Savannah is standing over the sink, her head partially submerged in inky water.

"Are you seriously dyeing your hair right now?"

"Yeah. Almost done."

Georgina stares at the murky color. "Why? Blue? Black?"

"Blue-black," Savannah says matter-of-factly, lifting her head and giving her hair a quick squeeze before wrapping it up in a towel. "Midnight Fantasy, to be more specific."

Georgina screams internally. Because it's not just any towel—it's a white, fluffy, pristine Harp House towel that will almost certainly be stained blue-black for the rest of its life. She looks down and sees a faint blue rim on the sink, too. Lila probably won't appreciate that.

"Did the urge just strike you or something?"

Savannah shrugs. "I was bored."

Georgina bites back a complaint as Savannah rubs at a drop of dye near her hairline. At least Poppy is on her way to meet Jared and Olivia for a few hours and not here breathing in toxic fumes.

Savannah starts riffling through Georgina's makeup next—an extremely rare occurrence—and Georgina wonders if her mentioning Sawyer Stokes's presence in Tarragon yesterday has anything to do with the sudden makeover.

Thankfully, he seems pretty enthralled by his new wife, an adorable black-haired beauty who had beamed with excitement when he handed his phone over to Georgina to say hello. She was surprisingly supportive of him staying an extra week to help with the project, so hopefully Savannah isn't planning something stupid.

Suddenly, Savannah gasps. "Oh, snap. You have Addies in here?"

"What?"

"These are your secret weapon, huh? Solid choice."

Georgina's stomach drops as Savannah holds up the bottle of Adderall and shakes it smugly. A rush of anger comes next, swiftly followed by embarrassment. "Why are you going through my stuff, Savannah—"

"Calm down, I was just looking for Chapstick—"

"Of course you don't have your own," Georgina snaps, grabbing the bottle.

"Chill out, Georgie. I'm not judging you—"

173

"They're not even mine. They're Lance's."

"Then why do you have them?"

"He left them in the apartment."

"And you brought them all the way to Tarragon?"

Georgina searches for a not-stupid-sounding explanation, but her embarrassment ties her tongue. "I take one, like, every two months," she finally grumbles.

"Cool, so I can have one, right? Since you obviously don't need them."

Georgina frowns at the hopeful look on her face.

"What, Georgie? You're being so dramatic right now. People take these all the time."

Georgina's discomfort deepens as Savannah goes on because she wasn't exactly being truthful about the one-every-two-months thing. She's slowly becoming one of those people Savannah is talking about. "Why do you need one, Sav?"

"Why do *you* need them?"

Georgina meets her sister's narrowed eyes with a scowl, but the answer to Savannah's question bubbles up under the surface. It's the late nights and early mornings. It's the rushed timeline. It's the pressure. It's the fear of failure when she's *so* close. "I—"

Suddenly, "Don't Stop Believin'" plays on the other side of the door—Savannah's obnoxious-on-purpose ringtone—and she hurries off to find her phone in her messy corner of the room.

As Georgina stands alone in the bathroom, she feels a surprisingly strong nudge to flush what's left of the Adderall. She frowns down at the bottle in her hands. She hates the idea of wasting them, but she doesn't give herself time to fight it. In one quick motion, she dumps the rest of the pills into the toilet and flushes them away. Relief fills her as they disappear.

"That was Mom, by the way," Savannah announces, startling

her as she pokes her head through the door again. "Now she's blowing up your phone instead. I was like, not today, Satan—"

Georgina's alarm grows as she finishes scrubbing away her makeup and joins Savannah in the bedroom. She has missed calls from Annette, too.

"Just answer it, Georgie," Savannah says with a defeated sigh as her mother calls again. "She's not going to give up. Don't tell her I'm here," she adds quickly as Georgina finally answers.

"Hi, Mom—"

"Hey, where'd you put the Addies—"

Savannah's question fades as her mother's shrill voice fills her ear.

"Did you and Lance break up? And are you dating someone on your show? A crew member? Georgina?"

Her mother is talking so loudly that Savannah can hear everything, and her stunned face matches Georgina's. Georgina's heart races, but she tries to keep her voice light.

"What? No—"

"Macy Higgins just sent me something that says you and Lance broke up." Georgina hears some frantic movements in the background. "And that he isn't part of your show anymore? You've got lawyers involved?"

Georgina can't speak for a moment, too shocked by the stream of mostly accurate information pouring from her mother's mouth. She races to her laptop and searches her name with Lance's, and her worst fears are confirmed. A hundred images pop up—all the same—of her and Cassidy standing in the cottage, standing closer than they should've been.

Rumors continue to swirl around Georgina Havoc and Lance Broussard. The couple has spent most of the summer apart, filming in separate locations, and the presence of a rugged mystery man on Havoc's set and an ongoing meeting with lawyers seem to suggest there's even more drama behind the scenes.

Georgina's heart sinks as she stares at Cassidy's happy, handsome face in the picture.

"Are they lying? Please tell me they're lying," her mother begs as Savannah grabs the laptop to see for herself.

"Um . . ." Brigitte's name suddenly flashes on Georgina's phone screen.

"Georgina!"

"Mom, I'll have to call you back."

"Georgina—"

"Brigitte!" she says, frantically switching calls. "The press—"

"I know. I saw. Don't panic."

Georgina bites her tongue to keep from cursing. It's way too late for that. "Someone *leaked* it? Who would do that—"

"Isabel."

Confusion fills Georgina. Then shock. "Your new assistant?"

"I'm taking care of it."

Georgina's surprise gives way to paranoia. Was the leak somehow Lance-related? Did he have some influence over Isabel, like he supposedly did with Damien? A text from Annette pings her phone.

Don't panic, babe. It hasn't hit the glossies yet, just the rags. Benny and I are on it. UpScale's not happy.

Georgina's stomach churns as she rereads that last part.

"Lance called me this morning," Brigitte suddenly announces as her stomach tumbles further. "From the Philippines."

Georgina's eyes widen. "That's where he is?" She's seen a few speculations floating around, but they were surprisingly easy to push out of her mind, thanks to Cassidy. "Is it part of his pilot? Is he—"

"He didn't say why he's there," Brigitte interjects. "But he does want to talk to you. Without lawyers."

Stunned silence follows.

"Georgina . . ." Brigitte's voice turns uncharacteristically gentle. "In normal circumstances, this wouldn't be any of my business, but, unfortunately, it is my business. You understand, right?"

Georgina mumbles out a yes.

"Do you want to talk to him? Is there any chance you can work it out?"

Georgina's head spins as she ponders the unexpected question. Her dreams for their future come to mind, but Georgina can still pull up that devastating night when she lost the baby and feel his cold silence all over again. "No," she says, ignoring the weaker part of her heart.

"Good. We have to move forward, then. I'll fix this mess with Isabel—"

"Do you think UpScale will really give me a chance, Brigitte?" Georgina blurts out, finally letting some of her insecurity spill to the surface. "I think they like Lance more—"

"Some of them do," she says simply, as Georgina's confidence takes another hit. "He has a proven track record. You're still the wild card."

Georgina winces. It stings to think that everything she's built over the years might come crumbling down, but it seems unlikely they can pull off a win and oust Lance after so many setbacks.

"But you have a chance," Brigitte adds, surprising her again. "Let's make the most of it."

A tiny ray of hope hits her as Brigitte's words land. "What did he sound like?" she asks before they hang up, unable to stop herself.

There's a brief silence. "Sad," she finally answers, snapping back to her matter-of-fact tone. "I'll see you soon."

Georgina blinks as the call ends. Sad wasn't the answer she was expecting, but Savannah's puzzled face demands her attention again.

"What just happened?"

Georgina drops her phone. *An absolute dumpster fire.* She rubs her temples. "Um . . ."

"Are you dating Sawyer's brother?"

Georgina's eyes snap to hers. She hasn't told Savannah about Cassidy yet, other than he exists and he's nice—not revealing that she has firsthand knowledge of his kissing prowess. Sawyer's arrival in Tarragon seemed like enough of a shock. "We're—"

They both turn sharply when someone knocks on the door.

"Who's that?" Savannah asks.

Georgina suddenly realizes what time it is. She was supposed to meet Cassidy ten minutes ago. "Don't answer it yet, Sav—"

"Hi there," Cassidy says as Savannah opens the door. "I'm just looking for Georgina."

Savannah doesn't respond.

"I'm Cassidy," he adds when the silence lingers longer than it should.

Georgina nearly trips as she pulls on her shoes at record speed.

"You're Savannah, right?"

There's another too-long silence, but Savannah finally nods.

"Nice to meet you—"

"Hi!" Georgina rushes over, breaking up the unnecessarily tense exchange. "Sorry. Busy morning. Anyway, we can go. Bye, Sav," she says quickly, hurrying through the door and beckoning Cassidy to follow, which he gladly does. Georgina looks back long enough to catch Savannah's betrayed gaze before they disappear down the stairwell.

"Is your sister all right? She looked a little—"

"She's fine," Georgina says dismissively as they walk toward his truck. After the train wreck she just experienced, she's not going to let Savannah's attitude spoil her short escape with Cassidy. "How are you?" she asks, focusing on him instead.

"Pretty good." His admiring eyes travel over her outfit, but he frowns at her pristine sneakers. "You got any uglier shoes than those?"

"You think these are ugly?"

"You know what I meant."

"No, sorry. I don't believe in ugly shoes. What are we doing, anyway?" she asks as he opens the door to his truck, and she climbs in. "Is it still a surprise?"

He smiles mysteriously. "Yep. There's gonna be a little bit of mud, though."

"Just a little?"

He nods.

"Then I'll take my chances."

"All right, good." He gets in on his side. "You look nice, by the way. Shoes and all."

She smiles. "Thanks."

"Overalls are a little on the nose, though," he adds teasingly. "For a farm date."

Her mouth falls open as he turns the key. "Excuse me? I'm not taking fashion advice from a man who only owns seven shirts."

"You've been counting them?"

"It's easy when there's only seven."

He laughs. "What's wrong with that? That's one for every day of the week."

Their teasing continues as he drives until her phone goes

berserk inside her pocket. She glances at it, intending to be quick, but her eyes stick to the screen as Annette bombards her with questions and lays out a new damage control strategy. There's a cryptic text from Savannah, too.

he seems nice

Georgina glances at Cassidy's profile and sighs inwardly. If he knows anything about random people splashing his face all over the internet and labeling him a "rugged mystery man," he's remarkably relaxed about it, but he doesn't strike her as the type who would pay any attention to celebrity gossip. Her mood falls as she realizes she'll probably have to tell him herself.

"Bad news?"

Her eyes meet his. "What?"

"On your phone?"

"Oh." *Yes.* "No. Just . . . work stuff." It's the obvious moment to mention his newfound fame, but she can't bring herself to do it. Her life always feels so much simpler in his presence, and she's not ready to overcomplicate it yet. "Sorry, though," she adds, silencing it and putting it away. "That was rude."

He shrugs. "It doesn't bother me, other than it seems like it bothers you."

"What do you mean?"

"Just that you looked happy before, but now you look . . . less happy."

"Oh." She frowns. He can read her face better than she thought. "Yeah, it's kind of a love-hate thing. I need it for work, but I kind of hate it, too."

"Seems like a lot of people feel that way."

She nods, secretly envious of him. He doesn't seem tied to his phone at all. "I am happy, by the way," she adds, meaning it.

He smiles.

The farm turns out to be a nice distraction from her racing thoughts as they pass by a smattering of old barns and greenhouses, followed by a gurgling creek and noisy chickens. It gets more beautiful the longer Cassidy drives, with tons of trees and thick grass and pink-purple cosmos dancing in the breeze, and the sky is another awe-inspiring shade of blue.

"So, what does an operations manager do exactly?" Georgina asks when a few workers nod at Cassidy, and he nods back. As far as she can tell, other people do most of the actual farming.

"The boring stuff, mostly," he says with a small frown. "Oversee workers, write the schedules, make the budgets, keep people happy—"

"That guy is wearing overalls," she interjects.

He looks over her shoulder. "Yeah, you're right. I might lose you out here, you're gonna blend in so much."

She laughs. "So, you're like the boss of the farmers."

He smiles, but his face turns wistful as he surveys the landscape. "Kind of." He parks near a thick patch of trees. "I still get to do fun stuff sometimes, though, which is where you come in."

"I'm ready," she says, bracing herself for the great outdoors until she remembers her bare face. "Oh, wait." She digs some sunscreen out of her purse and opens the mirror above her head. Embarrassment fills her. "Yikes. Sorry."

"For what?"

"My face," she says, rubbing it in. "It was either clown makeup or no makeup for you today, nothing in between—"

"Your face is as pretty as the rest of you," he says tersely. "And, besides, no makeup is better for . . . you know . . ."

Her brows lift when his sentence trails off. "Kissing?"

He nods as she bursts out laughing.

"You're such a good boy."

There's an edge to his smile that says otherwise. "Come on," he finally says as the air crackles between them. "We got work to do."

They hop out of the truck, and she watches curiously as he unloads two pipe-and-canvas contraptions out of the back, followed by a bucket and a heavy-looking bag.

"Any guesses?" he asks, handing her the bucket and taking the rest.

"None whatsoever."

He nods toward a wooded spot in the distance, and she falls in step with him as they walk in that direction. "So," he begins, suddenly turning more serious, "you're twenty-nine, you and Savannah are twins, you grew up in Nashville, you played tennis, you wake up early, you like cooking, clothes, crafts, cats, decorating, kissing . . ."

She laughs. "Are you writing my biography?"

"How am I doing?"

"Pretty good, but you forgot that I'm also a graduate of the highly esteemed Lake Chervil Bible Camp."

He smiles. "That's right. How'd y'all end up there, anyway? It's not exactly easy to find."

"My dad," she explains, her mood dipping a little. "He lived in Red Bank for a little while, so it wasn't that far."

"What took him out there?"

"A job, I think? Or a friend, maybe. I can't remember. Honestly, he probably picked it because it was far enough away from my mother to stay sane but close enough to make some demands." Not that her mother acquiesced to most of them. He finally gave up and took a job in Atlanta a couple years later. Georgina frowns. Her mother was always the more determined one.

Sympathy flickers across Cassidy's face. "When did they split up?"

"When I was twelve. I think it was just the classic married-

182

too-young thing," she adds, throwing out her own theory for why everything fell apart. Her mother also loves to talk about the "trauma" of having twins in her early twenties, so that was probably part of it, too. "Plus, they're just kind of opposite people." Hugh Havoc is very much the scattered artist type, just like Savannah, which had enchanted and irritated her mother at the same time.

"What about *your* dad?" she asks, taking over the questions before he can ask more. "Were you close? Or was he gone all the time?"

"Yeah, he was gone a lot, but we were close."

"Is he the reason you joined the military?"

"Probably, but I think I would've done it anyway. It's the only thing I ever really wanted to do."

She hides a frown as his face lights up, like it always does when he talks about that part of his life. "Did Melody like military life?"

"Not really, but she loved me, so she put up with it." As the conversation meanders to their marriage, Georgina learns a little more about Melody Harp—that she was a rebellious pageant-girl-turned-tomboy, a killer softball player, and a fierce animal advocate. They finally talk about her death, too.

"She had juvenile diabetes. That's the random genetic kind," he explains when Georgina looks confused. "Most people who have it are fine, but it was one of those things. . . ."

Georgina tries to wrap her mind around what that kind of loss must be like—to have a love like that, and then to lose it because of something neither of you can control—but she can't imagine it. Divorce is one thing, but death is entirely another.

"We're here," he announces, dropping the supplies by a shady glen.

"Are you finally going to tell me what we're doing—"

"Hans! Mabel!"

Georgina jumps as he yells, and then he follows it up with the strangest sound she's ever heard—something between a grunt and squeal. He grins as Georgina gapes at him, but her attention is pulled toward the trees as answering grunts and squeals fill the air. She gasps as two little pigs come running in their direction.

"Oh my gosh! They are *so* cute."

Cassidy smiles at her reaction. Hans and Mabel are pale pink with mottled black spots and happy faces, but they turn feistier as they reach the wire fence. It keeps them in, but they get close enough to root around Cassidy's boots. He crouches to pet their bristly heads. "Y'all are moving up in the world today."

Her eyes widen. "Where are they going?" she asks, hoping it's not to the butcher's.

"They're getting a new pen," he explains, pointing to another fenced-in spot a few yards away. "They ate all the grass in this one." He nods at their current pen, where all that's left is a few weedy clumps. "We move them every time they run out."

"That's so nice—"

"Until it's time to go to the butcher's—"

"No!" Her heart sinks as he scratches Mabel's floppy ears. "Don't talk about that part. I was a vegan once."

He grimaces. "Good thing you came to your senses."

"Don't pretend like it's not sad! Look at their precious little faces."

"It is sad, but that's life."

She frowns as Mabel trots over for more scratches. They are the cleanest, happiest pigs she's ever seen, and at least they get to live in a storybook forest with fresh grass whenever they need it. That makes her feel a little better about the fact that she couldn't give up bacon for more than a few months.

"We make sure every animal on the farm gets a good life and an easy death. All the Harps are passionate about that. Melody, especially," Cassidy adds, giving Mabel one more gentle pat before pouring the contents of the bag inside the bucket. Whatever's inside smells like salt and oats, and it makes Hans go crazy as Cassidy hands it to Georgina.

Georgina listens, eyes wide, as he explains the next steps. Apparently, he wants to lure them to their new home with food instead of a prod. It seems like a lot of things could go wrong, but he doesn't give her any time to doubt the plan.

"Just hold on tight until they're in the other pen, all right? That's all you gotta do. Easy."

She grips the bucket as he switches off the electric fence and lowers a section, but the pigs don't rush out like she was expecting. They just peer through the gap and squeal for their food instead.

"Come on, guys," Cassidy says, grabbing the pieces of canvas and holding them ready. "Let's go! Be brave."

"Why don't they want to come out?" Georgina asks, still gripping the bucket. She thought they would sprint around like crazy once they realized they were free.

"They've been shocked by the fence a few times, so they're skittish," he explains, gently pulling the bucket—and her—closer to the opening. "That's it, get that food, Hans," he encourages when the bigger pig takes a tentative step in Georgina's direction. "Be brave, buddy."

Georgina waits as Hans takes a few more careful steps and finally embraces his freedom. Her nerves spike as he makes a beeline straight for her, with Mabel right behind him.

"Start walking," Cassidy instructs calmly, following closely with the canvas squares. "They're about to get real rude, so don't slow down."

Georgina tries to listen to his instructions and walk backward at the same time, all while keeping greedy Hans from knocking the bucket out of her hands with his snout. Cassidy is inches away, holding the canvas pieces on either side of the pigs as they follow Georgina.

"It helps them stay focused on the goal," he explains, keeping the canvases steady. "They get stressed by new surroundings, so I'm blocking them out."

"I had no idea pigs were so complex. It's like they need therapy, too."

As Cassidy's laughter fills her ears, she realizes it's slowly becoming her favorite sound.

"Almost there," he says after another minute of careful team-work. When the new pen is in sight, they lure them inside, and Georgina finally drops the bucket, to Hans's and Mabel's delight.

"You know, most people do coffee on their first date." She finds a somewhat shaded spot under a persimmon tree as Cassidy closes up their new home. "Or brunch. Or a walk. Without pigs." She sits down and fans herself in the heavy June heat. "But this is very on brand for you, I suppose."

"We can do that stuff on our next date."

Georgina's heart drums happily until she realizes her misstep. She's the one who called it a date.

He frowns at the conflicted look on her face. "Unless you're already sick of me?"

She sighs inwardly. "Not yet." Unfortunately, she's the opposite of sick of him. She craves his closeness, with or without the kissing.

"You did great, by the way," he says, joining her in the shade. "If television doesn't work out, at least you know you can put those overalls to good use."

She laughs. "Yeah, no. I could *never* be a farmer. I would die. That's more Poppy's style."

His eyes turn curious as he leans his back against the tree. "What's your style, then? What kind of life do you want?"

She ponders the unexpected, deep-ish question for a moment. "Have you ever heard of Joanna Gaines?"

Unsurprisingly, he shakes his head.

"Well, basically, I want her life. She's a designer, and she has a bunch of other things, too, like products and shops and a cookbook—"

"Like you," he interjects with a smile.

Georgina's face warms. "Yeah, but she's, like, the greatest. I'm not on that level." Sadness fills her as she thinks about the biggest difference between her and Jo. "And her husband helps her with everything. They're super cute together. She's a mom, too—"

"You want kids?"

Her surprised eyes flick to his, but he looks as relaxed as always. Apparently, he doesn't know that most men avoid that question for as long as possible. "Yeah," she finally answers, scooting an orange-pink persimmon around with her foot. "If it makes sense," she adds.

"With your career?"

She nods.

"Poppy does both, right?"

She shakes her head. "She tried." Understanding fills his face as she explains Poppy's departure from *Nail Breakers*. "Her husband has kind of a weird job, and she and I were traveling a bunch for events and stuff, so they were just pulled in different directions all the time, and they were also trying to be there for Olivia, who's the absolute cutest, and it was just a *mess*, so . . ." Georgina sighs. "She left. I don't blame her, though," she adds, hoping she doesn't sound ungrateful. "It was basically single-parent life between their crazy schedules, and I couldn't do that, either." As her mind travels back to her own chaotic childhood, her respect for Poppy grows. "It just has to make sense," she repeats.

He nods along with what she's saying, but she can sense something different in the silence that follows. "So you—"

"What kind of life do *you* want?" she asks, flipping the question back on him.

He smiles and thinks it over for a moment. "Nothing that specific. I just want a life that helps people. However long or short it is, I just hope it makes a difference."

"That's a beauty pageant answer."

He bursts out laughing.

"I can tell you really mean it, though," she adds, smiling. The more time they spend together, the more obvious it becomes how much he cares about people, whether it's her or Goldie or Gavin or random stressed-out crew members. He goes out of his way to help others.

"Thanks."

"Do you think animals go to heaven?" she asks, changing the subject again as their differing visions hang in the air. The question popped into her head when he mentioned the butcher's earlier, and now it's tugging at her heart again as Hans and Mabel trot around their grassy new digs.

"I don't know." He ponders that, too. "Ecclesiastes says some stuff about it." He lifts his shirt to wipe the sweat from his neck. "What do you think?"

Insecurity floods her. First, because she's never even heard of Ecclesiastes, let alone read it. And, second, his magnificent abs are extremely distracting. "I don't know, either," she says, finally tearing her eyes away. "I hope they're there, though. It would be kind of lame if they weren't."

"Yeah . . ." He mulls it over for another moment. "Humans answer to God and animals don't, but that doesn't mean they won't be there."

Her confidence takes another hit as she remembers the Bible verses on his desk. Clearly, he knows a lot more than she does. Camp was the last place she heard about the Bible semi-regularly, but the gist of it was "Jesus loves you" and not much else.

"Have you been a Christian your whole life?" she asks, assuming he and Poppy have that in common, but he surprises her and shakes his head.

His eyes drift upward as he counts the years in his head. "Been about three years now. I didn't take it seriously until I started drinking too much."

Alarm bells ring in Georgina's head as her mind jolts back to her father—his drinking was a constant pain point between her parents, along with his short, shaky spurts of faith—but she relaxes again as Cassidy describes his own story. Apparently, it took a lot of prayer and counseling and nosy people, but he's been sober since his conversion.

"Good for you," she says, trying to sound encouraging, but amusement flickers across his face. "What? I mean it! Seriously. That's, like, super hard, but you did it."

"I know you mean it." He smiles reassuringly. "It's just the way you said it. Like I told you I'm getting a dog or something."

She bursts out laughing, which makes him laugh, too.

"What about you? Are you a Christian?"

Her laughter fades. "Um . . ." He's the only man she's ever met who moves from silly to serious in a matter of seconds and makes it seem normal. "Yeah?" She tries to think of a simple way to describe her haphazard faith. "My dad took us to church sometimes." Poppy and Jared come to mind, followed by Savannah with her sermons. Georgina still has no idea where she fits in. "I definitely think God exists," she finally answers. "And I pray, but . . . that's basically it." She expects disappointment to flicker across his face, but he just looks intrigued.

"Do you read the Bible?"

She shakes her head. "You do, obviously."

His brows lift—probably because the statement accidentally comes out like an accusation—but then he nods. "Yeah, it takes a while to get into it, but now it's just part of my routine. I like it."

"So, do you believe *all* of it?" She doesn't know much, but she does know the parts most people complain about. "Like, you think people need to go to church and only have sex after marriage and talk about Jesus all the time? All that stuff?" She makes the list sound as lame as possible, but he nods along with it.

Surprise fills her—and disappointment. "Why, though? Isn't that kind of outdated?"

His brows crease. "Why? Because some people think so?" He tosses Hans a piece of fruit when he trots over. "People are wrong all the time. What's fashionable today is outdated tomorrow." He shrugs. "I'm betting on God."

She frowns.

"And, just for the record, waiting until you're married isn't some kind of punishment. It just makes things a whole lot simpler."

Georgina's face warms at the bold statement. It dawns on her that he probably did that—waited to be with Melody until they were married—and she has no idea what that's like. From her first boyfriend through Lance, she's always thought of sex as a given. And it did complicate things.

"Okay, but what about hell?" she asks.

"What about it?"

"You really think a bunch of people are going there?"

"Oh." He shakes his head. "No, I don't think that. I know it."

Her eyes widen. "*What*? You actually think—"

"Once you've seen a war, it's pretty easy to believe in hell."

"But you think God sends people there?" Her voice is turning shrill now, but his face is calm as their eyes meet.

"No. I think people are going there because that's where they want to be." He shrugs as more shock colors her face. "Why is that so surprising? Heaven is all about God, and you know as well as I do that there's a bunch of people who want nothing to do with Him. He's not going to force them in."

She shakes her head. "That doesn't seem very nice. . . ."

"You think you're nicer than God?"

She breaks eye contact as a smile plays on his lips. "I'm not saying I'm nicer, I just don't understand how that's loving. Or fair. Maybe some people just don't know? Or maybe they had the worst childhood ever."

"I'm not worried about it."

She misreads his statement as apathy and throws him a horrified look, but his eyes correct her.

"God is nicer and fairer than anybody, Georgina. If someone really wants to be with Him, they will be."

Confusion fills her, along with a twinge of discomfort as his words unearth an unexpected question—does *she* want to be with God forever? She's never thought about it like that. She wants a happy life, obviously, and if hell exists, she doesn't want to go there . . . but God himself has never really been an important part of that equation.

"Georgina," Cassidy says gently, sensing her uneasiness. "I know it sounds like a lot of weird rules, but when you actually understand the whole story, it makes sense."

She hides another frown.

"And, really, it all just boils down to one simple question—is what Jesus said true or not? Because it is or it isn't, right? There's no in between." His face is understanding as her conflicted eyes meet his. "If you really think it's true, it'll change your whole life."

Her heart races as she listens, and she almost asks him another question about heaven as the baby comes to mind—she's wondered more than once if God might have an answer for that—but she stops herself, remembering the rules she set after their first kiss. They've been breaking them all morning.

"We should head back," she says, springing up.

He throws her a questioning look, but she carefully avoids his gaze.

"I have to film soon," she adds, trying to soften her abrupt dismissal.

"Okay." He rises, too. "Do you want to see the orchard real quick? We're pretty close."

She nods and follows him, but her mind races with more questions as they walk. She didn't realize just how little she knows about Christianity until now, but she's not sure how much deeper she wants to get. Part of her hesitation is all the rules, like Cassidy said, but another fear suddenly springs to the surface. What if she does trust God and He doesn't come through?

"There it is."

Georgina temporarily sets her worries aside and gets lost in the sweeping view, trying to memorize all the details while she still can—the endless fruit trees and wildflowers, the hills, the winding road, her little work-in-progress cottage. And Cassidy.

"What do you think?" he asks as his eyes meet hers. "Not bad, right?"

14

"**How many more?**" Sawyer yells as Cassidy swims by.

Cassidy's head is light, there's water in his ears, and his lungs are fighting for air, but none of that stops his brother from trying to start a conversation whenever he passes by the dock.

"Eight? Or seven?" Sawyer calls out, lifting his sunglasses. "I lost count."

Cassidy doesn't answer him, but the correct answer is six. Six more laps out of eighty in ice-cold Lake Chervil. The one he's finishing is the worst by far.

"You're not gonna drown, right?"

Breathe.

Cassidy tunes everything out except that one simple command, listening to the water rising and falling on either side of him as he swims, trying to let the sound hypnotize him into finishing. This is the hardest part of the exercise—the final five—but he forces his exhausted body to catch up with his mind.

Accept the pain. Move through it. Finish.

He and Sawyer finally broke the news to his mother over breakfast yesterday, when she was feeling mostly back to normal. Her reaction was a mix of shock, sorrow, and pride as Cassidy told her about the mission. Thankfully, she didn't try to talk him out of it because she's probably the only person who could've. For his sake, she's always kept her worries about his safety to herself, but he could see the familiar fear in her eyes.

"*It might be time to start thinking about moving, Mama,*" Sawyer had bravely suggested while Cassidy prayed for a crack in her stubborn resolve.

At first, she was adamant she didn't need any help and that she was going to die in Tarragon, but an hour of intense negotiation whittled her down until she finally agreed to visit Jacksonville. Depending on how that goes, there could be a "possible" move in the next few years—with an accelerated timeline in the case of grandchildren. The victory was bittersweet, though, since it reminded Cassidy that she's getting too tired to put up as much of a fight as she used to.

"You better hurry up," Sawyer warns. "We got Emmeline's shower."

Cassidy grits his teeth and picks up the pace, even though a baby shower packed with beauty queens and their significant others is about the last place he wants to be.

When the deep fatigue finally sets in, he imagines he's swimming toward land and warmth rather than just pacing the lake and that helps him get through three more laps until his mind turns on him. He visualizes Georgina next, waiting for him, and feels another burst of motivation to finish the final laps. He keeps his exhausted arms and legs moving long enough to get back to the dock again and grip the rusty stepladder.

They've squeezed in almost daily quick meals and walks around the orchard together since their date on the farm a week ago, plus the occasional too-long kiss in his truck, but it's still not enough. She's steadily taking up more of his mind and schedule.

"Woah," Sawyer says when the platform sways. He offers him

his hand, but Cassidy doesn't take it. It's easier to just hang on for a minute and let his lungs recover.

"Yeesh." Sawyer grimaces at the exhausted look on his face. "What fresh nightmare you got cooked up for tomorrow?"

"Tomorrow is a rest day," Cassidy says, when he can talk again. He heaves himself up the ladder. "But then it's eighty laps with boots and cammies." He leaves for El Salvador in just a little over a month, so he can't let his training slip now.

Sawyer tosses a towel by the ladder. "Enjoy yourself."

"It feels good when you're done."

"I'll take your word for it."

Cassidy smiles. It's Sawyer's last day in Tarragon, and he's going to miss him, just like everyone else. They probably won't see each other again until Cassidy returns from the mission, unless he can somehow drag Goldie to Florida before then.

"Make it quick," Sawyer says when Cassidy takes over his abandoned lawn chair and stretches out in the sun. "You don't want to miss Georgina," he adds with a smirk.

Cassidy slips on sunglasses to hide his annoyance. It didn't take Sawyer very long to figure out that there was something going on between them, and he hasn't shut up about it since. "Georgina is busy enough without you roping her into more stuff, Sawyer—"

"Busy with her show or busy with you?"

Cassidy doesn't respond, but the answer is both. He never knew filming a television show was so complicated. She has shoots and reshoots all hours of the day, with dozens of other always-urgent tasks squeezed in between takes. He likes helping when he can, though. She's in her element when she's designing, and it's fun to see how she's carefully bringing it all together.

"Don't act all put out. Mom needs the help, and Georgina doesn't mind. Plus, y'all can do that googly-eye thing you do, Mystery Man." Sawyer grins. "I practically did you a favor."

Cassidy scowls, reminded of a part of Georgina's life he's not particularly fond of. When they parted ways after the farm last week, he could tell there was a lot on her mind, but he couldn't get it out of her. It wasn't until he was in his truck again that he got a text message.

I'm so sorry I dragged you into this mess, Cassidy.

He opened the link she sent, which took him to a picture he didn't even know existed, and then there were about a thousand comments from strangers who had dug up everything about him—his name, his age, a random award he earned in college, his military career, his father's career, his job at the Harp House, Sawyer's construction business, Rachel's Realtor photo, and every other mundane detail of his life. A few people had even been talking about Melody's obituary, which dissolved his shock into anger. Georgina sent more frantic apologies via text until he finally called her.

"Can you explain this to me? I've never been famous before."

He was trying to lighten the mood a little, but it didn't work because she burst into tears. *"I'm so sorry. . . ."* She cried harder as she told him about the "leaked" photo and more about her piece-of-work ex. *"I know this probably sounds crazy, so if you want to be done, I get it. I never wanted to mess with your life."*

Her words were spilling out in a teary rush, and he wanted to say something to stem the flow, but his mind was still reeling from the pileup of events—their date, the photo, the comments, her tears—so he didn't immediately respond.

"I really am sorry," she repeated, filling his silence. *"I was going to bring it up when we were together, but I was just . . . happy."* She sighed miserably into the phone. *"And I didn't want to ruin it."*

The silence deepened as her words sank in—because he knew

exactly what she meant. It's crossed his mind more than once over the last week that he should bring up his new job, but the light feeling in his heart stops him every time. They've taken a couple careful steps forward, and he doesn't want to take any back.

"*It's okay,*" he finally said. "*We'll figure it out.*"

His eyes settle on the glassy lake. He really meant that when he said it, but he has no idea how. He had known from the moment he kissed her in his truck that he was playing with fire, but he didn't put it out while he had the chance. And he still doesn't want to.

"What does Eddy think of your little summer romance?" Sawyer asks, breaking through his thoughts. "He told you it's a bad idea, didn't he? Just like I said."

Cassidy ignores him, irritated that he guessed correctly. When Cassidy brought up Georgina during their last check-in, Eddy's usually jovial face turned darkly serious before he asked Cassidy if he was losing his ever-loving mind.

"*Boy, what on earth are you thinking? You want a little extra heartbreak before you ship off? Knock it off already.*"

Cassidy mumbled in agreement, but, truthfully, he can't imagine ending it with Georgina. Eddy might be right that he and Georgina are heading straight toward disaster, but it's like they're magnets and nothing can pull them apart. Cassidy can sense the same conflict in her, too—she wants to stay closed off and not let him in, but she can't help herself. As soon as they part, they come right back together again.

"*And if she's not a Christian, y'all are gonna pull each other in directions you don't want to go.*"

He pushes Eddy's voice away, but his worries linger. Georgina's hesitation toward God reminds him a lot of his own. He had the same concerns about fairness and sex and heaven and all the rest, but Mel was patient. She cared way more about God than he ever did when they met, but she never acted like they were on opposing teams. She just asked plenty of good questions, so that's the same approach he's taking with Georgina.

"I don't think Georgina's a settle-down type of girl—"

"Shut up, Sawyer," Cassidy finally snaps, his frustration bubbling over as Sawyer's comment dredges up more doubts. "You don't know her."

Sawyer looks stunned for a moment. He lets out a long, low whistle. "You're getting in pretty deep, pal. What happened to having no expectations? Isn't that what y'all wanted?"

Cassidy's jaw tightens.

"Don't get me wrong, I like Georgina, but her life is all sparkly parties and fancy people and cameras. Like Renata," he adds with a look of warning. "That's never been your scene."

He frowns as Sawyer makes another decent point. He finally looked Georgina up online after the leaked-photo disaster and got a glimpse of her life back in Nashville, and it couldn't be more different than his. The hundreds of photos of her with her ex didn't help his mood, either.

"And there's the whole you-moving-to-a-different-country thing," Sawyer adds, twisting the knife in a little deeper. "Georgina's not gonna follow you anywhere, Cass. She's not like Mel—"

"She doesn't have to be," he snaps as Sawyer finally falls silent. That's one of the things Cassidy likes the most about Georgina—that he doesn't find himself constantly comparing her with Melody. They're both one of a kind.

"I'm just looking out for you. I think y'all are pretty caught up in this."

"I don't need you to look out for me, Sawyer. I know what I'm doing."

"You sure about that?"

Cassidy ignores him and fixes his eyes on Lake Chervil. He

doesn't know what the future holds for him and Georgina, or if they even have a future, but he does know that his feelings for her are getting much deeper than he ever expected.

"You're not coming with us to the cottage?"

It takes Georgina a moment to answer Savannah's question. "I'll be there later," she finally responds, tearing her eyes off Annette's latest publicity scheme. Georgina hasn't read the entire text yet, but her stomach churns when she notices Cassidy's name. "I'm helping with the brunch thing, remember?"

Poppy nods excitedly, but Savannah's eyes narrow. "For Cassidy?"

Georgina frowns at her sister's sullen tone. "No. For Goldie."

More annoyance flickers across Savannah's face.

"What, Savannah?"

"I just thought maybe you were gonna work on your own life today. My mistake."

Georgina narrows her eyes right back. "I put in a twelve-hour day yesterday."

"I'm just saying . . . he keeps you pretty busy."

Georgina almost mentions that Cassidy is the one who insisted she didn't have to help with the brunch—it was entirely Sawyer's idea—but that might upset Savannah even more. She's been following Sawyer around the cottage all week with a look that's a little too reminiscent of their camp days. Thankfully, he hasn't seemed to notice, but Georgina's still eager for him to head home to his wife tomorrow morning.

"I'll be there later," Georgina repeats coolly, refusing to take the bait. "You look cute, by the way," she adds, noting Savannah's flowy blue sundress. It's a sincere compliment since her sister lives in leggings, but Savannah ignores it and mopes out the door. Georgina throws Poppy a bewildered look.

"Is she on her period or something? She's being such a grouch."

"I think she's just feeling a little left out."

"Of what?"

"Your life."

"What?" Georgina's confusion grows. "I'm paying for everything, Poppy! I've brought her to the set even though she's acting like a total weirdo around Sawyer. And I would let her hang out with Cassidy, but she's so rude whenever he's around—"

"I know," Poppy says gently, cutting her off. "You're not doing anything wrong, Georgie. I think she's just dealing with her own stuff and taking it out on you."

"As if I don't have enough going on."

"I'll talk to her. You just have fun with your future mother-in-law," Poppy teases, pulling the door closed before Georgina can throw her a fiery look.

She sighs into the silence. Obviously, Poppy's just joking, but Georgina wishes she wouldn't. For one thing, the comments are ridiculous—she's only known Cassidy for a month, even if it feels like so much longer—but also because Poppy's words strike a tiny, scary match of hope in her heart, and she can't put it out. Part of her had hoped the leaked photo would be the last straw for him, but he surprised her yet again and didn't run away from the chaos. He steadied her instead.

She distracts herself from conflicted feelings by tidying up Savannah's side of the room, which is cluttered with clothes and a half-dozen forgotten coffee mugs, but she pauses when she notices Savannah's open sketchbook.

As her eyes scan the page, she feels a jolt of guilt. She had tasked Savannah with painting an orchard-inspired mural in the cottage bedroom to keep her busy and away from Sawyer, but Sav didn't do anything except stare at the walls for three days, so Georgina scrapped the project. Now, though, as she flips through more pages, she sees that Savannah had sketched out all four walls, and each one is painstakingly detailed.

The guilt deepens as she heads for the kitchen, but Annette calls with an update.

"Ask and you shall receive! Your arbitration meeting is officially set, babe. Two weeks!" she sings in Georgina's ear while Benson cheers in the background. "I'll start working on the press release—"

Georgina halts outside the kitchen. "Thank you," she mutters, letting relief wash over her. Two more weeks of silence and secrets, and then she's finally free.

"UpScale is going to choose you, babe," Annette adds smugly. "I can feel it."

Georgina's nerves spike. She's not nearly as confident, especially after the leaked-photo snafu last week, but Annette has big plans for that, too.

"We need to talk about your hot sniper soon."

"I don't want to get him involved."

"Gigi, he's already involved. The entire *Nail Breakers* fandom is obsessed with him."

"He's not part of it—"

"We'll talk later," Annette says cheerfully, cutting her off. "Ciao for now."

Georgina's mood darkens as she enters the bacon-scented kitchen, but Goldie's smile lifts it again. "Good morning, honey. How are you?"

"Pretty good." *Other than my publicist is plotting something involving your son, who is now exclusively known as "the hot sniper" in certain internet circles.* Goldie doesn't need to know all that. "How can I help?" She surveys the cluttered countertops, not sure where to begin between endless cannisters, twelve dozen eggs, and a rainbow-hued assortment of fruit.

"I've got it handled, dear, if you want to go enjoy your morning. Sawyer and Cassidy like to baby me, but I'm just fine."

Georgina frowns. Sawyer had warned her about this.

"*You're just gonna have to take charge in there, or she's gonna run interference all morning. She's good at it, so put your game face on.*"

Georgina steels herself. It's not in her nature to step on someone's toes, especially in their own kitchen, but the tired look on Goldie's face propels her forward. She washes her hands and grabs a recipe card off the countertop.

"I'll just work on this strawberry rhubarb sauce."

Goldie stops stirring the batter she's working on. She looks stunned by the announcement—and uncomfortable. "Are you sure?"

Georgina nods nervously.

"You can't let it simmer for too long. It'll change the color."

"What if I just prep everything, and then you can take over?"

That makes Goldie relax a bit, so Georgina starts slicing up ruby-red strawberries. She finally figured out why everything is so good at the Harp House, thanks to her excursion with Cassidy. It's because they use as much as they can from the farm, all the way down to the butter and spices.

"Cassidy said the cottage is coming together," Goldie says, making conversation as she measures out milk.

Georgina nods, grateful for so much unexpected help over the last week. Sawyer's cabinets are works of art, along with a simple but perfectly scaled dining room table for the tiny kitchen. He and Tom ended up having a good rapport as they worked on the loft-and-ladder element, which Brigitte loved, and it rubbed off on Savannah, who finally warmed up to the camera and answered a few questions without looking down at her shoes.

"Any news about your cookbook?"

Georgina's slicing slows. She's about to try to explain the situation—that her dreams depend on whether or not Up-Scale decides to drop her like a hot potato and go with Lance instead—but Goldie misunderstands her silence.

"Do you have baker's block? I get that way sometimes. I have to slow down and remember why I cook in the first place."

"Because you love it?"

"Bingo." Goldie smiles over the stove. "That's where you gotta start. If you get stuck on the dishes and clocks and hungry people, it's all downhill from there. Isn't it funny how that happens? You get good at something because you love it, and then you're tempted to just love being good at it and not the thing itself."

Georgina ponders the profound words. Deep thoughts must run in the family.

"For me, it started off as something I could do for myself when the boys were little," Goldie continues, whisking enough eggs to feed all of Tarragon. "I would get one of the fancy magazines and flip through recipes and give it a whirl." Her hazel eyes turn nostalgic. "And then, of course, the boys wanted to help, and it turned into a special thing."

Georgina smiles. She can imagine the little-boy versions of Cassidy and Sawyer "helping" Goldie in the kitchen since she and Savannah used to do the same thing with their mother. Their cozy memories together are sparse, but the ones they do have almost always involved the kitchen.

"Are you missing Nashville?" Goldie asks when she notices her smile fade.

"Um . . ." Georgina's thoughts flash between the strawberry-stained cutting board and Lance, then her darkened apartment and neglected friends—and the baby. "Sometimes," she finally answers, although she's not sure if that's even true anymore. "I left it in kind of a mess."

"Well, once you tackle one, there's always another waiting. I wonder if heaven will always be tidy. Or maybe the messes up there are beautiful, too. . . ." Her voice trails off before she laughs. "Just ignore me if I'm not making sense, honey. I usually don't have any company in here, so it's just me and my silly thoughts."

"I don't think they're silly." They do remind her of Cassidy with his probing questions and Bible factoids. She finally borrowed Poppy's Bible a few days ago and cracked it open to get on his level, and it's a little less confusing than she remembers.

"Oh my lanta, look what time it is. I gotta finish up this cake."

"I can do it!" Georgina volunteers. She's determined to contribute more than a simple sauce, but Goldie frowns at the offer.

"Have you ever made a hummingbird cake? It's a special request from the mother-to-be."

Her tone is polite, but Georgina catches the subtext. *You can't screw this up, honey.* Georgina drags a chair over and stations it near the ingredients. "I can figure it out."

Goldie looks surprised as Georgina motions to the chair. "You won't mind me looking over your shoulder? Cassidy says I'm too picky."

"I'm picky, too. Picky people are my people."

Goldie laughs and sinks down gratefully. "All right, then. I finished the rounds last night, so it's just the filling and the frosting."

Georgina diligently gets to work. Goldie is next-level picky, but she's also a great coach. Servers come and go as the party kicks off, taking her other creations to the party.

"Don't overdo it on the vanilla," Goldie warns, watching closely as Georgina lifts the tiny glass bottle. "You gotta get that just right . . . yes, that's it . . . perfect."

When Georgina finally earns her trust, she leaves to peek inside the dining room. "Cassidy and Sawyer are out there," she says when she returns, her voice lifting happily.

"Go enjoy the party, Goldie. I can manage the rest. I've decorated a lot of cakes."

"Are you sure? Emmeline wants the meringue frosting instead of the cream cheese, and it's such a pain."

"Give me a chance." Her recipe cards are unsurprisingly meticulous, so Georgina just has to follow the instructions. "I'll make you proud."

"Okay, then. I'll just pop in and say hello."

Georgina gets water and sugar simmering for the meringue as Goldie slips out. Minutes pass as she layers the buttery cake rounds with pineapple filling as carefully as she can. Once that's done, she pauses to read over the recipe one more time, but her pinging phone captures her attention.

Having girl talk with Sav . . .

Georgina frowns at a text from Poppy.

What's her deal?

There's a long moment as Poppy types back.

I think she's jealous of Cassidy. That he's getting your attention or something. She said he's your "distraction."

Georgina's eyes narrow.

And she said you're taking adderall???

Georgina's stomach drops. She starts to type a frenzied explanation but stops when she remembers that they're at the cottage right now—which means Brigitte and the rest of the crew are milling around. Her head goes light. They just had a "leak" a week ago, and now Savannah is going around blabbing about the Adderall?

"Georgina?"

Cassidy's voice startles her as she turns sharply in the direction of the stove. Suddenly, a burnt-sugar smell hits her nose, and her heart stops as he grabs a potholder and quickly moves the bubbling pot off the heat.

"No!"

"What were you making?" he asks as she rushes over, frowning into the saucepan, which is currently filled with blackened sugar goo.

"Meringue," she says miserably.

"Oh."

Georgina sighs. Not only did she burn something mere minutes after Goldie left, but, of course, Cassidy had to walk right into the middle of it.

"You don't add the sugar to the water." He sets the saucepan aside and rummages around for a new one. "You whisk the eggs and sugar on top of the water." She watches as he rolls up his sleeves and fills the pan with water, and her eyes move to his forearms, which somehow also have muscles. She sighs inwardly. He's wearing the light green flannel, which is her favorite. It makes his eyes look more gold than brown.

"See?" he says, showing her the right way. "You're gonna put your glass bowl on top of this, and then you whisk until your arm falls off."

Georgina nods. She usually hates being corrected, but there's nothing cocky about the way he does it. It's just matter-of-fact, like he's been watching someone make meringues all his life—which he obviously has. Goldie really did raise him right.

"No big deal," he adds, smiling as he hands her the eggs. "We just lost a little sugar."

She tries to regroup as he works beside her, but his presence in the kitchen is comforting and intimidating at the same time.

"You want me to whisk it?"

"I'll do it," she says quickly, snatching the whisk from him.

"All right, but you gotta do it like your life depends on it."

She nods somberly. It really *does* feel like her life depends on it, since she promised Goldie she wouldn't ruin this cake.

"Look at you go," he says a few moments later as she whisks like she's never whisked before. When the texture finally thickens, she exhales.

"Time to test it," she says, and he hands her a spoon right on cue. Nerves rising, she dips the spoon in, then rubs the frosting-in-progress between her fingers. Thankfully, there's no more granules, which means it's ready, so she licks her fingertip. When she glances at Cassidy again, the look on his face makes her blush.

He clears his throat. "I'll move it to the mixer. . . ."

He sets up the stand mixer while she washes her hands, and soon the machine is whirring at full speed. "Ten minutes," Georgina says, glancing at the recipe card and raising her voice over the noise. "Thanks—"

He pulls her in the pantry before she can finish, so she uses the kiss to express her thanks instead. As his hands tangle in her hair and the muffled mixer whirs in the background, she doubts that *Young Southern Style* could create a more romantic scene if they tried. His mouth is desperate, like she's water and he's on fire, and she feels the same way. She's falling for him *hard*. Too hard.

"You all right?" he asks, seeming surprised when she pulls away first for once. "You look a little overwhelmed."

"Oh, really?" She throws him a sarcastic look as she hurries off to check on the fragile, fluffy peaks in the mixer. "I can't imagine why."

His lips lift as he grabs the butter.

"One little bit at a time," he says as she carefully drops it in. "Then the vanilla. That's the last part—"

"And the salt," she adds.

"Oh, yeah. I forgot." He smiles. "See, you didn't need me after all."

His voice is light, but the words land with a thud in her heart. After everything with Lance, she really doesn't want to *need* anyone, which is why she had thought a no-strings-attached romance would be a lot less risky—but Cassidy is proving her wrong.

"Can I pick you up for Sawyer's party tonight?" he asks, surprising her when his face turns tense. "I want to talk to you before it gets crazy."

"Sure. Oh, shoot, no." She groans inwardly. "I promised Savannah we'd go together." And she needs to keep that promise, even if she doesn't want to. "Sorry."

His face falls.

"Is something wrong?"

"I—"

"Cassidy?"

Georgina turns swiftly at the sound of a voice in the doorway and scowls before she can stop herself as the infamous Renata click-clacks in their direction.

"Sorry to barge in," she says sweetly, even though she doesn't sound sorry at all. "But you're wanted in the dining room, Cassidy." She glances at him first before eyeing Georgina. "By Emmeline," she adds coolly.

Cassidy nods politely, but Georgina spots the tiniest scowl forming on his lips as Renata positions herself beside him and loops her arm with his. She's dressed in an orange minidress and one of those massive Kentucky Derby hats that no one except her could ever pull off.

"I'm Renata, by the way. We haven't officially met, but I've seen your show," she adds, eyes sparkling. "Love it."

"Thank you—"

"Lance, too. He's my favorite."

Georgina blinks. It's a jarring statement for multiple reasons, but mostly because Renata lobbed it over like a bomb. Maybe she wanted Cassidy to watch the explosion, but Georgina doesn't take the bait.

"Where is he?" she presses.

"The Philippines," Georgina says, keeping her voice smooth. "We're working on different projects."

Cassidy shifts suddenly and breaks Renata's hold on his arm. "I'm gonna head back in. You coming?"

Annoyance shadows her face as she hurries after him, but she looks back long enough to throw Georgina an impressively fake smile. "So nice to meet you in real life!"

Georgina's irritation simmers until she catches Cassidy's eye as he slips out the door. She can tell from the tortured look on his face that there is something going on between them, but it's painfully one-sided.

Georgina tries to focus on the cake instead, for Goldie's sake. It's difficult between Renata's smirk and Cassidy's kiss and Savannah stupidly spilling her secrets, but she remembers Goldie's musings and forces it all to the back of her mind. She gets lost in the simple pleasure of frosting a cake, then adds the shredded coconut next, plus a few sliced kumquats for color, and surveys her finished work.

When someone arrives to carry it out a few moments later, Georgina follows and discreetly observes through the French doors. Dozens of women and men, plus a handful of children, fill the dining room, most of them dressed in various summery shades of orange and pink, with a pile of endless color-coordinated gifts to match.

Georgina smiles to herself. Cassidy looks hilariously out of place in his too-casual green flannel, especially next to Renata and her ridiculous hat. Goldie is seated nearby, watching happily as the server places the cake in front of the beaming mother-to-be. Georgina's nerves rise, but Goldie's expression is priceless—a blend of admiration and relief.

Their voices are muted behind the glass, but Georgina can make out "oohs" and "aahs" as slices of cake are placed on delicate glass plates and passed around. Her eyes settle on Cassidy again as he takes a piece of cake, and she laughs to herself when he studies it closely—just like his mother. As he chews, he glances at Goldie, who glances back with an impressed look. Georgina feels like cheering, until her eyes settle on a banner she didn't notice before.

Her good mood crashes like a meteor. *Clementine Rose* shimmers in orange and pink—a name she's always loved. Lance said he did, too.

Her mind almost travels back to that night and all the dreams that shattered with it, but Cassidy draws her attention again as a little girl in a too-long dress races over to him. She says something that makes him lift his eyebrows in pretend shock before she zooms off again, laughing all the way.

15

"You got a lot of nerve showing your face around here, Cassidy Stokes!" Dylan Hayes yells when he walks into Mulvancy's, the old barn that Rhett Mulvaney Jr. turned into a booming bar years ago.

Sawyer laughs, but Cassidy barely cracks a smile as a chorus of whoops and hollers erupts across the room. The barn used to be a hotspot for teen parties until Rhett smartened up and turned it into an actual bar, with licenses and everything, to keep the nonsense to a minimum. Now it's decorated with a mishmash of left-behind wedding décor and kitschy plaques with sayings like, *Around here, we call our sushi "bait."*

He joins Sawyer's crew by the pool tables. Between Emmeline's baby shower, a too-long meeting with Gavin, and now a bustling barn full of Sawyer's old high school friends, he's nearly reached his limit for socializing, but he dragged himself out for his brother—and Georgina, too. His plans to talk to her before the party fell apart, but he's hoping they can sneak away later and have a real conversation about the last few weeks. And he finally has to tell her about the job, no matter how much he doesn't want to.

"Sawyer told us you're sneaking off to El Salvador," Dylan

211

continues, drunkenly lining up his pool cue. "And look at you, just walking in here like it's nothing."

"That ain't right, Cass!" someone else yells.

"Y'all are dramatic," Cassidy mutters, throwing Sawyer an annoyed look, but his brother is too drunk to notice.

"What about Goldie?" Dylan prods, taking his shot and narrowly missing the eight ball. "You're tellin' me you looked that sweet woman right in the face and told her you're shipping out again? Crushed her heart?"

Cassidy scowls. He can read his mother well enough to know that she *was* crushed beneath her happy exterior, which makes Dylan's face look even more punchable right now.

"And what about the Harps?" he continues. "What about Gav? You're just gonna leave him high—"

"Y'all shut up about me and buy Sawyer some drinks," he finally snaps. "Tonight is about him."

Thankfully, they do, and the next hour almost feels like old times, minus the fact that Cassidy is sober for all of it. He eventually retreats to the bar after a couple rounds of pool, craving some solitude, but Sawyer follows him. He glances down at Cassidy's water.

"You good?"

Cassidy smirks at his worried expression. Apparently, Sawyer is just now realizing it's frowned upon to invite a recovering alcoholic to a bar, but Cassidy doesn't hold it against him. He's obviously not going to make a habit of it, but these days his desire to drink is less like a vise grip and more like an irksome little nudge. "I'm fine," he says, clinking his glass against Sawyer's bottle.

"Are you still feeling good about El Salvador, Cass?" Sawyer asks out of the blue, surprising him with a sorrowful expression. "You're sure it's the right move? With Mom and everything?"

Cassidy's face darkens. "They got you, too, huh?"

A moment of silence passes until Sawyer shakes his head like he's slinging water out of his ears. "Nah, you're right, never mind. Sorry. Just ignore me. I'm in my feelings tonight. I'm just gonna miss you, that's all."

Cassidy's irritation fades.

"Mom told me this morning that she'll give Florida a real chance," Sawyer adds, trying to take back some of the guilt he just piled on. "I think we almost got her."

That gives Cassidy some relief, but the pressure builds. He knows it's a lot to ask of his mother, with all her ties to Tarragon, so he's praying it really is the right decision.

"Hey, wait a second. I got it." Sawyer suddenly snaps his fingers. "Georgina should get you a permanent gig on her show."

Cassidy throws him a weary look.

"You can be the manual labor guy who takes his shirt off for all the ladies."

"Sounds great."

Sawyer cackles at his own joke, but his face turns more serious when Cassidy doesn't. "You really do like her, huh?"

Cassidy takes a drink to buy himself some time, because he's still not quite sure how to answer that question. "Like" is a terrible understatement, but "love" scares the crap out of him. He wasn't expecting to feel anything close to love again after Melody, let alone toward a woman he's only known for a little less than a month.

"Yeah, I do," he says finally, sighing. "I need to talk to her."

"Here comes your chance."

Cassidy looks up sharply and sees Georgina gliding through the barn, moving in their direction. Savannah is with her, too, and for once they actually look like twins in their pretty dresses, aside from Savannah's straight ink-black hair.

"There y'all are," Sawyer says, sliding off his stool to greet them. "I was wondering if you were going to leave me hanging."

Cassidy raises an eyebrow as Savannah giggles and crashes into him. Like Sawyer, she appears to have already had a few drinks. He glances at Georgina next, who looks back at him with an apologetic expression.

"Hey, where's Poppy?" Sawyer asks, looking around. Some of the other UpScale crew members are there, too, including Tom, who's laughing it up with the bartender.

"She was super bummed to miss it, but she needed an early bedtime tonight," Georgina explains as Sawyer's face falls. "Plus the whole being-hugely-pregnant-in-a-bar thing," she adds.

Cassidy laughs, but Sawyer doesn't hear her as Savannah drags him toward the dance floor. His rowdy entourage follows.

"Away they go," Cassidy says, watching them fade into the growing crowd.

"Thank goodness. She was driving me nuts," Georgina mutters, taking Sawyer's abandoned seat.

"Why?"

She studies the drink menu for a moment and orders a vodka cranberry before looking up at him with her fluttery eyelashes. "Where do I even begin?"

Cassidy smiles. He still can't tell if she does that on purpose or if it's just the way her eyes work. Either way, it has a powerful effect.

"She's just being moody. And she insisted on us taking shots before we left, and then the Uber was late—"

"Y'all called an Uber?" Cassidy listens with wide eyes as she describes the hour-long hassle. "I didn't even know we had one."

"You do. Literally one."

He laughs at the tired look on her face. "You could've just called me. You know I'm not drinking."

"I thought about it, but I didn't want to subject you to me and my tipsy sister." Uncertainty shadows her face as the bar-

214

tender slides over her drink. "Should I even be drinking right now? Is that rude? I don't know the rules."

"I don't mind."

She hesitates for a moment, then takes a slow, careful sip.

"What, you think the alcohol's gonna jump in my mouth or something?"

She laughs so hard she almost spits out the drink. "Sorry. I don't know what I'm doing. Like I said . . . tipsy. It's been a *long* week."

He nods. "You knocked it out of the park at the shower this morning, though. I've never seen my mother eat a whole slice of cake that she didn't make."

The compliment makes her smile, and she finally takes a drink like a normal person as they fall into an easy conversation about the day's events as other people ebb and flow at the bar. She's dressed up like always, in a silky dress that dips down over one shoulder and an opal necklace that matches a ring on her thumb. Cassidy's never met a woman who thinks about every little detail so much.

"Are all these people here for Sawyer?" she asks, looking around at the full house.

"Most of them."

"That's nice. Brigitte loves him, too. She was in mourning today."

"Yeah, but it's good he's leaving. The fame was changing him."

She laughs. "Speaking of fame . . ."

"What?"

"Do you really want to know?"

"Probably not, but you're going to tell me, aren't you?"

She giggles at the wary look on his face. "My publicist called you 'the hot sniper' today. That's your new nickname on Instagram."

He shakes his head as she laughs harder, still not used to the bizarre feeling of having thousands of random women fawn over him. He barely skimmed some of the comments on the "leaked" photo before he had to put his phone down. "How do *you* feel about that? Since you hate guns so much?"

"Let's just say I'm glad you made a career change." She takes another long drink. "Working on a cute little farm is so much better, anyway."

Annoyance pricks him. He knows she meant it in a nice way, but it still feels a little condescending. "What's your real hang-up with guns? It can't be the whole they-kill-people thing."

She frowns. "No, yeah, that's basically it. I don't like when people die."

"What about bad people? Are you sad when a gun kills one of them?"

"How bad are they?"

"Rapists. Murderers. Terrorists. That kind of bad."

She takes another thoughtful sip. "I'm not *sad* about it," she finally answers. "But I still wouldn't want to go around shooting them."

"Thankfully, you don't have to."

Her brows raise at his cool tone.

"Congratulations!" a drunk woman yells suddenly, startling them both. She points to a pair of abandoned *Mr.* and *Mrs.* sashes on their chairs. "Y'all are real cute together!" she adds loudly as a few people glance in their direction. Another woman whips out her phone when she notices Georgina.

"Darts?" Cassidy suggests as color blooms in Georgina's face.

She nods gratefully. They rise from their seats and head for the dartboards, but a familiar voice in the crowd catches Cassidy's attention.

"What on earth are you doing, Julie Briar?" Gavin demands.

Cassidy halts beside him as Georgina bumps into his back,

and the two of them watch as Gavin reaches over the head of a stunned teenage boy and takes a bottle of beer out of Julie's hands before she can pull it out of his reach.

"I'm here for Sawyer's party," she hisses, throwing him a scathing look. If she wasn't five foot three, it might be pretty intimidating. "My mom said it was fine," she adds.

Gavin snorts. "You must think I'm pretty dense if you think I'm gonna believe that." He scrutinizes the young man she's with next, whose eyes dart to the floor.

"You're not my dad, Gavin," Julie snaps, her embarrassment rising swiftly. "You're not even my friend—"

"You don't need any more friends. You got plenty," he retorts sharply, although his face softens a bit as hers fills with surprise. "But you do need someone to look out for you." He points at an empty table nearby. "Now y'all go sit over there and drink a Sprite or something. Good grief."

Her face stays defiant as she sulks off with the boy, but they begrudgingly slide into the booth.

"Good job, Gav," Cassidy says, thumping him on the back. "You gonna text Lila?"

"On it," he mutters, pulling out his phone.

"Do Lila and Gavin have a thing?" Georgina asks a moment later when they finally reach the dartboards. "Poppy and I came up with a whole romantic storyline for them."

Cassidy smirks. "I think so, but I don't know for sure." He holds out both sets of darts. "It's hard for me to imagine Gavin having a girlfriend, though. In my mind, he's perpetually thirteen."

She laughs. "He did pretty good back there." She chooses the red. "I hated it when my mom's boyfriends pretended like we were such great pals. Better to just be honest, in my opinion."

Cassidy nods and adds another piece of her past to the picture she's been painting. An absent, hypocritical dad. An impressive but overbearing mom. An unpredictable sister who she loves more than she lets on. He can see how some of it shaped Georgina, but he can also see how she's determined to break as many patterns as she can.

"You want kids, right?" she asks, surprising him.

"Yeah . . ." She's been asking him more questions like that lately. "I'd like to be a dad one day."

She nods at his answer, but a too-long silence follows. "Anyway . . ." She moves toward the board. "Let's play."

He's not sure what to expect as they start, but her darts land within mere centimeters of the bullseye almost every time. She laughs at his impressed-but-worried expression when she finally lands one dead center.

"Decorating, cakes, darts." He ticks her talents off on his fingers. "Anything you don't do?"

"No, I'm good at pretty much everything," she teases with a look that almost sends his mind to forbidden places, but he focuses on the target instead.

"I just thought of something, though," she says, sidling up to him as he lifts his arm to throw."

"What's that?"

"It's about your shooting obsession."

His eyes narrow over the target.

"How does it work with being a Christian?" she asks right before he releases the dart. He scowls as it lands off-center.

"You're supposed to love your neighbor, right?" she prods. "So, why are you okay with killing them?"

Her smug tone irks him, but he's noticed a pattern over the last couple weeks. She'll be vulnerable for a moment, like bringing up her parents or her past, but then she'll follow it up with a joke or a smart little dig.

"How is it loving your neighbor to let them be raped or murdered?" he asks, raising another dart.

He waits a moment, expecting some kind of retort, but it doesn't come, so he takes aim and lands closer to the center this time. The third one lands on the bullseye and evens out the score.

"It just doesn't seem like Christians should be violent," she finally grumbles, grabbing her darts.

"Some Christians aren't. Which is fine." He waits as she raises the dart and squints at the board. "But they only get that option because other Christians are."

She curses softly as her dart lands near the edge of the board.

"Pacifism doesn't really make any sense if you actually love someone," he adds as she tries again. Her next two throws aren't much better. "People protect what they love—"

"So you think Jesus wanted you to kill those people?" she snaps.

"No," he snaps back. "I'm just saying there are times when it's admissible. It's never ideal. And I never killed anyone because I *wanted* to," he adds tersely. His military service was the hardest, most humbling thing he's ever done. He obsessed over every target, haunted by the fact that it was somebody's son or husband or brother—even if they were the scum of the earth. "I always did it to save other people."

Her frustrated eyes finally meet his again.

"Georgina . . ." He raises his darts in surrender. This isn't at all the way he imagined the conversation going. "You just don't get it—"

"Oh, look," she says, her eyes darkening further under the low light. "Renata's here. Yay."

He groans silently as Renata throws him a bold look on her way to meet Sawyer on the dance floor. She's in her element as Sawyer gives her a quick twirl and releases her into the crowd of gawking admirers.

Georgina, however, is not. "Let's get out of here," Cassidy says, reaching for her hand, but she surprises him by pulling away.

"No," she says regretfully. "You can't touch me right now."
Confusion fills him. "Why not?"

"It can't seem like I'm single."

"Are you serious?"

"Yes?" She frowns at his exasperated expression. "Because of the NDA—"

"Yeah, but aren't we kind of past that by now? With the whole leaked-picture thing?"

"That's *why* we should be more discreet."

"Is your ex being as 'discreet' as you are? Didn't you say he's posted all about it online? But I can't hold your hand?" Unexpected jealousy makes his voice sharp. "When Renata brought him up earlier, you made it seem like y'all are still together." His mind has gone to that moment more than once today. "That just seems messed up—"

"It's because of the NDA, Cassidy," she snaps, cutting him off again. "I can't talk about it yet. I already told you that." Her tone is just as sharp as his now, but she looks hurt when he doesn't respond.

"Look, I'm sorry, okay?" she continues. "I know it sucks. I honestly don't know why you still hang out with me."

Her self-deprecation softens him a bit, but some of his frustration lingers. "It'd just be nice if you were done with him."

"I'm working on it. I really don't appreciate your attitude right now, though. Especially since I always feel like I'm stepping on someone else's property whenever Renata's around."

He scowls as her eyes flick back to the dance floor, annoyed that she brought up Renata again, but he's also relieved to know he's not the only jealous one. "If you knew how many times I've told that woman I'm not interested, you wouldn't feel that way."

"And if you knew how many calls and texts I've ignored from Lance, you wouldn't be acting like this," she interrupts. "I hardly even think about him anymore, Cassidy," she admits with an embarrassed look that warms his blood. "We're together for three years, and you come along and wipe them out with one kiss. . . ."

He's about to pull her out the door and redo their disastrous conversation when Savannah suddenly beckons her from the dance floor. Georgina reluctantly trudges over.

"Dance, Georgie!" Savannah commands, grabbing her arm. Georgina looks less than enthusiastic, but she's a good sport and shimmies along with her sister. Sawyer and his friends try dragging Cassidy out there, too, but he stays on the sidelines.

"Come on, Cass!" Dylan yells.

"Y'all are doing just fine without me—"

"Come on, James Bond," Sawyer says, bopping his head as Georgina and Savannah glide by. "It's your last chance until your secret mission—"

Cassidy's back stiffens. He glances at Georgina as her curious eyes meet his.

"What?" she mouths, her voice drowned out by the music.

"You gotta talk him out of it, Sawyer," Dylan continues, talking louder. "Tarragon ain't the most exciting place on earth, but it's better than the middle of the jungle."

Cassidy reaches into the fray and pulls Georgina out, stunning her and Savannah in the process, but he's not about to let drunk Dylan Hayes break the news before he does.

"What were they talking about?" Georgina asks, looking between his tense face and the dance floor with scrunched brows. Cassidy leads her out the back door as quickly as he can, searching for anywhere quiet, but the outside is just as busy, with people crowded under glowing string lights, listening to some young guy croon into a microphone. There's always his truck, but they get pretty distracted in there most of the time, so he opts for a nearby cornfield instead.

"Let's take a walk," he says, glancing down at her fancy-looking shoes, which aren't ideal, but at least they're flat.

221

She throws him another confused look but doesn't protest, and soon her light footsteps alternate with his as they walk through the maze. His mind races for the perfect words, but they don't come.

"Cassidy, you have to speak soon, or I'm going to freak out," she says after another long moment passes.

He finally stops walking. "Okay . . ." He drags a hand through his hair. "I, uh, gotta talk to you about something."

"I got that part," she says, her eyes widening. "Oh my gosh, your face is *so* serious right now. I don't like it."

Uncertainty floods him as she nervously fills in the silence, and he suddenly wishes he had her abandoned drink in his hand. *She might take the news better than you think*, he tells himself. That's the possibility he's been praying for. "It's about my job," he says, forcing the words out as she falls silent again.

Her head tilts. "At the Harp House?"

He nods, then shakes his head. "No." He sighs. "It's about a different job." *A job you're probably going to hate*, he thinks, recalling her various complaints.

"What kind of job?"

He does his best to explain it in civilian terms, but her face clouds with confusion the longer he talks. "It's kind of like being a bodyguard," he finally says, taking the most straightforward approach. "I'll protect people and property and—"

"In El Salvador?"

He nods.

"Why, though? That's so random?"

He fights back a laugh. As frustrating as it is that she has no idea what he's talking about, it's also one of his favorite things about her. "There's a drug war going on there." He tries to explain that, too, while also trying to make it sound as non-scary as possible. "So, there's this gang—multiple, actually, but one main one—and they do all kinds of crazy stuff to get money—"

"So, it's super dangerous?" she interjects.

"Um . . ." He shrugs, downplaying it as fear fills her face. "I mean, relatively dangerous, yeah." *That's why they need my help.* He doesn't say that out loud, though, since the last thing he needs to do right now is accidentally sound condescending. He's already upset her enough.

"How long does it take?"

His stomach sinks as she waits for his answer. "It's hard to say. It's sort of ongoing, and they might move me around a little for other missions, depending on how things go."

His words fall flat at the crushed look on her face. He's learned that she's a master at keeping her expression smooth when people are watching, even when she's overwhelmed, but her disappointment is slowly breaking through the surface.

"I don't think it would take more than nine months, though," he adds quickly, as her eyes drop to the ground. "Maybe not that long."

"You leave in August?"

The silence deepens as she looks up again and he nods, and it hits them both that they only have a few more weeks together. Sadness darkens her eyes.

"I know it's bad timing." *What part of our relationship isn't?* he wonders miserably. "I didn't know when to bring it up since we just started . . . you know . . ." What? Talking? Kissing? Dating? He struggles to pick the right word for their whirlwind-turned-F5 tornado. "I took the job before I met you," he adds quickly, trying to soften the blow somehow, but it doesn't work as she looks up at him through those lashes.

"And after I left the military, I never thought I'd get a second chance—"

"This is really what you want to do?"

Cassidy's feelings war within him as she waits for his answer. "I want to help people," he says finally, ignoring the torn-apart feeling in his chest. "And this is the best way I can do that."

Her face softens, but the sorrow lingers.

"And I never wanted to stay in Tarragon forever."

"I get that."

He falls silent as she mumbles the words out. He knows she understands on some level, but he still doesn't like it one bit now that she's looking at him like that.

Suddenly, anger flashes across her face. "What's wrong with you?" she demands, surprising him as tears start to fill her eyes. "Why didn't you tell me sooner? Did you just want me to fall totally in love with you before you broke my heart?"

She rages on, but Cassidy's ears momentarily shut down, and he can't hear anything except what she just said. First off, breaking her heart is the last thing he ever wanted to do, and secondly . . . does that mean she was at least falling a little bit in love with him?

"And, like, what are we supposed to do now?" she continues, throwing her hands up. "You're leaving, and I'm leaving—"

"Can't we just keep going?"

She stares at him like he's lost his mind.

"What, Georgina? People have long-distance relationships all the time—"

"We don't even have a relationship yet!" she yells as the tears finally fall from her eyes. "And we would never see each other—"

"Yes, we would—"

"When?" she demands. "For a few random days whenever you come back from a war zone? *If* you come back?" Her face turns pale as she shakes her head. "No. No. No," she says like she's trying to convince herself. "That's not what I want."

Understanding dawns as he listens. Her careful, tidy plans for the future begin coming to mind. It has to "make sense" to her, and, clearly, this doesn't.

"We have to end it," she says, so quietly that he almost doesn't hear her. He half-expected it, but the whispered words still hit him like a bullet.

"No we don't—"

"Yes we do! We can't be anything, so we have to stop pretending like we can—"

"What if I want to be something?"

The question stuns her for a moment. "We can't, Cassidy," she says again, her voice breaking. "It's over—"

He silences her with a kiss, unwilling to hear any more reasons. She desperately kisses him back, her arms clinging to his neck as he pulls her closer, unwilling to let her go. He wants the kiss to say everything he can't and erase her doubts, but she drags herself away.

"We can't do that anymore," she murmurs, trying to catch her breath as he fights for self-control. She always grazes her fingertips across her neckline after they kiss, and she has no idea how crazy it drives him. "It's over."

"Your eyes say it's not."

Her cheeks flush, but she vehemently shakes her head. "It is."

"Georgina—"

"I don't want to hurt you, and I don't want you to hurt me. That's what's going to happen if we don't—"

"Doesn't it hurt now?"

Her anguished face says yes, but he can see the determination in her eyes before she turns away.

Georgina does her best to revert back into the happy, smiling version of herself as she passes curious faces in the barn, but her façade is breaking. Thankfully, the bathroom only has two stalls and she has both to herself, so she locks herself in the larger one.

Country music pulses through the walls and softens her crying, which she's thankful for, but it's a pitiful scene that reminds her of her mother. She didn't have a choice, though. It was either a private sob session or having a full-blown breakdown in front of Cassidy, and he probably would've just kissed her again and slipped her back into the daydream.

She presses her hands to her eyes, willing the tears to stop, but it's too much—the kiss, his voice, his worried expression when he told her about the job, her own silly fantasies about their future. She'd caught a glimpse of it at the shower today when she saw him smile at the little girl. *That's what I want*, she had thought, surprised by how hard the realization struck her heart. But that fragile little dream just turned to dust, too.

She wipes the rest of her tears away, careful to keep her makeup in place. She should've known the last month was too good to be true. All the signs were there. The most terrible part is that she actually thought he was going to say he loved her in that deep, tense silence in the middle of the maze. She had no idea what she would've done if he had, but she had wanted him to, and that expectation made his announcement ten thousand times worse.

"What if I want to be something?"

She closes her eyes, remembering his question. *Then you wouldn't leave*, she replies silently, then scolds herself. It's unfair, and she knows it. She can't ask him to give up a job he obviously wants for a woman he's known for a month, especially when they're so mismatched. Between his previous marriage, career, and the fact that he can pull up random ideas from Ecclesiastes, she feels totally out of her depth, and he probably feels the same way about her, even if he won't admit it yet.

She exhales as the song changes to something slower and sadder, and her eyes drift to a stall wall scribbled with love notes and song lyrics mixed in with curse words and Bible verses.

Thank goodness Cassidy told her now, or she would've spilled it all soon—the depths of her father's abandonment, the baby she had to flush away, her barely-under-control anxiety. Little by little, she had been showing him what's under the pretty exterior to see if he would run away or not, but now there's no point.

The bathroom door creaks open, and she freezes as footsteps follow. She lowers her head to peek under the stall and sees Savannah's chipped toenail polish and Birkenstocks.

"Georgie?"

She quickly grabs a wad of toilet paper and drags it across her tear-streaked face. "What?"

"Are you okay?"

"Yes."

"Are you crying?"

Georgina stiffens. "No."

Savannah moves closer to the stall. "Yes, you are."

"I'm just going to the bathroom, Sav—"

"You never use public bathrooms."

"I had to go."

"Open the door," Savannah demands, but Georgina doesn't. "Please," she adds more gently.

"No, Sav, just leave me alone."

"Is it Lance? Did he do something else?"

Georgina sighs tiredly. Clearly, Savannah's not going to let her cry in peace. At least she sounds slightly sobered up. Georgina wouldn't be able to deal with drunk Savannah right now. "No."

"Is it your show? Did I screw it up?"

Surprise fills her. "What?"

"With the Adderall thing?"

Georgina's confusion grows until she remembers their conversation earlier that day. She lit into Savannah about spilling her secret to Poppy, reminding her sister how terrible it could be for her brand if people knew she'd popped some pills to keep her life together, but Savannah swore no one was around. "No," she repeats.

Savannah sighs with relief, which is a nice surprise since she only offered a bare-minimum apology earlier. A long silence passes. "Cassidy?"

Fresh tears fall as Savannah guesses correctly, and she feels the loss of her favorite lifeline all over again.

"Dang. That majorly sucks," Savannah mutters after Georgina explains his announcement. "He seemed cool."

Georgina finally flings open the stall door.

"I actually liked him," Savannah continues. "Way more than Lance."

Georgina's mouth falls open. "You could've fooled literally everyone, Savannah," she says shrilly as Savannah's face turns sheepish. "You acted like he was the worst."

"I know. Sorry. That was dumb."

"It doesn't matter now. You were right. He was just a distraction."

"I was just being mean, Georgie."

The honest statement stuns her speechless.

"I was mad that you were happy again."

Georgina's eyes widen. "Why?" Hurt follows. "Why would that make you mad?"

"Look, I know it was messed up." Savannah's eyes turn apologetic and defensive at the same time. "Obviously, I want you to be happy. I just . . ."

"What?"

"It was just nice feeling like I wasn't totally alone for once," she snaps, her eyes darkening with embarrassment. "You always get it together and you never need help, but for one hot minute, your life wasn't totally perfect. And I wasn't happy about *that*, but . . . it just made me feel better. Like I wasn't totally falling behind—"

"I'm not perfect, Savannah," Georgina interjects, moved by the defeated look on her sister's face. "You of all people know that. And you're not falling behind—"

"Yes, I am," Savannah insists, ignoring her. "Don't lie about it. It doesn't make me feel better," she adds. Her eyes darken before drifting to the scribbles on the wall. "I want to change, though. And I want to be me. At the same time." She traces a tiny, Sharpie-drawn mountainscape with her fingertip. "But, like, can you even do that? I don't know. . . ."

Her plea almost brings Georgina to tears again—because she understands. "You're doing that, Sav," she insists. Like Georgina, she's still far from perfect, but she *is* changing. Georgina was just too consumed with her own life to notice until now. "Just don't give up."

"Stop it." Savannah surprises her and rips off a piece of toilet paper as a rogue teardrop slides down Georgina's cheek. "No more crying about stupid boys," she adds gently, pulling her in for a hug. "You're too good for that."

16

"It kind of looks like blood. . . ."

Georgina frowns down at the canvas. That's not what she was going for.

"It's kind of cool, though," Poppy adds, turning the color-streaked paper upside down. "Seeds, fruit, flowers, blood. There's something deep in there for sure."

Georgina stares at her test swatch, thinking fast. She thought her idea for nature-inspired art was brilliant at first—pressing flowers and berries and whatever else she could find in the orchard against a crisp white background and seeing what kind of colors they left behind. But now that she and Poppy are dripping in sweat and the results are subpar, she's less enthused. There's also the fun fact that Tarragonians won't stop shooting off exceptionally loud fireworks in preparation for the Fourth of July on Friday.

"Are you ready yet?" Brigitte asks, antsy to shoot their signature scene. Georgina and Poppy always did at least one piece of pretty-but-easy-to-duplicate DIY art in their *Nail Breakers* renovations, so Georgina is planning on carrying on the tradition—if UpScale gives her the chance.

Her stomach churns as she remembers her meeting with Lance and their lawyers is only a week away. Seeing him face-to-face will be hard enough, but there's also his super-secret pilot. Benson tried digging up some dirt, but, unlike her, Lance hasn't suffered any "leaks."

"Almost," Georgina answers Brigitte, grabbing waxed paper to try a different technique.

"Five minutes," she mutters, racing off to find Nathan.

Poppy watches as Georgina slips the paper over the flowers and uses a lighter touch with the hammer. "That one isn't totally hideous," she says encouragingly. "Oh, look, there's Savannah and her new bestie."

Georgina looks up to see Savannah and Julie Briar hurrying inside the cottage with fountain drinks in hand. Apparently, Sav found a fellow kindred spirit who can drink Cherry Coke at ten in the morning. "Better late than never," she mutters as Savannah expertly dodges Brigitte.

"Sav as a big sister is the cutest thing ever," Poppy adds, watching Julie scurry after her.

Georgina smiles. It is cute. Ever since Lila gave them a ride after Sawyer's party on Saturday, Julie's been Savannah's almost-constant shadow, and it seems to have had a positive effect on both of them.

Georgina still winces as her mind travels back to that terrible night, once she and Savannah finally reemerged from the barn bathroom. Cassidy had offered to drive them back to the Harp House, but Lila Briar swooped in and saved the day, since she was already there to retrieve Julie.

"*Hang out with your brother,*" Lila had said to Cassidy, not realizing she just spared them all the most awkward ride of their lives.

Georgina caught his disappointment, but he forced out a polite good-bye and disappeared into the crowd again. She and Savannah slid into the back of Lila's old Subaru as Julie went from silent and sullen to speaking so fast Georgina could barely keep track of her questions about *Nail Breakers*. Georgina felt

231

bad that their first real conversation happened when she was so exhausted, but Savannah had picked up the social slack and secured a sidekick in the process.

"I'm still mad about the you-know-what, by the way," Poppy whispers, pulling her back to the present. It's a rare moment without Savannah around and no cameras. "Since when do we keep secrets? You know I wouldn't have judged you—"

"It wasn't *you*, Pop," Georgina whispers back, feeling another rush of regret about the Adderall. "It was just . . . stupid. I was embarrassed." The more she reflects on it, the more she cringes. Some people actually need that medication, and she had been taking it like it was shots of espresso.

"I could've given you some of my camu camu if you told me. That stuff saved my life."

Georgina smiles weakly as Poppy goes on, familiar with her and Jared's arsenal of crunchy home remedies. "I'm okay, Poppy," she interjects, sensing the sweet concern underneath a long list of herbal supplements. "I promise."

Poppy looks relieved, but her concern returns when Georgina lets a tired sigh slip out.

"Has Cassidy texted you yet?"

Georgina shakes her head, grateful and devastated at the same time. He did send a text on Saturday to ask if they made it to the Harp House okay. She had replied yes, then waited, anxiously watching the dots as he typed something else. It should've been at least a paragraph long, based on all the time it took, but the final message was painfully short.

I'm sorry.

"I'm just going to focus on myself," Georgina announces when Poppy looks like she's about to say more about Cassidy. Talking about it just dredges up the heartbreak all over again.

"And God?" Poppy asks gently.

Surprise fills Georgina. And annoyance. "Sure . . ." she finally says, even though her feelings toward God are pretty mixed at the moment.

"I just think focusing on yourself too much can make it worse sometimes," Poppy adds, pressing her hammer against a sprig of purple passionflowers.

Georgina nods but secretly bristles, even though she knows she shouldn't. Poppy loves her more than anyone she knows, aside from her mother and Savannah, and she's just trying to help. But between losing the baby and Lance and now Cassidy, she has no idea why God would put those things in her life just to yank them away like this. Her already-fragile faith feels pulled up by the roots.

"God can get you through anything, Georgie."

Georgina doesn't respond. A lot of people say that, but where exactly is God in this mess? He's not making it terribly obvious. Suddenly, a painful possibility pops into her head. Maybe Poppy's wrong, and it doesn't have anything to do with God at all—maybe it really is just about *her*. Maybe she's not worth sticking around for.

"You just have to trust—"

"Let's roll!"

Brigitte's impatient voice drowns out Poppy's as she returns with Nathan.

"Hey, y'all!" Georgina begins, forcing a bright smile once the red light on Nathan's camera glows. "We're focusing on natural elements with this renovation, so we turned to the great outdoors to create some unique art pieces."

She mentally escapes for a bit as she and Poppy pound flowers and berries into abstract art, but Brigitte's voice swiftly brings her back to reality when the scene ends.

"Your countertops are missing," she announces flatly, glancing at her phone.

Georgina's mouth falls open. "Which ones?"

"All of them. It's fine, though. We needed more mishaps."

Georgina scowls. Unlike Brigitte, she's not happy about the fact that her beautiful sage-green slabs of quartz are lost on a truck somewhere.

"I want to get Georgina talking to Cassidy about it," Brigitte continues, talking Nathan through her new artistic vision. "And then he can suggest an alternative—"

"I don't think Cassidy is coming today," Georgina interjects. She hasn't asked for his help lately for obvious reasons.

Brigitte frowns and checks her watch, then glances up the road. "He's here."

Georgina's stomach drops as her eyes follow Brigitte's. Sure enough, his truck is slowly coming down the drive, followed by another truck with *Eddy's Range* printed on the dusty exterior.

"Is there an issue?" Brigitte asks, noticing the troubled look on her face.

"Um . . ." Georgina avoids her eyes and zeroes in on the fanny pack instead. "No—"

"Good. Poppy, come with me," Brigitte says, whisking her away to reshoot something.

Georgina refuses to greet Cassidy alone, so she walks to the cottage. They finally installed the new HVAC system, so it's not miserably hot anymore, and the gross neglected-house smells have been replaced by fresh paint as Tom covers the kitchen in a pink sunlight-on-apples color Poppy picked out. It looks perfect with Sawyer's custom cabinets. Georgina misses his silliness, as does the rest of the crew, but Savannah is taking his absence surprisingly well. Georgina showed her a picture he texted yesterday, of him grinning with his wife.

"They're cute," Sav had conceded with a small but sincere smile.

Speaking of Savannah, Georgina heads to the bedroom to check on her progress. Georgina made the risky decision to resurrect the mural project with only a few weeks to spare, but, thankfully, Savannah is working at a slightly faster pace this time. A mounted camera captures her slow but steady progress as she paints careful cascades of leaves and fruit and flowers dripping from the ceiling, with Julie circling around to add gold leaf to every few petals.

"No means of measure can define His limitless love. He's enduringly strong. He's entirely sincere. He's eternally steadfast—"

S. M. Lockridge's familiar voice competes with Tom's classic rock station blaring in the kitchen as Georgina enters the room. Savannah and Julie don't hear her come in.

"Savannah—"

"He supplies strength for the weak. He's available for the tempted and the tried. He sympathizes and He saves. He strengthens and He sustains. He guards and He guides—"

Georgina reaches for Savannah's phone and turns down the sermon, which finally catches her sister's attention.

"What?" Savannah says with mild annoyance.

"This looks *amazing.*"

"Oh. Thanks," she mutters, quickly refocusing on a half-formed piece of fruit, but Georgina is still in awe. It was already the most beautiful room in the house with a pear-green color on the ceiling and the warm wood floor, but Savannah's mural is the showstopper.

"It really does," Julie chimes in, her voice reaching an excited new pitch. "And I love the bed so much!" she adds, pointing at the elegant canopy bed. "Do the people get to keep all the furniture you pick out?"

"No." That's the question Georgina gets asked more than any other. "It's just for staging. They can buy it if they want to, but most people use their own stuff once the show is over."

"I knew it!" Julie says triumphantly. "I told my mom that there was no way they could afford it, even with their crazy budgets."

Georgina smiles. "It's actually not the money most of the time. A lot of people just like what they're used to."

"Well, if y'all did our house, I wouldn't change a single thing," Julie says with exhausting but adorable enthusiasm. "I like how you mix in old stuff with the new. I feel like Lance's style is kind of cold. . . ."

Georgina nods but doesn't say anything specific. Julie has prodded her about Lance ever-so-gently a few times since the car ride. "Yeah, we like a more eclectic feel—"

Bang!

Georgina freezes.

"What was that?" Savannah demands, almost falling off her ladder.

Georgina can't speak. She's still frozen in place. She's used to all kinds of sounds on set, whether it's hammers or buzzsaws or paint cans clattering, but that one was different.

Bang!

She shrieks in surprise when it goes off again, but this time she hears laughter in its wake. She forces herself to look out the window and search for the source.

She curses softly when she finds it. "Are you freaking kidding me?"

Cassidy is off in the distance, facing the trees with a giant gun on a table in front of him.

"He's shooting a gun," she mutters in disbelief. "A literal gun." There are probably a million rules about firearm safety and licenses, but apparently none of that matters, not even to

Brigitte, who's watching the whole thing with Nathan by her side.

Georgina flies out of the house and stomps in that direction, followed closely by Julie and Savannah. The crew parts as she gets closer.

"Calm down, Rambo," Cassidy says to a man she's never seen before as the laughter continues.

"It's for television," the man retorts. He's older than Cassidy, with an alarming number of tattoos, but his face is friendly. "You need something extra special."

Georgina watches in horror as he clicks some other scary-looking thing onto the already-oversized gun.

"What are you doing?" she demands. Curious faces dart between her and Cassidy as he looks in her direction. Her heart races as his eyes meet hers. A familiar jolt of electricity passes between them, but she pretends not to notice. "Does this look like a gun range to you?"

Her sarcasm makes his mouth curve up. "Kind of," he says, moving aside so she can see the targets a few yards away—shadowy silhouettes—plus a table currently loaded up with gun parts and little boxes. She scowls. He's been busy.

"Eddy Alvarez. Nice to meet you," the other man says, extending his hand, which is inked with a fiery scroll. "Don't worry, we got the area all cleared out," he adds when her bewilderment lingers. "Plus, Cass can shoot that distance in his sleep."

Georgina's face swivels between him and Cassidy before finally landing on Brigitte. "We need guns in the pilot?"

"It's not for the pilot," Brigitte replies tersely. "It's a promotional thing. For Annette," she adds, throwing her a pointed look.

Confusion fills Georgina until Annette's hot sniper comments come to mind. She screams internally, but Cassidy interrupts it with a box of earplugs.

"You'll want these," he offers, but she doesn't move.

"Is the drone ready?" Brigitte asks Nathan.

Georgina's eyes widen as Nathan nods and fiddles with buttons on a remote control until a clunky drone takes flight and hovers overheard. Savannah and Julie watch with excited faces, along with Tom. Georgina didn't even know they had a drone.

"Where's Poppy?" she demands, wanting an ally.

"In the little cottage," Brigitte answers.

Georgina's disappointed but relieved, too. At least Poppy is safe with the snacks and protecting the baby's tiny eardrums. She begrudgingly takes a set of earplugs when Cassidy offers them again.

"Why don't you give it a try?" he suggests with an innocent look, but she can hear the amusement in his voice.

"Absolutely not."

"Yes, we definitely want that," Brigitte interjects, making sure Nathan is ready with the main camera, too. "It'll be a great HLSN moment."

Cassidy frowns. "A what?"

"Host Learns Something New," Georgina mutters miserably, throwing Brigitte an unhappy look. She had a detailed strategy for keeping herself and Cassidy apart on set, but Brigitte's wrecking her plans—and the rest of the crew is cheering her on.

"One shot," Georgina snaps in frustration as Cassidy smiles triumphantly.

"Is that a Remington 700?" Tom asks, his eyes lighting up as Cassidy gets the monstrous gun ready.

Cassidy nods.

"I'm gonna need to shoot that before y'all leave—"

"I can't even lift that," Georgina interjects, looking down at the beast sitting on the table between them. It looks as long as Savannah is tall. "And I don't want to look completely ridiculous," she adds, glancing at the cameras.

Cassidy frowns at the worried look on her face. "Okay." He thinks for a moment. "How about this instead?"

Georgina watches, stunned and horrified, as he lifts his shirt and reveals a holster—and a tiny sliver of his beautiful abs—and sets a much smaller gun on the table. Her confused eyes meet his. "You seriously carry that around all day? In your pants?"

He snorts. "It's in a holster, not my pants."

"What if it goes off?"

He closes his eyes for a moment, like he's praying for patience. "That's not how guns work. At all. Come over here, please."

Georgina reluctantly obeys, but her nerves spike when she feels every pair of eyes follow her and Cassidy.

"So, rule number one: if you're holding a gun, you always keep it pointed on your target and nowhere else," he begins when the crew hushes, and Brigitte gives him a signal. "And you don't put your finger on the trigger unless you're certain you're ready to shoot it. Okay?"

His voice is low and calm, but she still panics on the inside. What if her hand slips? What if she accidentally pulls the trigger somehow? "Okay . . ."

"Now, see how I'm standing with my knees a little bent, and I'm leaning forward, like this? And my hands look like this, see?" He leans in closer to show her his right thumb resting on the knuckle of his left thumb. "That gives you control when you press the trigger."

Sweat rolls down her back as he sets it down on the table. He motions for her to take it, but she doesn't.

"You don't have to shoot it yet. We'll just focus on the other stuff first."

She wills herself to pick it up, but her body feels rooted in place.

"The safety's on," he adds, like she knows what that means.

"I . . ." Her heart races as her eyes dart between his concerned face and the gun, and she knows her anxiety is about to take over. "I can't do it," she murmurs. It's the combination of the gun, Cassidy's dizzying closeness, and the excited cheers from the crew. It's too much.

"Georgina," Brigitte finally snaps. "It's just one shot—"

"I don't want to do it," she repeats desperately.

"You're being silly," Brigitte presses. "Just listen to Cassidy—"

"No," he interjects firmly, surprising them both as he focuses on Brigitte. "She doesn't have to if she's not ready."

Brigitte scowls, but Georgina doesn't see the aftermath because she books it out of there to avoid further embarrassment.

"I want a turn!" she hears Julie shout behind her as she races back to the empty cottage and shuts herself in the bedroom.

She leans against the door, and her mind finally goes to all the places she's been avoiding. To Saturday night, to Cassidy's conflicted face, to the excitement in his voice when he described the job, to the growing ache in her heart when she thinks about her life without him in it. She covers her eyes as fresh tears try to break through the surface.

There's silence, then another gunshot, followed by cheers. The pattern continues until there's a light knock on the door.

"Can I come in?"

Her heart races at the sound of Cassidy's voice.

He slowly opens the door before she answers. His face falls as he sees the sorrowful look on hers. "Are you okay?"

She nods, but the near tears give her away.

"Can we talk?"

She nods again, sure that her voice is going to come out funny and tight, but she finally breaks her silence when he starts to sit down on the bed. "No!" she yells, startling him as he straightens.

"What?"

"It needs a mattress protector," she explains, searching around Savannah's endless paint cans and rags for the bag with bedding. "Your butt is probably dusty."

"It's not." He sits down before she can stop him, so she reaches for his arm and tries to heave him up again, but his body doesn't move an inch.

"Get up, Cassidy," she hisses, still gripping his arm, but she falls silent as his eyes lock with hers. Her heart is already racing, but it skyrockets when he suddenly catches her other arm and pulls her toward him. "The camera," she squeaks when he's close enough to kiss.

There's a moment of surprised silence before he groans and drags himself up again. "Give us a minute, Brigitte," he mutters, tossing Savannah's rags over the mounted cameras. Georgina knows it's her chance to run away, but she doesn't take it, so he pulls her on the bed with him again.

Her heart jumps again as her body briefly tangles with his, unprepared for the sudden rush of closeness and whatever might follow, but he surprises her by pulling her to one side, then into the crook of his arm. *We're cuddling*, she realizes as her eyes settle on his profile, and it's the sweetest, strangest, saddest feeling she's ever had.

"How have you been?" he asks, his chin lightly brushing against her hair.

Georgina sighs at the perfectly normal question. He makes everything feel so gloriously simple, like her world isn't falling apart in a million different ways. It's her favorite thing about him, aside from the longing look in his eyes as they meet hers. "Not good. You?"

"Been better."

Her heart aches. He sounds as sad as she feels. "You haven't even tried to talk to me since Saturday," she whines.

His body stiffens against hers. "You told me it was over and literally ran away, Georgina. What was I supposed to do?"

She winces at the confusion in his voice. He's got a point. She's sending exceptionally mixed signals—and somehow he's still here. "Sorry. You're right. You shouldn't do anything. I'm just being stupid."

She falls silent as he turns and moves her along with him so they're facing each other, with her chest lightly pressed against his, and his drumming heartbeat finally makes the tears fall. He drapes his arm over her as she cries against his shirt. It's the blue cottony one, which makes her even sadder since she's getting mascara all over it, but she can't help herself. His arm feels like a warm, heavy blanket—and it's eventually going to be snatched away.

17

"How's it going, Cass?"

Cassidy looks up from the bulletin in his hands and meets the eyes of Derek Boggs. "Pretty good," he lies, shaking the pastor's hand. He doesn't like lying, especially to a preacher, but he also can't pour his troubles out in the middle of First Baptist social hour. "How are you?"

"Just getting ready for the Cornbread Festival."

"Your favorite time of the year."

Boggs smiles at his sarcasm. Being an introvert makes his profession a real challenge at times, especially since the previous pastor was a prolific talker.

"Goldie told me she's got a trip to Florida planned," Boggs says with a sad smile in Goldie's direction as she chats with her bridge friends. "Between you and me, I hope she doesn't like it. How are we gonna survive without her? The prayer chain is gonna fall apart, and no potluck will ever be the same."

Cassidy forces a smile. Boggs is the last person who would try to make him feel bad on purpose, but guilt tugs at him. His mother's been going to this little church since before he was born, and it's the main reason why she refused to follow his dad around the world. The fellowship here made his absence a little more bearable.

"What about you?" Boggs asks, changing the subject. "August, right? That's coming up quick. Everything coming together for you?"

Cassidy's mind flies through what's left to pack and prepare, but he's not as motivated as he should be. "Getting there." At least Gavin finally found a "good enough" replacement for him at the Harp House, so he can get that squared away. Beyond that, he's filling his time with training and target practice and trying to figure out what's going on with him and Georgina.

He was hopeful their conversation in the cottage might help steady her, but she seems as conflicted as ever—sometimes painfully distant and sometimes so close it's hard to tell where they start and end. Their conversation during the Harp House fireworks show two days ago threw him for another loop.

"You should come to Nashville. . . ."

His brows had raised as she waited for his response. *"With you?"* he had asked, not realizing how stupid that sounded until it was too late. She and Poppy are traveling back to Nashville soon for some kind of meeting with her ex, so he'd thought that's what she meant until embarrassment filled her face.

"No," she'd said quickly. *"I just mean, like . . . one day."*

"Hey, you ever seen *Machine Gun Preacher*?" Boggs asks randomly, breaking him out of the puzzling memory. "That movie with the Irish guy? That could be you out there one day. Start a ministry running guns to defenseless folks and spreading the gospel."

Cassidy smiles weakly, reminded of one of the many reasons he likes Boggs so much. "Sounds good to me—"

"We have some new faces today, Pastor!" Their conversation gets cut short when Marie Marsh hurries over. "Two young ladies," she adds excitedly. "They came with Lila."

Boggs looks over her shoulder. "Oh, that's your friend with the TV show, right?"

"Georgina," he says as she moves through the lobby with Savannah by her side. Cassidy hasn't told him much about Georgina yet other than they've spent some time together, but Boggs is no dummy. His curious eyes glance between them, but Georgina keeps her gaze firmly fixed on Lila as she leads her and Savannah to a pew.

The service starts a few minutes later, and his mother smiles up at him from her place in the choir. He's in the near-empty balcony, as usual—a quiet spot he picked after Melody died. He watches as a toddler peers over the pew to grin at Georgina and offer up his pacifier during the worship time, and she returns the gesture with a big smile.

"'Pain insists on being attended to,'" Boggs begins moments later, taking his place in the pulpit. "'God whispers to us in our pleasures, speaks in our consciences, but shouts in our pain: it is His megaphone to rouse a deaf world.'"

The sanctuary hushes as his voice rings out.

"That quote was from the late, great C. S. Lewis. It's true, isn't it? Pain insists on being attended to . . ."

Boggs has been taking the congregation through the book of Job, and they've settled on a verse in chapter three.

"*I am not at ease, nor am I quiet; I have no rest, but trouble comes.*"

"Sadly, a lot of folks take pain as a sign that God is far away when it's really a sign that's He's near. Pain tells us something has gone terribly wrong in this world, and Somebody's gotta make it right. . . ."

As Boggs's words hang in the air, Cassidy knows they're true. He's felt that wrongness of life down to his bones. And hope.

"Some of us reach out to God in those painful moments, begging for some Band-Aids, whether it's money or relationships or just something shiny and new to keep our minds off what hurts." Boggs smiles weakly. "And you know what? There's actually nothing wrong with a Band-Aid most of the time. You just can't pretend like it'll save your life."

Cassidy listens as Boggs moves on to Job's story, then to Jesus, and connects the two. That's how he preaches every sermon—threading everything back to the gospel. Job was humbled by the crushing wrongness of life and turned to God as his refuge. Jesus Christ was crucified for that same wrongness to draw humanity to life-saving humility.

Cassidy's eyes eventually drift in Georgina's direction, but her eyes are fixed on Boggs. Savannah quietly sketches something on her bulletin.

Later, when the sermon ends and the hymns fade, a small crowd gathers around Georgina and Savannah. Cassidy smiles at the overwhelmed looks on their faces. He feels for them— First Baptist folks take their hospitality seriously—so he doesn't add to the barrage of small talk and slips outside instead.

His mother is sitting on a bench near a shaded playground, praying with her eyes open. He knows because her face is thoughtful but distant, and it's part of her little Sunday routine to pray through the sermon while it's still fresh on her mind.

"I hear this is what Florida's like most of the time," he says, joining her on the bench. It's perfect, not-too-hot weather for once, so a father is pushing his little girl on the swing set.

"Sawyer says it gets even hotter there than here sometimes," she retorts. "Did you see Georgina?"

"I did."

"When does she go back to Nashville?"

"Tomorrow."

"But she's coming back?"

He nods, more aware of the calendar than ever before. "She's got a couple more weeks to finish up the cottage."

"And how do you feel about that?"

Cassidy frowns as his mother's curious eyes meet his. He

hadn't had to tell her much before she figured out he was falling for Georgina. She saw it with Melody, too. "I'm not happy about it, but I don't know what I expected." Goldie listens closely as he revisits his doubts—the whirlwind nature of it, the impending distance, their diverging careers, and the lingering walls around Georgina's heart when it comes to him. And to God.

She frowns at the conflicted look on his face. "I think y'all are making it a bigger mess than it needs to be, Cass. You know there's no one recipe for love. Some people fall fast, others take a long time. Some do okay with time apart, and other folks like every minute together. Two people in love can make just about anything work. Y'all really only have one problem, as far as I can tell."

"What's that?"

As sympathy fills her face, he knows he's not going to like what she's about to say, but she'll tell him anyway. "As much as you care about Georgina, she's got doubts about love. And I think you do, too," she adds gently. "And that's what will break y'all apart in the end. Love comes with risks."

He forces himself to nod. He guessed right—he didn't like hearing that very much—but he knows she's right.

"Just do what Melody did for you," she adds. "Keep praying."

18

"Please help me tomorrow . . ."

That's the last thing Georgina remembers praying before she finally fell asleep in her neglected apartment after she had finished the drive to Nashville with Poppy and Savannah. It was the tossing-and-turning kind of sleep you have in an unfamiliar place, but she's still grateful for it as her alarm chimes in her ear.

She groggily quiets it, then stares at the too-bright phone screen as her eyes adjust. She's been trying to read through some Psalms in the mornings, but a text message captures her attention first.

This isn't what I want.

Georgina's tired body stiffens as she reads Lance's latest message. He sent it at five o'clock in the morning—probably before he went for a run.

She tosses the phone aside and gets ready for the surreal day ahead. She and Savannah are going to Poppy's house for officially-breaking-up-with-Lance mimosas. Savannah found a recipe and renamed it for the occasion.

Georgina's Sweet Revenge: Three freshly squeezed blood oranges, a bottle of prosecco, and plenty of ice.

"This playlist is straight fire, Poppy," Savannah says when

they arrive an hour later. She bops her head along to the remixed version of "I Will Survive" blaring in Poppy's kitchen.

"Thank you!" Poppy says with vindication. "Jared doesn't appreciate my fine musical tastes." She sways around the room, which is cute and hilarious since her belly looks like a little watermelon now, even in a billowy sundress. And Olivia's corresponding dance moves only make it better. She moves like Elaine from *Seinfeld*, but with even more passion.

"I made it just for you," Poppy adds, throwing Georgina a celebratory smile.

Georgina returns it and finishes sliding on her strappy Gucci heels. It is a good breakup playlist—full of Shania Twain and Carrie Underwood, with a dash of Adele—but it doesn't make Georgina feel any more prepared for her meeting with Lance. Her heart has been racing since the moment she woke up.

"'It took all the strength I had not to fall apart,'" Poppy croons, holding her champagne flute of orange juice. "'Kept trying hard to mend the pieces of my broken heart—'"

"We should go out tonight!" Savannah exclaims excitedly, but Georgina firmly shakes her head.

"No. I want tacos and an early bedtime. That's it. It's a non-negotiable."

Savannah frowns, but thankfully she lets it go. They have to get back on the road first thing tomorrow morning and hammer out the next two weeks before the Seelys arrive for the big reveal. Georgina's stomach churns every time she thinks about it. The cottage doesn't have all the fancy amenities the Seelys wanted, but it's turning out better than she ever imagined.

"Well, you should at least dance on a table or something," Savannah suggests, finishing off her mimosa. "This is a big deal."

"I will if you hoist me up there," Poppy offers as Sav laughs. She lifts Olivia instead, who loves her view from the countertop while Savannah holds her steady.

"Don't celebrate yet," Georgina reminds them, her nerves rising. She's excited about finally being able to move on, but UpScale still has to decide if she's getting a show, and Lance is probably just as determined as she is.

"We should pray," Poppy suggests, surprising everyone, but they take her hands while Olivia wiggles to the middle of the circle and grins up at them before they close their eyes. "God, please help Georgina today. Let her walk out happy and free. Help UpScale make the right decision. Help Lance to deal with whatever he needs to deal with. . . ."

Georgina smiles as Poppy forces out that last request.

"Thanks for loving us," she adds softly, her hand tightening over Georgina's. "We love you, too. Amen."

Georgina smiles gratefully as they cheer her out the door, steeled by the precious prayer. As she drives toward downtown Nashville, it slowly sinks in that this random sunny Tuesday in July will change the trajectory of her career—and life—forever.

As she passes a beautiful old church with boards on the windows, she's reminded of the sermon she heard on Sunday. Her first impulse was to resist when Savannah asked her to go with her and Lila. It hadn't felt right after years of listening to her mother complain about all the hypocrites who go to church, but Savannah's hopeful face made her realize she's a hypocrite, too. She falls short of her own standards all the time, let alone God's, so that made it a little easier to sit and listen with minimal squirming, even when the pastor's words struck an uncomfortable chord in her heart.

That's what I do, isn't it? she'd thought silently when he started talking about asking God for Band-Aids. She yells for help when she feels desperate, but otherwise she clings to her own plans for the future and prays nothing gets in the way. That humbling realization made her feel light and heavy at the same time.

When she enters a conference room inside the courthouse moments later, Lance is already there, and his dark eyes feel like a blazing spotlight as she sits down across from him. Her heart thuds as his expression turns sorrowful.

"Hi," he says quietly.

Georgina nods, but she swiftly turns her face away to look at Talia instead, unprepared for the tidal wave of emotions his presence stirred up. He looks fit and tan in an Armani suit, but his face is almost unrecognizable as it fills with regret. She's more used to his confident smiles.

"Good morning, Miss Havoc. How are you?"

Georgina's head snaps in the direction of the infamous Mr. Malonetti, and she greets him with another nod. She met him at Lance's birthday party two years ago, when he was tipsy and cheerful, but today he looks sharp and serious.

Talia and Malonetti straighten as the arbiter—Ryan something—takes his place, along with an emotionless UpScale representative and the middle-aged secretary who can't keep her eyes off Lance.

Talia came prepared, so the first hour is uneventful as they finalize the statement she proposed and revise the NDA. Once that's signed, they can finally publicize the breakup, but other subjects are forbidden, like sex, finances, family members, health-related issues, and basically anything and everything Talia and Malonetti could think of that might endanger their reputations. It's a wildly uncomfortable conversation, especially since Georgina can feel Lance's eyes drift to her more than once, but she doesn't look up from the papers in front of her.

"*The breakup announcement is going to be insane in terms of publicity,*" Annette had explained yesterday, walking Georgina through what to expect. "*And you know Lance is going to capitalize on it, so we will, too.*"

Georgina had hidden a frown. The businesslike statement was sad but true.

"And he's going to try to make you look like the bad guy, so we have to be ready for that, too. The next few weeks will get ugly. . . ."

"That covers the statement, and the revised terms," Ryan announces, bringing her back to the tense present. He seems to be in a hurry because he's discreetly glanced at his watch more than once. "Let's move on to the partnerships." He passes out more papers, even though they're already swimming in them. "These companies are still interested in retaining you as separate entities, so we just need to split them up—"

"Georgina can have whatever she wants," Lance interjects, causing a stunned silence.

Talia's brows raise as Malonetti's eyes dart to Lance, but he's still focused on Georgina. She finally looks at him.

"You mean she can have the ones we talked about," Malonetti suggests nervously, but Lance waves his words away.

"No," he says tersely. "Let her have them. It doesn't matter."

Talia's knee knocks against Georgina's underneath the table.

"Can we take a quick break?" Malonetti throws a pleading look to Ryan. "It's almost lunch—"

"We don't need one," Talia counters sweetly. "Since we're nearly done."

"We *are* done," Lance says, letting out a frustrated sigh. "I'm serious." He looks at Ryan, too, who looks as surprised as everyone else. "Just give her what she wants."

He frowns at the resolved look on Lance's face. "I guess we are done, then." The room falls silent as he scrawls something on the paper in front of him. Malonetti looks tempted to snatch it away. "Miss Havoc gets the partnerships outlined here . . ." He keeps talking, but Georgina can't hear him anymore. She throws Lance a questioning look.

"I'm sorry," he mouths.

"Georgina!" Talia whisper-screams a few minutes later when they're alone in an empty hallway. "What just happened back there?"

"I have no idea." Georgina's still reeling, too—partly from the outcome, and partly from the heartbroken look on Lance's face. The strange combination makes her stomach hurt.

"Get some air," Talia suggests, reading the discomfort on her face. "And celebrate, babe." A triumphant smile breaks across her face. "I don't think it could've worked out any better for you."

Georgina thanks her with a hug and takes her advice by circling the building. The walking helps a little, but her discomfort lingers as she sits down on the courthouse steps and slips off her fabulous shoes. The heavy feeling in her heart lifts a little as a cool breeze touches her skin, and she closes her eyes to pray, but a familiar voice interrupts her.

"Can we talk now?"

Her eyes fly open. Lance is standing at the bottom of the steps.

"Those are new," he says, nodding at her shoes.

She doesn't respond.

"You look great," he adds.

She stares at him in disbelief. "Are you being serious right now? You want to make small talk?"

He looks surprised for a moment, then properly embarrassed. Finally. "I'm sorry. I just . . ." He sighs. "I screwed up, Georgina."

Her mouth falls open. "You can't just now be realizing this?"

"Of course not! I've been trying to talk to you for weeks."

"Right, except there was a whole month that went by where you didn't talk to me at all, remember?" Her anger simmers hotter than ever as she relives his rejection all over again. "Right after I told you about the baby? Remember, Lance? Because I remember. It was kind of devastating, believe it or not."

"I was sad about that, too."

The sincere look on his face silences her.

"I just didn't know how to deal with it," he continues, hanging his head. His dark hair swishes as he lifts it again. "My emotions were all over the place, and I didn't want you to see me like that. Since you were already going through your stuff—"

"No," she hisses. "Don't."

"Don't what?"

"Don't act like you cared about me."

His brows rise at her sharp tone, but she doesn't soften it. "You don't run away from the people you care about."

"I wasn't running away, G. I just . . . I can't make you understand, okay?" He sighs heavily. "Look, I don't expect anything from you, okay? I mean that. I just wanted to say I'm sorry. And that I did love you, and I still do—"

"How was your trip?" she interjects coldly, unwilling to listen to his monologue any longer. "To the Philippines, right?" It's supposed to be a reminder that he left the country at a time when she needed him most, but his defiant eyes lock with hers.

"It was good. How was Tarragon?"

Her eyes narrow as she catches the accusation in his voice. *You ran away, too.*

She doesn't answer.

"I did a meditation retreat in Manila," he explains when the silence lingers for too long. His eyes darken at the suspicious look on her face. "I know it was weird and kind of random, but I was desperate."

She frowns at that new revelation—if it's even true.

"I was trying to clear my head, and it was too hard to do that here. Everything reminded me of you and how much I screwed up—"

"Did you learn anything?" she asks sarcastically. "From your little *Eat, Pray, Love* experience?"

"Yeah, I learned a lot, actually. Mostly that I'm an idiot." His eyes turn pleading as he waits for her to speak again, but she doesn't, so he lifts his hands in surrender. "I get it, G. I'll leave you alone. That's all I needed to say."

"That's *all* you were doing that whole time? Meditating?"

"No," he finally admits as her eyes narrow. "I had work stuff, too. I just hate that we have to compete with each other," he adds. "I want you to get your dream, Georgina. You deserve it."

Georgina's stomach twists at the strange way he says it—like he means it, but also with a hint of pity.

"Regardless of what happens, you're amazing—"

"Is that why you didn't fight today?" She cuts him off as her panicked feelings rise. "You think it's a done deal?"

"What? Of course not." He shakes his head, but he looks a lot less rattled than she does. "I honestly don't care about that stuff anymore." His eyes shine as they meet hers. "I already lost the only thing I really want."

19

Gavin finally looks up from his phone when Cassidy honks.

"Can we stop at Ground Up real quick?" he asks, hurrying from the Harp House porch to Cassidy's truck.

"We don't have time, Gav." Cassidy glances at the clock. "They have coffee there—"

"Terrible coffee."

"That's all part of the experience."

Gavin grimaces. A sweet old lady named Cheryl Dunnard runs the coffee table at the local Alcoholics Anonymous meeting, and apparently it's not up to his standards. But he's extra snappish without his caffeine, so Cassidy relents and lets him run inside the Ground Up Café to order his fancy espresso steamer thing. An UpScale van passes by as he waits—a sight most Tarragonians have gotten used to by now—but a few folks still stop and stare.

Cassidy frowns as it glides by. He knows Georgina and Savannah drove back from Nashville yesterday—and that Poppy's cheerful presence is already missed at the Harp House—but he hasn't heard from Georgina yet. He texted her last night asking how the big meeting with her ex went, but for once she didn't immediately write back.

Gavin returns in record time with a to-go cup in each hand. "I got some real creamer for all those poor, unfortunate souls who are gonna drink Cheryl's coffee," he explains, plopping one cup in the cupholder.

Cassidy smiles. Hospitality runs in the Harp bloodstream.

They make it to the meeting with one minute to spare, and Cassidy signs them in while Gavin arranges the creamer by the coffee, to the delight of everyone except Cheryl. He doesn't typically come to meetings with Cassidy—he rarely even drinks—but he's getting more sentimental as Cassidy's last day at the Harp House approaches.

As usual, it's a mix of men and women, young and old, rich people and poor folks, but everyone looks relatively comfortable, thanks to Boggs's easygoing style. Eddy is there, too, with a Bible open on his lap.

Cassidy never imagined he'd actually enjoy AA meetings, especially since people get talking about some pretty tough topics—drugged-up parents, cruel spouses, random accidents, lost jobs, the list goes on—but he's found that an hour of brutal honesty is strangely healing for the soul even if he feels exhausted afterward.

"Hello, gentlemen," Lila says when they pass by, but her eyes linger on Gavin as he smiles shyly.

"Hey, Lila."

She's not an alcoholic, either, but Julie's dad is, so she uses her firsthand experience to mentor some of the ladies.

"You want some coffee?" Gavin asks her, pushing through his usual nervousness. Cassidy shoots him a proud look as she happily follows him to the table, and then he takes his usual seat next to Eddy.

"How goes it?" Eddy mumbles, his eyes still on his Bible.

"All right."

"You going to the Cornbread Festival tomorrow?"

"What do you think?"

Eddy's mouth curves up.

Goldie wouldn't let him miss it for anything, especially with him leaving soon. And she roped him into judging the controversial pie contest, so his presence is even more important now.

"Did you get your lady troubles sorted out yet?"

"Working on it—"

"Do it before you go, Cass," Eddy says sternly before turning to the Bible again. "Last thing you need is a soap opera at home when you're in the middle of a mission."

"I said I'm working on—"

Boggs signals for everyone to take their seats. "Y'all ready to join us over here?" he asks with a smile aimed at Gavin and Lila, who are laughing like it's happy hour.

Cassidy's phone buzzes as they make their way over.

Poor girl. I'm praying for her.

Disappointment fills him. It's a text from Renata, not Georgina. But the picture is Georgina. He clicks on the link below it.

Georgina Havoc and Lance Broussard announced the end of their three-year relationship two days ago with a statement expressing their respect and admiration for one another. The news comes after the pair spent months apart, with Broussard overseas, while Havoc films in Tarragon, Tennessee. A source close to both claims the breakup came after a devastating miscarriage. Broussard took to Instagram to add that he hopes the pair can rekindle the relationship with time.

The words hit Cassidy like a punch to his gut. Georgina was pregnant? That new detail fills him with shock—and confusion. Why didn't she tell him? He's known enough couples to know losing a baby can rock any relationship, even solid ones. His discomfort grows as he studies the photo included in the article.

Georgina is sitting on stone steps, and the Lance guy is standing at the bottom with his foot resting a few steps above the ground—almost looks like he's down on one knee even though he's standing. His movie star face is hopeful. Georgina looks surprised.

Suddenly, Cassidy's phone buzzes again.

"No soldier gets entangled with civilian pursuits.
His aim is to please the One who enlisted him."
Look that one up.

Cassidy's eyes narrow over Eddy's text. Apparently, he's got a Bible verse for everything.

"Let's get this party started," Boggs says, passing out copies of the Serenity Prayer. Cassidy finally tears his eyes off his phone to skim the familiar words. "God, grant me the serenity to accept the things I cannot change . . ."

Eddy recites it next to him.

". . . accepting hardship as a pathway to peace. Taking, as Jesus did, this sinful world as it is, not as I would have it, trusting that You will make all things right if I surrender to your will . . ."

Cassidy tries to listen, but his mind is racing for answers. Georgina Havoc is driving him crazy in pretty much every way possible—crazy with frustration, crazy with desire, and crazy with doubts. She's also tempting him to do something he's never done in his entire life, which is slog through celebrity gossip to try to figure out what the heck is going on.

He almost reaches for his phone again but stops himself as it dawns on him that ever since that very first kiss, she's been trying everything she can think of to push him away—so maybe he should just let her.

20

"Brigitte absolutely killed it," Savannah cheers, peering over Georgina's shoulder to watch the video again.

Annette posted it to Georgina's Instagram a few minutes ago.

Georgina still can't form words. She's watched the video at least a dozen times already, but she can't stop. She's hiding her tears from Savannah, since a two-minute montage is such a silly thing to cry about, but Brigitte really did pull it together so beautifully.

"And Poppy's parts are *so* cute," Savannah says, plopping on the bed beside Georgina. "Has she seen it?"

Georgina nods, recalling Poppy's happy shrieking.

"*Georgie, if UpScale doesn't pick you after that, I'm going to die!*" Poppy had yelled as Jared hushed her in the background. "*That video is the most amazing thing I've ever seen in my entire life!*"

Brigitte chose mostly candid, strategic moments without showing off too much of the cottage—it still has to be a big reveal, regardless of if UpScale decides to turn the project into a special *Nail Breakers* reunion or the kickoff for *Georgina Rebuilds*—but she captured the essence of Georgina's time in Tarragon perfectly. Georgina sketching in the sunroom, Poppy picking colors, Sawyer grinning for the camera, Savannah painting with a focused frown, Cassidy tearing down walls. There's a part where he pauses long enough to smile across the room at Georgina, and it fills her with bittersweetness every time she watches it. There's another part, too—per Annette's request—of him shooting his gun in super slow motion that's so absurdly sexy Georgina had briefly reconsidered her gun aversion.

"Are you reading the comments?" Savannah asks, capturing her attention again. "People are losing their minds."

Georgina shakes her head. The comments are pouring in so fast she can't keep track anymore, but it only took a few minutes of scrolling before she realized why Annette was so adamant on the Cassidy cameo.

> oooooh yes
>
> I love this upgrade for Georgina!
>
> this man out here sniping hearts
>
> Get it, girl!
>
> That's the way to rebound . . .

In the last three days since she and Lance met in Nashville, Georgina's been bombarded by the press with questions about the breakup and the miscarriage, and it's been one of the worst feelings of her life. Her secret loss resulted in stunned, awkward calls from Benson and Annette, a weird mix of sympathy and irritation from UpScale, and endless speculations from random strangers on the internet.

Georgina tried to find the source of the leak, wondering if Savannah accidentally let it slip to Lila or Julie, or if Lance leaked it for some unknown reason, but, ultimately, it didn't matter. The damage was done—until Cassidy. His moments in the montage eclipsed it all in a matter of minutes.

Savannah gleefully reads the most ridiculous comments aloud until Georgina finally snatches the phone away.

"Oh, stop. I bet Cassidy thinks it's funny," Savannah says dismissively, but Georgina isn't so sure.

She finally texted him back yesterday after an insanely busy day at the cottage—they only have a little over a week to finish everything before the Seelys arrive—but now he's the one taking his sweet time writing back.

"Anyway, we need to get ready," she announces, tossing the phone aside to hold two dresses to her chest. "Which one?"

Savannah studies them. "It's a festival about cornbread, Georgie. Dial it down a notch."

Georgina frowns. Savannah is not the most fashionable person in the world, but she does have a point. Georgina searches for an alternate and finds a white top with doily edging and pairs it with jeans and white vintage cowboy boots. "What are you wearing?"

Savannah glances down at her rumpled attire—an oversized USA sweater over leggings. "Nope! Don't look at me like that," she says when Georgina's eyes turn hopeful. "I'm not one of your projects." She leaps from the bed.

"You can run, but you can't hide," Georgina whispers, dreaming of a makeover. Most people want their sisters to stay out of their clothes, but Georgina is the opposite. "At least let me do your makeup?"

"Fine, but I want the kind where it looks like I don't have any on."

"I'll take what I can get." Georgina fetches her makeup bag and makes a few careful selections. As she studies her sister's lightly freckled face, nostalgia hits her, along with gratitude. Savannah has talked her through the bad press over the last couple days and made her laugh whenever she felt like crying.

"Your phone's going off," Savannah mumbles, trying to keep her lips still as Georgina swipes her lashes with mascara.

Georgina glances at the phone and stiffens.

"What?"

"It's Mom."

Savannah groans. "Don't answer it!"

Georgina panics as she remembers her last conversation with their mother. Georgina had called her when she and Savannah were on their way back to Tarragon—she had to, since the news about her and Lance was about to be splashed on every magazine—and, unsurprisingly, her mother acted like she'd heard about a new world war. Georgina hasn't heard her cry that much in years.

"I just don't want to talk about Lance anymore."

"Then don't, Georgie. And don't feel bad about it," Savannah adds, looking up sternly through the mascara brush. "It's your life, not hers. Someday maybe she'll figure that out."

Georgina's uneasiness lingers as the call goes to voicemail, but the memory of her mother's words keeps her focused on her sister's face instead of the phone.

"*I just don't understand,*" her mother had sobbed when Georgina finally explained the pause and what followed. "*Why didn't you tell him about the baby?*"

Georgina had winced through most of the call. Her mother made it sound like it was entirely her fault. "*I'd only known about it for two weeks, Mom. It wasn't like this big secret I was keeping.*"

"*Well, what did you expect him to do when you dropped it on him like that?*"

Georgina's heart sank as she tried to form an answer. "*I . . .*" Her mother wasn't bothered about the baby at all, so Georgina knew she wouldn't understand.

"*You scared him away,*" her mother insisted.

Savannah listened to the whole exchange with darkened eyes.

"*You're making a big mistake, Georgina,*" her mother went on weepily. "*A huge mistake. You should fight for him. For your future together.*"

"*I don't need Lance.*"

"*It's not about needing him. It's about the fact that life is easier when you have someone to live it with. You two should work it out—*"

"*No, Mom.*" Georgina had tried to sound firm, but her mother steamrolled her for another ten minutes, reminding her of all of Lance's great qualities and why Georgina shouldn't be so hard on him.

"*It's just . . . over,*" Georgina finally said when she couldn't take it any more. Her mother's voice reached a panicked new volume as Georgina hung up on her.

"I love Mom," Savannah says, drawing her back to the present as Georgina finishes with the lightest shade of lipstick she can find. "But . . ." Savannah shrugs sadly. "She's just wrong sometimes. Let her cry over Lance if she really wants to," she adds with a torn expression, like she's sad for their mother but unmoved at the same time. "You don't have to."

Savannah must sense Georgina's lingering guilt because she lets her curl her hair and pick her outfit, too. Georgina takes the opportunity to wrestle her into a dress with an actual waist. Savannah's annoyance turns to shock as she looks in the mirror.

"Dang, okay . . ." She strikes a dramatic pose as Georgina laughs. "I'm kind of hot, aren't I?"

"Amazing what the absolute minimum can do."

Savannah throws a ruffly pillow at her.

It's off to Goldie's next to help transport caramel apples— apparently, there's over five hundred of them, so reinforcements were needed—but, to Georgina's dismay, Cassidy is the one who greets them on the porch.

"Hey," she says softly when his eyes meet hers. He's wearing her favorite green flannel, but for the first time maybe ever he doesn't look happy to see her.

"Hey," he says flatly.

Savannah glances between them. "Hey," she adds, throwing another awkward greeting in the mix.

"Where's Goldie?" Georgina asks, breaking up the tension. "Inside."

She and Savannah watch as he silently counts a row, then moves a box to another part of the porch. He seems to have some kind of complicated system going on. "She's still assembling," he adds.

Georgina glances through the open door. Her eyes widen. The entire entryway is full of boxes, too.

"Give me a second and I'll load your car," he says, still not looking up from his counting.

"No, we can do it." She lifts a box, then regrets it. All the apples shift, and a few topple over.

"No, trust me." He takes the box from her. "I've been doing this for years. There's a whole science to it. Plus, y'all look too nice for manual labor."

She smiles at the compliment, but his eyes drift away from hers.

"You can go in and see if she'll let you do anything."

They try, but Goldie's too frenzied to let them help as she dusts the last few apples with crushed candy bars, then spears them. "Please forgive the mess," she says, rushing around. "I was sorting a few things in the attic, but my timing was terrible."

Georgina's eyes move to the pile of random objects cluttering up the dining room table—delicate dishes, punch bowls, board games, and an array of military uniforms that were probably Clive's, given their faded colors. Cassidy taught her that the fancier-looking outfits are called "dress blues." Sadness hits her hard as she's reminded of his departure, but Goldie's frazzled voice recaptures her attention.

"Thank you again for your help with the contest tonight, honey. It's a new thing we're trying out, and it's not nearly as organized as it should be—"

Georgina blinks, confused for a moment, until she suddenly remembers the pie contest she agreed to judge last week. "Of course." A pile of pies isn't included in her diet, but she'll do anything for Goldie.

"I'll be right behind you," Cassidy says, expertly avoiding her eyes again when she and Savannah head back toward her car, which is now full of tightly packed boxes.

"Well, that was a wee bit tense," she says, throwing Georgina a curious glance once they're safely sealed inside the Lexus again, but Georgina is too wrapped up in her disappointment to respond.

As Georgina reverses down the driveway, Savannah's eyes move between her and Cassidy, who's watching from the porch. Suddenly, Savannah makes a startled sound. "You're, like, totally in love with each other, aren't you?"

The Lexus bounces over a bump as Georgina presses the gas pedal too hard, but, amazingly, none of the boxes move. "What? No—"

"Yeah, you are. It's like . . . palpable. I literally felt it. That's what was so weird. It's like your feelings for each other take up actual physical space. Like, there's pink smoke and petals floating around you or something." Savannah continues in her weird Savannah way as Georgina's embarrassment grows.

"What are you even talking about, Savannah? He was acting like he hates me."

"No he wasn't."

"Yes he was," Georgina snaps. "But I don't even care. It's actually better that way." She wills her heart to believe her words, but her mind still races for an explanation for his sudden distance that won't turn her into a blubbering mess.

"Why you'd end it, Georgie?" Savannah finally asks after a long silence passes. "Just because of the leaving-for-another-country part?"

"Um, yeah? That's a pretty big part. And then there's the living-in-constant-danger part. And the we-have-nothing-in-common part. Can you imagine Cassidy in Nashville, Savannah? With my friends? He would hate it."

"Your friends are pretty terrible."

Georgina throws her a fiery look.

"I'm kidding. I get what you're saying." Savannah thinks for a long moment. "But doesn't it just depend on how much you care about each other?"

"No." Georgina sighs miserably. "He's going to be doing crazy stuff, we'll never see each other, he could literally die . . ." Just the sheer thought of that possibility makes Georgina's breath catch in her throat. "And if he doesn't go, it'll throw off his whole dream, and probably mine, too, and then what if it doesn't even work out? It's just way too risky. For both of us."

Savannah looks unconvinced as they pull into the festival parking, but Cassidy takes the empty spot next to theirs a few minutes later, so Georgina throws her a pleading look.

"Just let it go, okay? That's what I'm doing."

Savannah scowls but dutifully shuts up, and they get out of the car and wait for further instruction. Georgina can hear Cassidy rounding up troops on his phone before he starts unloading the boxes. Goldie tries to lift one while they wait for more help, but Georgina stops her.

"I got this, Goldie," she says, taking it from her. "I do Pilates all the time," she adds with a quick flex, which makes Goldie laugh.

"All right, fine. I'll let you baby me, too."

Savannah helps Goldie up the grassy slope toward the festival entrance while Georgina walks after them, trying to keep all the apples upright. Cassidy falls in step next to her with a box of his own.

"Thanks for helping her," he says with a small but grateful smile. "She stays up all night making 'em, and then she wants to carry 'em, too."

Georgina smiles weakly. "She's a very determined lady."

"Yeah, something like that. . . ."

She waits, her heart picking up its pace as he looks like he wants to say something else—maybe something to melt away his previous coldness—but he doesn't, and they go their separate ways when they reach the food stalls. Georgina tries to focus on helping Goldie carefully space each apple on the tables, but her mind fixates on the unfamiliar distance Cassidy is putting between them. She thought he would be happy to see her now that she's officially rid of Lance, but apparently she was wrong.

"What's the matter?" Savannah asks, breaking away from a conversation with Lila and Gavin. "Your face is all tight—"

"Nothing," Georgina says quickly, pretending to be engrossed by her surroundings, which is easy enough to do. She's been to the statewide Cornbread Festival plenty of times, but Tarragon's tiny one has a cuter, cozier feel.

"I'm going to explore a little," she says, hurrying off before Savannah can press her. She quickly passes by fried tomato stalls, woodworkers, funnel cake trucks, and a bow-tied banjo player. The First Baptist Church provides a perfect, picturesque backdrop, with its white bricks and crisp black doors and pops of color from quilts swaying in the evening breeze. Carnival rides blink and twinkle in the distance, and rows of cornbread samples, flavored honeys, and fudge squares line a sea of checkered tablecloths. It's a perfect scene, but the memory of Cassidy's stormy eyes casts a shadow over all of it.

She slows down by an old pallet arranged with beautiful handmade crosses. Her eyes linger on one of the simpler ones—just wood and metal with a sprig of lavender. It would be perfect in the cottage.

"Oh my gosh, there she is!"

Georgina's eyes dart from the cross to the crowd as a gaggle of women rushes toward her. Georgina's never seen so much flowing hair or spray tans in her life.

"I love your show," one of them shrieks, reaching her first. She's curly-haired and petite, and a satiny sash stretches against her baby bump. "When Cassidy told me you made my cake, I just about died," she adds excitedly. Georgina suddenly recognizes her from the baby shower—Emmeline.

"Oh, right. Hi." Georgina forces a smile as the mother-to-be beams back at her. She seems sweet, but more pageant queens are closing in, and the presence of so many bright smiles and mingling perfumes is overwhelming.

"Can we get a quick picture?" Emmeline asks hopefully. When Georgina nods reluctantly, she hands her phone over to Miss Cumberland County, who diligently works on finding the perfect angle. Suddenly, Georgina hears a familiar name in the fray.

"You need to whip that man into shape, Renata. He's such a mess."

Georgina stiffens as Renata's laughter fills the air.

"You like the messy ones, though," the voice adds teasingly as Renata giggles harder.

Georgina keeps her smile plastered on as Miss Cumberland finally finishes snapping photos—she must have given Emmeline at least thirty to choose from—but Georgina's mood darkens as Renata and her friend chatter on about Cassidy. She's about to escape and find Savannah again, but Renata's light voice stops her.

"I just wanted to say, I think it was *so* clever of you to use Cassidy for your show," she says, pretending not to notice the surprised look on Georgina's face. "He probably doesn't even realize it," she adds. "I was just telling Lauren that maybe you and Lance planned this whole thing as a big publicity stunt." She throws her a knowing look. "No judgment, though. I get that you have to stay relevant."

Georgina's eyes narrow. She's heard about the cutthroat cattiness in pageant circles before, but Renata takes it to another level.

"That's a really interesting theory, but, thankfully, not everything is fake." She forces a sweet smile of her own. "I can see why you might have a hard time believing that, though."

A brief stare-down follows as Renata's sweetness fades, but Georgina lets her win and books it out of there. She probably looks like a crazy person zooming through the festival, but she wants as much space between her and Renata's posse as possible.

"Ouch," she yelps, bumping into the corner of a picnic table hard enough that she almost falls backward. A strong hand catches her arm and steadies her. Her embarrassment flames as she realizes it's Cassidy.

"You good?" he asks, his eyes widening.

"Yes," she says quickly, rubbing the sore spot on her hip. "Thanks." She wants to run all over again, but she makes herself face him. A loaded silence follows as their eyes meet. She lets out a frustrated sigh when he doesn't break it. "Well, I guess I'll see you later—"

He catches her hand.

"What, Cassidy?" she snaps, irritated by the conflicted look on his face. "Do you want to talk to me or not?"

He throws her a frustrated look of his own, but he doesn't let her go. "For the first time in my life, I don't know what I want, thanks to you."

She scowls to hide her hurt. She's not entirely sure what he means, but it sounds like regret. He probably regrets meeting her, but he's just too nice to ever say that out loud. A terrible thought crosses her mind as she remembers Renata's accusation. Does he think that, too?

She pulls away when he pulls her closer, still in the habit of hiding in public.

"You don't know what you want, either," he mutters, letting her go.

Her heart sinks. "Yes, I do—"

"Y'all ready for the pie contest?"

They both turn sharply at the sound of Goldie's happy voice behind them. "Yes," they say in unison, surprising each other.

"I'm judging it," Georgina says, throwing him a questioning look.

"*I'm* judging it," he says.

"You're both judging it," Goldie explains.

Georgina and Cassidy exchange glances and try to keep their mutual frustration under the surface for Goldie's sake.

"Let's get y'all set up at the table," she says, beckoning them to a bunting-covered stage. Georgina's stomach churns as Cassidy takes the seat beside hers. A small crowd is already starting to form in front of them.

"How was Nashville?" he asks, keeping his voice low as more people gather around.

"Good, like I already told you. Lance and I worked it out," she mutters, remembering the text update she sent that he never responded to. She frowns as his eyes search hers. "What? Why are you looking at me like that?"

"Y'all are really over?"

271

Surprise fills her. And anger. "Cassidy, if you ask me that one more time, I'm going to—"

"I saw a picture," he grumbles, cutting her off. "And it didn't look that over."

Shock washes over her as she realizes what he's talking about. She saw the same stupid picture a million times before Brigitte's video finally drowned it out. As she meets his troubled gaze, his eyes tell her there's more. He knows about the miscarriage, too. Her stomach sinks. She had wanted to talk about that in person.

"Why didn't you tell me what was really going on, Georgina? With the baby—"

"The NDA," she hisses, flustered. And embarrassed.

"That's the real reason?"

Her irritation shifts to hurt. "You don't trust me at all, do you?"

"Do you trust *me*?" he counters, his own face darkening. "Because it sure doesn't seem like it—"

"Ladies and gentlemen!"

Georgina jumps when a man in a massive cowboy hat yells into an ancient megaphone.

"I'm pleased to announce that we've got two very highly qualified judges for our first ever First Baptist Pie Contest this evening. All the way from Nashville, please welcome Miss Georgina Havoc, a real-life television star—"

She smiles weakly at the strange introduction and the smattering of applause that follows.

"And Cassidy Stokes, a beloved Tarragonian and war hero—"

"Why do you even care?" she demands in a whisper as his applause eclipses hers. "Soon we'll both be gone, and you won't have me around wrecking your life anymore."

The announcer drowns her out with the rules—entries are anonymous, they get forty seconds to chew, thirty to score, no signals from the audience—but Cassidy's face suggests he sees right through her sarcasm.

"You know why I care," he mutters back as her heart races.

"First up, we've got one of my personal favorites, the classic chess pie," the megaphone man booms again, and Goldie places two huge slices of pie in front of them, along with forks and two glasses of milk. "And, folks, just a little reminder, this contest is totally anonymous, so don't y'all go giving anything away, you hear?"

"Actually, never mind. I was wrong earlier," Cassidy says, cutting into his slice with more force than necessary. "I do know what I want. But I'm trying to let you decide what you want."

Georgina reaches shakily for her fork. *Do not cry into a pie, Georgina Havoc*, she commands herself, avoiding his eyes as she takes a bite and chews. The sincerity in his voice hurts. And her mother's chess pie is *way* better than this one, which reminds her of that maddening conversation about Lance all over again.

"You should fight for him, Georgina. For your future."

Why? Georgina demands, taking a bite out of a too-soft slice of cinnamon apple pie next. Why should she? What did all her mother's fighting do in the end?

"I'd quit the job tomorrow if I thought that would be enough," Cassidy adds, barely moving his mouth. They both force smiles when someone snaps their picture. "But I don't think it is. You have to trust me if this is going to work, and you don't."

He waits for a response, but she can't deny what he's saying, so she stays silent. Distance and danger or not, she's terrified of the way he makes her feel—like she needs him. Lance made her feel that way, too, but it's even stronger with Cassidy.

"Georgina," he says again, more gently this time as his hand moves toward hers, but she pulls it away.

"Not here," she snaps, throwing him a desperate look. His

touch is overwhelming enough without fifty strangers watching. "Not now."

Her heart sinks at the defeated look on his face.

"You worry too much," he mutters as she reaches for the next pie and nearly knocks his milk over in the process. He catches it just in time.

"And you don't worry enough," she snaps softly.

"You're trying to plan everything down to the last little detail, and you can't—"

She hurries through the rest of the contest, eager to escape her warring feelings. The pies blur together. There are a few clear standouts, like the peanut butter and a blackberry custard that holds up impressively despite the heat, but the clear winner is a simple golden-hued peach pie. The cream part is melting by the time she and Cassidy get to it, but she knows it's the winner because she wants to keep eating it, despite the fact that she never wants to see another pie again in her life.

She gulps what's left of the milk before handing the megaphone man her scorecard. She tries to listen as he reads, but Cassidy's voice fills her ear.

"You're just scared. You think I'm gonna break your heart, so you want to break mine first—"

"Whew, folks, it got real close there toward the end, but our judges agree," the man booms. "The winner is . . ."

A few people drum their hands dramatically on the picnic table. Georgina's heart drums, too, but for different reasons.

"You can't be mad at me," she finally whispers, avoiding his eyes. "I'm doing what's best for both of us—"

"I'm not mad at you," he whispers back. "I just want you to trust God—"

"Why are you bringing God into this right now?" she hisses, surprising them both with her sharp tone, but he doesn't back down.

"Because God is part of it, whether you like it or not. And if you believed that, you wouldn't be so scared."

She scowls at the sincere, stubborn look on his face. Cassidy Stokes has made her life infinitely more difficult with his deep questions and the even deeper feelings he stirs within her, and sometimes she still yearns for the safe, familiar shallows.

"Southern fried peaches and cream pie!" the megaphone man shouts, breaking through their conversation as applause erupts. "Let's see here, that one was submitted by participant number eleven, who I'm sure y'all want to congratulate in just a moment here." His eyes quickly scan another piece of paper that matches the pies to participants. "Oh, well, here's a plot twist, folks! Participant number eleven wants to stay anonymous, but they did request that the prize money be donated back to the church. Ain't that nice?"

There's another polite round of applause, but Georgina sees a few sour faces, too. First Baptist Tarragonians take their pies seriously.

"Let's thank our judges one more time. . . ."

Georgina stands up to take a small bouquet of yellow roses from Goldie, while Cassidy gets a motherly kiss on the cheek.

"Now y'all go have some pie!"

As people converge on the tables, Georgina takes the opportunity to slip away before Cassidy can stop her, ignoring the growing weight in her heart as she searches for the Lexus in a sea of cars and trucks. When she finally reaches it, she sighs in relief, but her abandoned phone glows with a dozen missed calls from Brigitte.

"What is it?" she asks frantically when Brigitte picks up on the first ring.

There's a short, tense silence.

"What, Brigitte? Why are you—"

"Lance is in Tarragon."

275

21

Georgina nearly drops the phone. "He must be losing his mind."

"Do you want me to send Nathan over?" Brigitte asks, her voice turning tense.

Georgina's unsettled, too, thanks to a bizarre recording of Lance pacing on the porch of the cottage. Nathan set up a cheap outdoor camera in case anyone took an interest in any of their equipment, but apparently ex-boyfriends are more of an issue.

"Or I could call Cassidy?" Brigitte offers.

"No," Georgina says sharply, putting her on speakerphone before hitting the gas pedal. The last thing she wants is Cassidy getting involved. His suspicion stings all over again. "Don't tell anyone," she says firmly, flying toward the cottage. "I'll handle it."

"Okay . . ." Brigitte still sounds worried, but she understands the risk of making a big scene. "Call me after."

When Georgina hangs up moments later, she tries to calm down. Part of her still can't believe Lance is actually in Tarragon, but it's true.

where are you??

Georgina dictates a response to Savannah's question as she drives.

Migraine. Sorry. Ride with Lila?

She feels bad about the lie, but she can't afford Savannah freaking out, which she'll almost certainly do if she knows Lance is camped out at the cottage.

She arrives minutes later and parks next to his Audi, then stomps toward the steps where he's sitting. His face brightens as he rises to greet her, but it fades when he sees the look on hers.

"Georgina—"

"Is this supposed to be some grand romantic gesture?" she snaps, her eyes narrowing at the flowers in his hand. "Because it's more of a crazy stalker vibe."

"I had to talk to you."

"Lance." She groans in exasperation as he drops the flowers. "We already talked."

"I want to talk about the miscarriage."

Her eyes widen. She wasn't expecting to revisit that topic, given how much he's avoided it so far.

"I didn't leak it to the press. I swear," he continues, his voice turning more desperate. "I would never do that to you."

"I didn't think you did."

Now he's the one who looks surprised. "You didn't?"

"No? Why would you? It makes you look terrible."

More shock flickers across his face.

"'Lance Broussard flees to a tropical island and leaves devastated Georgina Havoc in her hour of need.'" She mimics a robotic reporter voice. "It's not a great look for you."

His eyes flash defensively. "Or maybe Lance Broussard just didn't want to dump his emotions on his already-traumatized girlfriend?"

277

Georgina throws him a skeptical look.

"Look, we don't have to get into it again," he says, throwing up his hands. "I wasn't there for you when I should've been. I said that already. But I want to be here now."

She frowns as his eyes turn earnest. "What do you mean? We're done, Lance. It's over."

"I'm just saying, I know it doesn't feel good to have your private life dissected by losers on the internet. It hurts. Especially on top of everything else."

Her guard drops a tiny bit. That is something he can sympathize with—the scrutiny. They've both been under a relentless microscope since the moment they met.

"Are you really okay, G?" he asks, sensing a crack in her cold exterior. "That's all I want to know."

"I'm fine," she lies, trying to seal her heart up again. As nice as it is to commiserate with someone, she reminds herself that Lance isn't the person to do that with anymore. "You should go—"

"I think this is some of your best work, by the way," he says quickly, shifting the subject to the cottage. "I was admiring it before you got here." He cups his hands against the glass and peers through the darkened window. "It feels very you."

"Thanks," she says warily, studying him just as closely as he's studying the house. "Poppy thought of the inspiration," she adds when the silence eventually gets too uncomfortable.

"What are you going to do with the porch, though?"

"What do you mean?"

"This is just the primer, right?"

"No?"

"Oh." He frowns down at the freshly painted wood. "The white is nice, but I thought maybe you were going to go with something bolder. It would make for a bigger transformation."

Annoyance pricks at her, but she doesn't respond.

"That was something I was looking forward to," he adds cautiously, tapping his tanned fingers against the porch railing. "Merging our styles. We were going to be unstoppable."

"Apparently not."

His eyes darken.

"You should go."

"I want us to work together, Georgina," he announces, drowning out her dismissal yet again. "I want *us* to rebuild."

Her eyes widen, but the rest of his pitch comes tumbling out of his mouth before she can respond.

"I know I acted like an idiot, okay? How many times can I say that? I got stereotypical cold feet. I lost it. I did run away, like you said. I'm sorry, babe. It was just the timing. . . ." His tone softens, but the desperation in his voice grows stronger. "I just wasn't ready for that, and I don't think you were, either."

She winces. He's still never used the word *baby*.

"I clearly had some inner work to do, and I just needed some space to do it. It wasn't you, G. It was me, but I've been growing. . . ."

Georgina swallows back a bitter taste and decides to mention God and her own "inner work," just to see where that conversation leads. Lance has never talked about faith much, other than in vague, catchall terms, but she decides to push through her hesitation and tell him what she's been thinking about ever since he left her reeling in a dark apartment two and a half months ago. She wonders if he's pondered any of the same things, but the uncomfortable look on his face answers her question.

"I think that's great," he says when her voice eventually trails off. "I think that stuff really helps some people. I'm happy for you."

His response is unsurprising—she would've said something similar before her time in Tarragon—but Cassidy's words suddenly come to mind.

"*Is what Jesus said true or not? Because it is or it isn't, right? There's no in between.*"

The memory sends her thoughts racing back to him, and she's reminded of how he and Lance are different in just about every way possible.

"I know I can't fix everything with one conversation, G," Lance continues, dragging her back to the present against her will. "I don't even know if I can fix it at all, but we have to try, right? We're too close . . ."

Uneasiness washes over her as he goes on, repainting the dream she was working toward for so long.

"I have to show you something."

Georgina waits stiffly as his fingers fly over his phone before he hands it to her. She studies the image on the screen.

"What's this?"

"Our next project."

Confusion fills her as she studies the grainy picture. It's an aging modern house on the outskirts of Manila with lots of glass and sharp, slanted lines. The landscaping is beautiful, too, with leafy palm trees and jewel-toned jade vines.

"UpScale is ready to go international, G. They're *finally* ready to take some risks."

Georgina's heart feels heavy as Lance's words sink in. They chose him?

"I don't want to do it without you, though."

As his dark, hopeful eyes meet hers, she considers his offer for one brief, weak moment. Her mother's pained voice comes to mind and reminds her how awful her life will be without him, or how many opportunities she'll miss if she doesn't take this one, but other voices speak up, too, and tell her that's not true. Poppy. Savannah. Cassidy. And God. God finally speaks in a way that cuts through what's left of her doubts.

"We need each other, G—"

"No," she says, forcing the word out as shock shadows Lance's face.

"No?"

She shakes her head as the weight lifts off her heart. "No. That's not my dream anymore."

22

A Rascal Flatts cover band blasts a love ballad while Cassidy searches for Georgina in the crowd at the Cornbread Festival. She's nowhere in sight, and she's not answering her phone, either, so he looks for Savannah instead, hoping she might be able to help.

A long row of booths is the only place left to search. He passes one for a local politician, another selling leftover fireworks, and one recruiting volunteers for Habitat for Humanity before his eyes finally fall on the First Baptists for Life display at the end of the row. That's Lila's passion project, but Savannah's the one manning the booth.

"Oh hey," she says, waving when she sees him. Thankfully, whatever grudge she used to have toward him seems to have faded. "How was the pie contest thingy?"

He smiles weakly. *A disaster.* "Good." He glances around. "Where's Lila?"

"With Gavin." She points at the twinkling Ferris wheel in the distance.

Cassidy looks up in disbelief. "Gavin is up there?"

She nods.

"He's afraid of heights."

"Not anymore. That's their third go-around," Savannah says with an amused smile.

He smiles, too, but his mind races back to Georgina. "Hey, you haven't seen Georgina around, have you?" He tries to keep his voice light, but Savannah's brows lift with surprise.

"No, she left. She said she had a migraine."

"Oh . . ." His mood falls as he realizes he was probably the cause. "Okay. Thanks." His mind is already darting to his next move, but a strong breeze blows some of Lila's flyers off the table. He manages to pin most of them down with his hand, but Savannah has to capture the rest.

"Shoot," she mutters, grabbing an armful of fluttering papers. "Let me get a rock or something."

While she searches around the booth, Cassidy's eyes drift over the pictures on the table—a smiling young mother, a sleeping toddler, a baby in the womb. The tiny baby is small and curled up tight, almost like it's protecting itself. He frowns. He could sense some of Georgina's pain under the surface ever since they met, but he didn't realize the depth of it until tonight when he mentioned the baby.

"Found one," Savannah says, returning to the table with a handful of pebbles-turned-paperweights. Cassidy lifts his hand as she secures the flyers again. "Thanks."

"Sure. I'll see you later—"

"Did you need her for something?" she asks, gently cutting him off. "I can try calling her."

"Uh . . ." He hesitates. It suddenly sinks in that even if Georgina were standing right in front of him, he still probably wouldn't know what to say to her—so he should probably figure that out first. "No, it's all right. Thanks, though. Have a good night."

"You too."

Cassidy catches the disappointment in Savannah's voice but

hurriedly moves through the festival toward the exit, ignoring familiar voices calling out his name.

Georgina takes slow, careful steps over broken branches and damp dirt, making her way toward the lake. When she had arrived a few minutes ago, she was alarmed by the heavy darkness, but she doesn't want to turn back yet. Her adrenaline is still going strong, the night air is cool, and her mind craves quiet.

Her cellphone flashlight is helpful, too, but it's draining the battery, which is already low, thanks to Lance. He had called her incessantly after she left him stunned and sputtering on the cottage porch and she finally blocked his number. But then Cassidy had called her, too, and Savannah, and Brigitte, until it was too much, so she set her phone to Do Not Disturb mode, not ready for more voices yet. There's only one voice she wants to hear right now.

Georgina slows down as she passes by a small, slanted cabin, suddenly recognizing it. She expects the door to be locked, but it isn't, so she steps inside and lifts her phone screen, illuminating the empty room as nostalgia wraps around her like a hug. The twin beds are gone now, along with everything else, but their doorframe fork carvings remain. Savannah's side is decorated with tiny musical notes and a million little S. S. initials, either for Sawyer Stokes, or Savannah Stokes, or maybe Sawyer and Savannah.

She heads to the aging dock next, and the wood sways over the water as she slowly steps onto it. The quiet stillness draws her closer until she's right on the edge. She tugs off her boots and socks, then sits down and lets her feet dangle in the cool water. And she finally breathes.

As much as she and Savannah griped about their father sending them off to Lake Chervil, it's unquestionably beautiful. The moon is so big and bright that she can finally turn off the flash-light and bask in the moonlight instead, which streams between the trees and spills out over the glasslike water. It's all shades of deep blue now—the sky, the water, even her reflection—but in the daylight, lush green trees contrast with sharp gray rocks. Georgina used to sit in this spot every chance she could get.

It doesn't take long for her mind to drift to the baby, and, for once, she lets it linger there. The baby is still the saddest part—the fact that she and Lance had a child together, a real-life person with a million little pieces from each of them, whether it was their eyes or their height or their personality—and he never cared like she did, and he never will.

Lance and the baby eventually fade, and her father's emotionless face comes next, surprising her. Her body tenses up, but she breathes deeper and lets her memories of him sink into the deep blue water. She thought she'd already forgiven him a long time ago when her life became so full that she barely thought of him anymore, but now she knows the forgiveness is real this time because her chest feels a thousand times lighter, like she could float on the water, or in the clouds, or both at the same time.

"Thank you," she murmurs gratefully. Now that she knows what this kind of forgiveness feels like, she understands why God cares about it so much. Conviction fills her as she realizes He's offered her this feeling countless times over the course of her life, and she's never accepted it until now.

"I'm sorry," she whispers, her voice breaking because she means it. She's sorry for running and hiding. She's sorry for rebelling. She's sorry for questioning the love of a God who dies for people who don't even love Him back. "You've been a good friend to me. You've been . . . a good father."

God has been moving toward her ever since that awful night in Nashville when she couldn't distract herself anymore. She was moving toward Him, too, but she had retreated again when Cassidy told her he was leaving. It had felt like God was closing yet another door, so she tried to close one on Him instead, but it dawns on her now that Cassidy was still a gift to her, even without the happy ending she wanted.

What has she been so afraid to let go of? Love, which she thought she lost in the form of Lance, but she was *so* wrong. Cassidy showed her that, too, because the idea of losing him hurts a million times worse. Her career was the next thing on the list, but the hopeful look on Lance's face jolted her out of that, too. It doesn't matter if she has all the success in the world if she doesn't have God.

"I do choose you," she whispers, finally deciding. "I can lose everything else, but I can't lose you." She understands the difference now—a life with God's gentle, relentless love and a life without it—and she can't go back. Her eyes move from the moon to the water, and she finally feels like jumping into the deep.

It takes an hour of driving around Tarragon, but Cassidy's thoughts finally start to slow down. "Talk to me," he mutters as the silence deepens. He makes himself wait, even though waiting is the last thing he wants to do when he still hasn't heard from Georgina. Worry gnaws at him as he surveys the darkness. Where else would she go?

"Please help her," he prays—his most frequent prayer these days. He's been praying it ever since that day on the farm.

He heads for Kit's cottage next, the only other place that comes to mind besides the Harp House, which he's already checked. "I love her," he says, finally admitting it.

Obviously, God already knew that, but Cassidy had wanted some kind of clear sign before he said the words out loud, since they fill him with a dread he hasn't felt since Melody. Love is the best and worst thing in the world. Love means you can have everything, but you also risk losing it. When that nightmare became his reality, his heart bled all over everything until he sealed it up tight, but now it feels uncomfortably exposed again.

His worries return when he arrives at the cottage and she's not there, either. He calls her, but it goes straight to voicemail.

He looks up helplessly at the blue-black sky. He's never gotten a clear answer about his feelings for her—no voice, no slammed door, no settled feeling in his gut one way or the other. Instead, he just felt the gentle nudge to keep praying and asking questions and showing her his own heart, piece by piece, with a cautious hope that she might love him, too.

"Help her trust me," he prays, until he realizes that's the wrong prayer. He exhales and finally lets go. "Help her trust you."

Suddenly, his phone pings in the silence. His hope rises as he reaches for it, but it's a text from Savannah.

heard anything?

> Not yet.

There's a long pause before Savannah's next message arrives.

maybe try the lake?

Cassidy frowns. The lake is one of the few places he hasn't tried yet, but it isn't that easy to get to in the daytime, let alone at night. Surely Georgina wouldn't go there by herself? He reverses out of Kit's driveway and heads in that direction, willing to go anywhere.

When he arrives at one of the wooded parking areas twenty minutes later, he doesn't see her car, but he gets out anyway. There are a couple ways to get to the lake, but he heads toward the campsite, since that's the part she'd be most familiar with. Thankfully, he's pretty familiar with it, too, since he and Sawyer spent most of their childhood either in the woods or water.

Memories return as mud slides under his boots and branches graze his arms, but his hope sinks when he sees the water shimmering in the distance. He squints at the darkened dock, but there's still no sign of Georgina. He almost turns around, but something propels him the rest of the way, and his footsteps echo against the wood as he steps over the water.

Suddenly, he sees a phone. And a pair of white cowboy boots.

"Cassidy?"

He turns in the direction of her voice, half-expecting he just imagined it—but he didn't. She's *in* the lake, with a stunned look of her own.

"Hi," she says as his eyes widen.

"What on earth are you doing?"

"Swimming."

His heart lifts, but his thoughts race between shock, relief, and the fact that she's breaking just about every water safety rule he can think of. He glances up at the night sky, then back at her. "Is now really the best time?"

Embarrassment flickers across her face. "Probably not. But it is pretty fun," she adds. Little waves rise and fall on the endless water as she keeps herself afloat. When their eyes meet again, she smiles up at his concerned expression. "If you knew the context, it would make more sense."

"What's the context?"

She opens her mouth but closes it again. "It's kind of hard to explain."

"Maybe just start with the part where you jumped in a lake with all your clothes on?"

She laughs. "Are you getting in, too?"

He raises an eyebrow at the invitation.

"Don't forget to take the gun out of your pants," she adds.

He snorts and pulls off his boots and socks, then undoes his belt and holster. Her eyes widen when he lifts off his shirt.

"Just take those off, too," she suggests when his jeans are the only thing left, with more than a hint of hopefulness.

He laughs and jumps in, shattering the smooth surface of the lake. The water is cold but exhilarating. It's up to his shoulders, but his feet still skim the bottom as he makes his way over.

"Hmm, well, you don't *look* like you're losing your mind," he says when they're finally face-to-face. She does look breathtakingly beautiful, though, with her wet hair and moonlit skin.

"Told you. How'd you find me out here, anyway?"

"Savannah thought you might be here. And I'd already looked everywhere else," he adds wearily.

When her eyes turn apologetic, he briefly forgets about the emotional roller coaster she just put him through.

"I was going to call you. I just . . ."

He waits, anxious for her to explain why they're both currently swimming in Lake Chervil in the middle of the night, but she hesitates again when his eyes search hers.

"That peach pie was totally your mom's, wasn't it?"

He smiles at the familiar deflection. "Yep."

Georgina smiles, too, but his fades as he recalls the moment she pushed his hand away from hers. As much as he'd like to stay in this light, happy moment, he knows there are deeper things going on under the surface, so he gently nudges her again.

"Are you finally going to tell me what inspired your midnight swim?"

"Yeah . . ." Her eyes drift upward, like she's searching for words that are just out of reach. "I think it was God."

More surprise fills him, but he waits for her to go on. Embarrassment colors her face again, but she pushes through it and tells him everything, starting with the baby and ending with her last muttered prayer for God to finally save her. She turns quiet again when tears start to fall.

"How do you keep your face like that all the time?" she demands when he doesn't immediately fill the silence.

"Like what?"

"All calm and normal while I'm spilling my guts out," she says tearily, wiping her wet face with her equally wet hands. "Most people would feel so awkward right now."

He smiles. "I'm just listening. And I'm happy for you," he adds with a hint of teasing.

She laughs and relief slowly fills her face, but it fades when Cassidy brings another unspoken subject to the surface.

She shushes him. "Don't."

"Don't what?"

"Don't talk about leaving," she pleads, reading his thoughts. "Let's pretend a little long—"

"Just let me finish, Georgina. Please."

She falls silent, but sorrow shadows her face and makes his heart race. He's almost certain she feels the same way he does—but that still might not be enough.

"If these were normal circumstances, I would say we can just walk away. You could have your life, I could have mine, we could see what happens. But nothing about you is normal."

His heart feels heavy as her laughter fills the air. It's a sound he wants to listen to for the rest of his life, like a favorite song on repeat.

"I have to go to El Salvador," he adds sadly when her eyes turn hopeful. "I made a commitment, and I gotta keep it." He prays she might finally understand, but the fear lingers in her face. "I know you don't like the danger, or the guns, or any of it, really, but it's what I was made to do, and I think you get that part. I see the same thing on your face when you're designing something. It's just part of you. And I love . . . that part of you."

A moment of heavy silence passes between them, but for once, she doesn't rush to fill it. She waits.

"And I love *you*," he adds, forcing the words out before the moment slips away.

"What did you just say?"

His heart thuds as her surprised eyes meet his. "You heard me."

A tiny gasp escapes her lips, and he doesn't know what to make of it.

"What kind of love?" she demands.

It's a strange, surprising question, but Cassidy knows exactly how to answer it. He's felt love before—real, once-in-a-lifetime love—and he's determined not to lose it again.

"The fireworks kind. The can't-sleep kind. The build-a-life-with-you kind."

Her breath catches in her throat.

"The happily-ever-after-meets-boring-regular-life kind. The forever kind. I want it all. With you."

Her eyes shine.

"And I know it doesn't look like what you wanted, but—"

"I love you, too."

Relief fills him until she lets out a tortured sigh.

"Ugh, I'm stupidly, overwhelmingly, happily in love with you," she adds, making him laugh. She shakes her head as he pulls her close. "You're wrecking all my plans, and I don't even care."

He smiles and lifts her chin. "We can make new plans."

As her hopeful eyes shine in the moonlight, he could stay like this for a long time—just memorizing her beautiful face—but she turns impatient.

"Kiss me already," she mutters as his lips lift into a smile. "I've been waiting for like five minutes."

He doesn't waste another moment of her time, and it's a kiss unlike any other because she finally trusts him. Wet hands, warm skin, cold water, desperate breaths—the love between them is like a steadying anchor, or the water itself, endless and wild, or some impossible combination of both.

23

Georgina pokes her head into the bedroom. "Savannah, can you please be done?"

Savannah doesn't stop painting.

"Savannah!" she yells louder, but Savannah still doesn't turn from the intricate magnolia blossom she's working on.

Georgina crosses the room and sees that she's got her Air-Pods in. Only when Georgina pokes her shoulder does she reluctantly takes one out.

"What? Stop rushing me—"

"Savannah, just stop. It looks fantastic, seriously. Ethereal. Whimsical. Stunning. Better than I ever imagined." Savannah rolls her eyes at her dramatic tone, but she means it. The bedroom is hands down the best room in the cottage because of Savannah's mural, which looks complete to everyone except for her.

"I'm almost done," she insists, grabbing another paintbrush as Georgina fights back a frustrated scream.

"Now is not the time for perfectionism." Her stomach churns as she glances at the time glowing on Savannah's phone. The Seelys are arriving in half an hour, and, as usual, everything is behind schedule. "I need your help with—"

"I can't not finish it, Georgie. Not when I'm this close. Like . . . I just can't. Go away."

Georgina sighs in exasperation, but she keeps her composure for Nathan's sake, who's trailing closer than ever, determined to capture every moment of stress. At her sister's current pace, she's still going to be stubbornly painting leafy veins and petals in the middle of Georgina's walk-through with the Seelys, but she doesn't have time to argue with her. She's also not thrilled that the room is going to smell like paint when they arrive—she's learned over the years that smells matter when it comes to the first impression—but hopefully Goldie's cookies will overpower it.

"We're clearing your stuff out in fifteen minutes."

"Fine, whatever," Savannah mutters, popping the AirPod back in, but Georgina senses a tiny increase in urgency. "Go freak out somewhere else while I finish."

Georgina adjusts the luxurious bedspread on her way out, but she nearly trips over Gavin Harp as she enters the living room. "Sorry," she exclaims, almost stepping on his hand, but he's too focused on wiping dusty baseboards with Lila to notice.

"I love you both," Georgina says, carefully stepping over Lila next. "You're my new best friends."

They pause long enough to smile, but they couldn't look any happier despite ending up with everyone's least favorite task. The cleaning is the worst part, thanks to the endless layers of dust that accumulate throughout the renovating and filming process, but it helps that Lila is the speediest cleaner Georgina has ever met, and she puts the UpScale crew to shame.

"Georgina, if it's okay with you, I'm going to go ahead and put these in the oven."

She swivels around at the sound of Goldie's gentle but antsy voice. "Let's wait just a little bit longer, okay?" She glances at the closest clock, trying to time it perfectly. "Two minutes."

"If you think so, honey."

Georgina smiles gratefully, glad that she doesn't have to worry about baking Poppy's orange-vanilla cookies on top of everything else. They became a signature on *Nail Breakers* after a few clients raved about the heavenly scent.

"Don't forget to breathe, dear," Goldie adds, frowning at the tense look on her face. "You've done a wonderful job in here."

Georgina thanks her, but she can't slow down yet, even though it feels like she's been running a marathon for the last week and a half. Lance's jarring arrival in Tarragon set off a chain reaction of events between the press and UpScale, but she's barely had time to think about any of that, too focused on this particular finish line.

This is the moment, she reminds herself when fatigue pulls at her. This is why she came to Tarragon in the first place—to build something new and beautiful—and it's almost time to reveal it. And contrary to what Lance suggested, she doesn't have any reason to give up now. According to Benson's birdies, she's still in the running.

"You're killing it, Tom," she says, passing by as he screws in outlet covers at an impressive pace.

He pauses from his diligent work to throw her a confused look. "Huh? Killing what?"

"Nothing, never mind. Keep going." She skims the room and reviews the list in her brain. The adorable kitchen is done, thank goodness—Goldie just has to clean up after the cookies. The lofted space is styled, too, and it looks like a childhood dream with colorful quilts, twinkly lights, and vintage posters pinned to the dark wood walls. "What's missing . . ."

"The coffee table," Julie answers, surprising her.

Georgina's eyes widen. Julie's right, and she has no idea how that massive, ornate piece of furniture slipped her mind. It's the living room statement piece.

"Cassidy is getting it now," Julie adds, sensing her panic.

Georgina looks at the clock again and tries to stay calm. They have sixteen minutes left, and they're ticking away. She forces herself to focus on something else. "Julie, can you scoot that just a tiny bit to the right before you hang it?"

Julie moves the wooden cross half an inch. "Like this?"

"Yes! Right there." She feels vindicated as Julie carefully nails it against the wall. Georgina and Cassidy had to scour Tarragon to find it after the festival, but it was worth the hunt. It's the perfect finishing touch centered between her and Poppy's nature-turned-art.

"That bookshelf looks phenomenal, by the way," she adds, admiring Julie's styling. "Just do that same spacing again with the little crystal decanters in the bathroom. You'll see them."

Julie nods soberly, like Georgina just tasked her with flying to the moon, but it does sort of feel that way as the pressure mounts and everyone picks up the pace. Georgina moves at lighting speed as she takes out trash and hides clutter, while Gavin and Lila move on from wiping the floors to polishing the rest of the surfaces until they shine. Georgina inhales deeply as the smell of citrus and vanilla hits her nose. It's coming together before her eyes—better than she ever imagined—but the coffee table is *still* missing. She's about to call Cassidy, but Brigitte interrupts her.

"It smells like paint in the bedroom," she announces, sniffing the air with a scowl as she frantically fluffs pillows. "Get flowers!" she barks.

Georgina races outside with a basket, thankful for Brigitte's brusque brilliance as she searches the garden for the most fragrant flowers she can find, plus a few sprigs of green. They finished the landscaping late last night, thanks to a dedicated band of Tarragonian teens Cassidy rounded up. The garden is still pretty wild—that felt like the right move, given the style of the house—but Georgina had picked out a few new beautyberry shrubs and a precious little picket fence to tidy it up. She prays the Seelys love it as much as she does.

There's less than ten minutes to go when Cassidy's truck finally rolls down the driveway. She leaps up, ready to direct him, but he's already on top of it. "Get Gav!" she hears him yell at Brigitte as he hops out of the truck and works on untying the coffee table. Georgina observes a little longer than necessary, torn between feeling bad that she picked the world's heaviest coffee table at an estate sale two days ago but also not feeling sad about the fact that hauling it around inspired him to strip down to his undershirt.

"Georgina!" Brigitte yells, getting her attention again.

She hurries to meet them on the porch, handing her basket of lilacs to Brigitte.

Cassidy's eyes light up when he sees her, but his frustration returns as he and Gavin struggle to get it through the door. "You didn't measure this, did you?"

"Yes, I did!" she says defensively. She actually measured twice, since it's a smaller-than-average door and a larger-than-average coffee table. "It fits."

Cassidy looks skeptical, but he tries every angle he can think of with Gavin working on the other side. When an exhausted breath escapes his lips, Georgina finally realizes the problem.

"Julie," she yells, peeking through the only little gap of space not currently blocked by the coffee table. "Grab the rug!" She winces as Julie darts over. "And please don't get crushed."

Julie shimmies a woven runner away from Gavin's feet, which provides the extra quarter of a centimeter needed for him and Cassidy to finally heave the table into the living room.

"The Seelys better buy that one," Cassidy pants once it's finally in its new home. "Because it's never leaving this house again."

Georgina smiles apologetically. She wants to reward his efforts with a kiss, but there's no time. And Nathan is poised to invade their privacy, per usual.

"What else is left?" Cassidy asks, finally recovered.

Georgina's mind races. "Um . . ."

Brigitte points to the bedroom with a panicked look.

"I'm done, I'm done," Savannah gripes, hurrying out with an armful of brushes and paint. Georgina wants to be annoyed, but Savannah's face is so bright that her irritation dissolves. She almost looks like a little girl again, delightedly showing their mother her latest creation, and she beckons Georgina to come see it.

Georgina's mouth falls open as she surveys the final result, with every last leaf and petal painted. Hints of gold shimmer in the sunlight, thanks to Julie. Georgina almost gets teary.

"It's a masterpiece, I know," Savannah says smugly, ruining the emotional moment. "You owe me one million coffees."

Georgina shoos her out. "Okay, yes, whatever, go." Brigitte's arrangements of lilacs are waiting on the kitchen counter, and Georgina places one in every room.

Goldie's the very last one out—because Georgina wasn't about to rush her—but she's adorable in there, arranging cookies on a platter, and Nathan captures that before racing to film the Seelys' car pulling up the drive.

Georgina inhales and tries to slow her fluttering heart. It's a surreal moment as it sinks in that this will be her first time ever doing a walk-through alone—no Poppy, no Lance—but Cassidy's hand over hers reminds her she's not alone. She couldn't have pulled it off without him.

"If they don't love it, they're crazy," he says.

She smiles in agreement, but her nerves return as Brigitte greets the Seelys and explains what they need—an honest, emotional reaction, good or bad. Georgina's mind races between the before and after, trying to remember everything in between, but Cassidy's hopeful eyes make the moment stand still and remind her of an even bigger transformation.

"I'll say a prayer," he says, bringing her back to the present as the Seelys approach, outfitted with their microphones.

She whispers a thank-you and greets them, nerves buzzing, but it's off to a good start as they study the restored porch and freshly painted exterior. Poppy's egg-blue door pops against Georgina's favorite buttery yellow paint.

"How'd y'all do this? It doesn't even look like the same house," Curt says, his brows raising.

"I love the white porch!" Monica exclaims, hurrying up the steps. "Oh, and the little fence is so cute!"

Georgina cheers silently and opens the door, with Nathan's camera trained on their anxious faces.

"What is that smell? It's incredible," Monica says as the citrus-vanilla-lilac smell fills the air. "It's like cookies and—oh my gosh!"

Georgina jumps as she gets the coveted doubled-over scream from Monica as they step inside, plus the classic speechless husband reaction from Curt when he sees the lofted space. The bedroom takes the cake, though. That's when the tears fall, and Monica tries to suffocate her with a hug. Georgina catches Brigitte's proud smile over her shoulder, and that might be the best part of all. They've heard through Benson's birdies that Lance has been on the warpath at UpScale ever since he returned to Nashville, but it's going to be hard for him to top this.

The next few minutes are a blur as the walk-through ends and Brigitte quickly shuffles the Seelys away for their interviews, wanting to capture more of their awestruck sputtering before they settle down again. Cassidy meets Georgina on the porch for a high five that turns into a discreet kiss.

Georgina still has more work to do, too, like reshoots with

the Seelys and final tweaks to each room before they take the "after" photos—but she sets it all aside for a moment and sinks into the rocking chair to catch her breath while the weary crew converges on Goldie's cookies. She smiles when Cassidy takes the seat across from her.

"This isn't as easy as y'all make it look."

She smiles at the tired look on his face. "I know, right? All that work, just to haul it all back out again."

She laughs as he makes a pained expression.

"It's kind of worth it, though, right?" she asks, hoping she hasn't totally worn him out yet.

He thinks for a moment, looking around at Goldie laughing with Gavin and Lila in the kitchen, then at Savannah and Julie testing out the loft. "I'd say so."

24

"You're a little off today, my friend."

Cassidy scowls as he misses yet another target. He's been off for a few days now, and Eddy's scrutiny isn't helping.

"You're tense," Eddy adds unhelpfully. "Relax."

Cassidy's eyes narrow as he repositions the rifle.

"Drop your shoulder a little—"

"You wanna take over, Eddy?"

Eddy looks surprised for a moment, then falls silent.

"Sorry," Cassidy mutters. "I'm just . . ." *Tense*, he realizes, frowning.

"Nah, it's all right. I don't like when Denise does that to me, either. I'll shut up."

Cassidy lets his breath out slowly. He should relax, but his thoughts have been shooting around like fireworks ever since he got the call two days ago. He had been in the middle of training his replacement at the Harp House when one of his new bosses called to let him know he was needed in Tapachula, Mexico, tomorrow morning for an emergency briefing before they fly him into El Salvador. Apparently, the situation is escalating faster than they expected.

The call churned up all kinds of mixed emotions, but Georgina took the news better than he'd expected.

"That means you get back sooner, right?"

He had smiled at the hopeful look on her face, wishing that were true. But he does have a surprise for her today before they say good-bye. He refocuses his eyes on the dot in the distance—and begrudgingly drops his shoulder.

Bang!

"There ya go," Eddy says with a hint of smugness as the target sways and Cassidy puts down his gun. "Your girl should be here soon, right?"

Cassidy glances at the clock and nods, but unexpected nerves hit as he second-guesses his brilliant idea. He was just teasing when he suggested shooting as their last date—since her first shooting lesson didn't exactly go well—but she agreed as long as there was food afterward. His mother is taking care of that part, and they've got the Harp House dining room all to themselves.

"Oh, I almost forgot," Eddy says, capturing Cassidy's attention again as he pats his pockets. "I got you a little present since this is our last hurrah for a while."

Cassidy stares as he holds out a tiny stuffed chipmunk.

"Alvin," Eddy explains with a fond look. "A friend for your travels."

"Uh . . ."

Eddy bursts out laughing louder than Cassidy's ever heard him.

"What, you don't want him?" he asks, howling harder as Cassidy finally realizes it's a joke. "You shoulda seen your face," he wheezes, clutching the startled-looking chipmunk to his heart, which makes Cassidy laugh just as hard. "I'm gonna tell Denise what you think of her work."

"Tell her I'll take that guy instead," he says, pointing to the newest member of the gun range—the little buck he dropped off after his close encounter with a certain Lexus. "She did a good job with him."

"Yeah, she did, but I'm still gonna tell her about the way you treated poor Alvin."

Cassidy lets him finish cackling while he takes a closer look at the buck. He still has that same resolute look on his baby face, but now he doesn't have a scratch on him. No one would ever know what he'd been through.

Eddy wipes his eyes and sets Alvin on the table. "All right, all right. Enough of that." He pulls a small box out of his rifle bag instead. "Here's your real present."

Surprise fills Cassidy as he studies the vintage box of black powder ammo. "Dang. This is a lot better than a chipmunk."

Eddy smiles. The packaging is worn with age—the last box of this stuff was made sometime around 1899—but Cassidy can still read the brown-and-green label.

"Your dad brought that in shortly before he died."

Cassidy looks up as Eddy's face turns wistful.

"I told him he could get at least a thousand bucks if he sold it to a collector, but he didn't care." Eddy chuckles. "He said it was my lucky day."

Cassidy smiles. That does sound like his dad. Eddy's reaction to owning it would've been more fun to him than the payday. Cassidy misses him most of the time but even more lately. "Thanks, Eddy," he says, fighting back the emotion rising in his chest.

"You're welcome. You already know he'd be proud of you. You never take the easy way out."

Cassidy nods. The truth is, he's thought about taking the "easy way" more than once, but Eddy's right—he can't do it. He made a commitment to help people who need him. That's what God would want, and it's what his father taught him to do.

Suddenly, the door to the range chimes.

"Hello?" Georgina's nervous voice echoes through the lobby.

Cassidy's heart drums as he goes to greet her. Apparently,

she's trying to make their good-bye as difficult as possible because she looks the prettiest he's ever seen her in a long, curve-hugging dress with a pattern like one of those fancy blue-and-white teacups in the Harp House china cabinet. Cassidy's certain no one's ever worn anything like it to Eddy's gun range before, and no one ever will again.

She looks pleased by the awed look on his face, but it's shadowed by sadness as their eyes meet.

"Come on," he says, leading her to the range as his doubts return. Sadness and fear aren't ideal emotions for a good-bye date, and he might accidentally cause both, thanks to his choice of location. Fortunately, her polite smile returns as Eddy greets her, and they have a more pleasant interaction than last time. Her face brightens when she notices the chipmunk.

"Oh, cute!"

"She has better taste than you, Cass."

Cassidy smirks.

"Cass is too good for Alvin," Eddy adds.

"Oh my gosh! That's my therapist's name."

Cassidy listens with a smile as they chitchat about Eddy's days as a chaplain, and Georgina's mood seems to lift a little.

"Anyway, y'all have fun," Eddy finally says, leaving them to it, but not before he gives Cassidy a tight, fatherly hug.

"Thanks, Eddy."

"You know I'll be praying," he says, patting Cassidy's shoulder. "God's gonna be sick of me and your mama by the time you get back."

Cassidy smiles gratefully, but the mood dampens again as Eddy closes the door behind him, leaving him and Georgina in the heavy silence.

"Ready?"

As he gets his pistol ready for her, it strikes him how different it is from that day at Kit's cottage. Georgina is still nervous, but she trusts him enough to carefully take the gun from his hands. She throws him an embarrassed look, aware that her stance and hands are totally wrong, but he slowly adjusts everything.

"Bend your knees," he says, lightly tapping one through her dress. She does, so he moves on to her hands and carefully moves her thumb to the right position, leaving a trail of heat between them with every touch. He steps back. "Looking good."

Cute color fills her face as she tries to hold still, determined not to slip into the wrong stance again. "How do I shoot it, though?"

He shows her how to look down the barrel next, then how to aim at the target. "When you're ready, you'll put your finger on the trigger and press. Don't pull."

She nods slowly, but then shakes her head. "I don't get the difference."

"It's okay. You will."

She frowns.

"See this? That's called the safety, and when it looks like this"—he flips it—"that means it's ready to shoot if you are."

More fear flickers across her face but she nods. The determination in her eyes touches his heart.

"Oh, wait a second. I almost forgot." He slips the headphone-style earmuffs off his neck and places them on her head instead. "You'll want these," he says, adjusting them over her hair. A strand falls in front of her eyes, so he lightly brushes it aside. "There you go. You're ready." He widens the distance between them. "You don't need me," he adds with an encouraging smile when she looks back.

A small sigh escapes her lips. She seems frozen for a moment as she peers down the barrel, and he almost intervenes, but then she finally pulls the trigger.

Bang!

She jumps, startled by the muffled blast and sudden burst

of pressure, but her face slowly changes from shock to relief as he cheers behind her.

"You're on the paper!"

"What? I am?" She squints at the silhouette. "That's just the background, though," she says with a frown, her perfectionism kicking in. "Not the actual bad guy."

"So? That's good for your first shot ever."

He's surprised when she asks to try again, but the next shot lands in a similar spot. She carefully readjusts and tries one more time, but it's still off.

"You're doing great, Georgina. Honestly—"

"Why can't I hit the actual target, though? Just, like, his belly button or something?"

"Maybe because you've never done this before in your entire life?"

She smiles weakly, but her frustration lingers.

"You're just anticipating the shot. It's normal," he adds, standing behind her with his chest against her back. He wraps his arms around her so he can place his hands over hers. "I'm not going to shoot it," he says quickly, flipping the safety on when she tenses against him. "I just want you to feel what's happening."

He hears another soft sigh. "Okay . . ."

"Now that you know it's gonna kick when you shoot, you're lifting the gun at the last second," he explains, mimicking the motion. "That little bit of fear is throwing off the whole shot. You have to keep it steady in spite of that. That's why you press, don't pull. And say a prayer, too. That never hurts."

He steps back again, and she tears her eyes off the target long enough to meet his.

"It doesn't have to be perfect," he reminds her. "Just stay steady. That's all you have to do."

She nods as her face turns more focused, like she's silencing all those demanding voices in her head and trying to listen to him instead.

He's observed her growing resilience since that night at the lake. So much has competed for her attention lately, whether it's Brigitte's final demands or phone calls from her panic-stricken mother or Lance's ongoing antics, but none of it has shaken her new resolve. Still, he knows their good-bye is what's weighing most heavily on her heart.

He sees her mouth move in a quick prayer before she flips the safety and presses the trigger, and the blast doesn't shock her as much this time. He watches, pride growing, as the bullet hits the paper villain close to his heart.

"There you go. He's dead."

She bursts out laughing but still carefully holds the gun until he takes it from her and sets it down.

"Maybe we should end on that note? Go get some dinner?"

"Yeah . . ."

He starts packing up, but her face makes him stop. He frowns as her eyes darken. "What's wrong?"

"What am I supposed to do if you don't come back?"

Her shaky voice breaks his heart. "You'd be okay."

She vehemently shakes her head. "No, I wouldn't—"

"Yes, you would," he says gently, silencing her fears. He holds her close. "I promise you will. If you have God, you have everything you need."

25

Savannah delivers another rocket-fire serve, but Georgina finally sends the tiny ball flying back across the table and surprises them both.

"About time!" Savannah yells, lunging for it but missing by a hair.

It's an exceptionally warm October evening in Nashville, so Jared busted out every outdoor game he could think of, including table tennis—Savannah's favorite.

She retrieves the ball and raises her paddle again, but Georgina lifts her finger and hurries over to a nearby patio table.

"Are you going to do that every time?" Savannah whines.

Georgina makes no apologies as she checks her phone again. She hasn't heard from Cassidy in almost seventy-two hours— a development that sends nerves crashing through her body every time she thinks about it. Poppy's "Hipster BBQ" playlist blares from a hidden speaker, but the upbeat songs don't match Georgina's sinking mood.

The last goofy message he sent fills her with bittersweetness every time she looks at it. Goldie had sent him a copy of *Country Home* magazine with Georgina's face on the cover, and he took a picture of himself with it.

Meet my new girlfriend.

"And she's gone," Savannah says with a sigh as Georgina gets lost in his old messages. "Take over, Jared."

Georgina happily hands over the paddle and focuses on her phone again. *Please let him send something soon,* she prays silently, missing their almost daily communication. Goldie and Sawyer haven't heard anything either, and even the lively Stokes family group chat has gone unnervingly silent.

She scrolls on, looking for any clues she might've missed that explain his silence. Cassidy's life in El Salvador is surprisingly normal in some ways—he drinks coffee and has internet and plays foosball and leads a Bible study—but she knows he doesn't tell her everything, and after last night, she knows why. As his silence dragged on, she'd made the mistake of scouring the news and stumbled upon a story about a jungle basecamp being raided and people's heads being chopped off. It was from a year ago, but the harrowing story was enough to send her into a spiral that only Jesus could drag her out of.

She exhales and closes her messages, trying to force her mind somewhere else, but a picture makes her heart ache all over again. It's Cassidy with a shaggy Malinois named Steve, his sidekick. Georgina frowns down at Cassidy's grinning, stubbled face. That's the other part that scares her, even though she won't admit it—he's happy. She can see the purpose in his eyes whenever they video chat.

"Anything yet?" Poppy asks hopefully, sensing Georgina's concern when she passes by with fruit skewers.

"Not yet."

Poppy keeps her face calm, but Georgina sees a tiny crease of concern between her eyebrows, so she forces herself to stop moping. Poppy and Savannah went above and beyond with the party tonight, with Jared's master-level grilling skills, Georgina's favorite but hard-to-find tiramisu cupcakes, and Poppy's decked-out patio covered with fresh flowers and string lights. The least she can do is pretend to be happy.

Cassidy would want her to celebrate, too. She hasn't told him yet that *Georgina Rebuilds* launches next summer—she wants to wait until they talk—but he wouldn't want a dark cloud of worry hanging over her head on such a special night.

Her mind races back to the moment Benson called three days ago and announced the official-but-not-public news. Before the call, she was still cautiously optimistic UpScale might choose her since Brigitte and the rest of the crew pulled off an amazing pilot, but Lance's words mingled together with her own doubts—until Benson's voice thundered in her ear.

"You did it, you beautiful little baby Joanna Gaines! You really did it!"

The moments that followed were a blur of happy shrieking, shouted thank-yous to God, and Savannah wildly punching her fists in the air.

Georgina is about to join again, hoping more table tennis might distract her, but she halts when she sees who took her place.

"Poppy, who's that?"

Poppy glances over. "Oh, that's Mason." A small, sneaky smile touches her lips. "Jared's friend."

Georgina watches as Savannah giggles at something Mason says. "Is he also a lumberjack?"

"No, he's like an accountant or something."

"An *accountant*?"

Poppy laughs at her stunned tone. "Yeah, something with numbers or computers, I can't remember. But he works out, obviously."

Georgina studies him discreetly. He's got the same wood-chopping, elk-eating build as Jared, but he's dressed in ripped skinny jeans and his shaggy hair droops over his eyebrows.

"Did I mention he loves comic books?"

Georgina raises an eyebrow.

"And wait, there's more," Poppy whispers in a dramatic infomercial voice as Georgina leans in. "He listens to sermon jams. He sends Jared new ones all the time."

Georgina grins at the mention of Savannah's latest obsession—fiery, passionate sermons set to epic music.

"Hold your applause," Poppy says smugly.

Georgina smiles as Savannah smokes Mason with her signature rocket-speed serve, and he hurries off to retrieve the ball. She's been on a winning streak ever since she moved into Georgina's apartment two months ago. She's the one who diligently scoured Nashville for a church and found a small but growing chapel they both love. Then she surprised Georgina again by job-hunting like a madwoman and finding one she actually enjoys at a nursing home, organizing activities for the residents or just chitchatting in their rooms. She's even painting again—mostly lakes or barns or starry night skies.

They've fallen into an unexpected pattern ever since their time in Tarragon—sort of old and new at the same time—with easier conversations and a growing pile of ideas for the future. Brigitte's already trying to rope her into *Georgina Rebuilds*. Surprisingly, Savannah hasn't said no.

"Gigi, get over here!" Annette says, capturing her attention. She beckons her over to one of the empty seats beside Benson.

Georgina smiles to herself. They arrived separately, but Annette's chic dress is the same smoky gray color as his sweater.

"Have you seen this yet?" she asks, holding up her phone.

Georgina studies the screen and feels a twinge of secondhand embarrassment. Benson's birdies gave him some intel on Lance's show, too, and the news wasn't as good for him as it was for Georgina. Instead of renewing his contract, they're going to make him the host of a new show for up-and-coming designers. It's a subtle demotion, since he'll still get a big paycheck and keep his fan base, but he's not taking it well. His Instagram is an almost constant barrage of shirtless selfies and careful jabs at Georgina.

"He's putting off *very* desperate vibes, but, who knows, maybe that'll work for him." Annette shrugs. "Bad publicity is still publicity."

Georgina nods wearily. She's been having her fair share of that, too, thanks to the steady stream of rumors about her "reckless rebound" with Cassidy and growing criticism that she's "getting too religious" ever since she returned from Tarragon. Those kinds of comments don't bother her as much as flippant statements about the miscarriage or her mental state, but Cassidy has reminded her more than once that she can't control that part of her life.

"You just have to hand it over to God, Georgina. He knows every single thing about you, good and bad, and He still loves you, so who cares about some strangers on the internet?"

She sighs, missing him all over again.

"Oh, there's my little blobby blob," Poppy sings when Jared brings two-month-old Auggie out, wrapped up in a star-patterned blanket. His exceptionally chubby presence is greeted with oohs and ahs before Poppy expertly slips his fuzzy head under her shirt.

"Do you need anything?" Georgina asks as Poppy readjusts Auggie.

Poppy shakes her head, and Georgina throws her an impressed look. She's basically a pro mom now, throwing an incredible party and nursing a squiggling baby at the same time—something she never would've attempted doing when Olivia was so small. It helps that Jared took more time off to help her transition from one child to two, but Georgina can see the growing confidence in her eyes as they meet hers.

"My offer still stands, Poppy," Benson says, floating his idea by her one more time. "People love the visiting best friend. You pop in on set with some great curtains and then pop back out again to chase your rug rats. Easy."

Poppy smiles weakly—but, like Savannah, she doesn't say no. "Oh," she says, suddenly straightening. "Your mom's here."

Surprise fills Georgina as she turns and sees her mother coming through the gate. And uneasiness. Thanks to her mother's vague reply to Poppy, she wasn't sure if she was coming or not, and most of their conversations since she left Tarragon have been consistently terrible. Georgina understood her mother's irritation, since she had to find out most of the details of Georgina's life from over-the-top tabloids, but her mother's main contention is Cassidy. She decided from the moment Georgina described her feelings for him that she was making a mistake.

"It won't last."

Her reasons were varied—that he's too country and too Christian, among others—but the primary one was the distance.

"I know you, Georgina, and you can't handle that. You simply can't. It's not how you're built. And why would you want to, anyway?"

Georgina almost told Poppy not to invite her to the barbeque, but she prayed instead and muddled through her conflicted feelings about it. Ultimately, she realized her mother's concerns aren't really about Cassidy, or even Georgina. They're about her.

"Hi," her mother says coolly, kissing Georgina's cheek.

The familiar smell of Shalimar perfume touches Georgina's nose. Her mother fits right in with the fashionable crowd in her pretty tailored dress, but the fine lines on her face are deeper than Georgina remembers.

"Who should I give this to?" she asks, holding out a home-made chess pie. When Poppy's mother sweetly carries it away, she settles into the seat beside Poppy's.

"How are you, Faye?" Poppy asks, smiling over the Auggie-sized lump on her chest. "I'm glad you made it."

"Tired," she says with a sigh. But then she flashes Georgina a small, unexpected smile. "But I'm happy to be here."

Georgina's heart lifts at the hint of pride in her voice, but her mother swiftly changes the subject.

"Where's Savannah?" Her eyes scan the party until she spots Savannah chatting with Mason near the food tables. She looks like she's about to stand up again and head in that direction, but Auggie's reemergence distracts her.

"Remind me of his name again?" she asks as Poppy gently pats his back.

"August. But we call him Auggie."

"Unique."

Georgina frowns at her forced tone, but she catches Poppy's unbothered smile.

"Do you want to hold him?" Poppy asks. "He already pooped, so we're good for a while."

Georgina's mother hesitates for a moment, but then she carefully takes Auggie and gently maneuvers him until his little blinky eyes are gazing up at hers. Georgina hears a happy sigh escape her mother's lips.

"He's precious, Poppy."

A semi-awkward conversation follows, with a few sweet moments intermixed with annoying ones as her mother sprinkles in complaints about Georgina's silence and questions about Cassidy, but Poppy gently tries to bring the conversation back to the reason they're celebrating—Georgina's exciting new chapter.

"I just don't understand, though," her mother says, refusing to be deterred. "Why can't Cassidy just get a regular job?"

Georgina bites her tongue as Benson and Annette exchange uncomfortable glances.

"Cassidy is kind of like Jared," Poppy says, still valiantly trying to help. "He just couldn't do a normal desk job. I mean, he could, obviously, but it's not what he wants—"

"And you're just expected to suffer through his little adventure?" her mother interjects. "That doesn't seem fair."

Georgina's embarrassment grows, but Poppy still looks unruffled.

"Yeah, but would it really be fair for me to ask him to give up something he loves?" she asks, keeping her voice light, even when Georgina's mother throws her a weary look.

"He should put your relationship first—"

"He does, but that doesn't look like him just doing whatever I want all the time. Because I want him to be happy, too. That's love—"

"A few months together isn't *love*," Georgina's mother snaps, and Poppy falls silent. Clearly, the conversation isn't about her and Jared anymore.

Georgina rises from her seat.

"Where are you going?" her mother demands.

"I'll be back," she lies, moving swiftly in the opposite direction and taking her phone with her. Her heart dips lower when there's still nothing from Cassidy.

"Ow!" Savannah says when their elbows bang together. "Look up, Georgie."

"Sorry."

Savannah's face softens when their eyes meet. "Still nothing from Cassidy?"

Georgina feigns calm and shakes her head. "Nothing. And Mom is just being super annoying."

Savannah glances in that direction just as Poppy rescues Auggie from their irate mother. "Maybe she's going to ignore me tonight," Savannah says hopefully.

"Not a chance. She already asked about you."

Savannah's optimism fades. "Oh, well, whatever. I'm ready. Bring it on, Faye."

Georgina smiles weakly as a moment of solidarity passes between them. "Just keep her away from your new friend," she adds, glancing at Mason. He's over by the fire pit with Jared, but his eyes have drifted to Savannah more than once. "She's in an opinionated mood, per usual."

Savannah's face warms, but she looks grateful for the tip.

Suddenly, Georgina feels buzzing in her pocket, and her heart stops. Savannah hears it, too.

"Is that your phone?" she asks as Georgina immediately grabs for it. "Is it Cassidy?"

Georgina almost screams as her eyes scan the screen. "No." Somehow her mood plummets even further. "It's Dad."

"Dad?" Savannah's eyes widen before they snap back to their mother, who's watching them with wounded eyes. "This is literally my nightmare."

"Should I answer it?"

"Um . . ."

Georgina had asked Poppy to text him an invitation as a mere courtesy—he hasn't shown up to anything in-person in years—so she feels compelled to take the call. Savannah looks shocked when she lifts the phone to her ear.

"Hello?"

"Georgina?"

Georgina inhales as her father's voice fills her ear. It's familiar and not at the same time.

"How are you—"

316

"Go, go, go." Savannah cuts through his question with a panicked whisper. "Mom's coming."

Georgina hurries toward a half-painted gazebo in a shady corner of Poppy's sprawling yard. She looks back long enough to see Savannah intercept their mother by the food tables.

"Georgie? Are you there?"

"Yes, sorry. I am." She focuses on her father again. "I'm good. How are you?"

"Good."

Nostalgia fills her, along with intense discomfort. She can't even remember the last time they talked, especially since most of their conversations usually follow the same surface-level, one-word patterns. Tonight is no exception as he offers her a simple congratulations, which she returns with a polite thank-you. Unlike her mother, he's never had a lot to say, even when Georgina wishes he did.

"How's Savannah?" he finally asks when the silence takes over.

"Good. She's here, actually. Do you want me to get her—"

"That's okay. I'll catch her next time."

Georgina's disappointment deepens, but she doesn't press him. "Anyway, I'll let you enjoy your party."

"Okay—"

"Oh, and thanks for the books. I'm going to read them."

It takes her a minute to figure out what he's talking about, until her late birthday gift to him comes to mind. Usually she sends an obligatory text, but she felt a nudge to do more this time, so she enlisted Cassidy's help and settled on a sturdy collection of C. S. Lewis stories.

"You're welcome."

"I, uh . . ." He hesitates. "Yeah, anyway, have a good night."

"You too." *I love you*, she adds silently as he hangs up, more out of habit than anything else, but there's some truth to it.

Her eyes drift back to her mother, and it sinks in how much she loves her, too, even when she's in the middle of lecturing Savannah about something with a familiar scowl on her face. Her parents' flaws seem even more glaring than usual tonight, but they don't bother her as much as they used to. She's spent a long time chasing that tidy, pretty, "finished" feeling with them, but God's been freeing her from that, too.

She's just about to rescue Savannah when an unknown number flashes across her phone. Her mind sprints between two possibilities—the good being that it's finally Cassidy, the bad being that it's someone else calling about Cassidy.

"Hello?"

Her heart drums as light static fills the line.

"Hello?" she repeats, praying for someone to speak. A muted beeping sound follows, and the call ends as her chest tightens with panic. She's about to call the number back when she gets a text.

It's me.

Georgina nearly faints with happiness as he types another message.

Sorry. Phone issues. I'll try again soon.

Tears of relief spring into her eyes. She types back with shaky fingers.

I can never forgive you for this.

?

I've been losing my mind, Cassidy.

Worrying?

YES.

318

I'm sorry. Perfect storm situation here. They
took down one of our helicopters.

Georgina drops down on the bench and drags in another deep, happy-but-totally-worn-out breath.

How are you?

Now that she knows he's safe—or relatively safe, at least—she can't wait another second to tell him the news.

I got the show!

!!!!!!! 👏👏👏👏👏👏👏

Poppy and Sav are throwing me a party. I wish
you were here.

🎵 • •

Sorry. Not trying to make you feel bad.

I just miss you and love you and this doesn't feel as good as I thought it would without you. She doesn't write any of that in the text since he has enough on his mind without her wild emotions, but it's true.

I know.

Her mother's words suddenly come to mind—that Georgina's not "built" for this kind of love—and she wonders if she's right. He seems to take it all in stride, but every minute he's in El Salvador feels like she's missing a piece of her own heart.

I wish I was there, too.

26

FOUR MONTHS LATER

"I just don't think it's going to work out, Pop."

"Hush," Poppy says, waving Georgina's complaints away as they walk against a chilly breeze. A bundled-up, six-month-old Auggie is nestled in his stroller and snoozing through most of their conversation.

Georgina sighs inwardly as they pass house after house in one of Nashville's historic neighborhoods, keeping an eye out for a *For Sale* sign. The trees are huge and old, and almost every house has a porch or a swing, but there are definitely signs of neglect.

"I love this neighborhood so much," Poppy says when they pass by one of the better-kept houses. It's decorated for Valentine's Day, with haphazard hearts in the windows and a lace-and-rose-covered wreath on the front door. A few toys and bikes crowd the porch.

"It's super cute, but we already decided on the Harding house—"

"Not officially," Poppy interjects, throwing her a knowing look. Technically, she's right—Georgina hasn't submitted her next project proposal to UpScale yet—but her mind is already made up. After sifting through thousands of homeowner applications and renovating two massive, side-by-side fixer-uppers for *Georgina Rebuilds*, she wants something smaller and simpler. And she's stressed out enough already, thanks to Cassidy's latest announcement about Guatemala.

"The Harding house is just kind of blah—"

"Poppy—"

"Does this look blah to you?"

Georgina halts as Poppy stops the stroller in front of a rusted wrought-iron gate. She missed the *For Sale* sign thanks to a row of overgrown gardenias. She peers through the gate and raises an eyebrow.

"You have my attention."

Poppy grins. "Let's go."

Georgina wrestles open the gate while Poppy maneuvers Auggie's stroller up a path of broken stones. The rest of the yard is in decent shape, though, besides some weeds and a few too many tree branches grazing the roof. Georgina looks up in awe. It's truly a rare find—a French-inspired square tower house with red-and-white brick and an arched front door. She's never designed anything like it.

Poppy scans her phone for a moment, then punches in the code to get a key from the lockbox as Georgina's anticipation grows. Her awe only grows as they tour the inside, despite the long list of flaws. The kitchen is outdated but sprawling, the primary bedroom has a dangerous but potentially fabulous balcony, and Savannah could paint the mural of a lifetime in the attic-turned-bedroom, which has a breathtaking set of windows overlooking the backyard. Savannah decided to knock out her final semester of school in Sewanee, but she should be done by the time they'd actually start filming.

Poppy looks just as excited as Georgina as they walk through the house.

"Like, *imagine* cooking in this kitchen once we make it fabulous," she says, talking a million miles a minute. "And you could make an amazing office over here—"

"I know, Pop." Georgina finally snaps back to her senses. "But let's just do the Harding house."

Poppy stares at her. "Are you not seeing what I'm seeing?"

"It *is* cool, but . . ."

"But what?"

Georgina fumbles for a good reason, but the truth is, she just feels drained. Not even her upcoming cookbook project makes her feel better, thanks to Cassidy's announcement that he took an emergency assignment in Guatemala two days ago. He promised her a long reunion after that, but it still felt like a blow to her heart.

"I think you should go big or go home," Poppy continues, misunderstanding her hesitation. "Like, won't you totally regret it if you let this one slip away?"

It's a tough question, but Georgina doesn't have to answer it, thanks to a well-timed wail from Auggie. Poppy whisks him away to the backyard—he's a lover of the outdoors, just like his father—and leaves Georgina alone in the kitchen with her conflicted thoughts.

She frowns up at a stained-glass window over the kitchen sink. It's yet another stunning detail, featuring jewel-toned hummingbirds drinking from pearl-hued flowers, but her heart just isn't in it. She sighs. As usual, it's a few thousand miles away.

She's about to ask God for His opinion on the house, but her prayer is only half-formed when a door quietly opens and closes again.

"Poppy?"

Poppy doesn't answer but footsteps echo across the empty foyer. Her eyes narrow as she walks in that direction, wondering if it's a nosy neighbor or a rogue Realtor, but her heart stops when she turns the corner.

"Oh, hey, aren't you that famous girl?"

She claps a hand over her mouth as Cassidy smiles down at her.

She blinks a few times, which makes him laugh, but she wants to make sure it's not a dream because it would be the absolute best and worst dream of her life.

"You're not in Guatemala?" she finally squeaks.

"Nope."

"Why didn't you tell me you were coming?" she demands.

He smiles at her shrill tone. "For dramatic effect."

She throws him a horrified look, unsure if she wants to slap him or kiss him. "Well, it worked." She looks around for Poppy, but she's still nowhere in sight. "Oh my gosh." She suddenly figures it out. "You roped her into this, didn't you?"

He smiles sneakily.

"This is literally the worst idea you've ever had—"

He quiets her with a kiss, which sends her already-thudding heart into overdrive. She still doesn't dare open her eyes in case she wakes up, but it goes on long enough that she finally melts against him. He feels so wonderfully solid that tears spring into her eyes.

"It's really me, Georgina," he says gently when she traces his smile. His eyes turn apologetic when tears spill out of hers. "Do you like the house?"

Surprise fills her. She already forgot all about it.

"It's cool, right? It reminded me of you."

Her face scrunches. "You've seen it before?"

"Just pictures. I've been wanting to see it in person, though."

Her mind replays that puzzling sentence ten more times as confusion fills her. "Why are you looking at houses?"

"I'm in the market. And I wanted a professional opinion—"

"No, you're not." Her heart races as a smile touches his lips. "You have another scary mission in Guatemala."

"No, I don't. That was for dramatic effect, too."

She glares at him as hope soars in her chest. "Cassidy, if you're joking right now I'm going to—"

"I'm not joking," he says gently, pulling her close again. "I got a job at Fort Campbell. It's still a little bit of a commute but definitely closer than Guatemala," he adds, wiping another tear when it falls.

Georgina's head and heart feel light as her mind whirls with a million questions about his dreams, and hers, too, but the happy look on his face erases most of them. "Are you sure?" she finally asks, praying he is.

He nods. "I want to be home."

Discussion Questions

1. Have you ever wondered what it's like to be a television design star? What surprised you about Georgina's profession?

2. Do you think the saying "opposites attract" is true? Why or why not?

3. Georgina and Cassidy are obviously opposites in many ways, but in what ways are they similar?

4. Like most modern moms, Poppy struggles with feelings of guilt when she's away from Olivia. Why do you think so many women feel this way? How can their communities help?

5. Pastor Boggs says that people often seek out "Band-Aids" instead of life-saving treatments. What Band-Aids did you see the characters reaching out for? What Band-Aids do you see in your own life?

6. Georgina is initially very uncomfortable with the changes she sees in her sister. Why do you think we tend to be so skeptical of change? Especially when it comes to our own family?

7. In what ways are Georgina and Savannah similar to their parents? In what ways are they breaking familial patterns?

8. Georgina, like Cassidy, spent most of her life thinking she was a Christian without actually committing to Christ. Do you think is a common occurrence? If so, why?

9. S. M. Lockridge was a real minister known for his incredible sermons. Were you familiar with him before reading the book?

10. C. S. Lewis once said, "Whatever is not eternal is eternally out of date." What do you think he meant by that?

Acknowledgments

As I write this, it was almost a year ago that I received the not-so-great news from my editors that I needed to drastically re-imagine this book. I was just days away from going into labor and not ready to face the fact that there would be a lot of re-writing in my future—with a three-year-old, a one-year-old, and a newborn baby in tow. Oh, and another book to promote.

(It's called *After She Falls*, by the way. You should read it.)

Anyway, it always hurts when your confidence takes a hit, but the good news is, God can work with that in some pretty incredible ways. This book you're holding—and my mostly intact sanity—is proof.

Now that we're finally here, some thank-yous are in order.

Thank you to Dave, Jen, Jess, and so many others at Bethany House for being gracious to me as I juggled two books and three babies at the same time. I could not have asked for a better, kinder team.

Thank you to Jessica for being my agent, ally, and friend.

Thank you to Rachel for helping me calmly (er, somewhat calmly) deliver my precious son during the busiest season of my life.

Thank you to Jan for loving my children so well while I wrote. You made a hard task so much easier.

Thank you to my parents for letting me sneak away and write in your basement and bringing me Cuban coffee when the creativity was running low. Your thoughtfulness never goes unnoticed.

Thank you to my sweet in-laws for coming to our rescue so many times this past year, whether it was postpartum struggles or a broken-down rental car in the middle of Illinois. You're lifesavers!

Thank you to Haley and Mike for answering my weird, random questions about the military. I would be as clueless as Georgina without you.

Thank you to Inga for being one of the greatest friends I've ever had. You are God's answer to a lifelong prayer.

The biggest thank you of all goes to Jeff. I love you and our family more than I'll ever be able to express.

Lastly, thank you to my readers who waited so patiently and cheered me on the whole way! C. S. Lewis famously said, "To love at all is to be vulnerable. Love anything and your heart will be wrung and possibly broken. If you want to make sure of keeping it intact you must give it to no one . . ." Well, here's my heart for a few hundred pages. I trust you with it.

Cheers,
Carmen

Carmen Schober, author of *After She Falls*, is a wife and mother, a proud Cuban-American, and a woman of eclectic interests, ranging from gritty combat sports to feminine design shows. She writes unexpected romance novels for the modern woman, with relatable but inspirational heroines and heroes. When she's not writing fiction, she blogs about Christianity, motherhood, writing, and everything in between. She earned a master's degree in English literature and creative writing from Kansas State, and she currently lives in Manhattan, Kansas. You can follow her at carmenschober.com.

Sign Up for Carmen's Newsletter

Keep up to date with Carmen's news on book releases and events by signing up for her email list at carmenschober.com.

More from Carmen Schober

After an abusive relationship derails her plans, Adri Rivera struggles to regain her independence and achieve her dream of becoming an MMA fighter. She gets a second chance, but the man who offers it to her is Max Lyons, her former training partner, whom she left heartbroken years before. As she fights for her future, will she be able to confront her past?

After She Falls

You May Also Like . . .

When Luke Dempsey's fellow inmate lay dying, Luke promised to protect the man's daughter, Finley, and help her find the treasure he had hidden. Upon Luke's release, he and Finley uncover the clues, and their reasons for resisting each other begin to crumble. Luke will shield her from unseen threats, but who's going to shield him from losing his heart?

Turn to Me by Becky Wade
A MISTY RIVER ROMANCE
beckywade.com

When Cameron Lee's music career takes a nose dive, he reluctantly returns home, where he falls fast for single mom Lexie Walters. But fantasies only last so long, and soon they have to face the real world, one fraught with heartbreak and disappointment and questions that can only be answered on your knees.

Love and the Dream Come True by Tammy L. Gray
STATE OF GRACE
tammylgray.com

Allie Massey's dream to use her grandparents' estate for equine therapy is crushed when she discovers the property has been sold to a contractor. With weeks until demolition, Allie unearths some of Nana Dale's best-kept secrets—including her champion filly, a handsome man, and one fateful night during WWII—and perhaps a clue to keep her own dream alive.

By Way of the Moonlight by Elizabeth Musser
elizabethmusser.com

⬦ BETHANYHOUSE

More from Bethany House

Coast Guard flight medic Brooke Kesler was caught in a mass shooting at a Coast Guard graduation—and little does she know that she overheard something that could expose the mastermind's identity. With targets on their backs, Brooke and CGIS agent Noah Rowley must race to find the killer before he strikes again.

The Deadly Shallows by Dani Pettrey
COASTAL GUARDIANS #3
danipettrey.com

Libby has been given a powerful gift: to live one life in 1774 Colonial Williamsburg and the other in 1914 Gilded Age New York City. When she falls asleep in one life, she wakes up in the other without any time passing. On her twenty-first birthday, Libby must choose one path and forfeit the other—but how can she possibly decide when she has so much to lose?

When the Day Comes by Gabrielle Meyer
TIMELESS #1
gabriellemeyer.com

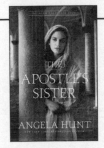

After moving to Jerusalem, Aya expects to be bored in her role as wife to a Torah student but finds herself fascinated by her husband's studies. And when her brother Sha'ul makes a life-altering decision, she is faced with a troubling question: How can she remain true to all she's been taught since infancy and still love her blasphemous brother?

The Apostle's Sister by Angela Hunt
JERUSALEM ROAD #4
angelahuntbooks.com

◊ BETHANYHOUSE